Camelot 30K

Robert L. Forward

A TOM DOHERTY ASSOCIATES BOOK
NEW YORK

This is a work of fiction. All the characters and events portrayed in this book are either products of the author's imagination or are used fictitiously.

CAMELOT 30K

Copyright © 1993 by Robert L. Forward

Cover art by Shigemi Numaza
Edited by David G. Hartwell

A Tor Book
Published by Tom Doherty Associates, Inc.
175 Fifth Avenue
New York, NY 10010

Tor Books on the World Wide Web:
http://www.tor.com

Tor® is a registered trademark of Tom Doherty Associates, Inc.

ISBN: 0-812-51647-8

First edition: September 1993
First mass market edition: August 1996

Printed in the United States of America

0 9 8 7 6 5 4 3 2 1

ACKNOWLEDGMENTS

I WOULD LIKE to acknowledge the technical assistance of the following people in the preparation of this manuscript: Dana Andrews, Gregory Benford, C.B., Margaret Devine, James Gole, David Hartwell, Seichi Kiyohara, Dave Lynch, Daryl Mallett, Vonda McIntyre, Morris Pottinger, Steve Rogers, Johndale Solem, Harry C. (Hal Clement) Stubbs, and Fred Winterberg. Connie Hood of Hood Graphics prepared the illustrations in the technical appendix.

I would also like to thank Freeman Dyson for taking the time to give me some excellent technical advice which I didn't take. For if I had, I wouldn't have followed the Final Law of Storytelling, which is:

"Never let the facts get in the way of a good story."

Camelot
30K

PROLOGUE

OUT PAST THE planets lie the comets. Some of them are so large that although they are ice-covered on the surface like a comet, they have a rocky core like an asteroid. They can be considered cometoids—half comet and half asteroid.

Some think that Pluto is the outermost planet. But Pluto is not a planet. Pluto is a double cometoid consisting of Pluto itself, only two-thirds as big across as the Moon, and Charon, half as large as Pluto. The orbit of Pluto-Charon is highly elliptical and tilted 17 degrees out of the ecliptic plane where all *real* planets orbit. Pluto's density is only 2.4 times that of ice, indicating a small rocky core with a thick covering of ice, but Charon, with its density of only 1.4, is almost all ice. Certainly these are cometoids, not planets.

The true outer planet of the solar system is Neptune. Its major moon, Triton, is also a cometoid. Triton is made mostly of ice, boasts liquid-nitrogen-driven geysers, and has a tenuous atmosphere. Its average surface temperature is a frigid 38 K, or 38 degrees above absolute zero. Triton's inclined, retrograde orbit indicates that it was originally a giant cometoid that was formed elsewhere. When it wandered too close to Neptune, it collided with one of Neptune's original moons or its upper atmosphere and was captured, the heat generated by its capture evaporating much of its original ice.

It is thought that these giant cometoids originated in the Kuiper Belt, a wide band of icy bodies of varying size postulated to surround the Sun. The Kuiper Belt is thought to merge into the Oort Cloud, a spherical collection of ice-covered bodies loosely bound to the Sun which stretches out to the nearest stars. Before 1992, except for Pluto, which was found only after decades of searching, and the occasional in-falling comet with an apogee calculated to be out in the Kuiper Belt or the Oort Cloud, no object had been observed in those regions.

Then, in 1992, a large ice-covered cometoid was found in the Kuiper Belt. Called 1992 QB1, it had an orbit at 42 AU. This put 1992 QB1 far out past Neptune, whose orbit is at 30 AU. Now that the Kuiper Belt was shown to really exist, the search for its inhabitants intensified. A few years later, shortly before the beginning of the new millennium, the European Infrared Space Observatory was launched. One of its major finds was 1999 ZX. It was the size of Pluto and Triton combined, and orbited at 35 AU. Everyone was amazed that it had been overlooked in previous searches, but when its orbital elements were determined, they understood why. Its position in the sky was near the center of the Milky Way in the constellation Sagittarius, where the background clutter of stars made it difficult to find. Also, 1999 ZX was just approaching its perigee in its highly elliptical orbit and so had been much farther away in previous years. Once the orbit of 1999 ZX was known, its image could be found in retrospective searches of old photographic plates and CCD imager data files, but in each image, bad luck had placed it either near a background star or galaxy, a flaw in the emulsion, or at breaks between CCD pixels.

Fortunately, there had been a breakthrough in high-speed interplanetary transport. It was called the cable catapult. Once a payload had been lifted into Earth orbit using large, slow, and costly chemical rockets, the cable catapult could shoot it out through the solar system at high speed. The catapult consisted of a power supply connected to a long cable that stretched for thousands of kilometers, and a launching motor that rode on the cable. The payload capsule was connected to the launching motor at one end of the cable. The heavy nuclear-thermal-electric power supply then generated a sustained burst of radio frequency energy, which traveled down the conductive cable where it was absorbed by the launching motor. The launching motor then used magnetic coupling to pull on the conducting cable like a monkey climbing a rope, and accelerated toward the power supply and the distant planet. Just before the motor reached the power supply it released the payload capsule, which would travel on to the planet, while the launching motor decelerated to a stop on a short stretch of cable on the other side of the power supply, in a position to accelerate again in order to catch an incoming payload.

The cable catapult was used to launch a flyby robotic probe that passed close to 1999 ZX to take pictures. The scientists and engineers who launched the probe expected the imaging cameras to see an icy surface with many impact craters and perhaps a tenuous atmosphere. They were hoping that they might find something more exciting, like the liquid-nitrogen geysers that had been found on Neptune's cometoid-moon, Triton. When the images came back, however, they contained something that was even *more* exciting than active geysers . . .

There were cities on 1999 ZX!

The cities seemed to be concentrated on relatively flat regions of snow and ice that formed the "plains" between the rocky mountain ranges and a multitude of geyser craters. All the cities had a road network in the form of a spiderweb—a spoke-and-ring pattern that radiated outward from a central, circular "park." At the center of each park was a flat, round "plaza" made of some dark material. The circular cities essentially filled the plains, and were separated from each other by bands of unoccupied ice. What was most amazing about the cities was their small size. An entire city was only a few hundred meters across, and the broadest streets were barely big enough for a human to walk on! The inhabitants must be small indeed.

The finding of cities on 1999 ZX sparked a short resurgence of interest in space exploration. The cable catapult was used to launch a small robotic lander and its massive retrorocket toward the distant cometoid. In 2009, after a long journey through space, the lander settled in the foothills of a mountain chain not too far outside one of the cities. Although the ten-hour round-trip communications time delay made conversation difficult, the scientists on Earth were finally able to establish a dialogue with one of the alien scientists. Her name was Merlene, her people called themselves keracks, and she was the wizard of the city of Camalor, on the planetoid the humans called 1999 ZX and the keracks called Ice.

Although the Earth scientists were overjoyed with the scientific knowledge they were gathering from Merlene, Earth politicians were highly disappointed. The technology of the keracks was far behind that of Earth. There would be no miracles from space to save the human race from its increasingly severe internal problems. Because of the cost of chemical rockets and the protests of environmentalists over the pollution that rockets caused, the rest of the space program was in the process of being contracted. Mars had been abandoned, and the Moon bases were being closed down. Despite this contraction, the scientists and engineers pleaded for a manned mission to 1999 ZX. Finally the politicians relented and gave the technologists their mission—but only if it could be done cheaply. However, propelling a human crew and tons of support equipment over a distance of 35 AU, bringing them to a halt, and landing them on 1999 ZX in less than two decades would require billions of tons of chemical rocket fuel. Even nuclear rockets would require millions of tons of expellant mass. Rockets were too costly.

The space engineers had a simple solution. If rockets were too costly—they wouldn't use them. A second cable catapult was constructed in high Earth orbit. Then the two catapults tossed dummy capsules back and forth at each other over the curved horizon of the Earth that lay between them. With each toss and each catch of a capsule, the catapults reacted by moving slightly farther apart. The catapult in high Earth orbit was pushed off in the direction of Ice; the other was kept tied to Earth by gravity pulling on it one way while the capsule's impulses pushed it the other way. Once the traveling cable catapult had attained cruise velocity, it stopped tossing dummy capsules back to Earth and saved them instead. In 2029, after nearly two decades en route, the traveling catapult approached Ice and shot off the saved capsules to bring itself to a halt.

Now that the two cable catapults were in place, the crewed mission could start. Shelters, equipment, and robotic cargo landers were launched from the cable catapult at Earth and captured by the cable catapult at Ice. The robotic landers then landed their cargo in an unoccupied valley deep in a mountain range far from any of the alien cities. Once the equipment for the base was in place, a capsule containing six humans was launched with an acceleration of 30 gees down the 4200-kilometer cable. It reached the cruise velocity of 50 kilometers per second after three minutes. To survive this high level of acceleration, the crew submerged themselves in water tanks after filling their lungs with oxygen-bearing liquid. Their capsule was followed by another containing food and other supplies. When it caught up with the crew capsule, the two were tied together with a small cable and set into rotation to provide artificial gravity on the way out. After over three years of travel in the cramped capsule, the humans finally arrived at their destination. After another short sojourn in the acceleration tanks while the cable catapult near

Ice brought them to a halt, the crew rode a waiting rocket down to the surface and set up their base. It was now time for the human crew to met the alien wizard Merlene and the rest of the keracks . . .

1

MEETING WITH THE HUMANS

BRIGHTSTAR WAS JUST rising to join the other stars in the jet-black sky of Ice when Merlene, tired from the long climb up the foothills at the base of the northern mountain chain, came to a stop beside the giant machine from space. She looked up again at the mechanical monster that towered over her. The shape, though familiar through long association, was still alien to her eye. The planetary lander from Earth had come long ago, over five plus four twoffdays—nearly twenty human years. It had traveled through space from one of the specks of light near Brightstar, which the human called Sol. Although Merlene, with her large single eyeglobe, could easily see the larger gas-giant planets orbiting Brightstar, the speck of light the humans called Earth was so small that she could observe it only with her best diamond eyepiece on her best telescope.

Over time, the round pads at the ends of the three legs of the lander had sunk deep into the dirty white surface of Ice. The legs themselves were covered with layer after layer of rime crust that had been deposited by the occasional frost storms that followed when a geyser spouted. The central body of the machine, however, was warm and clear of frost.

Merlene could see the various emblems of the nations of Earth that had sponsored this expedition to the home world of the kerack race on the outskirts of the solar system—out past the planets, where the comets originated. But, although ice-covered, Merlene's world was no comet. Ice was as big as many of the moons around the giant planets that orbited Brightstar.

Merlene had spent many days conversing with the alien humans through the lander since it had dropped down on Ice long ago. The effort of learning how to communicate with them had been a tedious task, but as Wizard of Camalor it was one of her primary duties, for certainly there was much she could learn from the humans, and they certainly seemed to be willing to share their knowledge. The first task, of course, had been for them to learn to speak to each other. Fortunately the humans were prepared for this, and the lander machine contained not only a voice that could talk to Merlene, but an eye with which it could see her and anything she brought for the machine to look at. It also contained a thing like a smoothboard, but more magical—not only could she draw on it, but the humans could see what she drew from a distance and draw on it in return, sometimes sending moving drawings that were so complex and detailed they looked like real objects.

At first, the most difficult problem was the long time lag between asking a question and getting a reply. Merlene would first listen to a long speech by the humans, then make a similarly long response, and then wait for a third of a day before a reply came. But, with the help of a semi-intelligent intermediator inside the lander that the humans called a "computer-translator," and aided by her excellent memory and the notes she made in her notebook, Merlene soon developed the ability to carry on discussions about many different topics at the same time.

Thus, over time, despite the long round-trip communications delay, the humans had learned to talk to her in the kerack language, while she had learned some human words. More importantly, she had learned a number of new technologies. Now, with the recent landing of six humans behind the mountains to the north, the response time between question and answer was almost instantaneous. The keracks and the humans were now ready to meet eyeglobe-to-eyeglobe.

Merlene, wanting to look her best, used the small claws on her second pair of legs to adjust the skirt surrounding her ample abdomen, making sure the back of the skirt properly covered her wide, finned tail. The bottom of her tail was splayed out on the ice, cooling her off after her climb to the landing site. She would normally have ridden up to the lander on a heuller, letting the beast do the work. But on this trip she had left the heuller back in the pen on her husband's farm. She wasn't sure how the beast would react to the presence of humans.

She noticed that the exertion of the climb had caused her chestcoat to twist around, wrinkling some of the ornate designs in front. Standing tall on her two hind legs and tail, and straightening up her body, she used her eight other legs to adjust the star-embroidered black velvet chestcoat on her ebony-shelled thorax. Then, one by one, she pulled the ten puffed black velvet sleeves down to their proper position on her legs. A final check of the black constellation-sprinkled wizard's Cape o'Trade around her shoulders, and her discreet, five-layered, black gauze mouthveil around her waist, and she was ready to welcome the visiting humans.

Actually, she would still not see the humans in person, for they were too big to walk the streets of Camalor. They were taller than the lander beside her. She looked up at it, towering over her, and tried to imagine a being that was even taller, a being that was somehow able to stand upright on only two legs without a tail for balance. The image made her dizzy. Not only were the humans too big to visit Camalor in person, they were too hot. Their bodies were so hot they glowed. They were probably even too hot to touch. So, instead of visiting in person, the humans were going to visit Camalor in proxy, in machines the size and shape of keracks, called telebots.

The humans, just six of them, had landed in a small valley far back in the middle of the northern mountain chain, where the flames spewing from the gigantic engines on their large flying flamewagon would cause the least amount of disruption to the people living in the cities on Ice. The humans had set up a small base to live in, and would now transport the telebots for a visit with Merlene using a small flamewagon they called a microhopper. The microhopper would shuttle the telebots back and forth between the human base and Merlene's city of Camalor, and later other cities on Ice. Merlene hoped, however, to convince the humans to stay in Camalor so she could learn as much as possible from them. She especially wanted to learn the powers of the human wizards that allowed them to build machines that used flame to fly through the sky. To keep them in Camalor, she would do her best to satisfy their inquisitive desire to learn all about kerack culture. But that would not be hard, for Camalor was indisputably the best city on Ice.

Merlene stretched out the two antennae on either side of her single large eye. Through her antennae she received, off in the background, the constant murmur over the electromagnetic aether that was generated by the many thoughts that made up the Spirit o'Camalor. Now, being quite distant from the city, she felt dull in intelligence, and lonely—almost bereft. She would be glad when she was back in the middle of the city and participating directly in the thoughts of the Spirit, for then she would not only be happier, she would be smarter and her memory more acute. Suddenly her antennae picked up an alien radio signal from the aether, a signal that came from the opposite direction from Camalor.

"Rob Young calling Merlene," said the rough, hissing mechanical voice of the human. Overlaid on the voice were confusing, twittering, mechanical noises. "We have you in sight and should be arriving there shortly."

Merlene turned to look northward with her eye—an eye that was so sensitive it could see as well by the starlight at night as by Brightstar during the day. With her antennae acting as direction finders, she soon spotted a tiny speck approaching low in the sky over the mountains. The speck grew larger, and Merlene could now see that the microhopper was a vehicle similar in shape to the lander, with three legs sticking out from a central body. It emitted a few short bursts of flame, which caused it to slowly turn around until it was traveling backwards. Then another burst of bright flames and soon the microhopper came to a halt in the sky overhead, hovering in the air on its roaring hot flame. Then, slowly, it settled to the surface in a cloud of blowing ice and hissing vapor.

Merlene was surprised to see that the microhopper was actually slightly smaller than the ancient lander, but then she realized that it wasn't built to carry heavy equipment like interplanetary communicators or the heavy, hot things called power supplies that kept the communicators operating for long periods of time. All the microhopper had to do was deliver the two telebots with their proxy human inside them. As Merlene waited for the landing site to cool down and the door on the side of the microhopper to open, she took her wizard's notebook out of her carrying pouch and made a quick sketch of the vehicle on a foil page with her diamond scribe.

The door slid open. Two keracklike creatures tentatively emerged, and with an awkward gait they made their way out onto the ice. The creatures were obviously artificial, like kerack statues that had come to life. As on a kerack body, the head of each was small and consisted mostly of a large, single eyeglobe with two antennae emanating from either side of it. The head sat directly on the thorax, from which sprouted ten legs, five on each side. The first legs had large claws with three opposable pincers, while the rest had smaller pincers that could be either brought together to grasp something or splayed out to provide support. The thorax was connected to a large abdomen by a thin waist. At the top of the abdomen, just below the waist, was the mouth, which in the human telebots was nonfunctional, and at the base was the tail, which supplied cooling and balance. One of the telebots had the two normal front claws of a kerack female and was wearing the female mouthveil at her waist, while the other had a large male warclaw on his right front leg and was wearing the male mouthbelt around his waist with a modest tonguepouch hanging from it.

The shells of the telebots were structured in the form of kerack shells, but instead of ebony-colored boron carbide with a rich sheen, they were made of slickly shining brown-black metal. In the eyeglobe of each robot Merlene could see projected images of the soft faces of the humans, as if their heads were inside it. Having seen humans before in the lander viewing screen, she was used to the strange organization of the features, with the two small eyes that could only look in one direction, and the naked mouth right below the eyes through which she could see flashes of naked white teeth and pink tongue. The humans didn't have antennae for carrying on conversations by radio signals; instead they used their mouths for talking, using acoustical noises. For listening, they had basin-shaped, acoustical focusing structures on either side of their heads.

In order to provide communication between the two alien species, the computer-translator in the lander and in the telebots took the audio tones coming from the human mouths, translated them into kerack language, and broadcast the kerack words through the telebot's antennae into the aether as radio waves. The radio waves Merlene sent in answer were detected by the antennae, translated from kerack to human, and then broadcast by audio speakers to the human ears.

Merlene was abruptly taken aback by the crude clothing of the human telebots. Being aware of the sensitivity of keracks to seeing naked shells, and especially naked mouths, the humans had attempted to cover the bodies of the telebots with chestcoats, skirts, and mouth covers. But Merlene was appalled to see that the style of their clothing was atrocious and the fabric so flimsy as to be almost transparent. Revising her initial estimate of the infinite wisdom of the human wizards, she resolved that their first stop in town would be at the workshop of the clothier. Meanwhile, not wanting to alienate her most intelligent, but perhaps not most knowledgeable friends, she would make the best of things.

"Merlene be greeting her new friends," she said, bowing low to the two telebots as if they were noble ladies.

"I'm Rob Young," said the telebot with the warclaw. "And this is Selke Bergen." Selke attempted a bow, but, not used to her new body in the low 15 percent Earth gravity of Ice, she lost her balance and splayed her front claws out on the crust to keep herself from falling. Merlene politely didn't see the slip.

"Merlene be taking human wizard friends into Camalor. It be a long distance, so we be best moving onward." She started down the slope at her usual eight-legged scurrying gait but soon realized she was leaving the humans far behind, and slowed down. The humans followed as fast as they could go, but their gait was restricted by the limits on the mechanical transfer characteristics between human bodies and the kerack-shaped bodies of the telebots.

"I can see this is going to get tiring fast," Rob griped to Selke over their private audiolink, which worked through encrypted spread-spectrum channels linking the telebots with the home base and each other. With the thumb and first two fingers on each hand engaged in control-ring levers that were mapped onto the three-fingered major front claws of the telebot, he was left with only the two remaining fingers on each hand to activate the walking mechanism. Unfortunately, there were four walking legs on each side of the kerack body to control. The final engineering solution had been to map the human feet into the kerack tail to provide balance, with toe pedals controlling the communication links, map the thumb and first two fingers of each hand to the front claws, and map the two remaining fingers onto the four walking legs of the kerack body, each finger controlling two legs. The orientation and spread angle of the three-pincered "feet" of each walking leg were automatically controlled by force feedback to accommodate variations in ground contour. This produced an awkward two-pair by two-pair motion of the four pairs of walking legs instead of Merlene's fluid, multilegged gait.

After they had been traveling for a while, Rob and Selke called a halt and stopped at the peak of a foothill to rest their third and little "walking" fingers and take a look at the city of Camalor before them. Merlene politely came back to wait with them. Like all the similar-sized cities spread out on the plains of Ice, Camalor had a circular shape, with a central park region and six main roads radiating outward, crossed at intervals by concentric roads. At the very center of the park was a dark-colored, circular plaza devoid of plants or structures except for a black stepped tower, three stories tall, in the very center. The park had numerous low shrubs and paths wandering through the plantings, providing access from one area to another. Each area possessed different structures, plant arrangements, and ground features. In one was a gigantic maze of high hedges, probably too tall for a kerack to look over, with several circular spaces inside that looked like picnic areas.

"That smooth area over there next to the maze looks like a lake, with islands in it," said Selke, pointing with her right claw.

"If it's on Ice, it can't be a lake," Rob replied. "No element or compound known is a liquid at thirty degrees above absolute zero at almost zero pressure. They are either gases, like hydrogen, helium, and neon, or they are solids, like everything else." Then he saw a kerack workman dragging something like a board across the surface of the pond, legs splaying to the sides as he moved across the surface like an eight-legged ice skater. The board was steaming slightly, and behind it, the surface of the pond had been changed from a frosty white to a jet black. Rob realized that he could see stars in the black area, that the blackness was the reflection of the sky.

"It's an ice-skating rink!" he exclaimed. Turning to Merlene he asked, "What is the lake made of? Water ice?"

"Water ice be too dry for good sliding," Merlene replied. "The Basin o'Sliding be covered with nitrogen ice."

Selke pointed in another direction. "I assume the large oval area over there is the amphitheater."

"Selke be correct," said Merlene. "The Oval o'All be large enough to hold all those that live in Camalor."

"What is that large rectangular building on the other side, with the many small buildings and the fenced-off areas around it?" Rob asked.

"That be the Courtyard o'Warriors, where the warriors be living and training in their trade. The outbuildings be for the workshops of the armorers, weapon-makers, harness-makers, victuallers, and stablers. The pens be for the war-heullers."

Merlene pointed to another structure off to the right. "That be the final school for the older children. When the children be young, they be taught reading, writing, and counting in neighborhood crèches. They be then going to final school for instruction in the finer arts and crafts, where they be exposed to artisans from all disciplines. They be choosing then a trade and be apprenticed to an artisan to learn that trade."

"I understand from our briefing that most of the buildings in the city are underground, which is why most of Camalor looks like a park with streets running through it," Selke said.

"What are those low buildings in the area around the park?"

"That be Old Camalor. The elder artisans be living there. They be now having so many apprentices that they be expanding their workshops up to the surface. Merlene be taking you there." She started off down the slope again, and with a groan, Rob and Selke wiggled their smaller fingers and followed her down.

At the outskirts of the city they had to pass through a gate guarded by a bored warrior patrolling the boundary walls on a large, caterpillarlike animal. Upon seeing and smelling the mechanical bodies of the telebots, the beast became agitated, and it took all the riding abilities of the young warrior to stay on the back of the frightened animal as it rolled sideways again and again.

"That must be the beast of burden Merlene described earlier—the heuller," said Selke. "Built like a caterpillar, but with four sets of legs, two on the top and two on the bottom."

"That baby is big—even by Earth caterpillar standards!" Rob said, impressed. "Must be a whole eight centimeters high. Tall as a kerack—and some twenty-four centimeters long."

The heuller had a single large eye and two antennae up front, quite similar in size and shape to the head of a kerack. But it had no thorax and no waist, just a head stuck onto a long abdomenlike body. There were four sets of legs going down the length of the body, two above and two below, and forty-eight feet in each set. Each foot had three stubby, clawed, opposable "toes." The feet near the head were larger, designed for digging, while the feet along the body were designed like those of an Earth mole, equally good for walking or pushing through a tunnel.

The warrior finally got the heuller under control and forced it slowly back toward them. The kerack was larger than Merlene and had the one large warclaw that indicated that he was a male. His antennae had a number of gold and silver rings spaced at intervals along them, and his red-edged cape carried on it the multipointed mace symbol of a warrior, embroidered in silver thread. Below the mace symbol was the portrait of the Queen of Camalor.

In the warrior's warclaw rested a long lance with a striated shaft made of a light plastic material bonded to metal strengthening fibers, and a sharp point made of what looked like titanium. The warrior held a shield in his other claw. At the top of the shield was a clear dome, obviously for protecting his large, single eye from damage while still allowing vision. A well-used mace hung by his side. Some of its points had obviously once been bent over and then straightened out and sharpened again. The chain mail that covered his carapace from eye to tail was of a businesslike gray metal alloy over a heavy underpad. Across his thorax were broad belts of crimson that bound dagger scabbards to his back, with the handles of the daggers sticking forward where he could quickly grab them with the claws on his second pair of legs. The brightest spot on the warrior was the broad mouth-belt around his waist, made of a shimmering green satinlike fabric. At the point where the belt covered the warrior's mouth there emerged a grotesquely long tonguepouch of heavily embroidered golden-yellow fabric that hung halfway down his abdomen.

Like all those in Camalor, the warrior was in constant radio contact with the whole community and, like everyone else, had known Merlene would be bringing the humans into the city today.

"The Wizard Merlene be best keeping the human strangers away from the stables," warned the warrior, resuming his seat on his mount.

The heuller had finally calmed down, and its upper two sets of legs had re-formed into a saddle that held the warrior up on top of the beast. As they passed through the gate in the wall guarded by the nervous beast and its rider, Rob could now see the large mouth of the heuller between two of the

front digging feet. The mouth was full of huge, well-worn
transparent teeth with flat facets.

"Look at those teeth!" Rob exclaimed to Selke. "I didn't
believe it when we were told in the briefing that the heullers
had grinding molars made of diamond. Those must be a
couple of carats each."

Selke snorted. "Those teeth may be made of pure diamond, but they aren't worth the cost of shipping them back
to Earth—except perhaps as curiosities."

Leaving the warrior behind, they stepped from the crusty
irregular ice that covered the open country onto the paved
roads inside the wall.

"All roads lead to Camalor," Selke said wryly as they set
out on the long, broad highway. "This looks as straight and
level as the proverbial Roman roads."

"It looks like it's been paved with crushed rock cemented
with ice," said Rob. He stopped to look down and used his
toes to operate the zoom on the camera built into the eyeglobe of his telebot so he could get a close-up record of the
texture of the surface.

"Rob be correct," Merlene said. "Specially trained heullers be tunneling through the ice to the rock below. There
they be grinding up rock and be bringing it up to the surface
and regurgitating it to make the roads."

"Useful animals," Rob mused. "Cement mixers you can
ride on."

Now that they were on a smooth paved road, the going
was easier for the humans, for they could put their telebots
into autopilot mode and let their fingers go along for the
ride. As they went along the road, they could see that
the outskirts of the city had been divided into farming plots,
roughly rectangular in shape, each tended by male keracks.
Out on the periphery were newer plots tended by older,
larger males assisted by two or three younger male apprentices. Most of these farms were undergoing what looked like
ice-mining operations, with waste heaps covered with a

black, funguslike growth. Closer to the center of the city were more established plots with rows and rows of shrubs carrying multicolored berries growing out of the fungus-covered mounds. These plots were tended by smaller, younger males. All of the farmers had at least one heuller.

"They have the beasts well trained," Selke noted, pointing to a heuller pulling a two-wheeled cart loaded with dirty ice. "See how the heuller grasps the drawbars of the cart with its upper hind feet. No wagon harnesses needed."

"I see," said Rob. "In that last field I saw a farmer riding up front on a heuller, and behind him were baskets of berries, held in place by the animal's upper set of feet. Didn't even need straps to tie the load on." He paused, then said very deliberately, "I would say it is a very *handy* pet, wouldn't you?"

He looked sideways out of his eyeglobe at the image of Selke projected on her eyeglobe to see if she got the pun. She didn't, but Rob was pleased to hear Elizabeth burst into a giggle over the audiolink between the telebot and the base. Elizabeth Mackay was back at the base monitoring the video screens showing the views picked up by the visual, infrared, and microwave imagers looking out the eyeglobes of the telebots. Her primary task was to make sure that the data link was functioning and that the recording equipment was set at a data rate appropriate to the information in that spectral channel, but she also acted as "data fetcher" in case the two humans working the telebots needed some information stored in the base computer.

As Rob and Selke left the fields and entered the outskirts of the city, Merlene was relieved to feel the Spirit o'Camalor flood back into her through her antennae. She connected into the Spirit and, looking carefully and thoroughly at each of the two humans in turn, forced a memory of their likeness and smell.

From now on, the kerack-shaped bodies of the human wizards would be instantly recognized and accepted by everyone in the community. Remembering the incident with the heuller at the city gate, she also searched out the indistinct sector of the Spirit that represented the blurred thinking of the many heullers in the city, and forced the same memories on them, along with the reassuring thought that one normally used to pacify the giant creatures.

"Merlene be first taking you to a clothier's," she said, stopping at a hole in the ground with steps that led downward. She headed down the stairs, and the humans two-stepped their way after her. As they descended below the surface, Rob audiolinked a query back to Elizabeth.

"How is the base-to-'bot link holding up as we go underground?"

"The 'hopper-to-'bot radio link has only dropped a few db in signal strength," Elizabeth reported. "It looks like the ice on Ice is so cold that it's almost transparent to radio waves, despite the dust in it. There is plenty of margin in the signal level."

With the starlight blocked, the humans switched from the visible-image intensifiers to the infrared arrays in the telebots' eyeglobes. After passing through a first-floor landing leading to a kerack home, the stairs ended in a large workroom containing rolls of woven cloth, cutting tables, and a couple of busy young female apprentices sewing by the light of some glowworms. The visitors were greeted by a neatly but simply attired clothier standing next to racks and racks of clothing.

"May Homene be of service to the Wizard Merlene?" asked the clothier.

"Merlene be requesting some appropriate sets of clothing for her human friends," Merlene answered.

Rob looked down at the serviceable cloth chestcoat and skirt that covered his telebot. He thought that the seamstresses back on Earth had done an excellent job of fitting the multilegged thorax. The fabric even had woven ornate patterns that had been copied from kerack patterns transmitted back to Earth.

"What's wrong with these clothes?" he asked.

"They be crude in fabric, style, and pattern," Merlene said sharply. "If humans be Wizards o'Earth, they should be dressing like wizards, not like slop-bucket menders from Harvamor."

In the meantime, Selke had wandered over to look at some of the clothing hanging from the racks. "I begin to see what she means." She held a chestcoat up to her eyeglobe and illuminated the ornate pattern on the coat with an electric light built into the base of the eyeglobe. "Back on Earth, when we were designing the clothing to cover our 'bots, all we had as examples to copy from were long-distance shots of clothing Merlene brought for the lander video camera to look at. We got the general overall patterns, but none of the finer detail. The work is extremely intricate, down to the limit of vision of the cameras on my 'bot."

"Must be due to the large size of the kerack eye compared to the kerack body," said Rob, coming over to see for himself. "We thought the large eye size was primarily for collecting as much light as possible out here, where the only light to see by is starlight and infrared emission from warm objects. But the large lens would also let them see finer detail than the small lenses in our lander cameras." He held a chestcoat up to his thorax and turned to look in a nearby mirror that resembled finely polished aluminum. "Say, that *does* look good. I wouldn't mind switching to some fancier duds."

"Merlene be happy," she said with obvious relief. "Now humans be not looking . . ." She struggled to find some euphemism for the naughty word. ". . . uncovered."

"I don't understand," said Rob, bewildered. He'd been well briefed and was well aware of the strong kerack taboos on nakedness. He looked down at the thick, heavy-duty clothing that covered the metallic carapace of his 'bot.

"Rob, switch to microwave vision only," said Selke. She was obviously using that mode now, for she was moving her eyeglobe around from Rob to Merlene and back again. Rob twitched a few toes in his telebot controller back at the base, and the visible and infrared seeing modes in the telebot switched off, leaving only the backup microwave vision operating. Whereas in the visible and infrared modes Selke's telebot had been decently clothed, in the microwave region of the spectrum the telebot was naked! No wonder Merlene had been too embarrassed to parade them through the city.

Rob looked at Merlene, the clothier, and the two apprentices with his microwave vision. They were all not only properly covered, their clothing had equally striking patterns in the microwave that were different from the patterns in the visible. Rob looked at the racks of clothing and rolls of cloth—all reflected microwaves. He decided the fabric had wire threads woven into it.

Rob switched the telebot vision from microwave only to infrared only to visible only, and with each switch, the clothing on the keracks changed in pattern and color. The microwave and infrared vision systems in the telebots had been designed to provide different false colors for different wavelengths. In each imager, the microwave and infrared patterns were just as ornate and colorful as the visible patterns, but they were distinctly different. Rob also realized that the false colors of the human imagers, probably produced images for the humans that were colored differently than the "real" images that keracks "saw."

Rob and Selke were soon outfitted in relatively plain but microwave-opaque clothing. The clothier then took their measurements for a more ornate set of clothing that would be more appropriate for wizards of Earth. Rob watched as Merlene gave Homene a large pouch of berries in payment. Suddenly Merlene's antennae stood straight up in the air, followed by the antennae of Homene and the apprentices.

"Lady Vivane!" they all cried, and bowed low toward the

stairway. Rob and Selke just stood there, bewildered, for they had heard nothing over their radio antennae except the general background murmur that pervaded Camalor.

There was a bustle on the stairway and a large female swept into the room. She was dressed in an ornate, bejeweled chestcoat with diamond-stud buttons, a long, sweeping, equally ornate skirt that she expertly kept under control with kicks of her fifth set of legs, a multilayered mouthveil that was so long it looked like a floor-length apron, and a white-on-white patterned cape with a portrait of the Queen on the back.

Her chestcoat had two large bumps under it that looked remarkably like the matronly bosom on a grande dame, but it was obvious that the chestcoat had not been designed to cover one of those bumps, for the fabric was under considerable strain in that region, distorting the ornate patterns in the cloth. In each of her two front leg claws was a furry animal. The animals were the size, shape, and structure of the claws that held them, with three large leg pincers that lay along the inside of the three pincers on her claws. Each animal was so large that it prevented her from using the claw for anything else, but the animal's pincers took over the task of grasping. One of the animals was holding a single-lensed lorgnette that Lady Vivane used to haughtily examine the detail of the patterns on some of the fabrics on the table. The other animal was holding a piece of food, which the lady tucked under her mouthveil occasionally in order to take a bite. The animal alternated bites of the food with its owner, its actions seemingly unnoticed by her.

"May Homene be of service to the Lady Vivane?" asked the clothier, holding her low bow. Merlene, also bowing, scuttled backward toward the humans and herded them into a far corner.

Lady Vivane addressed the clothier as if the humans and Merlene were not there. "Lady Vivane be blessed with a new beautybump and needs a new chestcoat immediately."

Merlene touched her antennae to those of the two humans and whispered, "Humans be following Merlene." She bowed again toward Lady Vivane and sidled toward the stairwell. Rob and Selke followed, also bowing as low as they dared. Merlene ushered them up the stairwell to the surface.

"We be returning to the clothier Homene later when Lady Vivane be gone," she said. She paused to look at them critically. "Those clothes be doing for now, but Merlene must be getting you clothing and capes appropriate to your standing and trade."

"This certainly seems to be a class-ridden society," Selke remarked over the audiolink.

"Reminds me of the royal family and the aristocracy back home," Elizabeth audiolinked back. "By the way, I just looked up the word *beautybump* in the kerack dictionary that Merlene helped us develop. A beautybump is a furry pet that the keracks wear on their bodies, usually on their chests. Those animals that you saw Lady Vivane carrying in her claws are also pets. Reasonably enough, the translation program calls them 'clawpets.' The dictionary also notes that ownership of pets is limited to the ladies of the nobility."

"Merlene be now taking her human friends to visit her home and workshop," said Merlene. She led the way inward toward the older part of the city. As they traveled, the streets became more crowded.

"That's the trouble with the spoke-and-concentric-ring road pattern," Rob said. "Had the same problem in the Pentagon. The shortest route to practically anywhere involves first going inward, so the inner ring corridor is always crowded."

The parklike atmosphere of the outer suburbs slowly degraded into the crowded, noisy city center as they moved inward. The more established merchants in the older part of the city had outgrown their underground workshops and had expanded up to the surface, where they displayed their goods. Nearly all the merchants were females, with the ex-

ception of a few dealing in crafts that required the large size
or large claw of a male.

One shop, with a male butcher and male apprentices,
specialized in slaughtering heullers. It was a gory sight. They
used heavy, swordlike axes to cut apart the 48 armored
segments in the long, fat, caterpillarlike animal. Yellow-
brown blood dripped from the carcass to the floor, where it
froze into slippery piles of gore.

"Ask Merlene to get us a sample of that heuller for me to
analyze," Hiroshi Yazawa requested over the audiolink from
the base.

"Good thought," Selke replied, then she turned to Merlene. "Could we get a section of that heuller? One quarter of
one section would be a sufficient sample. Tell them we want
the internal organs, blood, outer shell, foot, and all. Also, if
it isn't too heavy to carry, we'd like the whole head section
too."

"Merlene be understanding the desires of the human wizards," she said, and went over to talk to the butcher.

The butcher, Roklart, required a little persuading, since
his pride objected to selling an uncleaned carcass, but when
he understood that the humans were not going to eat it, but
just dissect it to see how the heuller body was constructed, he
relented. He was relieved to get rid of the head section so
easily. Although the juices of a heuller eyeglobe could be
used as the base for a dipping sauce, and a heuller tongue
was edible if you cut it into tiny chunks so it didn't look like
a tongue, the hard teeth were of no use to anyone.

Rob and Selke watched while Merlene paid the butcher
with some berries from her carrying pouch, and the three
continued on their way, Selke carrying the quarter section
and Rob the head.

"I feel like an ant that is proudly carrying home the head
from a dead fly," said Rob, easily holding the large, single-
eyed heuller head in his warclaw.

"You're just demonstrating the square-cube strength-to-mass law for living creatures," Selke said. "Plus the fact tha the gravity on Ice is only fifteen percent of Earth gravity."

There was a commotion up ahead.

"Make way!" came a loud cry. "Make way for Princess Onlone!"

"The humans be fortunate this day," Merlene said excit edly. "The wizards from Earth be getting to see the Princess Regent herself!"

The call grew louder, and soon a warrior could be seen over the heads of the crowd, riding on the back of a large heuller. He was dressed in gold chain mail with the image of the Queen picked out in links of silver. His only weapon was an obviously ceremonial mace held straight out before him in his warclaw. The head of the mace was a multifaceted diamond that glittered in the light from Brightstar. Behind him was a wedge of other warriors that filled the street. The lead warrior's gold-ringed antennae straightened.

"Make way for the Princess Onlone!" he called again, his voice over the aether overloading the radio receiver in Rob's telebot.

The crowd, pushed back to the sides of the street by the advancing wedge of heullers, stood as the procession made its way. Following in the wake of the wedge was a gigantic kerack warrior on an even more gigantic war-heuller. His antennae were nearly solidly packed with golden rings. One antenna ended in a gold ball with spikes on it, like a miniature mace or star; the other ended in a silver star.

His gold chain mail was the finest that Rob had seen yet, with intricate patterns formed from the shape, surface roughness, and interconnections of the rings. His cape was made of gold chain mail so fine it moved almost like cloth. His war-heuller was also covered in golden chain mail, and considering the size of the beast, it must have taken an armorer ages to make the enormous blanket.

"That be Mordet, the consort to Princess Onlone," said Merlene.

Behind Mordet came four young warriors on foot, easily carrying between them an open sedan chair in their war-claws. Riding in the chair was a large female in an ornate dress woven of silver threads and bejeweled with sparkling diamonds. Around her eyeglobe was a circlet of silver, also encrusted with diamonds. She was looking straight ahead, ignoring the crowd, who were all bowing low as she passed. The humans also bowed, but not too far, in order that they could capture a good video record of the procession. It was hard to see because of the crowds, but the thorax of the female seemed bigger than normal, as if she had four large breasts under her chestcoat. She was also carrying something white and furry in both her first and second claws—obviously clawpets, very large clawpets.

"That be the Princess Regent Onlone," whispered Merlene to the humans from her low bow. "She be the only one allowed to speak to the Queen."

The procession finally passed by, with a final rank of warriors on heullers bringing up the rear. Merlene and the humans continued on their way toward the center of Camalor. They entered the park, and Merlene led them along a winding pathway that led past the final school. The icy crust in the park was lightly covered with a black fungus, and through the growth sprouted small bushes that came up about waist-high on the keracks.

Rob looked at them closely. "They have berries on them. Can I pick one for a sample?"

"One be not an adequate sample," Merlene replied. "These bushes be similar to those on the farms, and the berries on those bushes be larger and more ripe than these in the park."

"Let me get those heuller meat samples analyzed first," Hiroshi reminded over the audiolink. "Then I'll be ready to cope with samples of the vegetation."

As they walked by the final school, they noticed a class of young females gathered around an older and larger female outside the building. There was an intense glare of light coming from what looked like a brick kiln. The older female was dressed in a plain chestcoat and skirt, not much different from the simple dress Selke wore, but her whole front was covered with a heavy apron and she wore what looked like a welder's helmet with a circular pane of dark glass covering her eyeglobe. Using a three-pincered set of tongs, she reached into the oven and pulled out a glowing metal vase. Holding it above a mold, she poured out a clear glowing liquid that gave off clouds of vapor that turned to snow and fell to the ground all around the mold. Intrigued, Merlene and the humans stopped to watch. A few moments later the instructor opened the mold to show the class the crystal-clear cart spoke she had cast.

"That be dihydrogen oxide, or what you humans call water ice," said Merlene. "It be plentiful on Ice and quite strong, especially under compression. It be much stronger than nitrogen or methane ice."

As they were leaving the school Rob asked, "Why do you build structures with walls and ceilings like this final school? There is almost no atmosphere on Ice, and therefore no weather. Why do you bother with shelters?"

"It be true that there seldom be weather on Ice," replied Merlene. "But when there be weather, it be quite strong."

"You forgot the geysers, Rob," Selke reminded him. "This planetoid is big enough to have a hot interior, and once every few years a geyser erupts, throwing out nitrogen, methane, and ammonia-water. Then for a few months the atmosphere gets much thicker and there is much weather."

"That be why most homes and workshops be underground," Merlene added. "Merlene be taking you next to her home and workshop."

"Then this would be a good time to make a shift change," Rob said to Selke.

"Shift change is past due!" complained the voice of Gabrielle over the audiolink. "Get out of these 'bots so Boris and I can see what Camalor is like!"

"We must go now," Selke said to Merlene. "Boris Chekhov and Gabrielle Mercerau will be here shortly to replace us." Her visage in the eyeglobe blinked off, leaving the mechanical kerack body still and devoid of life. Rob put down the huge heuller head he had been carrying, and his eyeglobe blinked off too. Merlene didn't like the abrupt departure of the humans, or the disturbing simulations of dead keracks they left behind, but she supposed she would soon get used to it.

2

BACK AT THE BASE

A HUNCHED-OVER, cocoonlike object at one end of the cramped room split open along the back, and a tall, thin body clothed in white cotton long johns raised its black-helmeted head. Selke Bergen pulled her hands loose from the arms of the sensuit and, sitting up, took off the verihelm, revealing a strong-jawed face with serious blue eyes and a long sharp nose. Her short cap of sensibly cut yellow hair was damp with perspiration from being in the helmet for the past four hours. She reached down through the fly front in her long johns and pulled loose the urinal tube from the gathering device. Unfortunately for her, she had been forced to use it, and it had leaked a little. Fortunately for her, it was time for her once-a-day shower—if only she could get into the communal bathroom before Rob. She emerged from the sensuit somewhat awkwardly, like a newly hatched butterfly emerging from a cocoon. The tilted orientation of the cushioned front of the sensuit was what made it possible to operate the telebot in relative comfort for hours at a time, but the tilt also made it difficult to get out.

"Sorry—had a little accident," she apologized to Gabrielle Mercerau as the smaller woman came to take her place. Gabrielle had short, curly brown hair and deep brown eyes. She too was dressed in long johns, ready to start her shift in the telebot controller. Selke trotted gingerly on bare feet across the cold metal floor into the bathroom and locked the door behind her.

Gabrielle had arrived for her shift with a towel in one hand and a replacement cushion under her other arm. In a practiced series of motions learned during many training sessions, she used the towel to dry the inside of the verihelm, then moved on down to wipe out the body and limbs of the close-fitting sensuit. After removing Selke's damp body cushion and setting it aside to dry, she replaced it with her dry cushion and, climbing in, settled her body into the cocoon.

Next to her, the other sensuit split open and Rob Young raised his head and took off his verihelm. Tall, muscular, and handsome, with gray eyes and long, beautiful, curly brown hair, he looked like the Hollywood version of a medieval knight.

"What a fascinating place!" he said. "And in the telebot it's just like you're really there in person."

"Except you are a bug instead of a person," Gabrielle said dryly as she hooked up her urine tube.

"You're going to love it!" Rob struggled out of the tilted sensuit, getting a little help from Boris Chekhov, who had just come over for the shift change. Boris was the same age as Rob, also tall, muscular, and handsome, but with his balding pate and short fringe of graying hair, he looked much older—more like the Hollywood version of an experienced astronaut than a medieval knight.

"I'll sure be glad to get my s-'n'-s," Rob said with a grin, which rapidly faded as he looked around the shelter. The two communal bunks were open and empty, and Selke was not in the commons room, so that meant that she was behind the locked door of the only other room in the small shelter. He would have to wait his turn at the single toilet and shower. He took the towel from Boris and wiped down the leg and arm holes of the sensuit while Boris changed the body cushion.

Watching them both from one of the two telebot monitor consoles above and behind the sensuits was Hiroshi Yazawa, a thin, medium-sized man with straight black hair and almost black almond-shaped eyes. In front of him were the two main video monitors that showed the view out of the eyeglobes of the telebots now resting on the surface of Ice. Each monitor held a view of the alien shape of the wizard Merlene. To Hiroshi, Merlene looked like a large, one-eyed prawn that some child had dressed in fancy clothing. Now, considering that they were becoming close friends with the kerack wizard, Hiroshi was beginning to wonder if he would ever be able to eat shrimp tempura again.

"That is, if I survive this mission and make it back to Japan," he muttered to himself. Although the cable catapults set up at Earth and Ice were able to boost their interplanetary spacecraft to speeds of 50 kilometers per second, it still took over three years to travel from the inner solar system out to the inner portions of the Kuiper Belt where they were. Also, to attain that speed required that the crew be accelerated and decelerated at thirty gees for almost three minutes. Despite the immersion tank that helped them survive the strain, it had taken desperate measures by Elizabeth and Selke to revive Hiroshi after the deceleration period at Ice. Although the others made it through without much difficulty, Hiroshi's heart, after so many years at low gravity, had stopped under the strain. He was not sure he would survive the trip back.

Still, Hiroshi was glad he had come to explore Ice and interact with the keracks. A Reiyūkai Buddhist, he believed strongly in the philosophy of "dependent origination"—that every thing and being in the universe comes into existence through its relationship with other things and beings. Hiroshi was pleased that he would be extending this philosophy to things and beings not of Earth. He considered himself fortunate that he had been one of the six picked for this mission, out of all the discontented and unhappy billions on increasingly crowded Earth. He felt that he had been guided in his life by the spirits of his ancestors.

His meditation was interrupted by a commotion behind him. He turned around just in time to see Elizabeth Mackay heading for the fold-up table in front of the one window in the small shelter.

"Lucifer! You damn cat! Get out of my dinner!"

There was a slap, an enraged yowl, and a large bundle of bristling black fur flew across the room in the low gravity and landed in one of the two sleeping bunks built into the far wall, ripping a hole in a sheet as sharp claws brought it to a halt. Lucifer was no longer the cute, tiny, fluff-ball kitten that Gabrielle had smuggled onto the mission in her personal baggage. He was now a big, black, frustrated male cat that refused to accept dominance by the six humans he lived with.

Elizabeth picked up her midshift meal where she had temporarily left it in order to refill her coffee cup from the galley spigot. She brought her food over to the telebot monitor console and stood next to Hiroshi. Elizabeth was tall, large, and heavy-boned, with Celtic curly red hair, green eyes, and pale white complexion sprinkled with a few freckles. She looked carefully at the plastic tray with its various reconstituted portions of microwaved food in their individual compartments. She could tell from the fang marks that Lucifer had taken a number of mouthfuls of her Caithness wild-salmon casserole. During the early years of the mission she would have carefully cut out the portion that the cat had touched, but now she just dug in with her spork and finished the whole thing off.

"It's not like we don't all share the same germs, anyway," she said with a resigned sigh as she watched Gabrielle hunker down into one of the sensuits.

Gabrielle put on her verihelm and leaned forward in her sensuit to slide her arms down so she could reach the ringed finger levers that controlled the claws and legs of the telebot. She tapped a suit control with one of her toes and the sensuit automatically closed around her body, leaving her in darkness. Another tap with her left big toe and the wraparound viewing screen inside the verihelm lit up with a high-resolution picture of Merlene in the park at the center of Camalor. The picture still looked like it was on a television screen, so Gabrielle deliberately moved the verihelm on her head back and forth a few times.

The signals from the verihelm shot out through a radio link to a communications satellite high overhead, then back down to the microhopper that had taken the telebots to the hillside outside Camalor. There the signal was amplified and beamed down to the antennae of the telebot. The head of the telebot in Camalor swung back and forth in imitation of the verihelm at the base, and the view seen by the video camera inside the eyeglobe changed with each motion. The moving series of video pictures were shot back through the communications link and brought before Gabrielle's eyes by the wraparound display in the helmet. By the time Gabrielle's head had moved twice, with the picture before her eyes changing in synchronism with the movements of her head, her brain had switched viewpoints. She was no longer at the base looking at a television screen inside a helmet. She was living in the virtual world that was the kerack city of Camalor, some thirty kilometers distant.

Hiroshi and Elizabeth watched the monitor move as Gabrielle shook herself into the scene. The image stabilized on the patiently waiting kerack, and they heard Gabrielle greet Merlene.

"Bonjour, Merlene! I am Gabrielle. Boris will be joining us shortly."

"Remember," Hiroshi called out as Boris sank down into the all-encompassing sensuit. "We have not yet found the missing energy source for the kerack civilization."

Boris nodded back in reply. Everyone on the mission

knew full well that what the keracks called "Brightstar" did not supply anywhere near the total amount of energy that was needed to support the obviously thriving life-forms on Ice. Everyone was interested in finding the missing energy source that allowed these aliens to survive out where there was almost no sunlight and therefore almost no energy.

Once Boris and Gabrielle had been teleported into their robotic bodies and had started their journey through the park to visit the home of Merlene, Elizabeth turned away from the monitor screens and spoke to Rob.

"We got a message from Grippen while you were away."

"Did he have anything nice to say?"

"Does he ever?"

"We might as well get it over with." Rob was technically mission commander, with Elizabeth in second command when he was busy operating one of the telebots. Leaving Hiroshi to monitor the progress of Boris and Gabrielle as they piloted the telebots through Camalor, Elizabeth went to one of the sleeping bunks, took out a Lookman that Gabrielle had been using to put herself to sleep, and brought it over to the single table in their cramped quarters. The table was opened up at mealtime. But when it was up there was only standing room for four of the six crew members, so it was usually folded against the wall under the window. Rob joined her as she removed Gabrielle's movie videochip from the pocketbook-sized video display device and replaced it with another from the communications rack that contained the message from Frank Grippen, program manager for the Kuiper Belt Contact Mission, the only mission left of the almost defunct United Nations Space Consortium Organization. UNSCO had been patched together after the Soviet Union had fragmented, the European Community had faltered, and the United States of the Americas had lost its verve.

No one nation felt it could afford space exploration alone, but the abortive attempt to form a cooperative consortium to revive space exploration under the auspices of the

UN had also failed, partly because of political bickering over the nationalities of the astronauts chosen for the missions and partly because of the paucity of contributions from the participants. Only because life had been found on Ice had there been sufficient interest to launch the present mission. But even then it had to be done on the cheap, since the politicians supplying the money complained that there was no likelihood that the human race would ever derive any financial return from the backward race of keracks that would cover the enormous cost of sending an exploration crew of humans far past the orbit of Neptune. Only the invention of the cable catapult, with its inherent ability to fly itself out of the solar system and place itself in orbit around the kerack planet, had made the mission feasible. To insure success, Frank Grippen had been appointed program manager. He had been chosen by the politicians and their captive bureaucrats for one reason and one reason only: it was known he could do things cheaply.

Elizabeth set the Lookman up on the table and turned it on. The face of a handsome middle-aged man appeared on the screen. His distinguished-looking gray hair was long, in the American style, and combed over in an attempt to hide a balding forehead. He wore distinctive, heavy-rimmed glasses in an age when most refraction problems could be handled by auto-focusing active contact lenses. There was a permanent, suspicious frown on his countenance, and his eyes and face muscles twitched nervously as he talked. The severe video compression algorithms used for planetary links normally made a person look like a cheap cartoon—a stationary head with just the lips moving. Unfortunately, the frame delays produced by the attempts of the algorithm to cope with Grippen's nervous facial twitches and eye movements usually resulted in a hilarious image. Hiroshi sometimes amused them by giving formal-sounding Grippen-like speeches, interspersed with Grippen-like inappropriate or delayed word gaps and exaggerated eye and mouth twitches.

"Grippen here," said the frowning image, mouth twitching during the pause after the greeting. Then, remembering that because of the long communications delay there would be no reply to his greeting for at least ten hours, he continued. *"You're two weeks behind schedule. My ass is going to be in hot water unless you six produce some data and pictures, and quickly!"*

"We're two weeks behind because of the cheap design of this tin balloon you gave us to live in," Rob grumbled.

Instead of a heavy and energy-expensive waste collector and dehydrator, the shelter had a single toilet that simply emptied out onto the surface of the planetoid. Before the crew could move from their landing rocket into the shelter, they'd had to dig a crude septic tank while wearing space suits, and that had taken time.

Rob sighed. Just then, Lucifer jumped back up on the table. Finding the food all gone, he deliberately sat in front of the Lookman, where his body effectively blocked the screen, and started licking his fur. Elizabeth reached out, and Lucifer responded with a warning hiss, raising a paw with his claws outstretched. Knowing better than to try to move the cat, Elizabeth reached around behind him and pulled the Lookman out where she and Rob could see it again. Lucifer continued licking. Grippen continued talking.

"By the time you get this, you should have made your first contact with that wizard person. Make sure you get some good videos of the meeting and send them to me immediately. The President is leaving for Camp David on Friday afternoon for a long weekend, and I want to get on her calendar to show the video clips to her in person before she leaves."

"He could release them to the press, or to his real boss, Lord Farquar, the head of UNSCO. But no—he has to pander to the US President," Elizabeth complained.

"That's where his real bureaucratic future lies," said Rob. "Besides, I wouldn't mind pandering to her myself—the most beautiful, richest, and most powerful bachelor-bitch in the world."

"She'd eat you alive," Elizabeth growled.

"Ah . . . but what a way to go."

"Whatever you do, take care of those 'bots. My career depends on them staying healthy. What with the cost of the antihydrogen in their trapchips, each one of them is worth more than all six of you combined."

"What about *us* staying healthy?" Rob interjected. "We already got a radiation dose on the way out that would mean automatic retirement in the nuclear industry. It's a good thing we're not near the 'bots anymore. Those things are dangerous."

"They sure *are* dangerous," Elizabeth said. *"I'm* concerned about the effect on the keracks of the gamma rays and pions from the antihydrogen annihilations taking place in those 'bots."

"So are most people who have looked at the numbers," Rob replied. "But Grippen only listened to the experts who told him what he wanted to hear. The keracks seem to be thriving on a nearly airless planet that is constantly bombarded by lots of radiation from cosmic rays, so Grippen decided a little extra dose of radiation from the 'bots shouldn't hurt them—too much."

Just then Selke appeared in the bathroom doorway in her nightgown and slippers. She had a disgusted wrinkle on her face.

"The toilet doesn't flush," she reported.

"Shit!" Rob exclaimed. "The outflow pipe must be frozen up." He started to get up.

Hiroshi spoke up. "If one of you will monitor Boris and Gabrielle in the 'bots, I will be glad to go out and take care of it." No matter how menial a task was, Hiroshi was always the first to volunteer.

"I'll cycle Hiroshi through the lock," said Rob, relieved. "Why don't you take over the monitoring, Elizabeth, since it's your shift anyway."

"Unless you need me for something, I'm going to bed," said Selke.

Rob was twisting uncomfortably. "I can't go to bed until the toilet's fixed. But why don't you help Hiroshi suit up while I use the urinal. At least that way we'll have plenty of liquid to flush the toilet with, once Hiroshi has cleared the blockage." Taking a deep breath, he opened the bathroom door and went in.

As Selke helped Hiroshi on with his helmet and checked his air tanks, her frilly blue silk nightgown contrasting with his hard, silver canvas outer coat, she suddenly realized that while Hiroshi might be facing a long stretch of hard, tedious, and probably messy duty, at least for the next few hours he would be breathing clean, pure air without the oppressive smell of human sweat and cat urine pervading it.

By the time Selke had taken Hiroshi through the suit checkout, Rob had returned from his visit to the bathroom, being careful to shut the door tightly behind him. There wasn't room for all three of them near the airlock unless the table was folded down, and Lucifer was on the table, so rather than attempt to move the cat, Selke just climbed into the upper bunk to get out of the way. Lucifer, seeing her in bed, jumped down off the table, bounded up into the bunk next to her, and demanded to be petted, the claws on his kneading feet adding more pinpoint holes through the already tattered lap of her silk nightgown.

Rob ushered Hiroshi into the airlock, with its ever-present and powerful cat box; then, making sure that Lucifer had not slipped inside to visit his box, he shut the door and cycled Hiroshi out onto the surface of Ice. He left the outer door open so that the cat box would undergo a thorough vacuum dehydration while Hiroshi was outside. After finishing the airlock cycle, he went over to the upper bunk and looked in on Selke and Lucifer. Selke was reading a book on another Lookman and patting Lucifer, who was purring loudly. There were only two bunks in the tiny shelter, and tradition was that the female member of the sleep shift got the upper bunk and the male member the lower bunk. The bunks were large enough to sit up in with the door closed, so a person could get dressed in private if the bathroom was occupied. They were also wide enough to accommodate two people at once, if they didn't mind a little friendly contact.

"Like a little company before you go to sleep?" Rob asked Selke hopefully.

She gave him a sweet smile and shook her head. "Not tonight. Already have some company." She patted Lucifer on the head.

"It was worth a try." Rob shrugged and went to the console, where he monitored Hiroshi's progress outside from a remote video camera mounted on the tall communications mast above their base.

The base had a roughly triangular layout. At one point of the triangle was the rocket that had brought them down from the cable catapult orbiting Ice and would take them back up again after the visit was over. The second point contained the supply tanks, the communications antennae complex, and the shelter they were in, the bright light from the single window making an oval spot on the crusty ice outside. The shelter was tiny, only two meters wide by four meters long by two meters high.

"Like six people having to live in a broken-down mini-camper all through the winter season at the North Pole on Mars," Rob had remarked one day shortly after they had arrived and taken up residence. The cramped quarters affected Rob the most, for although he was two centimeters short of two meters tall, and the shelter was designed to be a full two meters high, that measurement was an exterior one. By the time the thermal insulation and the cable run floors had been installed, the distance between floor and ceiling was six centimeters less than two meters. Rob had to keep his head bent over every time he stood up, and could only straighten his neck when he sat down.

The third point in the camp contained the buried nuclear reactor that supplied the power needed to run the base and make the liquid oxygen and hydrogen rocket fuel they were going to need to take off again. Fortunately, since the temperature on the surface of Ice never varied by more than a few degrees around 30 K, there was no problem keeping the fuels in a liquid state. Since oxygen solidified at 55 K, and hydrogen boiled at 20 K, a small refrigerator unit that took heat from the hydrogen storage tank and put it into the oxygen storage tank sufficed to keep both fuels liquid.

From his overhead view through the monitor camera, Rob watched as Hiroshi stepped from the airlock door and made his way around to the back of the shelter.

Hiroshi could almost feel the pressure of confinement lifting off him as he stepped out under the star-speckled black sky. The Sun was just another point-like star in the sky, although much brighter than all the others. Seen from the distant orbit of the kerack planetoid, Sol (or Brightstar, as the keracks called it) was above the head of Orion, near where the plane of the ecliptic crossed the plane of the Milky Way galaxy.

Hiroshi looked around until he could see the cable catapult terminal in orbit around Ice. Once he had spotted the 400-gigawatt power supply and its large radiators, it was easy to trace the 4200-kilometer cable attached to the power supply and pointing in a direction away from the Sun. There was a similar cable catapult terminal in orbit around Earth. Both had been constructed in space out of a small, carbonaceous chondrite Earth-crossing asteroid, the carbon being used to make the 1400-ton superstrong superconducting polybucky cables, and the metals used to make the equally heavy reactor shielding, thermal energy storage banks, and space radiators. All the builders needed to bring up from

Earth was the plutonium for the topping-off nuclear thermal reactor, the Boeing thermophotoelectric converters, and the sophisticated linear motor that rode the cable.

The terminal speed that the cable catapult could give a payload depended on the mass of the payload and the linear motor. The big linear motor could accelerate ten tons at thirty gees to fifty kilometers per second. There was also a smaller linear motor that could accelerate a ten-kilogram capsule at three thousand gees to five hundred kilometers per second. These smaller capsules could reach Earth in less than four months instead of over three years. They had already been used to send rock samples and ice cores back to Earth, and shortly would be sending samples of kerack food and artifacts to be analyzed where there were machines that were much more capable than the simplified, lightweight chemical analyzers Grippen had insisted on.

The sight of the cable catapult brought back to Hiroshi long-buried remembrances of the horrible feel of drowning, as the six submerged themselves in oxygen-bearing fluid in order to survive the 30-gee acceleration period. If only there had been enough money to build longer catapults that could launch decent-sized payloads to higher terminal velocities at lower and less dangerous accelerations . . .

Hiroshi admonished himself not to think futile thoughts about what might have been or what might happen to him on the return journey. He turned his mind to the present task of the frozen sewage line. It didn't take him long to find the problem. The teflon-lined sewage pipe was large enough in diameter and at enough of an angle that normally everything flushed down the toilet flowed through the pipe rapidly enough to make it to the septic pit without freezing. Over the weeks since it had been installed, however, the ice underneath one section had caved in, and the pipe had developed a bend that trapped some fluid, which had frozen to form a plug. Hiroshi propped up the pipe with some blocks of ice, gave the pipe a few taps, and the plug of dirty ice broke free and the line cleared.

"Great!" said Rob, after Hiroshi reported the good news over the outside communications link. "I'm relieved."

"In more ways than one, I'll bet," Elizabeth bantered, getting up from the telebot monitor console. "Why don't you go and get your s-'n'-s, as you so euphemistically call it, and I'll cycle Hiroshi back inside. I'll see you later."

When Rob finally came out of the bathroom, hair still wet from the shower, the tiny commons room seemed strangely empty. Boris and Gabrielle were still encased in the telebot sensuits, walking behind Merlene through the streets of Camalor, and Hiroshi was back at the telebot monitor console, watching their progress. Selke had closed the soundproof door on the upper bunk, and since Lucifer was nowhere in sight, he was probably inside with her. Then Rob noticed that the bottom bunk door was shut. He knew what he would see when he looked inside. He had been willing to take on Selke tonight——she was soft and tender once she had been talked into it——but he didn't know whether he was physically up to Elizabeth. But he had a macho reputation to live up to. Putting on his most charming smile and gritting his teeth, he reached down and opened the door to the lower bunk. A set of feminine overalls and some pale green silk underwear lay rolled up in a neat ball out of the way at the foot of the bed.

"Like a little company before you go to sleep?" asked a throaty voice from inside his bunk.

It was only fifteen minutes later when Elizabeth, still buttoning up her coverall, joined Hiroshi at the telebot monitor console. Hiroshi, ever polite, made no mention of her recent absence. Since he and Elizabeth worked on the same shift and had the same sleep periods, they had shared a bunk together many times. Hiroshi had been teaching her to take her time and try different and more relaxed techniques, and together they had been quite successful at prolonging the enjoyment, but when she was with the Russian or the American, it was . . . he couldn't quite remember the phrase . . . "Bang, bonk, thank you, sir?" No . . . that wasn't it.

"Boris and Gabrielle have arrived at the home of the Wizard Merlene," he said, turning to look at Elizabeth.

"I'll set the recorders at high resolution and high speed for all the spectral bands," Elizabeth replied as she reached for the controls. Together they watched the monitor screens as the view of a rectangular hole appeared in the ground alongside the road that the telebots were traveling.

3
DAY IN THE LIFE

FOLLOWING MERLENE ALONG one of the ring roads, Boris and Gabrielle passed by what were obviously individual plots of land, since the types and arrangements of the plants varied periodically. There were almost no structures, although occasionally they would see a storage shed or workshop or brick oven in one corner of the plot. Most of the plots, however, had a knobbed post in the middle, around which the ground had been cleared for some distance. Its function soon became clear when they came to a plot where a heuller stood hitched to the post by its antennae reins. The heuller wore a muzzle, but that didn't keep it from nibbling on a plant that had grown within its reach.

"There are no markings or numbers on the plots to indicate the address," Boris remarked. "There are no street signs, either."

"Camalor is a small town," replied Gabrielle. "In the rural villages in France we have no numbers and no names on the houses. There is no need—everyone knows where everyone else lives."

"I guess that is true in Camalor also," said Boris. "Since the keracks are in constant radio communication with each other, they probably even know the whereabouts of any person at any time."

Merlene finally came to a stop in front of a rectangular hole in the ground with steps leading downward.

"This be the residence o'Merlene," she said, pointing to the hole. "Merlene be honored with your visit." She turned and led the way down the steps, her eight walking legs moving in smooth precision.

The humans put down their burdens of heuller parts, and Boris started down the steps in the human's two-pair-by-two-pair gait and almost tipped his telebot over. As they descended into the darkness and the starlight decreased, the display on their verihelms shifted input from the visible-image intensifier camera to the infrared camera and the microwave scanner. The false-color mapping algorithm changed slightly with the change in spectrum, so things looked somewhat different. Whereas before, Merlene had worn black wizard clothing and cape over a black shell, the shell that covered her thorax and abdomen now glowed through varicolored, diffusely scattering cloth. There was an especially warm region right at the base of Merlene's thorax, just above her mouthveil. It was bright red in the false-color infrared image, indicating that it was a number of degrees warmer than the usual yellow body temperature. The coldest parts of Merlene were the three pincers at the end of each walking foot, splayed out on the cold tiled steps; and her eyeglobe, which was jet black in the infrared array.

If an eye is to see in the infrared it must be kept cold or it will blind itself, Boris reminded himself. *Her eye must be mounted on a highly efficient heat exchanger.*

The first landing of the stairwell was situated in one corner of a large underground room. In each of the four corners, up near the ceiling, was a small cage containing a few wormlike creatures that gave off a soft green glow. Together they lit up the room with green light that was as bright as starlight, and almost as bright as the illumination on the surface when Brightstar was overhead. The visible-image intensifier cameras in the telebots resumed domination of the display in the humans' verihelms.

"This be the living room for the family o'Merlene," she said as they entered. "We be using this room for eating, resting, and learning."

The floor and walls of the living room were constructed with rectangular bricks that insulated the room from the ice that surrounded it on all sides. On the floor were woven rugs for warmth and better footing, and tapestries covered the bare spots on the walls.

"The lack of windows and the tapestries give it the look of a cellar room in a medieval castle," Gabrielle remarked.

There was a large, ornate table in the middle of the room that held baskets containing a variety of berries. Beneath each corner lamp was a tilted, padded bench that looked like it might be a kerack reading chair, for beside each bench was a bookshelf with a selection of rolled-up scrolls as well as bound books with pages. There were numerous miniature statues around, each one highly detailed. The tiles that lined the ceiling of the room were supported by beams made of a clear material containing metallic-looking threads.

"Are those beams made of water ice?" asked Boris, pointing upward with his warclaw.

"Merlene be not knowing if that be true," she said, looking up. She had not paid any attention to the beams before. "This residence, like all residences in Camalor, be built by constructors. They be knowing the composition." She paused for a second, her antennae quivering slightly. Boris and Gabrielle heard their translators trying to cope with the flood of incomplete thoughts flowing from Merlene as she tapped into the Spirit o'Camalor. "Constructor Polnart . . . residences . . . composition . . ."

Shortly Merlene was back with them. "The beams be indeed made of cast water ice. The metal threads cast in the ice be giving the ice strength in tension. The tiles on the floor, walls, and between the beams be made of rock dust bound with a plastic compound extracted from heuller shells. Many fi'fifthdays ago, Merlene be studying the plastic by decomposing it in her workshop. It be made of two parts carbon and six parts fluorine."

"Hexafluoroethane," Gabrielle said.

"I'll look that up," came Hiroshi's voice over the audiolink.

Merlene then slid open a door in one end of the room, the door disappearing into a slot in the thick brick wall. Boris and Gabrielle could see a smaller room scattered with clothing and various objects. From the size of the chestcoats and skirts lying around, it seemed to be the room of a child. It was not a bedroom, since there was nothing in it that looked like a bed, but that didn't surprise them, since they already knew from prior conversations between Merlene and scientists on Earth that although the activity of the keracks slowed down when Brightstar set, there was still plenty of starlight to see by, so the keracks never slept. That fact had made it even tougher on the six people of the landing party, since it meant they had to remain on continuous shift duty to maintain constant surveillance of kerack activities.

On a reading bench, in the glowworm-illuminated corner of the room, was a young female kerack. She was lying on her front on the tilted bench, her eight walking legs hanging down on either side, her two front legs propped up holding a scroll in front of her eye. She was softly singing several different parts of an aria at the same time. When she saw the humans enter her room, she stopped.

"This be our young daughter, Solene," Merlene said. "These be two of the humans, Solene. He be Boris and she be Gabrielle."

"Boriset and Gabriellene," Solene repeated, adding the proper kerack endings to the names. "Those be strange names. Be they from Harvamor? Solene be not liking those from Harvamor."

"They not be from Harvamor," replied Merlene. "They be from a place that be even farther away. Solene be liking the humans."

Solene would reserve judgment. Her mother, being a wizard, was required to meet strangers occasionally. But, like most keracks, Solene had a strong, inborn prejudice against anyone who wasn't a subject of Queen Une of Camalor.

"That was beautiful music you were singing," Gabrielle said enthusiastically. "Please don't let us interrupt you."

"Solene be just practicing," the youngster replied. "Solene be now able to be singing four voices. But, to be joining the chorus, Solene must be able to be singing at least five. Someday Solene be the best singer in Camalor and be leading the whole chorus in *all* the voices!" Illustrating, she slid off the bench and started waving her front claws in time to her singing. She hadn't noticed, but in getting off the bench her mouthveil had been pulled to one side of her waist, revealing her mouth with its tiny, innocent, pale-yellow tongue behind the fine crystal-clear diamond baby teeth.

"Solene!" Her mother gasped in shock at her daughter's inadvertent nakedness. She wasn't quite sure what to say next, but Solene rapidly realized what was wrong and adjusted her mouthveil back in place.

"Your singing is most beautiful," said Gabrielle, ignoring the accidental indiscretion.

"Someday you will be leading the chorus," Boris added.

"Do you be really thinking so?"

"Merlene be sure Solene be doing that," Merlene replied. "Solene be continuing with practice." Visibly relieved, Merlene slid the door shut on the messy room, and they were back in the living room.

A voice message came in over the base-to-telebot audiolink from Hiroshi. "The hexafluoroethane monomer has a melting point of 173 K, highest of all the simple hydrocarbon and fluorocarbon monomers, including tetrafluoroethylene or teflon. It would make a good, strong binder for rock dust, especially if they used a catalyst or enzyme to polymerize it."

Merlene went to the second door on the same side of the room and paused before sliding it back. "This be the room of our son Jordat. We be very proud of Jordat. He be awarded five copper young-warrior rings in the final-school tournaments. He also be awarded a silver ball as a young warrior troop leader. Jordat be now finished with final school and be receiving his Cape o'Trade. Because of his awards, Jordat be chosen to apprentice with the great warrior Laslot as soon as he be completing his next molt. He be trying to hasten that time by eating and exercising."

She slid open the door. This room was relatively orderly, with large male chestcoats, skirts, and capes hung neatly from pegs along one wall. On the shelves in the back of the room were a few books, but most of the space was taken up with statuettes of kerack knights, some in golden plate armor on golden-mailed heullers, some in fierce action against the foes of Camalor.

In the middle of the room was a young male kerack with a larger than normal warclaw. On his right antenna were five copper rings, all closely packed together as if it had been difficult to cram them on. They were capped by a silver ball that covered the end of the antenna. Jordat was covered from head to tail with what looked like two suits of heavy-ringed chain mail that had obviously seen better days. He was going through a series of formal fighting postures in front of a floor-to-ceiling mirror. He had a heavy spikeless practice mace in his small claw, a heavy, blunt-tipped exercise rapier made of lead in his warclaw, and two real daggers in his second set of claws. His back was to them, and he was obviously busy, so Merlene slid the door shut again without bothering him.

She took them next into the kitchen and showed them around. Behind an insulated door was a walk-in larder with metal shelves embedded in the walls of ice. On the shelves were chunks of heuller meat, some whole gutted worms, stacks of small, white eggs, sacks of roots, and baskets of berries of various kinds.

The kitchen was simple, with a brick oven for baking and a metal hot plate for frying. Both were heated by a single fire chamber, from which a flue led up through the ceiling to the surface. At the base of the fire chamber was a bellows and some adjustable air vents.

"How does it work?" asked Gabrielle, bending down to peer into the fire chamber. "What is that silvery gauze inside?"

"We be calling it firemetal," Merlene replied. "It be what you call platinum. The fire be hard to start, but after the firemetal be getting hot, it be simple to keep going." She reached into a basket of white berries sitting to one side of the oven, took out a berry, and slipped it under her mouth-veil. While she was warming the berry in her mouth, she continued to talk through her antennae.

"The fireberries contain frozen oxygen. But after they be warmed up, the oxygen be a liquid. This one be warm enough now." Taking the berry out of her mouth with her pincers, she poked a tiny hole in it with a pin conveniently sticking out of the handle of the fireberry basket where it would always be handy. Reaching into the fire chamber, she squeezed a tiny, clear drop of liquid oxygen onto the platinum gauze, where it spread out to form a glistening wet spot. She pumped the bellows vigorously and said, "There! The fire be started." She then adjusted the air vents until she was satisfied with the result.

"Where is the fire?" Gabrielle asked. "I see no flame."

"Switch to infrared," Boris suggested. "She is using catalytic combustion. It produces heat without flame."

Gabrielle twitched a few toes to change her viewing camera and now could see an orange-red glow in the infrared where the liquid oxygen had wet the center of the platinum gauze. "I can see now," she said. "Instead of burning a hydrocarbon liquid or gas in an oxygen atmosphere, she is burning oxygen liquid in a hydrogen atmosphere. The platinum catalyst makes the reaction go even at these low temperatures."

"Now that the firemetal be warm," Merlene continued, "Merlene be adding the rest of the fireberry." She squirted the rest of the liquid onto the gauze, which soon began to glow all over. She tossed the skin of the berry in the fire chamber, where it shriveled up and burned away, then threw in another fireberry. "Now that the fire be started, there be no need to prick the fireberry. It can be tossed in whole." She reached into a different basket and pulled out another white berry. "For a strong fire, especially when the air be thin like it be now between geyser eruptions, Merlene be adding fuelberries. They be containing air bound with carbon, that the humans be calling methane. Merlene be not liking to use fuelberries, for they be coating the flue black with carbon." She then reached into yet another basket and drew out a berry that was off-white in color. "This flareberry be for making more heat quickly. It be containing carbon monoxide, which be a fuel like the hydrogen in the air, but more concentrated." From a fourth basket she removed a dark blue-black berry. "This hotberry be for making a very hot fire. It be containing three parts of oxygen in one molecule."

"Ozone! I have never seen it in solid form before," Boris exclaimed, reaching over to take the blue-black berry from Merlene's grasp and looking at it carefully. "It is normally unstable in bulk, but at room temperature on Ice, I assume it would last a long time. It is much more energetic than oxygen, and when used with a carbon monoxide berry it would make a very hot fire indeed!"

"Hmmm," Gabrielle mused, mentally checking what she could remember of the periodic table and oxidation chemistry. "Fluorine is a much stronger oxidizer than oxygen. Do you use it for fires?"

Merlene straightened her antennae in obvious surprise at the thought, and the humans began to worry that they had broken some kerack taboo. Suddenly she bent over at the waist, again and again, while her antennae emitted a series of hiccups. The hics grew louder and louder. She crossed her antennae over on themselves so that they shorted each other out, and the hics were muted to whispers. Finally Merlene got herself under control.

"It be true that spiritberries will burn," she said. "But there be *much* better uses for them."

"If the translator converted that word correctly, then I can understand your mirth," said Boris, the image on the eye-globe of his telebot smiling. "I would be laughing at the idea of burning vodka to cook dinner also."

Gabrielle, impressed, remarked, "The cooker uses a so-phisticated chemistry for such a simple device." She looked around the kitchen to see what else there was to see. She had seen the refrigerator and the cooker . . . "Where is the kitchen sink?"

"Sink?" Merlene queried, not understanding the word.

"There are no liquids at room temperature on Ice," Boris reminded Gabrielle. "That's why she had to warm up the fireberry on her tongue."

"Please!" Merlene interrupted in an irritated whisper. "Do not be using *that* word where Solene can hear."

"I am most apologetic," replied Boris, with a low bow to her. "In the future, I will watch my t——" He decided to quit right there.

Merlene then showed them the canister of solid ethane that she used for crisping meat and roots. "This be liquid at a little above body temperature and be not boiling away even at high temperatures. But it be getting hot enough to cook any food put into it."

"Kerack lard," Gabrielle remarked, taking a sample of it and putting the sample bag back into her collecting pouch. Merlene helped Boris collect and bag samples of the various fuel and food berries at the same time.

After Merlene showed them her collection of knives,

cooking pots, and serving dishes, she finally showed Gabrielle the kerack equivalent of the kitchen sink. It consisted of one bucket of clean sand and another for the waste sand that had been used to scrub the dirty dishes.

Merlene then took her visitors to her personal room and that of her husband, Fasart. Both rooms were mainly clothes closets, although Fasart kept some spare farming tools and harnesses in his.

"Since Merlene be having a workshop downstairs, she be keeping her tools there," she explained. She walked to the landing at base of the stairway that came down from the surface, and using the prehensile pincers on one of her back feet, she slid open a door in the floor that opened up on another stairway, this one leading down. "Shall we be visiting Merlene's workshop next?" she asked.

"What does this door lead to?" asked Boris, as he pointed to a small door under the stairwell.

"That be the slop bucket room," Merlene answered.

"Oh!" Gabrielle said. "Sorry to embarrass you. We can skip that room."

"There be no embarrassment." Merlene looked slightly puzzled. "Merlene be just forgetting that the room be there. Besides, since you be scientists studying the kerack people, you should be learning about slop buckets and their importance to the functioning of the city, especially the farms." She slid open the door, and they entered the smallest room in the house. Along one wall there was a row of empty buckets and along the other a row of buckets filled with frozen, yellow-brown sludge. Standing in the middle of the room, at some distance from a waist-high rail fastened firmly to the wall, was a half-full bucket.

"This be how you use it." Merlene went to the wall and held on to the rail with her front claws. With her balance thus assured, she raised her tail off the floor. The tail lifted her skirt while keeping the shell of the tail properly covered.

Boris, embarrassed, started for the door. "I'd best be leaving now."

"Why?" asked Merlene. "Merlene be about to show you how it be done."

"On Earth, it is not polite to watch someone eliminate waste from their bodies," Gabrielle explained.

"That be an unusual taboo," Merlene said. "It be a perfectly normal function of any living creature."

Boris seemed ambivalent. "If it is so normal, why do you have a door on the room?"

"It be the *smell*, of course," said Merlene, pointing to a hole in the ceiling. "That be why this room be having a vent to the surface. Will Boris be staying to watch and learn?"

"Very well," he said reluctantly.

Merlene grabbed the rail and raised her tail again.

"First, number one in the air," she said, and the acoustic sensors on the outside of their telebots picked up a loud hiss of escaping gas.

"The chemical sensors on your telebots just registered a big jump in the hydrogen and nitrogen content in the room, along with a little neon and helium," Elizabeth reported over the audiolink.

Merlene backed up until her tail was over the slop bucket. "Then, number two in the bucket." A mixed stream of warm liquids and solids emerged from under her tail and fell into the bucket.

Elizabeth's voice came over the audiolink again. "It's now registering nitrogen trifluoride, methane, ethane, and a lot of other hydrocarbons and fluorocarbons."

Merlene wagged her tail in a nearby box of sand to clean it, moved the now full slop bucket to the wall, and replaced it with an empty one.

"I guess I should really get a sample to analyze before it freezes," said Gabrielle, taking a sample bottle out of her carrying pouch.

"Make sure you get some representative samples of the

solids for me to analyze," Hiroshi advised over the audiolink.

"*Merde,*" Gabrielle muttered under her breath as she bent to the task.

Merlene's antennae straightened and turned upward. "Merlene be hearing grumble from heuller o'Fasart," she said. As soon as Gabrielle had her sample tucked safely away in her carrying pouch, Merlene led them up the stairs to the surface. Coming down the street was a good-sized kerack male riding near the head of a heuller, which was hauling a large, two-wheeled cart behind it.

"This be Fasart, husband o'Merlene," she said. "Fasart be now taking you to visit farm. Merlene be showing you workshop o'Merlene at a later time."

Fasart approached, and using the reins attached to the antennae of the heuller, he pulled the animal to a halt. Fasart was dressed in a simple, heavy-duty cloth chestcoat and skirt, and his Cape o'Trade had a stylized berry plant on it similar to those dotting the yard. He was armed with a single dagger in a well-worn but serviceable sheath tucked behind his back.

"Fasart be welcoming the humans." He did not loosen his firm grip on the reins, for the presence of the telebots obviously made the heuller nervous, its usual grumbling sound interspersed with nervous squeaks and splutters.

"It be not safe for humans to be riding on heuller," Fasart went on. "They be safer riding in cart."

"Excellent idea," said Boris, and he and Gabrielle moved around to the rear of the animal. As they passed out of sight of the large single eye of the heuller, the animal calmed considerably. By the time they had loaded up the frozen heuller parts and clambered aboard the cart, the nervous noises had stopped and the heuller had resumed its quiet grumbling. Fasart twitched the reins a few times and they started off. The gait of the multifooted heuller soon progressed to a rapid wave that took them along at speeds well in excess of what the telebots could have accomplished on their own.

"Good-bye!" Boris waved to Merlene, who was rapidly shrinking in the distance. Gabrielle was at the front of the cart, looking around at the scenery. Although the road was relatively smooth, the ride in the springless, hard-wheeled wagon was jolting.

"It is like being hauled to the guillotine in a tumbrel," Gabrielle remarked, holding on firmly to the guardrail.

They soon left the parklike suburbs of Camalor for the farms and fields, where they could see young male keracks picking berries from row after row of large bushes. Every dozen rows or so, there was a good-sized hole in the ground at the end of the row. The plants had no leaves, just a brownish-black central stem from which sprouted several small branches, some of them subdividing into twigs. At the end of each branch or twig was a berry, sometimes two or three. These were put into bags with drawstring tops and tossed on top of a heuller, who held them in its upward-facing set of feet.

"These be the older farms," said Fasart, his radio voice not significantly diminished by distance. "They be fully planted and most productive of the farms. Each be tended by apprentices who be learning about all the different crops."

They passed by another field. Here the rows of plants had been picked clean, and some young males were pulling up the plants with their large warclaws, each using the sharp pincers of his other claw to clip off the fat roots into bags held in his second pair of claws. The brushlike stalks of the plants were then heaped in a large pile, usually near one of the holes in the ground.

"They look like haystacks," Gabrielle remarked.

"They probably serve the same function." Boris pointed off in the distance. "If you look over there, you can see a heuller making a meal out of one of the stacks."

"Those be called brush stacks," said Fasart.

Fasart slowed the heuller down to a trot, and they pulled off the road onto a large farm plot. Here apprentices were picking berries in the fields, their capes off and draped over the pull shafts of a wagon nearby. Each wore a single dagger in a sheath worn on the back of the thorax.

Fasart proudly swung his warclaw over the broad expanse. "This be the farm o'Fasart." He tapped the head of the heuller behind its eye, and the heuller dropped the pull shafts of the wagon with a thump. He climbed down, led the heuller to a brush stack, muzzled it, and tied it to a nearby post.

"Why do you put a muzzle on it?" asked Gabrielle. "Surely it must be hungry after all that work."

"The muzzle be not keeping it from eating brush stacks," Fasart answered, and the heuller proved him right by using its long, almost prehensile tongue to snake a large bite out of the stack right through the gaps in the muzzle. "The muzzle be keeping it from eating too many holes in the ice. Fasart be showing you." He led them to one of the large holes in the ground that were scattered all over the farming plot.

"This be what heullers can do," he said, pointing to the heuller-sized hole. "They be of great help in expanding the farm down, but they be difficult to stop once they be started digging."

"Expanding the farm *down?*" Gabrielle repeated.

"Most of farm be underground. That be where best ice exist."

"We should have suspected," said Boris. "Your homes are underground, so it should not be surprising that your farms are underground."

"Especially since the plants aren't using photosynthesis," Elizabeth interjected over the audiolink. "I noticed that those plants you saw had no leaves, so all the nourishment must come through the root system. They probably would grow as well underground as on the surface. Observe things closely here. Those plants are collecting energy from somewhere, and it isn't the Sun. Whatever it is, it must be the mysterious missing energy source."

Gabrielle directed her telebot close to the hole to peer down, being careful not to get too close. One slip and Grippen would have her head. "How do you get down there?"

"Fasart and others climb down using that." Fasart pointed to a knotted rope hanging down in the hole. "But perhaps humans be not good at climbing down ropes. Fasart be arranging for help." His antennae pointed off in another direction. "Samart! Dirmat! Come here!"

Two of the young apprentices stopped picking berries and came toward them. Boris noticed that one of the young males wore two copper rings on his left antenna, while the other had one. Both were good-sized males, but neither one seemed to be as big as Jordat. Jordat was going to be an apprentice in the glamorous trade of being a warrior, while these males had been relegated to the farming trade.

As they waited for the apprentices, Boris remarked, "I notice that all the farmers and apprentices are males. Farming does not seem to require large size or a large warclaw. Why are all the farm workers male?"

Fasart was considering his reply when he was interrupted by one of the approaching apprentices, who had easily heard the query over the aether despite the distance.

"To be keeping those mother-licking Harvamors in their place!" the apprentice bellowed.

"Dirmat!" said Fasart severely. "You be not using field language in front of visitors."

Boris reminded himself again that he would have to learn to whisper with antennae touching if he was going to keep any conversations private.

Fasart turned and pointed with his antennae toward a distant rise in the ground where there were more farm plots and roads behind a low, wide wall. "The border wall of Harvamor be·just over there."

Boris realized that the farm plots he had originally

thought were part of Camalor were actually separated from the Camalor farms by boundary walls. Between the two walls was a wide stretch of uncultivated land.

Fasart went on, "The reason all farm workers be male is that all farm workers be also warriors defending the boundary o'Camalor from invaders. The fields along the border be farmed by those who have gone through many molts and are large and strong and have won tournament rings."

Boris noticed belatedly that Fasart had two copper rings on his left antenna. They had become dull brown with time, and no longer had the shiny red newness of the rings on the apprentices.

"Samart be farming the frontier one day," boasted the apprentice with two tournament rings. "And that farm be *next* to the boundary wall o'Harvamor."

Fasart ignored the outburst. "We be keeping our armor and weapons near at hand at all times."

Dirmat and Samart, eager to demonstrate their prowess, dashed to a long box near the entrance to the farm plot. Soon they were dressed in plain but serviceable chain-mail hauberks and sparring with pikes.

Fasart gave a suppressed hic or two of amusement at the impetuousness of youth. "There be time enough for battle when the cowardly Harvamors be sneaking over to steal. You two be putting those pikes away and be helping over here."

When Gabrielle realized that Fasart was planning to lower them into the seemingly bottomless pit, on the ends of ropes held negligently in the large warclaws of the two apprentices, she turned to Boris and said with an amused smile, "Grippen will shit in his pants when he sees today's video clips with his precious 'bots in danger."

With the rope safely tied around their middles and their claws holding on firmly, the two telebots were slowly lowered into the hole with Fasart leading the way, claw over claw down the knotted climbing rope. They soon came to a level where there were six heuller-sized holes drilled horizontally through the dirty ice. One of the tunnel roofs had caved in, and three others looked filled in.

"Farming on Ice is like mining on Earth," said Boris.

"That might be a clue to the missing energy source for this civilization," Gabrielle said, looking critically around her. The walls of the shaft had horizontal striations, whiter layers of snowy ice alternating with dirty layers of evaporated snow.

"It looks somewhat like the polar caps of Mars," said Boris, who had been lucky enough to be part of the last telebot exploration of the planet before the Mars program was terminated. "But Ice doesn't have yearly seasons like Mars does."

"Perhaps it has seasons, but all the seasons are cold. These layers must be due to geyser eruptions spreading new snow layers over old layers. There could be minerals in the erupted ice, but where is the energy source?"

They continued down past some more tunnels and finally came to a halt where some glowworms hung in cages. At this level there were only five tunnels, with a blank wall where the sixth would be. Fasart was waiting for them in the mouth of one of the tunnels, and he pulled them inside and unfastened the ropes. Shortly afterwards the two apprentices made their way down the rope and joined them.

A loud, acoustic grinding noise came from one of the tunnels across the shaft from them, accompanied by the complaining radio grumble of a heuller working under protest. Boris activated the illuminator inside the eyeglobe of his telebot and sent a beam of light down the tunnel, where it illuminated the hind end of a heuller. The beast was using its four sets of feet for purchase on the wall of the tunnel it was excavating, rotating and at the same time slowly inching forward, like a giant living drill. Between them and the heuller was a bored apprentice, antennae pointing straight at the heuller, acting as a driver. The apprentice turned around and, seeing them, called out a warning.

"The belly of the heuller now be full of ice and dirt. You be moving back."

The apprentice backed out of the tunnel, antennae still pointing at the heuller, while the gigantic beast also backed up. The apprentice clambered on to the climbing rope and hung there while the heuller backed down the shaft under his control. Once the head of the long animal came into view, the apprentice dropped down onto the beast just behind the eye and, giving the animal a few kicks, rode it up the shaft to the surface like an Indian mahout on an elephant. As the animal rose past their shaft, the five stepped back to avoid the sharp, scrabbling claws of the multitude of large three-toed feet as they passed the mouth of the tunnel.

Boris grinned. "I see how you dig these shafts and tunnels now. What will the heuller do with its belly-load of dirt and ice?"

"Since it be new ice and has not been farmed before, the apprentice be having the heuller regurgitate the ice in mounds for the next planting of the multiberry plants," replied Fasart.

"So you can only use the ice once?" Gabrielle asked. "That must be a clue to the missing energy source."

"It can be used more than once," Fasart admitted. "But each use be weakening it, until finally it be valueless and useful only for paving roads, making boundary walls, or filling in farmed-out tunnels."

Gabrielle frowned. "I still don't understand. From all the biochemistry I have learned, ice is a poor source of energy. What makes the ice here on Ice different from the ice on Earth, Mars, and Ganymede?"

"I think I may know," said Boris. "The ice here is colder, nearly at absolute zero, and has always been near absolute zero since it fell as snow after a geyser eruption. But it has also been subjected to cosmic radiation from space. That radiation would create energetic free radicals in the ice. On Earth, Mars, or inner planets and moons, those free radicals would recombine or decay, but here on Ice most would stay in their metastable state for long periods of time."

"I think you may have found the missing energy source," said Gabrielle. "I would take a sample of ice back to Hiroshi to analyze, but I am afraid that the heat and radiation from the body of this 'bot would alter it."

Hiroshi's voice came through the audiolink. "I will plan to send a special insulated sample case on the next trip of the microhopper."

"Excuse us for chattering," Gabrielle said to Fasart. "Please show us more of the farm."

"This be a typical working tunnel." Fasart, holding a glowworm, led the way down the long tunnel. "We be using full-sized heullers to be boring the tunnel, then we be planting iceworms to burrow through the ice and grow."

"Iceworms?" asked Gabrielle.

They came toward the end of the tunnel. The apprentices Samart and Dirmat were there, one working on each side of the tunnel. Between them was a large basket half-full of small white objects. Fasart went to the basket and picked up a couple of the objects.

"This be an egg," he said, holding out the small white ovoid.

"Like the ones we saw in Merlene's kitchen?" asked Gabrielle.

"They be the same, but these be ready to hatch. When the egg hatches, out be coming an iceworm, like this one." He held out the other object, a small plump worm with no feet, two small antennae, and a single blind, vestigial eye on the front. It had a large mouth and a number of separate orifices of different sizes in its tail. It gave off little whuffling noises as it was handled.

"We be planting the worms like this." Fasart poked the end of a sharp pincer into the icy wall to start a small tunnel.

He put the worm into the hole, and with a soft whuffling sound it soon burrowed out of sight, leaving behind a casting that was mostly ice, with a lot of the dirt taken out.

"The worms be avoiding the burrows of other worms, and soon the ice around the tunnel be full of interlaced burrows."

Fasart turned and walked back along the way they had come. Boris could now see that the walls were pockmarked with holes where previous iceworms had been planted; only now, the castings in the holes were black with some sort of fungus growth.

Fasart stopped at one of the holes, and, using the three opposing pincers of his large warclaw, he extracted a large conical core of ice containing the entrance to a burrow. Carefully breaking the core in half, he showed them a cross-sectional view.

"The casting of a healthy iceworm be containing fungus nodes. The roots of the fungus grow into the ice surrounding the burrow and extract the good there, which be concentrated in the nodes."

"Let me get a sample of that fungus," Gabrielle said, getting out a sample bag.

"From heuller tunnels to iceworm burrows to root channels," Boris commented. "Soon, every bit of ice in the entire volume of the farm has been worked."

Gabrielle was fascinated. "How do you harvest the fungus nodes?"

"The iceworms be doing it for us," Fasart replied. "If humans be now quiet, Fasart be attempting to demonstrate."

Boris and Gabrielle both twitched a third left toe back at the base, and the radio transmitters on the telebots in the tunnel turned off. They kept their receivers on and tried to imitate the configuration of Fasart's antennae as he searched the tunnel, listening intently. Finally they all picked out a faint, whuffling radio signal coming through the ice. Fasart pointed his antennae at the spot and emitted a high-pitched whistle. A little while later a plump iceworm broke through the surface of the wall, where Fasart caught it. It was slightly larger than the newly hatched ones the apprentices had been planting.

"They be not growing much at first planting," he said. "But when Fasart be replanting them in a burrow rich with fungus nodes, they be growing rapidly." He inserted the whuffling iceworm into a burrow black with fungus, and it eagerly dug back into the wall and out of sight, leaving behind a casting of clean ice.

"How often do you replant them?" asked Gabrielle.

"The biggest and healthiest ones be replanted many times. The smaller be culled at each replanting. They be the major meat crop of the farm."

"I guess the best ones are saved for breeding purposes," Gabrielle remarked.

"Fasart not be understanding."

"You are getting close to a kerack taboo subject, Gabrielle," Elizabeth warned over the audiolink. "Stay off the subject of sex."

"Are all the iceworms eventually eaten?" asked Gabrielle, trying to find the answer without bringing up the forbidden subject.

"Most be eaten. A few be allowed to pupate and become heullers."

Elizabeth gave an amused snort over the audiolink. "And we won't ask Fasart to tell us what the heullers do to each other so they can produce the eggs that hatch into the baby iceworms that turn into the mommy and daddy heullers."

By this time the apprentices had returned from down the tunnel, carrying the empty basket between them.

"It be culling time in the tunnels above," said Fasart. "Do you be wishing to observe or not? Merlene be telling Fasart that humans be having a taboo about killing animals."

"I don't think I want to monitor this part," audiolinked Elizabeth.

"The taboo is not strong," Boris said. "As scientists we should observe, but we do not wish to participate."

Fasart led them to the entrance to the tunnel. With the help of the apprentices the telebots were lifted up a level, where they entered another tunnel whose walls were honeycombed with large burrow entrances choked with fungus. Shortly, a production line was set up that moved slowly down the tunnel. Fasart would whistle into the ice, and when an iceworm appeared Fasart would pick it up and heft it. The larger iceworms he sent back into the wall until the next harvest. The smaller ones he held and stroked while one of the apprentices suspended a cup under the the creature's tail.

With the inducement of the stroking, the iceworm would emit some varicolored crystals, which the apprentice would catch in the cup. Once the milking process was over, Fasart pulled his plain-handled dagger from his well-worn, unornamented farmer's sheath and pithed the softly whuffling iceworm with a jab right through the vestigial eye into the brain beneath. Most iceworms died instantly, although in one or two cases the whuffles changed to screams, which required another jab to silence. The corpses were laid out on the floor of the tunnel to cool as the production line progressed.

Boris and Gabrielle kept silent as they watched the efficient and mostly silent harvesting process. At the end of the tunnel the two apprentices started off again, loading up the basket with the cooling corpses, and Gabrielle finally spoke.

"What is that substance that you obtained from the iceworms before you killed them?"

"It be fertilizer for the plants," said Fasart, holding up the cup.

"Like you collect in the slop buckets at home?" Boris asked, puzzled. "It seems like such a little amount to come from so many creatures."

Fasart broke into hics of laughter, then quickly got himself under control. "This be not number two! This be like number five or number fi'five. Although the crystals be poisonous to eat, they be very powerful fertilizer for plants. We be mixing the crystals with large quantities of ice and be placing them near the roots of the plants. The plants be then producing many berries and large roots."

"That must be powerful fertilizer indeed," Gabrielle said. "May I have a sample?" Fasart helped her get a representative sample of the many different kinds of crystals.

With the planting and harvesting of the iceworms completed, they returned to the surface. There, Fasart showed them his crop of surface plants.

"These be the multiberry plants," he said as they approached the first row of plants.

"Multiberry?" Gabrielle repeated. "Did the translator handle that word properly? Do you mean that this plant grows different kinds of berries?"

"Betruth," replied Fasart, both bewildered and annoyed that the humans could not immediately sense the veracity of his statement. Then he remembered that in this sense, the humans were like Harvamors. You could lie to someone from Harvamor and they would not be able to tell you were lying, but you could never lie to someone from Camalor—you were all part of the same Spirit.

Boris looked carefully at the berries on the plant. "He is right. I had not noticed it before, but the berries on this plant are of many different varieties. This branch looks like it is mostly producing fireberries, while this small twig over here has one berry with the distinctive blue-black color of the frozen ozone berries that Merlene had in her kitchen."

"That be a hotberry," said Fasart. He then pointed to some greenish ones. "These be spiritberries, and over here, these be bloodberries."

"This is amazing," Gabrielle said. "On Earth, we must plant a different type of plant for every different type of fruit. There are hundreds of different varieties of plants."

Fasart had a hard time believing that statement, but unless the human was exaggerating, she was probably telling the truth. "In Camalor there be only two plants. The fungus be in the tunnels and the multiberry plants be on the surface."

"Come to think of it, he is right," Hiroshi said over the audiolink, surprised that he had not noticed it before. "All the plants and trees in the park and on the lawns of the homes are just different-sized versions of the same basic plant. How strange. One would think the process of natural selection would produce more varieties than that."

Boris was still examining the berries. "I notice the tops of the plants have a spray of single twigs, each with a single tiny berry of a different color."

"That be the metal spray portion of the plant," Fasart explained. "Every plant be starting one, but few be completing a ripe metalberry. When we be harvesting the ripe berries and the root nodes from the plant, and before we be feeding the stalks to the heullers, we be taking the small metalberries to our metalberry plot and burying the unripe berries near the roots of the proper plant. After some time we be getting a large ripe metalberry to harvest."

"Then these berries have metal in them?"

"Fasart be showing you the berries in the metalberry plot. They be easier to see." He led them to one corner of the farm, to a plot protected by a heuller-proof wall made of bricks of ice mixed with chopped brush. He crawled through a hole in the wall that was too small to allow a heuller through, and they followed. Inside was row upon row of thick, gnarled plant stubs with just a few small twigs sprouting from the tops.

"It looks like an ancient vineyard just after pruning," Gabrielle remarked. "Except that there are no support stakes."

"These plants be the same as the others," said Fasart. "But all the branches have been cut off but one. The one that be left be from the metal-top spray, a different branch for each different metal." He walked down the row, pointing to each in turn. "Aluminum, beryllium, iron, copper, nickel, silver, gold, platinum . . ." He stopped near a stub with a single short stem containing a single, silver-gray berry at the tip. "This be a large magnificent queenberry. It soon be ripe enough to present to the Queen."

"Queenberry?" Boris queried. "The translator was unable to convert that word to the name of a metal. Do you have another name for it?"

"Fasart be unable to help. It be always called a queen-berry and nothing else. Perhaps Merlene be knowing what humans be calling it."

With Fasart's assistance, they took a sample of all the berries growing from the multiberry plants on his farm. They didn't get the ripe queenberry, but had to settle for a small one from a secondary plant. Fasart assured them that the unripe berries were not significantly different from the ripe ones except in size.

"That *is* strange," said Boris. "Size usually has some correlation with ripeness, but usually ripeness means sexual maturity."

"Ooooh!" Elizabeth interjected over the audiolink. "You just said that naughty word again."

Fasart interrupted. "That word be not translated. What be meaning of word *sek-su-al?*"

"That doesn't matter," said Gabrielle. "I have samples of all the berries that your multiberry plants produce, plus samples of the different roots, and the iceworms and fungi below." She tried to put the last sample bag back in her pouch and found the pouch full. "I think we'd best transfer these samples back to the base where Hiroshi can analyze them."

"Merlene be telling Fasart of the need for that task," said Fasart. "This farm be not far from the human flamewagon. Fasart be taking you there."

Fasart and his apprentices rounded up a heuller, attached the wagon they had come with, still carrying the heuller head and quarter segment, and soon the three of them were headed toward the foothills to the north of Camalor. They loaded up the microhopper rocket with the heuller parts and their large bagged collection of berries, fungus, and iceworm excrement, and sent it off to the base to be analyzed.

"Shall we be returning to the farm?" Fasart asked as the microhopper disappeared over the hill. "Fasart have much more to show to you."

Gabrielle was amazed at how nonchalant the alien had been at the sight of the rocket taking off. But then she realized that he was not a typical kerack, but the husband of the Wizard Merlene, and was probably used to seeing such unusual things.

"We are always interested in obtaining more knowledge," Boris replied.

They be talking just like Merlene, Fasart thought. *They must be truly wizards.*

"I've got the 'hopper on landing approach," came Hiroshi's voice over the audiolink. It was followed by that of Elizabeth.

"If you two can manage the ride back to the farm by yourselves, I'm going to suit up and take the samples around to the cold box so Hiroshi can take them through analysis."

After they arrived back at the farm, Fasart continued to tell them about life on the farm: how to take care of the 192 feet of a heuller, how best to mulch a multiberry plant, and how a good bed of black fungus around the base of a multiberry plant caused the berries to ripen faster.

Gabrielle and Boris, although continually expressing interest in all the details of farm life Fasart was expounding on, were both getting bored as the hours dragged on and wishing that their shift would soon come to an end. Their eyes started to blink . . .

"EMERGENCY!" came Elizabeth's voice over the audiolink. "An explosion has knocked Hiroshi down!"

Fasart saw a strange look suddenly appear on the faces of the humans. The flaps that partially covered their two small eyeballs, which had been blinking and drawing closer together during his long lecture, now suddenly raised wide open, and the eyeballs inside twitched back and forth nervously.

Elizabeth audiolinked again. "I hear air escaping. BAG DRILL! STAT!"

"Must to go!"

"Au revoir!"

Fasart was left staring in bewilderment at two blank eyeglobes on two lifeless, mechanical kerack bodies.

4
TRACK IN THE CHAMBER

IN A CONTROLLED panic, Boris cracked his sensuit. Not bothering to take off the verihelm—for he had practiced the bag drill many times in pitch darkness—he reached upward out of the sensuit toward the ceiling corner where he knew he would find two hand loops.

Grabbing the loops, he pulled an insulated silver bag out of the ceiling and down over his body, somersaulting head-first into the bag as he did so. When the lips of the bag contacted each other below his feet, supermagnets inside pulled the edges together in an airtight seal. Air gushed into the bag, inflating it.

He was safe—for a while.

He removed his verihelm, worked it down the cramped confines of the bag, and placed it out of the way between his legs. Looking out the crude oval window in the head of the rescue bag, he looked around the small commons room. He could see another bag wiggling behind the other cocoon as Gabrielle struggled to take off her verihelm and get it out of the way. The lights on the airlock door showed it was cycling, but no one else was visible. Both bunks, where Selke and Rob should have been sleeping, were still shut. He took command.

"Boris here! I see Gabrielle. Selke? Report!"

"Bagged," came the terse reply, muffled by the close confines of a bag inside a closed bunk.

"Rob here and bagged," came another muffled reply.

"Stay in your bunks until I determine what happened," Boris warned. "Liz? Hiroshi?" Concern was rising within him. There was a switch click over the aether and a voice answered that sounded like someone talking in a telephone booth. The voice, Elizabeth's, was intermittently drowned out by loud coughing.

"I'm in the airlock with Hiroshi. Careful! There's poisonous gas in the commons. Hiroshi got a whiff of it."

"What happened?"

"I don't quite know. Hiroshi was working in the cold box, using the manipulators to take some of the samples through analysis, when there was an explosion. He staggered back. Following him was some yellow vapor hissing through a breach in the manipulator controls. When I heard the hiss, I called 'Bag Drill.' Hiroshi was so doubled over with coughing that I decided it would be faster to get him into the airlock rather than try to bag us both."

Boris turned and looked at the wall where the warm ends of the cold-box manipulator controls entered the shelter at the end of the aisle between the two controller cocoons. There was no vapor entering now, but the wall was buckled inward as if a giant foot had kicked it in. The thick cold-box viewing window above the manipulator controls was bowed, but unbroken.

Boris made his way carefully to the window in an awkward, stiff-legged stride. One could walk in the legless rescue bag—it was sort of like walking in a potato sack—but having a verihelm between one's calves increased the difficulty.

When he looked inside the cold box, he could see traces of yellowish vapor still leaking out of a large rupture in one of the analyzer machines stacked in a rack at the back. The vapor was finding its way out a small air lock that was used to insert objects from Ice into the cold box for inspection and analysis. The wall of the cold box was bulging out, and the lock had been forced partially open. It was obvious there had been a powerful explosion inside the cold box.

Boris considered what to do next, and decided he needed to get rid of the poisonous vapor before he did anything else. Sliding his forearms into the air-bloated, oven-mitten appendages sticking out from the waist of the suit, he used a thumb to activate the lock control button. The lock door opened completely to the near-vacuum of Ice, and soon the cold box was clear. Now, however, Boris could hear an air leak, as air from the shelter made its way past the seals in the cold-box manipulators.

"We have a small air leak," he told the rest. "Nothing serious. I have gotten rid of the source of the poison gas, whatever it was."

The coughing from the air lock subsided as Hiroshi got himself under control. "Fluorine," he rasped.

"That's nasty stuff," said Elizabeth. "We'll have to take the shelter down to vacuum to get rid of it. I should be able to do that with the controls in here. Is everyone still safely bagged?" She checked through the roster again.

Suddenly Gabrielle screamed. "Lucifer!"

"He's in the bag with me," Selke called out.

"Dieu merci!"

"Down we go!" Elizabeth said, and air started whistling out the air vents. A temporary haze of fog formed in the room and a bowl of warm noodle soup on the table boiled over as the poison-laden air in the shelter was evacuated and replaced with pure oxygen and nitrogen from the tanks outside.

After they had all climbed out of their bags, Rob went to look at the leak around the manipulator controls.

"The seal popped loose when the bulkhead was bent inward," he said. "If I can seal off the cold box, I should have it fixed in no time." He tried the button for the air lock in the cold box and and discovered that it still worked. After letting cold nitrogen gas into the cold box to bring the pressure inside up to the pressure in the shelter, he undid the bolts holding the manipulators in the wall, readjusted the seal around them, and reinstalled them.

"We're safe now." Rob lowered the nitrogen pressure in the cold box back to the ambient pressure on Ice, then turned to Hiroshi. "What happened?"

"I was working in the cold box dissecting the frozen segment of heuller. I had it sitting in a pan of liquid nitrogen to bring it up to heuller body temperature. The meat was getting soft, and some of the body fluids started to liquefy. Using a syringe, I used the manipulators to take a good-sized sample of the yellow-brown liquid that looks like it serves as their blood, and injected it into the molecular weight analyzer. The next thing I knew, the syringe full of blood exploded, the manipulators bucked in my hands, and the viewing window struck me in the face, sending me backwards up the aisle." He stopped at this point to feel his sore nose. "I got a whiff of something sharp and started coughing, and Elizabeth got me in the lock. I have had time to think more about it while we were in the air lock, and I'm now sure that I got a dose of fluorine gas."

Gabrielle, who was sitting up on one of the monitor consoles, punched a few buttons and looked up at the monitor screen. It flashed a list of fluorine compounds and their properties.

"There it is," she said, pointing. "Difluorine oxide—or oxygen difluoride, if you prefer—melts at 49 K, boils at 128 K, so it would be liquid at kerack and heuller body temperature. Note that it is the only fluorine compound that is liquid at those low temperatures, except fluorine itself. Fluorine melts at 53 K and boils at 85 K."

Hiroshi added, "I have done some fluorine chemistry. That is how I knew the smell. It couldn't have been liquid fluorine in the syringe—wrong color. Besides, fluorine is so reactive it couldn't exist long in the free state without combining with something. Fluorine even burns water at room temperature. The blood sample must have been F-two-O."

"That's beginning to make some sense," Rob said thoughtfully. "We have H-two-O in our blood, but that's a solid at the low temperatures on Ice. The keracks must have liquid F-two-O instead of water in their blood as the solvent and carrier for the other constituents. It is the same compound as water, except each H is replaced with an F."

Hiroshi nodded in agreement and added, "It is well known in fluorine chemistry that for every hydrocarbon there is a matching fluorocarbon, as well as mixed variations of fluorohydrocarbons where only some of the hydrogen atoms are replaced by fluorine atoms. I had suspected that the kerack body chemistry was based on such fluorohydrocarbons, and was hoping the molecular weight analyses would prove me correct, but now the analyzer is damaged."

"Beyond repair." Rob shook his head. "It looks like the whole front end of the machine is blown off."

Gabrielle switched the view on the monitor screen. "Here are some details from the *Encyclopaedia Terra* on difluorine oxide, where it is compared to water, which has a similar structure." She read off the information, although everyone could read it for themselves. "Yellow-brown liquid. Hmmm. That is a good description of heuller blood color. There are two possible isomers, F-F-O and F-O-F. The only one known to exist is F-O-F, which is the same structure as water, which is H-O-H. The angle of the F-O-F bond is 103.2 degrees, which is almost identical to the H-O-H bond in water of 104.5 degrees—again making the compound a great deal like water. Wait. Here's a difference. The length of the F-O bonds is 1.418 angstroms—that is a lot longer than the H-O bond in water, which is only 0.958 angstroms. Hmmm. Fluorine atoms are not that much bigger than hydrogen atoms. That long bond length probably means that F-O-F is not as tightly bound as H-O-H, which would make it unstable."

"Unstable!" Rob echoed. "That's certainly a euphemism for what it did to the analyzer and the cold box. Explosive is more like it."

"I now see what caused the problem," said Hiroshi. "At the low temperatures of Ice, or even at kerack and heuller body temperatures, difluorine oxide is quite stable. But the boiling point of the liquid is only 128 K. If you heat the liquid slowly in an open container, there should be no problem. It will just evaporate into a gas and dissipate. But if the liquid is heated rapidly in a confined space so a high pressure develops, then vapor bubbles will form at the heated surface and collapse as they rise into the cooler liquid. At high pressures, those vapor bubble collapses can be quite violent and could trigger the instability, causing an explosive chain reaction where the difluorine oxide liquid decomposes into fluorine gas and oxygen gas. Although the analyzer is in the cold box and is cold on the *outside* of its case, it is electrically powered, and is likely to be well above the boiling point of kerack blood *inside*."

"And the blood certainly was confined inside there," said Rob. "But not for long."

Hiroshi groaned. "With the analyzer broken, I will be unable to do any molecular weight analyses on our organic samples. *Dame! Dekinai!!*"

"That's OK," said Rob. "Now that I've seen what can happen, I think I'll be just as happy to send all the organic samples to Grippen to analyze."

Selke asked, "What analysis machines *do* we have left?"

"I will check them out," Hiroshi said with a cough, getting up from the table and starting down between the two telebot controller cocoons toward the cold-box wall. But Gabrielle stepped down from the monitor console above one of the cocoons and blocked him.

"My experience with analytical equipment is equal to yours. I will do it. You had better get Liz and Selke to check your lungs."

"She's right," said Elizabeth, still sitting at the table. She picked up a chopstick lying next to a half-eaten bowl of now vacuum-dried noodles. "Come here, Hiroshi. Sit down and stick out your tongue so I can look at your throat. Selke, could you get our black bag out of storage and help me? The first thing we'll need is the stethoscope."

Gabrielle went to the cold box and started checking out the instruments there. Boris took the opportunity to use the bathroom, while Rob went to the galley and started brewing a large batch of instant coffee for everyone. He didn't want to leave Fasart staring at two empty kerack husks for too long, but he wasn't going to return to the normal shift schedule until he knew the status of his crew and equipment. Until everything got straightened up and people's nerves had quieted down, they were going to be short on sleep and the coffee would be needed to keep them alert—especially Selke and him. They had been asleep less than four hours when Elizabeth called the bag drill. While the coffee water was heating, he went to a monitor console, filled out the electronic management form for reporting accidents, and sent it off to Grippen. It was not going to make his day.

Over coffee, they reviewed their status. Elizabeth and Selke reported that Hiroshi's chest sounded clear, but to be safe they had sedated him and sent him off to bed. Gabrielle also had relatively good news.

"I put what was left of the heuller section back in storage and checked out the machines with small samples. The molecular weight analyzer is indeed nonfunctional. The laser-scanning optical spectrometer *is* functioning and can measure bulk optical properties and identify simple compounds, but not large molecules. The mass spectrometer can give us the relative atomic composition of any compound, but not its molecular weight or structure. The alpha-beta-gamma radiation spectrometer is also functioning and has already produced some interesting results."

"Like what?" asked Rob.

"Let me show you on a monitor screen." Gabrielle climbed up into the monitor chair. Rob, Boris, and Elizabeth gathered around, while Selke went to the bathroom for her morning ablutions. Gabrielle's fingers flew around the edges of the touch screen and soon a chart labeled *Beta particles* appeared.

"I didn't expect to get any significant radioactivity indications out of organic material, except perhaps carbon 14, so I used a small sample of the 'fertilizer' crystals that Fasart was so careful to milk out of the iceworms before killing them. This is what I got when I examined them with the radioactivity spectrometer. The alpha and gamma charts only showed a few events, but the beta chart was crowded." She pointed at the peaks on the charts. "There are so many events that the machine could identify a number of beta lines. Those are the ones it has labeled."

Boris read them off the screen. "Beryllium 10, carbon 14, aluminum 26, silicon 32, chlorine 36, argon 39, potassium 40 . . . those are all the beta emitters with long lifetimes measured in years to millions of years. It shows the machine is working, but one would expect to find a few atoms of those isotopes in practically any random inorganic sample."

"But look at the intensity level." Gabrielle pointed to a number in the upper corner of the chart. "The level of radioactivity per gram is so high a few of these crystals would kill you if you swallowed them. Here, let me show you the spectroscopy I did on a single black grain I teased out from the rest of the crystals. It weighed about three micrograms." She touched the screen and the display changed. The chart now showed a single peak, labeled ^{14}C.

"That black grain must have been a speck of graphite," said Boris. "It would certainly have a small quantity of carbon 14 in it."

"Look at the intensity number again," Gabrielle said "The only way you would get that high a reading of radioactivity per gram is if the graphite were almost pure carbon 14

The amount of normal nonradioactive carbon 12 and carbon 13 in that sample is negligible! I have not done it yet, but when we analyze the other crystals one by one, we will probably find the same thing—they are all pure samples of a single isotope, the radioactive isotope of that element."

Rob nodded slowly. "Then those iceworm creatures not only comb the ice for the free-radical energy stored there, but they also comb the dirt for the long-lived radioisotopes they contain. Fasart said the crystals were poisonous. That makes sense now. The crystals are so intensely radioactive they would be as deadly to the radiation-tough keracks as to humans." He paused, obviously puzzled. "But if the isotopes are poisonous, then why do the iceworms collect and concentrate them into crystals? Why don't they just leave them dispersed in the ice?"

"Because they are part of the energy source for the kerack civilization we have been looking for!" said Boris excitedly. "I wondered at the time why something that is poisonous could be used as fertilizer for plants. Now I see—the radioactive isotopes are mixed with ice and placed near the roots of the multiberry plants. The isotopes decay, emitting high-energy beta particles. The beta particles travel through the ice, energizing the electrons in the ice and dirt atoms and molecules, making long-lived free radicals. The free radicals are then used as an energy source by the plant roots. The energy source for the keracks is, firstly, the cosmic-ray-produced free radicals in the old ice, and secondly the radioactive-isotope-produced free radicals in the used ice. Together, they supply the energy needed to sustain life here so far from the Sun."

"I wonder if it *is* enough to sustain the observed level of activity," Elizabeth mused. "Those keracks run at a pretty high body temperature compared to their surroundings. I will have to run through some calculations on their total energy balance and see if the numbers check out. Hmmm. I wonder how one measures the temperature of a kerack—or a heuller, for that matter. Perhaps Merlene could be of some help."

"I am sure that Merlene would be interested in what we found and our speculations," said Gabrielle. "She might also be interested in helping us carry out our investigations."

Boris looked skeptical. "I doubt she would be knowledgeable enough about modern science to be of significant help. She probably knows nothing about radioactivity, and since the keracks obviously don't have electricity, they have no analytical instruments to make any measurements of anything."

"I spent a summer as a docent in the science exhibits section of the Glasgow museum," said Elizabeth. "It was amazing to see the quality of the instrumentation produced by Scots inventors and scientists in the 1700s and 1800s. You don't need electricity to measure radioactivity; you can do it with a Wilson cloud chamber. A glass bowl, a piston, and some alcohol, and you can detect charged particles by the cloud tracks they leave."

"I built an even simpler cloud chamber for a science fair project," Rob said. "All you need is a piece of dry ice covered with a piece of black velvet cloth soaked in alcohol, and a glass bowl over it. Give it time to stabilize, and soon you have a continuously operating cloud chamber."

Elizabeth waved at the window. "There's plenty of dry ice around here. But I wonder what Merlene could use for the dense vapor liquid instead of alcohol?"

"There are probably many other types of instruments Merlene could construct using the materials she has," Gabrielle suggested. "We could even get her started on electricity with batteries, thermocouples . . ."

"At the temperatures she lives at, she even has access to lots of superconducting metals," Rob reminded them. "A few thousand turns of superconducting wire and a battery, and she would be able to make strong persistent-current magnets the old-time Earth physicists would have traded away their handmade slide rules for."

Boris remarked, "That introduces a problem. We all know about those instruments, but in many cases the technology is so old that we do not know how best to make them, and so cannot tell Merlene."

"We shouldn't be telling her everything, anyway," said Gabrielle. "She should be doing some of the inventing herself. She needs to anyway, since the ambient temperature is so different."

"She could still use some help," Elizabeth said. She pointed to the monitor screen still holding the data on fluorine compounds. "Look at us. We're way ahead of her in knowledge, but we don't know everything, so we look it up in the *Encyclopaedia Terra Digital*. What Merlene needs is the equivalent of the encyclopaedia."

"Why the equivalent?" Rob asked. "Why not the original? The original Kerack contact team developed a human-kerack dictionary during their years-long dialogue with Merlene while the cable catapult system was being set into place. All we need to do is load the encyclopaedia and the dictionary onto a Lookman chip along with a simple program to provide a word-by-word translation interpolated between the lines of the encyclopaedia text. That way Merlene could use the Lookman to look up things in the encyclopaedia herself."

"I don't know if that is a good idea," said Elizabeth. "It might spoil the kerack culture."

Selke gave her a sardonic look. "Keep them in savagery, you mean. The typical Anglo-Saxon attitude toward the 'poor benighted heathen.' "

"Don't call me a bloody Anglo-Saxon," Elizabeth retorted. "I'm a Scot!"

Boris interrupted them. "The United Nations has already gone through that debate. It was decided long ago that it is unfair to deny knowledge to a savage people in the hopes that it will 'save' their native culture, especially after contact has been made and the savages can see, and appreciate, and want, the advantages of a superior technology. To then deny them the same advantages on the pretext that it is 'better' for them to develop the technology on their own is unjust."

"We *do* owe her some sort of payment for all the information she has given us over the years," Elizabeth agreed. "I'll fix up one of our Lookmans, suit up, and put it in the microhopper to be shipped back for Merlene's use."

Rob smiled at the thought. "For us, a Lookman is something you carry in your shirt pocket. For Merlene, it is going to be a large screen display that fills one wall of her workshop. That reminds me. The Lookman is so big and bulky it's going to be tricky for the 'bots to carry. Instead of sending the microhopper back to the lander, maybe we ought to deliver the Lookman to Fasart's farm so we can carry it back to Merlene in the wagon."

"Speaking of Fasart, he is still waiting for us to return." Boris pointed to the other monitor screen, where Fasart could be seen through the eyeglobes of the distant telebots. He was directing the apprentices to their tasks around the farm while occasionally looking in their direction to see if the telebots were occupied yet.

"I guess we had better get back to the 'bots," said Rob. "Since Hiroshi is perforce on sleep shift, you might as well start yours, Liz. Selke and I will soldier on and start our shifts early."

"Gott!" Selke burst out angrily, cross because she had had only a few hours' sleep. "You are certainly free with *my* time! Mission commander or not, you could have at least *consulted* me!"

Boris, trying to defuse the situation, suggested, "Perhaps we should break up the shifts into shorter segments. If you and Rob can run the 'bots for two hours instead of four, then Gabrielle and I will be rested up enough by then to go back in for a while."

"As soon as I get the Lookman loaded into the microhopper, I'll take a quick catnap," Elizabeth said. "Then, when Boris and Gabrielle are in the 'bots, I'll ride the monitor chair and Rob and Selke can catch up on their sleep." She paused for a second. "There's going to be a minor problem with that idea. Hiroshi will still be sedated and will be using one of the bunks. You two would have to share the other one."

"I wouldn't mind that . . ." Rob replied, not really knowing how Selke would take it after her outburst. He soon found out.

"We accept your offer," Selke said with a malicious look. "Except *I* sleep in the bunk, and Rob sleeps in the air lock . . . *with* the cat box!" She headed down the narrow aisle between the two cocoons, donned the verihelm, and was soon encased in the sensuit. The view of Fasart and his farm in the monitor display above her cocoon moved from side to side as she shook herself into the scene.

"Guten Tag," Selke said as she brought the telebot to life. Without waiting for Rob to teleport in, she twitched her smaller fingers to get her legs in motion, and, feeling the roughness of the crust through the sides of her feet as she dragged her tail behind her for balance, she made her way over to where Fasart waited.

"I apologize for the abrupt departure of Boris and Gabrielle," she said. "We had a problem back at our base that needed their immediate attention."

"Fasart be told by Merlene about often abrupt behavior of humans. Fasart be understanding."

There was an acoustic rustle behind Selke, and Rob came up to join them. He told Fasart, "We have a gift for Merlene. It will be brought back on the microhopper. Could we land the microhopper here on the farm? We need a large, clear space."

"Fasart be noticing the hole left in the ice when flame-wagon leave." He looked around and pointed to a corner of the field where the apprentices were forming a brush stack.

"Fasart be having apprentices move brush stack. Humans be setting flamewagon down there. Moving brush stack be taking some time. Fasart be continuing lecture on farming from the point where Boris and Gabrielle left."

Soon Rob and Selke, both operating on less than four hours' sleep, found their eyelids drooping as Fasart droned on.

After a number of trips with the wagon, the apprentices finally had the brush stack moved out of the way. Fasart finished his lecture on the techniques of multiberry mulching, which required just the right mixture of ice, organic manure from household slop buckets, iceworm excrement, and heuller-regurgitated, ground-up rock dust. They stood near the entrance of the farm to watch as Boris flew the microhopper in over the mountains by remote control and landed the small craft. The microhopper stood just one meter high on its three independent-suspension shock-absorber landing legs and had a body about thirty centimeters in diameter. It landed with its body raised high between its legs to prevent damage; then the legs lowered the body down to the surface. Not built for high speed, the microhopper had no aerodynamics, and looked like a fat bug with rocket nozzles on its bottom.

They unloaded the Lookman, loaded more samples of farm produce in its place, and the microhopper took off again. Loading the Lookman into the wagon with them, Rob and Selke rode back into Camalor behind Fasart on his heuller. As they arrived at the home of Merlene and Fasart, Merlene came to the surface and down the street to greet them. Her wizard-symbol-decorated chestcoat, mouthveil, and skirt were protected by a kitchen apron covered with dusty, flourlike spots where she had wiped her claws.

"She looks like she's been groped by the Pillsbury Dough boy," Rob joked over the audiolink. Selke didn't get it.

In one claw Merlene was carrying a brown morsel of something.

"The antennae of Fasart be smelling something tasty!" asart said as he approached.

Merlene held up a claw. "I have been cooking heuller incers for dinner."

Fasart reached down with his huge warclaw and easily wung her up behind him on the heuller and headed the nimal into their yard toward the tethering pole. Merlene eached around him, pulled open the bottom of his mouth-elt just a little, and slipped the morsel into his mouth.

Fasart twisted his body around so that the humans ouldn't see what she was doing. One of his antennae ouched hers and he tried to hold his voice to a whisper, but nough leaked through that Rob and Selke could hear his rotest.

"Merlene be not feeding Fasart in front of the humans!"

"They be not keracks."

Rob twitched a toe and switched to intersuit audiolink. Couple of interesting facts there. They use their antennae ot only for radio communication, but for smell, too. Also, here seems to be a taboo of sorts on helping someone eat."

Merlene was pleased with the gift of the Lookman and, arrying it herself, led the way down to her workshop. She ad to stop at the first landing, take the pot of hot frying fat ff the heating plate, and hang up her apron. Rob took a mall sample of the flourlike material that Merlene had used o coat the heuller pincers before frying them. It had a lightly yellow tinge. There was a hunk of similarly colored oot nearby, next to a grater with fine teeth.

"Freshly ground root flour," he remarked as he pouched he sample bag. He picked up one of many freshly fried euller pincers. "Kentucky-Fried Heuller Toes!" He bagged nd pouched that also.

They finally got to visit Merlene's workroom. Since there vere no apprentices to Camalor's solitary wizard, the work-oom was smaller than others they had visited. Like all the nderground rooms in Camalor, it was illuminated by glowworms installed in cages in the corners. Merlene went to each cage and pushed fireberries into the mouths of the compliant worms, and the room brightened.

There was a large worktable in the center of the room and shelves along the walls containing books, scrolls, pieces of equipment, and jars of chemicals. It looked a little like an alchemist's lab—which it was. Next to the table was a stand up writing desk with a writing stylus stuck into a convenient hole in the top, and a notebook on it opened to a blank page. Both the desk and the table seemed to be made of fiber-ice composite "boards" that had been cast into shape and bolted together with countersunk heads. Along one wall was a large, seamless board that reached from kerack waist level to the ceiling. It had a reflective metal surface that looked like aluminum, with a matte finish so the surface didn't act as a mirror but yet had no intrinsic color itself. There was a tray along the bottom containing a number of sticks of jet-black material that looked like compressed carbon dust. On either side of the board was a tall cylindrical pot with a top. There were similar pots on two corners of the worktable and the top of the writing desk. Merlene put the Lookman next to the writing desk where she could reach it easily.

"The Lookman box be warm on this side," she said, patting it on the left side.

"That's where the permanent battery is," Rob explained. "The Lookman is powered by radioactive particles called alpha particles coming from a small amount of americium inside. Since there is no way to turn off the radioactive source, it is always generating heat, even when the Lookman is off and not using the electricity."

"Merlene be not knowledgeable about meaning of words like 'radioactive.' She be learning of its existence in talks with Earth, but be knowing little about it."

"You don't need to know about radioactivity to operate the Lookman," Selke said. "And after learning how to operate the Lookman, you can use it to learn more about that subject and many others."

Rob added, "One of the reasons we want you to learn more about radioactivity is that we have found that some of the samples that we took back to the base have very large amounts of radioactive materials in them, much higher than would normally be found. We are interested in learning why that is so, and perhaps you could help us."

"Merlene be willing to help."

"Then let me show you how to operate the Lookman." Rob went over to the machine and stood next to Merlene. He pointed to a small, luminous white dot in the lower left corner. "Touch that dot with a pincer." Merlene did so, and immediately the screen came to life with a menu border. Rob was pleased to see that the translator program had placed words in kerack script underneath the English words so he and Merlene could read it together.

"Now touch the box with the word FIND in it," he said. Merlene easily identified the right box and did so. The menu blinked, some of the command options in the boxes changing as it did so, and at the top of the screen flashed the instruction: *SPELL OUT THE WORD YOU WISH INFORMATION ABOUT.*

"I can see a problem here," said Selke, who had been looking on. "I bet the program can only look up English words in the encyclopaedia, and Merlene's command of the vagaries of English spelling is going to be even worse than mine."

"I'm hoping the spelling routine will be able to cope." Rob turned to Merlene and showed her the letters of the alphabet along the bottom of the menu. Fortunately, Elizabeth had changed the screen options so the letters were in alphabetical order instead of the QWERTY keyboard system. At the top of the menu was a list of kerack phonemes. "You can enter a word in kerack language and the machine will automatically translate it and look it up for you. Or, if there is no kerack word, you can spell out the sound of the English word phonetically and the machine will attempt to find the correct meaning."

"This be a truly marvelous machine," Merlene said.

Rob smiled. "I am going to say a word. Tell me if my telebot audio-radio translator produces a kerack word." He paused. "Radioactive."

"That word be not translated."

"Then spell out how it sounds using kerack phonemes."

Merlene touched the upper menu and typed out a kerack nonsense word. Below it was the phonetic English translation: *ra-de-o-ak-tiv*

"Pretty close," said Selke.

Rob continued. "Now touch this box here that has the word SPELL in it," Merlene did so. Immediately below the phonetic spelling there appeared two words in individual boxes: *radioactive* and *reductive*. Below the words were their phonetic translations in kerack phonemes.

"Touch the word that is closest to what you heard and spelled." Merlene did so, and instantly the screen was filled with a text entry from the encyclopaedia that started with the word *Radioactivity*. Below each line of text in English was a line of text in kerack giving the translation.

"If the text has an English word that is not translated and you cannot guess the meaning from the rest of the sentence, touch the box labeled FIND, then the English word you want it to look up." He demonstrated by touching FIND, then the last name of the French physicist Henri Becquerel, who first discovered radioactivity. He was certain that the kerack word underneath was just a phonetic repetition. Instantly a box appeared in the bottom half of the screen with a biography of Becquerel. "When you have finished looking up that word, you return to the main menu by touching this little box labeled EXIT."

Merlene was a fast learner, and soon Rob had shown her through all the important options on the menu. He noticed that if she paused and "forced" herself to remember something new, she never forgot it. After a while, eyes glazed, Selke called a halt to the lesson.

"If you remember, we were going to do just a short shift," she reminded him with a yawn. Merlene was a little taken aback by Selke's blatant show of the inside of her mouth, but reminded herself that the humans were shameless in this aspect.

"Right," Rob agreed, yawning in reply. "I got carried away."

"It is time for us to rest," Selke said to Merlene. "Boris and Gabrielle will be taking our places." The image of her face on the eyeglobe of the telebot blinked out.

Merlene turned to face Rob. "Merlene be thanking you for bringing the Lookman and teaching Merlene about the human machine. Merlene be teaching Boris and Gabrielle about the machines o'Merlene."

Over the audiolink Boris said, "That sounds interesting. I am ready to teleport as soon as you get out of the cocoon."

"See you later, alligator," Rob said, and blinked out.

"That word not be translated," said Merlene, bewildered and left facing two empty kerack husks. Then she realized that she could now find out the answer on her own. She turned to the Lookman and phonetically spelled out: *a-li-ga-tor.*

When Boris and Gabrielle teleported back into the telebots, Merlene was busy looking at a picture on the Lookman showing the wide open mouth of an alligator facing the camera. When she heard the rustle of the telebot legs coming alive, she quickly punched the EXIT box, and the picture disappeared. As she turned around Gabrielle noticed that Merlene's second set of legs were fussing with each other as if she was nervous.

"She acting like she be caught looking at a naughty postcard," Gabrielle murmured over the audiolink.

"She was," Boris audiolinked back. "That huge mouth with its huge tongue and all those teeth, thrust right out where you can see it, and not a mouthbelt in sight. Merlene is certainly going to get a broadening education from that Lookman."

"Bonjour, Merlene," Gabrielle radioed out loud. "Boris and I will be visiting you for a while."

"We would like to see more of your laboratory," said Boris. He pointed to an object hanging from the wall that consisted of four rods attached to each other at points along their length. "That is obviously a pantograph."

"Merlene be inventing that, so she be able to make replicas of drawings either smaller or larger," Merlene replied. She reached for one of her creations on the shelf below. "Merlene also be inventing arrangements of lenses inside tubes that make objects appear larger and smaller to the eye." She picked up a long tube. "This be for seeing at a distance. Merlene be not able to show you how it works inside the workshop."

Boris looked at the arrangement of the lenses. "A Galilean telescope."

Merlene picked up another tube, much smaller this time, and looked through it at one of her pincers. "This Merlene be inventing for making small things look large."

"A very nice microscope," Boris took it from her and looked through it at one of his pincers. "Looks like one Leeuwenhoek might have made."

Merlene then showed them her jars of chemicals and her kerack equivalents of test tubes, beakers, retorts, bunsen burners, and hot plates. The bunsen burners had a gauze wick of platinum firemetal and produced a hot flame by burning methane from fuelberries and ozone from hotberries. The portable hot plates operated the same way as Merlene's kitchen oven, with a platinum mesh burner wetted with oxygen, glowing by reaction with the hydrogen "air" in the room. The tall pots worked in a similar fashion. They were designed by Merlene to be brighter sources of light and infrared radiation than the usual glowworm illuminators. They contained a long wick of firemetal that sucked up liquid oxygen and liquid methane from storage tanks in the base, where they recombined on the brightly glowing wick. All the heaters and lights were started up by the primitive technique of warming a fireberry under the tongue and placing a few drops of liquid oxygen on the firemetal wicks.

"This is a very sophisticated analytical balance," said Gabrielle, pointing to it on the shelf. "Even has knife-edge support points. Probably good to better than one percent."

"Merlene be able to distinguish heavy silver from light silver with it." she said proudly. Then she picked up an instrument that had a large disk with a crank handle and put it on her worktable. "This be Merlene's latest invention." She started to crank the handle.

"I didn't understand that remark about 'heavy' silver and 'light' silver," Elizabeth interjected over the audiolink. Her comment was drowned out by a loud cracking noise accompanied by bright sparks.

"Merlene be inventing a machine that makes lightning!" she said proudly, keeping the crank turning.

"A static electricity machine!" Gabrielle cried as she lowered the sensitivity of her image intensifier.

"Machine be making very hot sparks. It be capable of burning anything, even metals. Merlene be using it to be identifying metals in compounds." She stopped cranking the machine and the sparks ceased. She got down another machine and put it on the worktable.

"That must be an optical spectrometer." Boris pointed with a pincer instead of with his antennae. "There's the slit, the collimating lens, the prism, and the focusing lens."

"The prism seems to be strongly refracting—probably cleaved from a heuller tooth," Gabrielle noted.

Merlene hooked the static electricity generator to two electrodes on the spectrometer. As she cranked up the generator, a spark appeared between the electrodes and two strong yellow lines showed up on the curved display surface at the back of the spectrometer, along with other, less bright lines.

"It is a spark spectrometer," said Boris.

Gabrielle nodded. "There are the sodium D lines. She should be able to do a lot of analytical chemistry with that."

Boris looked carefully at the machine. To make the electricity, the wheel rubbed against something that looked a great deal like white cat fur. "What is that material?" he asked.

"That be the skin of a clawpet," said Merlene. "Lady Vivane be on the Basin o'Sliding one day and be colliding with her warrior escort while both be at a high speed. She be stretching out her claw to protect herself and the clawpet be crushed. Merlene be getting the skin from the butcher."

"I doubt that we will get an opportunity to get a whole clawpet, so we should take what we can get," Gabrielle said. "Could we have a sample to take back and analyze?"

"Besure." Merlene went to a shelf. "Merlene be having a scrap left over." Gabrielle bagged the sample of clawpet and added it to her carrying pouch.

Merlene then showed them more of her instruments. One was a set of bellows chamber barometers, one large chamber for measuring the normally low pressures on Ice and one smaller chamber for measuring the much higher pressures that followed a geyser eruption.

"Merlene be able to predict the arrival of snowstorms using the barometer and the thermometer. Here be the thermometer."

"Interesting! May I see that?" Gabrielle stretched out a claw. Merlene gave it to her and Gabrielle quickly figured out how it worked. "I see. A bimetallic strip. Simple and rugged. Very nice workmanship. What are the two metals?"

"They be cadmium and manganese."

"That will not be an efficient combination," Gabrielle

objected. "Those two metals have nearly the same coefficient of thermal expansion. We will have to teach you how to make Invar alloy. It has a very small coefficient of expansion compared to most metals."

The voice of Elizabeth broke through on the audiolink. "I just looked up the coefficients of linear expansion for cadmium and manganese. Don't forget that Merlene lives in a world with an average temperature of 30 K, not 300 K. At 30 K, the c-axis expansion of cadmium is at its peak—two or three times larger than most metals—while manganese is going through a transition from expansion to contraction and is near zero. She has the optimum materials for her temperature range."

"Elizabeth informs me that I am in error," Gabrielle said to Merlene, handing the thermometer back. "This is an excellent thermometer."

Merlene had known that she had the right metals in the thermometer. She had gone through many combinations before choosing this pair. It had taken her and the metalspinner Patene many tries before Patene had learned how to stroke her cadmium spinner worm to produce an oriented crystalline cadmium surface that gave the best thermal response.

"How do you calibrate it?" Boris asked as he looked more closely at the instrument. One end of the double-metal strip was affixed to a tip of beryllium that was placed in contact with the object whose temperature was to be measured. As the temperature changed, the indicator at the free end of the strip bent back and forth in front of an indicator plate with marks inscribed on it. "What do each of these marks represent?"

"The mark that be below the number zero be the position of the indicator when the thermometer be in a container of melting hydrogen frost Merlene be collecting during clear nights when Brightstar be not in the sky. The mark that be below the number five fi'fives be the position of the indicator when the thermometer be in hydrofluoric acid heated to melting by a methane-ozone flame."

"Hmmm." Elizabeth's voice came over the audiolink as she flipped her monitor screen through the encyclopedia. "Her zero mark is fourteen K, while her one hundred twenty-five mark is one hundred ninety K. This is going to be a lot like converting from Fahrenheit to Celsius. Ten marks on her thermometer equals fourteen degrees Kelvin, but she starts at fourteen K, so absolute zero is minus ten marks on her scale. Ask her what her body temperature is. I need it to develop my energy balance model for the keracks."

"Elizabeth is asking what is the temperature inside a kerack body," Gabrielle said.

"The temperature be one fi'five, three fives marks," said Merlene, demonstrating by putting the thermometer under her mouthveil and letting the indicator end show from beneath the veil.

"Hmmm." Elizabeth calculated quickly. "Twenty-five plus fifteen is forty marks, times one point four degrees per mark—that's fifty-six, plus fourteen because she doesn't start at absolute zero. That's a body temperature of seventy K. Significantly hotter than ambient."

"But not really that much different from humans," remarked Gabrielle. "Although ambient on Earth is about seventeen C, the human body is significantly higher at thirty-seven C."

"And to think she invented all of these devices on her own," Elizabeth said. "She is the Roger Bacon of Camalor. Why don't you tell her what you found out about the radioactive iceworm shit, and how we think it is part of the kerack energy source? Then we can ask for her help in identifying other possible sources of energy. Sometime I also want to ask her to keep a record of her weekly food intake and body temperature to help calibrate my energy balance model."

Gabrielle returned to talking with Merlene. While Merlene listened in fascination, Gabrielle told her about finding the high levels of radioactivity in the crystals Fasart extracted from the iceworms before butchering them, and how the radioactive crystals gave off charged particles that generated the energetic molecules in the ice that the multiberry plants needed for energy. Merlene, having never heard of radioactivity before, wanted to know how to detect this new phenomenon.

Boris joined in. "We have identified a device for detecting radioactivity that you could build with your available resources. It is called a cloud chamber. It is a container with a transparent top and a black bottom that is kept cold. A small amount of liquid is put inside, where it evaporates and forms a heavy vapor layer over the cold bottom. When the charged particle from the radioactive source passes through the cold vapor, it leaves a track in the form of a long, thin cloud. At the high temperatures that exist on Earth, we use frozen carbon dioxide as the cold source and ethyl alcohol for the liquid. Here, at the low temperatures on Ice, it is hard to find a liquid with the right properties, but after looking through the encyclopaedia we think that if you heat the apparatus so that the top of the chamber is hotter than the bottom, you could use a heavy molecule with a low boiling point like carbon monoxide or nitrogen trifluoride as the liquid."

"Merlene be having many flareberries in the kitchen. They be having carbon monoxide in them. Merlene be also thinking of how to have top of chamber be hot as well as transparent and be finding ideal solution." She went over to a stack of various sheets of material and pulled out what looked like a large pane of glass. "This be cleaved from a heuller tooth. Diamond be both transparent and a good heat conductor." From a shelf she pulled out a flat-bottomed container that was smaller in diameter than the sheet of diamond. She stacked some bricks up on the table and put the container on the bricks and the diamond sheet on top, the edges sticking out over the bricks. Around the chamber she put some hot plates so that the diamond contacted the hot surface.

Gabrielle quickly caught on. "That should work! We need a piece of black material in the bottom of the chamber."

Merlene shortly found a scrap of black velvet and after a few quick snips with a pair of scissors, installed it in the bottom of the chamber. Then she scampered up the stairs to the kitchen and returned with a pin and a mouthful of flare-berries. Soon the velvet cloth was wet, and the diamond lid was on and heating up.

"It will take some time for the chamber to stabilize and the cloud region to develop," Boris warned. "You must be patient."

"Patience be a required virtue of wizards," replied Merlene as she peered eagerly into the chamber.

"Fortunately we won't have too long a wait once the cloud region has formed," said Boris. "The high cosmic-ray intensity on Ice is certain to give us lots of showers to see."

Gabrielle frowned. "Wait. We are two stories underground. The mass of the ice above us is going to shield us from a lot of the incoming cosmic rays. We may have to move the apparatus up to the surface."

"We may be two stories underground," Boris said, "but those are kerack stories, which are only ten centimeters high. Considering that the room above us is essentially empty, there is less than ten centimeters of ice between us and space. The cosmic rays will make it through."

Patiently they waited and waited.

"I thought I saw something!" said Gabrielle excitedly.

"Merlene be seeing nothing."

"I wish we had better light inside the chamber," Boris said. "Maybe we should bring over one of those light pots and hang it overhead."

"Boris be wishing more light?" Merlene asked. "Merlene be getting a lightrod. They be much brighter than light pots." She reached under the table and pulled out a hollow glass cylinder with a cord trailing behind it. One of her middle feet cranked something else under the table, and the tube glowed a bright red color.

"A helium-neon light!" Boris exclaimed when he saw the familiar color.

"That makes sense," Elizabeth said over the audiolink. "Helium and neon are two of the elements that are still gases at the temperature of Ice. The others are frozen."

"She already has invented an electric light," Gabrielle said. "It won't be long before Camalor has streetlights."

"And lasers," Boris added. "All she needs to do is attach a few good mirrors to the ends of that tube and she will have a helium-neon laser."

Merlene stood the lightrod up on a brick so it was higher than the cloud chamber. Suddenly they saw three white streaks in the cloud chamber.

"Part of a cosmic ray shower," Boris said. "The cosmic ray particle came in from space, hit an atom in the ice above us, and generated many smaller particles, most of them electrons. What we saw are called beta particles or electrons. As they traveled through the carbon monoxide vapor they knocked some of the electrons off the carbon monoxide molecules, creating a charged ion. The charge attracted other carbon monoxide molecules until the clump of molecules became a tiny drop that was big enough to scatter light."

"Many words be not translated," said Merlene. "Boris be not attempting to explain. Merlene be learning from the Lookman."

"It is too bad we don't have some of those crystals that Fasart extracted from the iceworm," said Gabrielle. "Those were highly radioactive, and if we put just one tiny crystal in there, we would have lots of tracks."

"Does Gabrielle be meaning the iceworm crystals that Fasart be using as fertilizer?"

"Yes. They are tiny crystals of elements like carbon, beryllium, and aluminum."

"Merlene be knowing of those. Merlene be perhaps having some in cold room." She scampered rapidly up the stairs again and returned carefully carrying a spoon. In the bowl was a single crystal of aluminum. "Fasart be sometimes not cleaning the iceworm carcass properly. Merlene be finding this crystal on an iceworm Fasart be bringing home yesterday."

"Lift the top of the cloud chamber carefully and drop it in the middle," said Boris. The second the speck hit the velvet, white tracks spurted out from it in all directions.

Merlene was clearly fascinated with her new toy. "The longest ones be all about the same length."

"That is because there is a maximum energy to the emitted beta particles," Gabrielle said. "The length of the track is proportional to the energy. If you get Fasart to bring you home other crystals, you will find their tracks longer or shorter."

"Why be that?"

"Perhaps that is something you should look up yourself in the encyclopaedia."

There was a brief burst of static over the aether, and suddenly the chamber was full of streaks. The tracks all pointed at Gabrielle. She looked at Boris in surprise.

Boris smacked his eyeglobe with his warclaw. "I forgot the most obvious source—us! I mean these telebots we are in. Your trapchip just dumped a crystal of antihydrogen into your thermoelectric generator and those were the pions from the antiproton annihilations. If Merlene is going to use the cloud chamber, we had better keep the telebots a good distance away."

Elizabeth's dry voice came in over the audiolink. "One of these days Merlene is going to be able to figure out the dose of radiation she is getting from Grippen's unshielded 'bots. She isn't going to be pleased."

Gabrielle turned to look at Boris. "Merlene is going to be busy for some time with the new toys we have given her.

Why don't we take these 'bots up to the surface, park them in a corner of her yard, and 'port back. We need to take a day off, do our laundry, and catch up on our sleep."

"Good thought." Boris headed for the stairway leading to the surface. "We are going now, Merlene." But he was talking to Merlene's back. She was at the Lookman reading through an entry in the *Encyclopaedia Terra Digital* entitled "Beta Particles."

5

FIFTHDAY AT THE CONCERT

ELIZABETH WAS FEELING out of sorts when her alarm woke her up and turned on the lights inside the bunk. The previous evening, when she had gone to bed, she had started reading a collection of Jeeves stories on her Lookman, thinking they would put her to sleep, but they were so amusing that she had kept on reading "just another one" until she was halfway through her sleep shift. Now, her shift in the telebot controller was about to begin and she had gotten only four hours of sleep. Sitting up, she opened her locker at the foot of the bed, took off her pale green nightgown, and put on the long johns she would be wearing in the telebot controller. She didn't bother belting on the urine collector; she had long ago learned to just hold it in. Besides, ever since Lucifer had gotten hold of her collector and had batted it around for a while, it was prone to leaking.

She opened the soundproof door and left the cavernous, solitary, quiet comfort of the bunk for the cramped, crowded, noisy irritation of the shelter. The bathroom door was locked, meaning Hiroshi had beaten her to it, so she stepped down into the commons room. Selke was up on a monitor stool watching Boris and Gabrielle pilot the telebots through Camalor. Rob was at the galley. He turned to greet her.

"Made you some coffee," he said, handing her a steaming cup.

"Thanks." Elizabeth downed a good-sized swallow. He had put sugar in it again, but she had long ago learned not to stir.

"There's plenty of hot water. Do you want me to whip you up some instant oatmeal?"

Elizabeth didn't feel like facing a bowl of American-style oatmeal with milk and raisins and sugar and butter, and besides, Hiroshi was still in the bathroom and she had nothing else to do but wait, so she turned him down and stirred up some of her own Scottish porridge, made with oat groats—plain. She sat down at the table, and Lucifer instantly jumped up beside her bowl to see what she was eating. Feeling a little mean, Elizabeth dipped out some porridge with her spork and held it out to the jet-black beast with the malevolent yellow eyes.

"Have a taste of my yum-yum porridge, Lucifer," she said, knowing full well that he liked his porridge made with milk. Lucifer turned away in disgust and jumped up on Selke's monitor desk, activating a few keys that switched off the video recorder. Selke pushed him aside and restarted the machine. Boris's voice came over the audiolink from the telebots. He was addressing Merlene.

"It is time for our shift to end. We will be going now, and shortly Elizabeth and Hiroshi will be taking our places."

There was a creaking noise as the cocoon in front of Selke split open and Boris's verihelmeted head raised up. Then Elizabeth heard the welcome sound of the lock being opened on the bathroom door and Hiroshi emerging. She quickly finished off her porridge and stepped around the corner into the bathroom, leaving on the table an empty bowl and a coffee cup with a partially melted sugar cube at the bottom.

When she tried to leave the bathroom a few minutes later,

she couldn't. With five other people either trying to get something to eat or waiting in line for the bathroom, there wasn't room for her.

"Fifteen puzzle time!" Rob announced, seeing the problem. He backed up and sat on a vacant monitor stool. "I'll move into this slot."

"And I'll move down here," Hiroshi said, carrying his bowl of rice and vegetables as he sidled past Rob down the narrow access aisle between the two telebot controllers.

Selke swung her chair around the table. Elizabeth was now able to push past Gabrielle, who squeezed into the bathroom and out of the commons, relieving the crowding.

Hiroshi finished his breakfast, passed his bowl and chopsticks to Elizabeth to put in the galley sink, climbed into one of the two telebot controllers, and started inserting himself into the cocoon. As soon as he was out of the aisle, Elizabeth went down and climbed into the other controller. She knelt down in the knee pads, leaned forward on the chest pad, put on the verihelm, and lowered her arms down in the sleeves until her fingers reached the leg controllers. The cocoon closed around her and her display came on. This time it took only the slightest shake of her head to "leave" the cramped, dirty human base, with its lack of privacy, and be instantly teleported thirty kilometers away into Merlene's clean spacious home, where every occupant had a private room.

"Elizabeth has arrived!" Hiroshi said when he saw the eyeglobe of the telebot light up with a picture of her face.

"You be coming at a favorable time," said Merlene. "Fifthday approaches. It be a day of rest, with feasting and enjoyment for all. This Fifthday there will be a stage show in the amphitheater with dancing and choral singing."

The humans heard a faint wailing sound coming over the aether as from a distance. The eerie sound grew in volume, and as it did they could hear Merlene and her children adding their voices to the ancient call.

"A-i-e-e-i-i-i."

"Brightstar be rising," said Merlene. "It be the beginning of Fifthday. Merlene be now preparing the feastbasket." As she headed for the kitchen, the door to Solene's room opened and the child emerged, dressed in a bewilderingly ornate, intricately colored matching chestcoat and skirt. The pattern extended to her mouthveil. Having not yet graduated from final school or apprenticed to a trade, she wore no cape.

"That pattern looks awfully busy to me," Elizabeth muttered over the audiolink.

"You forget the large eye of the keracks has much better resolution than the video camera lens in your 'bot," Selke remarked from her monitor station. "It probably looks beautiful in hi-res."

"Solene be helping fill the feastbasket?" the child asked her mother.

Merlene suggested, "You be selecting the best berries from the baskets on the table." Solene picked up a large pouch and started filling it with the largest berries from the selection available on the center table and the sideboards.

The door to Jordat's room slid open and the voice of the young kerack boomed out. He had taken off his practice armor and was now wearing a dazzling outfit of white on white. The only color in his costume came from the five copper rings and the silver ball stacked on his left antenna.

"Jordat be taking the sharestand up the stairs, then be returning for the feastbasket," he announced. He entered his father's room and emerged a short while later, easily carrying in his warclaw what looked like a folded-up table. He took it up the stairs to the surface, taking the steps three at a time.

Shortly a call came down through the ice.

"Father be coming home from the fields on his heuller! Jordat be running to greet him!" Although the humans were still inexperienced at interpreting radio signals that were not deliberately directed at them, they could soon sense that a strongly radiating presence was moving rapidly away down the road. A little while later, three presences returned, moving more ponderously. Fasart and Jordat were exchanging light conversation, while beneath their voices there was the deep, constant grumbling sound of a heuller being forced to work. The acoustic receiver on Elizabeth's telebot picked up heavy footsteps coming down from above, and in the ceiling, an ice-beam creaked under the increased load.

Soon the entire family and the two humans were gathered in the living room, with Jordat carrying the heavy feast-basket. The keracks were in their best clothing. Merlene looked critically at the two telebots.

"Merlene must be getting you better-looking clothing for Fifthdays." She paused; then her antennae quivered and her eye glazed over as she went into a trance and broadcast a query over the aether into the continual background murmur that represented the Spirit o'Camalor. Since the query was not in the form of a spoken phrase, but more like an inner thought process, the translator program could only catch parts of it. "Homene! . . . be done? . . . now."

Merlene came out of her trance. "The clothier Homene be nearly finished with the clothing of the humans. Only the cape for the female telebot be not completed." She headed for her room. "Merlene be getting a wizard cape for Elizabeth to wear, then we be stopping at the clothier on the way to the park." She returned with a dressy wizard cape in dark blue-black velvet with star constellations formed out of ornate, multipointed stars embroidered with silver-colored thread. It was not as fancy as Merlene's best cape of black velvet, with its diamond jewels for stars, but it was much prettier than the plain cape that Elizabeth had been wearing.

"You look very nice," said Hiroshi as Elizabeth twirled around to show off the cape.

"I can't wait to see the rest of my costume," Elizabeth replied.

The six headed for the surface and started off down the

road, leaving the muzzled heuller tethered to the post in the center of the yard. Fasart was carrying the sharestand and Jordat carried the heavy feastbasket, occasionally lightening the load somewhat by picking out a berry with one of his second leg pincers, slipping it up under his mouthbelt, and eating it.

"Aren't you going to lock up your residence?" asked Hiroshi, pointing back at the open doorway.

Merlene turned to look at him with her antennae tips pointing directly at him. Hiroshi had learned enough about kerack antennae positioning to realize that Merlene was puzzled, as if she didn't believe what she had just heard.

"Lock?" she queried. "Perhaps it be wise that Merlene be sliding closed the door to her home in the rare chance a geyser be erupting and there be a snowstorm that fills the stairwell, but what be Hiroshi meaning by 'lock' for a home?" She paused and went into a temporary trance again to pull a memory back from where she had stored it in the spirit. She soon returned to them.

"From the language lessons, Merlene be learning that *lock* be meaning the fastening of the opening to a container so that it not be easily opened," she said. "One be locking a pen so a heuller be not escaping. But one be not locking a home. There be nothing in there to escape."

"My parents never locked their home in Caithness," remarked Elizabeth. "They never had any problem with thieves."

"Thivs?" Merlene repeated. "That word be not translated for Merlene."

Hiroshi explained. *'Dorobo.* People that enter your home while you are away and take things that do not belong to them."

"We be too far away from Harvamor for that to happen," said Merlene. "And it be unthinkable that someone in Camalor would do such a thing. If a person in Camalor be needing something, one be giving it to him willingly. Be sides, everyone be knowing that the person be entering the home and taking the thing."

Elizabeth nodded. "That's why stealing is so uncommon in Caithness. There are so few people there that everyone knows everyone else. In addition, everyone is so nosy that a thief is nearly always seen and reported to the police——if not to the thief's mother, who often hands out tougher punishment than the police."

"Po-leese?"

"Never mind," said Elizabeth. "Let's head for the park and the Fifthday festivities."

As they strolled along one of the main roads that led toward the center of the city, they were joined by more and more keracks streaming in from the suburbs, all of them dressed in their finest clothing. When they came to a ring road Merlene turned away from the crowd and led her family and visitors down the side street until they came to the home and workshop of the clothier Homene. Homene and her family had already left for the fifthday feast and celebrations, but the door was open, so they went down the steps into the workshop. There, displayed on dummy kerack bodies, one male and one female, were two magnificent sets of clothing. The male costume was of a dark green velvet that was so thick it looked black. On the chestcoat and skirt were anvil-shaped thunderclouds in gold thread. The mouthbelt was of bright green satin with a long yellow tonguepouch that hung halfway down the skirt. Hiroshi took the costume into the dressing room and soon emerged, twirling in front of the large dressing mirror to show off the cape. On the cape were realistic depictions of two lightning bolts, a gold one starting on one shoulder and a silver one starting on the other, both spreading out over the cape and intertwining.

"Those lightning bolts are much more realistic than the zigzag lightning bolts we humans draw," Elizabeth remarked. "Although these are also artistic representations rather than the real thing. They are so convoluted they are almost fractal in their detail."

Hiroshi paused in his preening. "I wonder how the artist knew about thunderclouds and lightning? There certainly are no rainstorms on Ice."

"Lightning be common during the heavy snowstorms that be occurring after the eruption of a geyser," Merlene replied. "They be the study of all wizards. If a wizard be controlling lightning, the enemies of her city be not daring to attack."

Elizabeth's suit of clothing was made of blue-black velvet covered with thousands of tiny snowflakes made of silver thread, no two alike, swirling around in streams and looking like the interior of a snowstorm. The chestcoat and dress went well with the blue-black wizard cape she had borrowed from Merlene, although Merlene expressed some reservations.

"The stars on the cape be made of platinum thread while the snowflakes on the skirt and chestcoat be of silver, but few will be noticing the difference."

"The keracks must have a terrific sense of color or something to be able to tell the difference between the two metals at a glance," Rob said over the audiolink.

Elizabeth was more bothered that the patterns didn't match and was looking forward to the day when she would be getting her matching cape. That cape, the storm of silver snowflakes on it only partially finished, could be seen at an apprentice's table on one side of the workshop.

After they had both completed dressing, Merlene looked at the telebots with approval. "You both be now properly dressed for the Fifthday festivities." She led them up the stairway to the surface.

"These costumes must have taken Homene and her apprentices days to make," Elizabeth remarked as she two stepped her way up. "How can we repay her?"

"They be gifts," Merlene replied. "Every artisan and

worker be giving their products away to those that desire them."

Hiroshi looked at her in surprise. "But didn't I see you giving some berries to Homene to pay for the first set of clothing these telebots wore?"

"Polnart, the husband of Homene, be a constructor instead of a farmer," Merlene replied, leading the group back down the ring road. "They always be needing food and berries, so Merlene give Homene some fireberries that Fasart be bringing home."

"I presume you don't get paid either?" asked Hiroshi. "I was wondering what a wizard produced in the way of research that she could sell to make a living."

"No one be paid. To each be given that what each be needing most, from each be giving that what each be doing best."

Boris's voice came over the audiolink. "True communism. I wonder how *they* made it work?"

"Merlene be focal point in Spirit o'Camalor for all knowledge about nature. There be only one wizard, since there must be only one point where all natural knowledge be collected. Every observation of nature by anyone in Camalor be transferred to Spirit o'Camalor, which be focusing it in Merlene. Merlene be then incorporating that observation with all the other observations and be attempting to find patterns."

"That doesn't sound right," Rob said over the audiolink. "We know Merlene's brain is in her thorax under her eye. Her thorax isn't much bigger than a walnut, so her brain is even smaller than that. How can she remember all that stuff? She doesn't have enough brainpower."

"She must function similarly to a complex memory synapse in the brain," Selke mused. "The continual radio linkage of all the keracks must make them somewhat like a gigantic brain, and Merlene is similar to a complex synapse that correlates knowledge about the physical world. Like when doctors stimulate a single brain cell and it generates a memory consisting of a complex series of images in full color and high detail."

Elizabeth added, "The memory must be stored somehow in the brains of the rest of the keracks. Probably holographically, somewhat like our brain. She must use her constant radio contact to access it through this 'spirit' she keeps referring to."

As Merlene joined the streaming throng heading for the center of the city, she continued to talk. "The knowledge Merlene be collecting be important to Camalor. Merlene be able to predict geyser eruptions, weather, and most icequakes. Merlene also be inventor of blood bomb that be decisive in last battle with Belator. The wizard Merlene be giving much to Camalor," she concluded proudly.

"What do the princesses and other ladies of the nobility give?" asked Hiroshi.

There was a long pause as Merlene searched the Spirit o'Camalor for information. "They be giving nothing but commands," she was finally forced to conclude. "They be taking always the most of the best that be available." This was a new fact, and Merlene wondered if she should be forcing a memory of it. But it was not about the physical world, so she stopped thinking about it and promptly forgot it.

"We have a similar situation in the UK," Elizabeth remarked under her breath. "It's called the civil list."

Hiroshi persisted. "They must serve some function. Otherwise why did their class evolve in a society that is so thoroughly interconnected and communally interdependent?"

"Easy answer to that one," Elizabeth remarked. "Ever heard of parasites? Some antiroyalists list all the royalty, except perhaps King William himself, in that category."

They came to the base of the main radial road and entered the park near the final school. Most of the keracks continued along the wide path that wound around the play yard of the school, but Merlene headed off in another direction to a large clear area.

"This area be reserved for the building of another play yard as Camalor be growing larger in the future and a larger final school be needed. Merlene be obtaining approval from park supervisor Lady Arbane for humans to land microhopper here in park close to Center o'Camalor."

"That will be of considerable help," Hiroshi said gratefully, walking to the center of the region Merlene had indicated. "Rob, can you get a fix on the position of my 'bot?"

"Give me a second to activate the commsat net," Rob replied. A few seconds later he added, "Got you to less than a meter."

"Then you can insert the coordinates in the microhopper navigation system and send it back here," said Hiroshi. "We can start loading it up with more samples for me to analyze or ship back to Earth."

"I can have it on the way in a few minutes, if it's OK with Merlene," said Rob.

Hiroshi turned to Merlene. "Shall I arrange to have the microhopper land now, or should I wait until Fifthday is over and the park is clear?"

Merlene looked around at the dwindling numbers of passersby on the path. She had seen the microhopper land out on the ice near the giant lander and knew that there was more than enough space here for a safe—though noisy—landing.

"It be best that the microhopper come now," she said. "There be no students in the final school and the Fifthday Service o'Giving be not starting for some time yet."

"Then she's on her way," said Rob. "The keracks are going to have a fireworks display at the beginning of the Fifthday festivities instead of the end."

When Merlene saw the tiny speck with the hot flaring tail rise over the mountain chain to the north, she broadcast a warning out through the Spirit, and all eyes in the park turned to watch the remotely controlled miniature rocket arc over Camalor, lower itself on its oxyhydrogen flame down near the surface, then drop the last few meters in the 15 percent gravity of Ice to come to a bouncy halt on its shock absorbers. Hiroshi cycled through the lock, checked out the systems, and came back out.

"Everything's fine. It's ready to take off anytime we would like to go. Shall we proceed on?"

They were among the last arrivals at the picnic area. Most of the other family groups were already there. They had set up their sharestands but had left feastbaskets closed and were slowly drifting inward toward the central plaza, talking with their neighbors.

A call came through the aether. It seemed to start deep within the icy crust below, but soon spread throughout the park as all the keracks responded by adding their voices to the ancient chant.

"*A-a-a O-o-o. A-a-a O-o-o.*"

"It be time for the Service o'Giving," Merlene explained. "We be going now. It be not proper for humans to come, so you must be waiting here until we return."

"Would it be all right if we erect a video camera on the end of a pole so we can record the activities in the park?" Elizabeth asked.

"Merlene be not thinking of any reason why you should not," she replied after a pause. She pointed one of her antennae toward the amphitheater, partially-sunk into the ice not too far away. "There be a rise where the ground be meeting the top of the viewing ramps in the Oval o'All. A viewing eye set there be seeing both the Park o'Pleasure and the interior of the Oval o'All."

Meanwhile, Fasart had found an empty spot on the picnic grounds and set up the sharestand. Jordat tucked the feast-basket underneath, sneaking one last nibble before he did so; then the family walked off together with the flowing crowd that was funneling down a ramp that led under the central plaza.

Looking at the size of the crowd, Hiroshi commented, "No matter how long the service takes, just getting 10,000 bodies down that ramp and back up again is going to take over an hour. We should have plenty of time."

"Let's put a hurry on anyway," said Elizabeth, heading back toward the microhopper as fast as her fingers could twitch.

Merlene and her family joined the others as they all slowly made their way toward the ramp that led under the Plaza o'Dance. As they approached the entrance to the ramp, Jordat and Fasart split off to the left and Merlene moved off to the right with Solene following her and holding on to the tip of her cape. Merlene and Solene went down the right ramp with the rest of the females and were soon underground. At the bottom of the ramp they turned right and walked along a long curving tunnel that followed the circular edge of the plaza overhead. All along one side of the tunnel were little cubicles, each with a female kerack in it. Finally Merlene spotted a female leaving a cubicle up ahead, and, ushering Solene ahead of her, she entered. The glowworm lighting the cubicle was fading, so Merlene took a fireberry from her pouch and poked it into the creature's mouth, and it brightened up again. The walls and floor were lined with plain tiles and there was a dark hole in the floor at the rear. Merlene spoke to Solene.

"Now, do you be remembering what I have been teaching you?"

"Yes, Mother." Solene proceeded to parrot what her mother had been drilling into her. "Number one for the air, number two for the bucket, number three for the privies, and number four for the altar."

"Did you be remembering to be doing number one and number two at home before we be leaving?"

"Yes, Mother."

"Now Solene be turning around and doing number three into the hole as Merlene be teaching you." The child turned and placed her tail over the hole. There was a hissing sound.

"Number three, not number one," Merlene reminded patiently. She was rewarded with a distant *thunk* echoing up from the bottom of the pit. With Solene finished, Merlene took her place and concentrated until a small, heavy metal pellet passed through her number-three orifice and fell to join the other equally heavy metal pellets in the bottom of the communal privies. She and Solene exited to the right and continued down the curving corridor, and someone else took their place in the cubicle.

At the end of the corridor, they met the stream of males exiting from the left-hand row of privies. Fasart and Jordat were waiting there for them. Their bodies now cleansed, the family joined together again and entered another tunnel leading to the Service o'Giving.

Merlene could feel her soul warming as she exited the tunnel. Ahead of her was the perfection of the shining golden surface of the Dome o'Holies, lit by the light from thousands of glowworms. The Dome o'Holies was a gigantic ellipsoid covered with gold, sitting inside an even larger hollow cylinder of gray metal. The whole complex was buried in the ice beneath the Palace o'Princesses and the Plaza o'Dance. The tunnel led to the top of the Spiral o'Holies, a spiral ramp that wound its way down the interior of the cylinder. At the bottom, the spiral ramp ascended again, this time up a metal cone that rose from the bottom of the cylinder to form a base to support the golden egg of the Dome o'Holies. Built in at intervals along the low railing of the ramp were small cages containing glowworms that provided illumination for the magnificent scene. As the family progressed down the spiral ramp, they came to a weakly glowing worm, and Merlene gave Solene a fireberry to feed it and brighten it up again.

Because of the delay caused by the arrival of the human

rocket, Merlene's family was among the last of the keracks to enter the Service o'Giving. Merlene didn't mind, for now the Spiral o'Holies was completely full and she could feel her soul warming even more as she sensed the Spirit o'Camalor suffusing her body.

Some keracks were spiraling down the outer ramp, some were spiraling up the inner cone and entering the Dome o'Holies to participate in the Service o'Giving, while the rest, who had completed the service, were spiraling back down the cone and up the outer cylinder along the exit spiral that was interleaved with the entrance spiral. Although all the keracks on the Spiral o'Holies remained reverentially silent during the long procession and service, Merlene could sense through her antennae the close presence of all those in Camalor. It produced a feeling of oneness and completeness that was the spirit and mind of Camalor, of which she was a small part.

Halfway down, the curved golden surface of the Dome o'Holies came close to the spiral ramp, and Merlene could see herself and all those around her in the shining, curved surface, reduced in size. It looked as though all the people in Camalor had been compressed into one large ovoid. Merlene had been intrigued with the optical illusion ever since she was a child, and when she had been appointed the wizard of Camalor, she had played with curved sheets of reflective metal and had invented mirrors that made things look larger rather than smaller.

The family reached the bottom of the entrance ramp at the base of the cylinder, and Merlene moved Solene in front of her as they started up the conical spiral leading into the Dome o'Holies. The golden dome now loomed large overhead, and Merlene could see Solene's large eye looking upward, awed at the sight. The spiral ramp passed through a hole in the base of the dome. The eyes of most keracks entering the dome were drawn to the spherical Altar o'Giving ahead. But as Merlene stood briefly in the entranceway, she looked upward once again at the strange, layered structure of the cross-section through the thick wall of the Dome o'Holies. It was obvious that the outer layer of gold on the dome was thin and that the wall consisted of many layers— Merlene had estimated almost two fi'fives. Some layers, like platinum, silver, copper, iron, sulfur, and diamond, were easily recognizable. Merlene had no idea why there were so many, or why they were there in that order.

They now entered the hollow interior of the Dome o'Holies. This was also a smooth ellipsoid, but it was covered with a silvery metal instead of gold. The conical spiral continued upward where it met the silvery sphere of the Altar o'Holies and continued to spiral up and around the sphere to the top. Far above them, hanging from the silver-colored curved ceiling, was a featureless black sphere—the Heaven o'All. Heaven had the soft, all-absorbing, total blackness of carbon. It was warm, and gave off a slight glow of broadband microwave and infrared radiation, as if it were alive inside.

As they finished their climb up the spiral ramp to the top of the altar, where the High Priest Princess Kitone was waiting, Merlene noticed Solene's eye staring upward in awe at the abject blackness that closed in around them. She could feel Solene's emotions leaking out through her antennae. Merlene could well remember those emotions, for she had experienced them when she was a child and had looked into the deep, bottomless blackness all around the altar. For everywhere one looked, the mirrored surface of the interior of the dome had been replaced by the soft blackness of the Heaven o'All.

Merlene knew that the interior of the dome was of polished silver-colored lithium, but it didn't look that way— instead it was black, as black as the sky between the stars on the clear nights that came between geyser eruptions. As a child, she had wondered how the Heaven o'All, which started out above the Altar o'Holies, suddenly was all around the altar, as if she were visiting the inside of heaven itself.

Now, however, being a wizard and having derived the laws of reflective optics, she knew that the altar was at one focal point of the ellipsoidal dome and heaven was at the other. Thus, no matter which direction the eye looked, the curved mirror of the inside of the dome directed one's view so that all one saw was the absorbing black surface of heaven.

"Be the child properly taught?" Princess Kitone whispered as Solene and Merlene at last took their places before the altar.

"Yes, Princess," replied Merlene. "Solene? You be bringing your tail forward. Remember, number four be for the altar."

Princess Kitone held forth a long-handled spoon and placed it under one of the four orifices in the tail that Solene presented. Solene discharged a small amount of white material. Princess Ketone looked at it critically, twitched the end of an antenna in approval, and deposited the gift into a tapered hole in the top of the altar. After Merlene and the rest of the family made their larger contributions, Princess Kitone lowered a close-fitting plug into the tapered hole and pushed the material down to join the rest that had been given in the past. Their solemn and awe-inspiring Service o'Giving completed, the family started down the winding downward ramp that took them in between the upward ramps of those still approaching the altar. They went faster now, for they were looking forward to the feasting and festivities of the rest of the day.

After climbing up the Spiral o'Holies again and out the exit ramp, they returned to the picnic area. The humans were waiting for them there. Merlene noticed that on the upper part of the bank near one end of the amphitheater there was now a tall pole made out of tubes of metal fitted one into another. The whole thing was supported by wires anchored into the crust. On top of the pole was a box with one of the mechanical eyes that the humans used for seeing at a distance.

While Merlene was greeting Hiroshi and Elizabeth, the rest of the family busied themselves with Fifthday activities. Solene went running off to play "Holler Me Find" in the maze with the other young children. Fasart set up the sharestand and started loading it up with the contents of their feastbasket. Jordat, always interested in food, wandered over to the neighboring sharestands and, loosening his mouthbelt, tasted samples of the delightful preparations that were spread out. The neighbors were pleased to see such a large and obviously hungry young male and plied him with sample after sample, hoping that he would make a large dent in the copious display on their sharestand—for a family could be justly proud of the quality of their sharings if their sharestand was the first to be eaten bare. Fasart, knowing the high quality of his farm produce and Merlene's cooking, ate from his own sharestand until Merlene shooed him away in embarrassment.

While the keracks were picnicking, the humans, whose robotic bodies were fed with antihydrogen instead of calories, wandered through the grounds visiting all the sharestands and taking two samples of each different berry, root, biscuit, cake, pie, fungus node, and meat slice.

Hiroshi and Elizabeth soon came upon the butcher's sharestand. The butcher and his apprentices were there with their families, running a communal barbecue. The joint sharestand was gigantic, with room for ten keracks to line up in front of it. A whole gutted heuller was roasting over an open brick pit lined with firemetal gauze. One apprentice had the task of turning the crank to keep the roast turning while occasionally throwing buckets of fireberries and fuelberries on the firemetal gauze to keep the fire going; other apprentices cut slices off the roast and served them to the crowd.

Their pouches soon full of samples to be analyzed, Hiro

shi and Elizabeth traveled to the microhopper and unloaded, then returned to Merlene and her family.

"It be soon time for the dance performance in the Oval o'All," said Merlene. "Humans be allowed in the Oval. Be you joining us?"

"It sounds fascinating," Elizabeth said. "I would love to see it."

"We ought to pick two spots with views of the performance that are different from each other and the video camera on the pole," Hiroshi suggested. "That way our 'bot cameras and the pole camera will record the performance from all angles."

"Merlene be understanding." She turned to her son. "Jordat? You be taking Hiroshi with you to stand with the warriors on Consort Rexart's side of the Oval. Merlene, Fasart, and Solene be taking Elizabeth to the other side with the commoners."

They headed for the amphitheater with the rest of the crowd. Their way took them around the sliding basin, and Solene ran out onto the ice and skated alongside them, showing off a number of routines she had been learning. One routine involved skating backward on one pincer of one middle claw, thorax bent downward until her eyeglobe almost touched the ice, two front legs spread wide, four bottom legs wrapped around her to insure that her skirt properly covered her raised abdomen.

"Solene be chosen to be in the snowflake chorus in the next skating production in the Oval o'All," Merlene said proudly as they watched the acrobatic young female show off.

As they entered the Oval o'All with the crowd, Hiroshi and Elizabeth could see that the nobility were already there. In the royal box stood a large male kerack in fine golden chain-mail armor. His antennae were covered in golden rings, and there were spiked golden balls, like miniature maces or multipointed stars, on the ends of both antennae.

He held a large golden mace in his warclaw. To his right stood another warrior, almost as large and also clad in golden armor, but there were slightly fewer gold rings on his antennae, and the star at the tip of his left antenna was silver instead of gold. Standing next to him was a large, buxom female kerack dressed in silver, her middle legs hooked under his, her first two pairs of claws encumbered with fluffy white clawpets. On either side of the three stood other pairs of well-dressed warriors and ladies of the nobility; the warrior armor showed less gold and the ladies boasted fewer beautybumps and clawpets the further away they were from the box of honor. All the nobility and most of the crowd were ingesting greenish spiritberries and enjoying themselves.

Merlene pointed with one antenna and touched the other to Elizabeth's antenna and whispered, "That be Commander Rexart, consort to Queen Une. Rexart be leader of all the warriors. Next to him be Subcommander Mordet, escort to Princess Regent Onlone. They be the ones Rob and Selke saw going through the streets on the first day."

"I recognize them," said Elizabeth. "I was on monitor shift at the time." She pointed a claw, not having rapid control over her antennae. "Look! You can certainly spot Hiroshi easily, with his dark green wizard outfit in the sea of young warrior apprentices all dressed in white."

"The performance be about to start," Merlene whispered.

"Where is the Queen? Isn't she coming to the performance?"

"The Queen?" Merlene repeated, drawing back and pointing her antennae at Elizabeth in bewilderment. There was a long pause as she thought. "Merlene be not thinking that question before. Betruth the Queen be never coming to the performances in the Oval o'All. She be at the dance held at the close of Fifthday, but not at the performance."

"Why?"

"Merlene be not knowing." For a brief moment Merlene thought about trying to find out why the Queen never came to the performances—certainly Princess Onlone and all the other ladies came with their escorts, but Consort Rexart always attended the performances alone while the Queen stayed in her tower. Then Merlene realized that the question was not one about the physical nature of things, so therefore it didn't concern her, and she promptly put it out of her mind.

The loud, commanding voice of a male kerack boomed throughout the Oval o'All, and Elizabeth noted that Consort Rexart had lifted his mace on high.

"Let the performance begin. The Queen be living ever!"

"The Queen be living ever!" echoed the crowd, and as the last voice died away, a multivoiced chorus welled up from underneath the stands, and out from tunnels in the walls marched a stream of singing females all dressed in full flowing capes that covered them from eyeglobe to tail. The capes were all plain, but they varied in color from one end of the spectrum to the other.

"It looks like a flowing rainbow," Elizabeth commented over the audiolink to base. "Except the ends are gray."

"I can stretch the spectrum here in my monitor," Rob said. "The kerack rainbow extends into the ultraviolet and infrared. Wonder how they know about rainbows?"

Selke offered a suggestion. "They don't have rain to make rainbows, but they do have access to lots of large crystals and have a good point source of white light in Brightstar to make a rainbow on a wall."

"I estimate there must be close to a thousand keracks in that chorus," Rob remarked.

As the chorus entered the amphitheater and arranged themselves around the central platform, their voices kept up a marching chant that was simple in vocal tone but complex in melody. It reminded Elizabeth a little of bagpipe music.

A single female kerack in a plain, pure white cape came from another entrance and marched to the podium, reaching it just as the chorus completed its maneuvers. She had stiff metal whips attached to the ends of her antennae that she waved expertly to bring the voices of the huge chorus to a halt at the end of the procession march.

"That be concertleader Arpene," Merlene whispered into Elizabeth's antenna. "She be composing the music for all the performances."

Arpene raised her antennae and the chorus broke into a multivoiced theme that sent shivers down the spines of all the humans who heard it. The song rose in power and complexity until it filled the aether.

"Wow . . ." Rob murmured at his monitor console back at the base. He made sure that the audio portion of the recording was set at maximum bandwidth and maximum bit rate so every nuance would be recorded.

Selke remarked, "She is Mozart and Bach and Haydn and Beethoven all at one time. Grippen is going to have the antiscience arts types turning in favor of the space program when he releases this one."

But the performance was not just music; there was dance too. From another tunnel under the stadium there emerged a chorus of dancers, both male and female. Instead of heavy, buttoned chestcoats, heavy skirts, and long capes, they were dressed in variously colored tights that properly covered their shells from eyeglobe to tail but left their ten legs unencumbered. The females had a gathered elastic ruffle around the waist as a cover for the mouth in place of the normal mouthveil, and the males had plain elastic mouthbelts with no long tonguepouches dangling from them to get in the way.

Over the audiolink Rob observed, "After being in Camalor for a while and getting used to those obscene-looking tonguepouches hanging down the front of all the males, these guys look like sissies."

The dancers whirled onto the stage in the center of the amphitheater and began to move through a series of patterns that were synchronized with the music, yet hypnotizing in their own right. The lead female dancers raised up on a single pincer of a back foot like a human ballerina on point and engaged in gigantic leaps that took them halfway across the stage, to be caught easily in the warclaw of a male dancer and thrown back again.

"Square-cube and low gee again," Selke reminded them.

"It *still* is remarkable," Rob said. "Prawns that are more graceful than humans. This video is going to be an instant hit in the classical video charts."

Shift change for the humans came in the middle of the performance; Hiroshi and Elizabeth had gone into the amphitheater, but Rob and Selke came out.

"That took quite a while," Selke said, pointing at the tiny, bright point of Sol in the sky. "Brightstar is almost setting."

"It be time for the closing dance," Merlene said. Then Selke noticed that instead of dispersing, the crowd leaving the amphitheater was all going in the same direction, toward the Plaza o'Dance at the center of the city. Baskets of spiritberries were being passed around, and both Merlene and Fasart took quite a few. Leading the procession was Consort Rexart, walking alone, followed by Princess Onlone and Mordet, then by the rest of the nobility and court paired off in order of rank.

When they reached the Plaza o'Dance, the nobility went toward the center and formed a circle around the three-storied Tower o'Queen while the commoners gathered in larger circles near the periphery of the plaza. Rexart made his way up the tower on a ramp that spiraled up the outside wall, until he reached the third and topmost level. He then walked around and slid open four heavy doors to reveal the Queen, who was sitting in the center of the tower covered completely in a full-length cape of gold. Around her eye-globe was a large tiara made of diamonds, so ornate that Selke wondered if it sometimes blocked her vision. Standing next to the Queen, Rexart raised his mace high.

"Let the dance begin! The Queen be living ever!"

"The Queen be living ever!" roared the crowd in reply, and as the last voice echoed away, its place was taken by a single voice, pure in tone but powerful in strength. It was the voice of the Queen, singing an eerie, ancient, hypnotic chant that had no words and almost no tune but a very complex rhythm. The crowd, knowing the tune well, took up the chant and began to dance.

"A-a E-e A-a E-e-e. A-a O-o A-a E-e-e."

"I'd tap my toes except that I'd louse up my communication channels," said Rob. "Sounds a little like an Indian war dance."

"It looks more like a formal Renaissance ball at the court of King Louis the Fourth," Selke said.

The keracks had formed circles around the central tower that held the queen, males alternating with females. Princesses and their warrior consorts were in circles close to the tower, while commoners circled farther out, with youngsters imitating them around the periphery. Rob and Selke, not joining in, watched from the edge of the plaza.

The circles moved, males one way and females the other; then each dancer took a partner from first an inner circle then an outer circle. As each new pair met, they grasped front claws, rose up on their hind legs until they were almost mouthveil to mouthbelt at their belly lines, then fell back again.

The Queen interrupted the chant with a call in a deep, commanding note.

"Come!"

All the circles took a step inward, bringing everyone closer together.

The chant started up again, faster this time, and the pattern of the dance was repeated. Another command of "Come!" and they all crowded even closer. The tempo of the chant increased and the dance became more frenzied and less formal.

Suddenly Rob and Selke heard an incoherent shout over

the aether from the other side of the plaza. Rexart looked down in that direction, drew his golden daggers, and leaped off the top of the tower and into the crowd. The dance broke up and everyone crowded toward the scene of the commotion.

Rob and Selke, curious but not wanting to interfere, trotted quickly around the periphery of the plaza to the other side. When they got there they saw two dead keracks being dragged to the edge of the plaza by angry members of the crowd. Behind the bodies paced the grim figure of Rexart. In his second set of claws were his two golden daggers, dripping with yellow-brown blood and clear ichor. The corpses had been summarily executed by a stab through the eyeball into the brain beneath.

"Like a pithed iceworm," Rob murmured over the audio channel.

At first the humans couldn't tell whether the dead keracks were male or female, since all their legs had been torn from their bodies. The limbs were tossed off the dance plaza and into the park along with the bodies.

"It was a male and a female," Rob said. "One has a tonguepouch and the other the remnants of a mouthveil."

The crowd returned to their positions. Rexart sheathed his daggers and climbed back up the tower to take his place beside the Queen, and the dance started again as if nothing had happened.

Merlene found the humans standing next to the abandoned corpses.

"What happened?" asked Rob.

"They be having too many spiritberries and be losing control of themselves," Merlene said angrily. Then she calmed herself down and changed her tone. "Fortunately, it be happening only occasionally."

"A very severe penalty for drunkenness," Selke remarked.

"That be not all they be doing. Too many spiritberries be

sometimes leading to behavior forbidden by the Queen. Behavior that be instantly punishable by death."

"What is that?" Rob asked, still puzzled by what he had seen.

There was a very long pause as Merlene—indicating her extreme agitation with twisting antennae and twitching second legs—attempted to find a way to explain.

"I think Rob has touched upon a taboo subject," Elizabeth warned them over the audiolink.

Trying to change the subject, Selke said, "Perhaps Rob and I should be taking our samples to the microhopper now."

"Merlene be unable to explain because there be no word for the forbidden behavior," Merlene explained. "There do be a human word for it. Merlene be noticing the word while searching through Lookman for information on copper. Following copper, Merlene be noticing entry on Coptic Church—very much like Service o'Holies. Beyond that entry be one on . . ." She struggled as she tried to force out the revolting word. "Cop-u-la-shun." She paused, antennae pulled back in disgust. "Merlene be not knowing humans be doing things like that."

Rob gasped, now regretting his previous questions.

"We *must* be going now," Selke said firmly. "Come help me, Rob." The two humans scuttled off to Merlene's sharestand to get their sample pouches, hoping they had not damaged their relationship with the keracks and the Wizard of Camalor.

"Sex must be an *extremely* delicate subject if they don't even have a word for it," Elizabeth remarked over the audiolink.

"I have just looked up the subject of sex in the data bank containing the information gleaned from the conversations that Merlene had with Earth before we arrived," Hiroshi added. "From what I am reading here, there indeed is no mention of sex, except for some delicate queries that the humans made. Hmmm. This is interesting. It says here that in every case, Merlene did not respond to those questions in her next reply, as if she hadn't heard the question being asked. The interrogators finally took the hint and stopped asking. It looks like we don't even know where their sex organs are located, much less what they look like or how they are used."

"Then," Selke said, "until we know a lot more, we had better just stay off the subject."

"Say," Rob said over the audiolink, "perhaps we could find out if we could get these two corpses to dissect."

"You're probably treading on taboo ground again," warned Elizabeth.

"I'll be careful." Rob headed back toward Merlene, switched on his radio, and touched one of his antennae to hers. "If this is a delicate subject, just don't answer. What will be done with these bodies?"

"They be fed to the heullers, like the garbage they be," replied Merlene angrily. "Even their souls will be fed to the heullers, for the Queen be having no use for them."

"Could we have them instead?" Rob asked. "It would help us understand how keracks are made."

"Certainly!" Merlene replied with alacrity. "No one, not even the butchers or the garbage collectors, be wishing the task of touching those two again." She went off to rejoin the dance.

It took Rob and Selke three trips, but soon the microhopper was loaded with their samples and the bodies and limbs of the unfortunate keracks. They returned to watch the rest of the dance. The pace was now faster, but the dancers, seemingly hypnotized by the chant, capered tirelessly on. Finally the Queen's voice rang out again over the aether.

"Flee!"

At the signal, everyone turned and ran from the plaza as fast as they could go, chattering joyfully.

The dance was over. Rexart slid shut the four doors of the

throne level, closing off the view of the Queen. Then, raising his mace high, he announced the obvious to the disappearing crowd as the Sun set below the distant horizon.

"Fifthday is over! The Queen be living ever!"

"The Queen be living ever!" the crowd repeated as they picked up their feastbaskets and sharestands and headed for home.

Fifthday ended the same way it had begun, with a fireworks display. Hiroshi activated the microhopper by remote control and flew it and its gruesome cargo back to the base. As unfortunate as this day had been for the two keracks, it was a fortuitous day for the Earth scientists. They now had a pair of kerack bodies in the prime of life to examine, only slightly the worse for wear from the rough handling of the crowds. Hiroshi would make sure that they were sent back to Earth on a sample return capsule the minute they got to the base. It would take a long time for the bodies to travel to the inner portions of the solar system, and even longer before the autopsy was completed—a minimum of four months before the group at the base on Ice would get the results back. Hiroshi didn't want to delay receiving that important knowledge by a single hour.

6

VISIT TO THE BASE

ROB WOKE UP feeling pretty good. After living for a few months on Ice, with its continual grind of shift work, he had trained himself to go to bed when it was his sleep shift and go directly to sleep instead of staying up reading or watching a video. He felt even better when he raised the bunk door and realized that he was going to beat Selke to the bathroom. While he was busy brushing his teeth there was a loud banging on the door and Selke hollered grumpily at him.

"Aus! You can brush your teeth in the galley."

Rob could only agree, so, still brushing his teeth, he exited the bathroom in his shorts and let the red-eyed Selke in. Head bent over to clear the low ceiling, he walked to the galley sink and rinsed his brush and teeth. Then he tucked the toothbrush away in his bed locker and got dressed.

"She sure is in a good mood today," he said to Boris as he returned to the galley, where he made himself a cup of coffee. There was a noise from one of the cocoons at the front of the shelter as Elizabeth rose and took off her verihelm. She was soon followed by Hiroshi.

"What does Merlene have planned for us this shift?" asked Rob.

"She is going to show us some artisans," Elizabeth answered. "We left the 'bots by the side of the road in the artists' district while Merlene went down into some of the workshops and studios to see which artists had something complete enough to show us. She said it would take some time, so we 'ported back early. You and Selke can wait to start your shifts until she shows up in the monitor."

"Don't tell Selke that," Rob said. "She could have used more sleep. I'd better get her coffee ready and microwave a frozen strudel for her breakfast."

"I don't see how she can eat that sweet stuff for breakfast," Elizabeth said with distaste. "Porridge for me . . . although sometimes I wish they had found a way to freeze-dry and reconstitute a decent slice of haggis."

Merlene went down the stairs leading to the workshop of the spinsculptor Dilene. She could sense that the painter Komart was there with Dilene. Komart was one of the few male artisans. He had lost his warclaw in an ancient skirmish with Belator, and without that, he was of no use in heavy work. He had learned to paint with a brush fastened to the end of his stump. Many in Camalor now had his paintings of stirring war scenes; the composition most closely identified with him was that of a central figure of a heuller raised up on its hindquarters with a golden-armored warrior nobly astride.

Dilene also did warriors, but hers were sculptures of famous Camalor heroes in silver and gold. It took her a long time to produce each one, since she had to use spinworms to spin each molecule into place. The two often conferred with each other on the subtleties of representing armor in an artistic manner.

Merlene entered Dilene's studio. In pens along the wall were some well-tended spinworms, a strand of their output dangling above the door of each pen to identify them.

"Merlene be greeting Dilene and Komart," she said. "Merlene be taking humans to visit artisans this day. Be you having suitable works for them to observe?"

"Komart be having many paintings in his workshop," Komart said. "The humans be most welcome to visit."

"Dilene be just completing a statue. It be not of a warrior this time." Dilene led Merlene to a small statue in the corner. It was of a formal dancer in a graceful pose, impossibly balanced on the tip of one hind claw on the top of a hemisphere, belly arched one way and torso the other. The hemisphere was large and extremely shiny, the dancer's carapace had a lifelike texture, and her dance costume looked amazingly delicate.

"This be the latest work o'Dilene," she announced proudly.

Merlene was impressed, and after walking around to view it from all sides, she scanned the work carefully with her antennae. Being a wizard, she was familiar with the color and smell of most metals.

"The figure be spun of beryllium, while the base be osmium." She was obviously perplexed. "Those be unusual metals for a spinsculptor. Most figures be spun of silver or gold."

"The dancer must be denoting strength with lightness, while the hemisphere must be denoting heaviness," Dilene replied. "Beryllium be strong and light, while osmium be the densest material known."

"But why be there such a large and massive base?" asked Merlene. "It be detracting from the dancer."

Komart answered for Dilene. "This statue be the symbol of the eternal struggle of the will and strength of the dancer against the gravity that be forever attempting to pull her down. It be the triumph of the dancer lifting her body against the enormous gravity pull of Ice that be giving the statue its meaning. Without the overly large and overly dense base, the message of the statue be lost."

"Merlene be understanding now." She turned to go back

up the steps to the surface. "Merlene be bringing the humans down shortly."

From the monitor chair Boris saw Merlene's head rise above the surface. "Here she comes! Time to start your shift in the 'bots."

"All right! I'm coming!" Selke irritably downed the last of her coffee. Rob was already crouched in his sensuit with his verihelm on. So far he had been just watching the screen inside the helmet as if he were a detached observer. He shook his head and was instantly teleported into Camalor.

"Hello, Merlene," Rob said. "Selke will be with us shortly. Did you find us some artists to visit?"

"Merlene be taking you to visit two artists. One be a spinsculptor and one be a painter."

"The translation program generated a word, and I suppose it makes sense, but what is a spinsculptor? How is that different from a plain sculptor?"

"It be obvious when you be seeing it."

They waited for Selke to arrive and then Merlene led them down the stairs to Dilene's workshop. Rob noticed that Selke's eyes looked just as tired in the telebot eyeglobe as they did in the flesh. He would have to make sure that she napped on the floor between the cocoons at the first break in shifts.

"These be spinsculptor Dilene and painter Komart," said Merlene. "And these be the human wizards Rob and Selke."

The two keracks gave the humans a low bow, and Komart said, "Komart be leaving now to prepare his workshop for the human visitors."

"We be coming to see you shortly." Merlene watched him leave, then turned to Dilene. "Rob be asking how a spinsculptor be doing her art."

"A spinsculptor be not cutting away material from a block to shape a figure. Instead, a spinsculptor be *adding* material, using spinworms." Dilene went to the wall of cages. "Komart be using brushes. Dilene be using these. This be a spinworm for spinning gold." She took the creature out of its pen and stroked it gently. From the base of the spinworm emerged a fine gold thread. With a deft nip of her pincers, she cut it loose and handed it to Selke. Selke, amazed by the performance, was now wide awake.

"May I keep this as a sample?" she asked, taking a bag out of her sample pouch.

"Of *course,*" said Dilene. "Anything the humans be desiring they be having."

"No doubt Grippen would like a worm that lays golden threads," Gabrielle audiolinked. "It would solve his budget problems in a hurry."

"Dilene be using the spinworm to build up a statue in this manner." She went to a small, partially completed statue of a warrior made of gold metal. Stroking the spinworm gently, she applied its tail to the unfinished golden warclaw and very slowly dragged the tail along a pincer to the point. Where the spinworm tail had passed, the pincer was now perceptibly thicker. She repeated the process again and again until she had built up the pincer to the right shape.

Dilene took the spinworm back to its pen in the wall, but before she put it inside, she stuffed a berry into its compliant mouth from the bowl inside the pen.

"What did you just feed that spinworm?" asked Rob.

"It be a goldberry. A spinworm be spinning the metalberry it be fed." Dilene went to another pen, and with one antenna pointed to the thread hanging over the door. "This spinworm be spinning silver. This next one be spinning platinum. And on-on."

"I do not see how the worm accomplishes that feat!" Boris interjected over the audiolink. "The melting points of those metals are thousands of degrees, and that boneless wormlike body can't be strong enough to cold-forge the metal into a wire."

"You physicists always think in terms of solids—like your brains," Gabrielle audiolinked. "In chemistry we learn that at the atomic level, like attracts like. If that worm orifice has many subchannels that deliver one gold atom at a time, they will either collect into a wire or, if a gold surface is nearby, they will be plated onto the surface. Don't forget that the air on Ice is mostly hydrogen, which is a reducing atmosphere. Nearly all metal surfaces here are clean and free of oxide coatings."

"It's still hard to believe," Rob said. "Even after seeing it with my own eyes. It's like those creatures have little tiny nanomachines inside them, taking apart the goldberry an atom at a time, transporting the metal atoms from the gut to the spinner orifice, and depositing the metal atoms one at a time at the desired place."

"You are as bad as Boris," Gabrielle retorted. "You mechanical engineers think only you can make nanomachines. Nature has been making nanomachines for billions of years, only we biologists call them enzymes. I can easily imagine an enzyme designed to do just what you described—even a single enzyme that can adjust itself to accommodate different metals. Although I suspect that with the selectivity the spinworms show, having a separate orifice for each element, there is a different enzyme for each element."

Selke snorted. "I do not believe I am saying this, but I want to examine that spinworm's arse with a microscope when we get back."

To Merlene Rob said, "Those spinworms look quite similar to the iceworms that Fasart showed us out at the farm."

"They be the same," said Merlene. "Iceworms be unplugged and most minerals and metals pass through them except fertilizer metals. The spinworms be plugged at the exit to the gut so metals be coming out through spin orifice. The spinworms be unplugged and fed each Fifthday while the artist be enjoying the festivities, then they be plugged and fed metalberries again until next Fifthday. Each metal be coming out through the number orifice corresponding to that metal."

Boris's voice came over the audiolink. "Number one in the air. Number two in the bucket. Gold and silver must be numbers fifty and sixty or something."

"How many orifices does a worm have?" asked Rob.

Both keracks paused and looked at each other. "Betruth, Merlene be not knowing," Merlene finally said. "Many more than five fi'fives. To be getting the true number you be counting the orifices in the iceworm that Fasart gave you."

Gabrielle audiolinked, "I'll let Selke count *les trous.*"

"They certainly are remarkable creatures," Boris added.

"Five fi'fives—that's more than a hundred and twenty-five. That sounds like an awfully large number," Rob said. "More than one for each of the ninety-two elements."

"Betruth," Merlene replied. "But there be separate orifices for heavy silver and light silver. There be eight orifices for cadmium alone. But we not be here to discuss spinworm orifices." She led them to the corner of the room where Dilene's latest figure was standing. "Dilene be creating this statue with the spinworms."

Merlene had mentioned heavy silver and light silver before, when discussing the sensitivity of her balance. Rob was anxious to continue the discussion, but now was not the time. Merlene took them around the statue of the dancer. It was small, only three centimeters tall, including the large base, but it was exquisite.

"It is beautiful!" Selke said, obviously impressed.

Rob agreed. "Every art collector and museum on Earth will be clamoring to have it."

"Betruth?" asked Dilene, not sensing the truth automatically from the radio emissions of the alien humans.

"Yes!" Selke and Rob both replied.

"Then it be yours." Dilene picked it up from the table and handed it to Rob.

Rob and Selke were taken aback. They hadn't expected this.

"Accept it!" came a loud whisper from Boris over the audiolink. "This culture is like those of the ancient nomadic tribes in Asia and Africa—admire something and it is yours. Remember the sharestands at the Fifthday feast and how everyone was eager to be the first to give all their food away? You will insult Dilene if you refuse her gift."

Rob bowed as low as he dared with the heavy statue in his grasp. "The human race is honored by your most magnificent gift. It will be placed where all may come and admire its artistry and inherent beauty."

"We be now going to visit the workshop of the painter Komart," said Merlene, nimbly climbing the stairway to the surface with her liquid gait. The humans two-stepped their way upward, Rob being careful not to tumble with the delicate, yet heavy sculpture. At Komart's yard, Rob put down the statue next to the stairway entrance, secure in the knowledge that in Camalor it would not be stolen, and followed Merlene and Selke down the stairs. Selke stopped at the first-floor landing and looked inside the living quarters. The room was small and cluttered, with only one reading bench, and the kitchen was full of unsanded dishes.

"It looks like a bachelor lives here," she said.

They continued down to the workshop below, which they found equally cluttered. On a table in the center of the room was a large frame made of cast-ice bars bolted together at the corners, with a blank, canvaslike material stretched over it. Along two walls were hung some pictures, some finished and some obviously awaiting additional inspiration. A third wall was taken up by a long brick oven with a series of hot plates on it, each holding a metal pot of a different-colored paint, glowing warmly in the infrared view of the multispectral telebot sensors. Komart and Merlene were standing at the far wall next to large painting of two war-heullers reared up on their hindquarters and clawing at each other. The warriors on their backs were reacting to the blows they had given each other with their lances, the shattered pieces of which could be seen flying through the air.

"His work reminds me of the famous Western painter, Remington," Rob audiolinked. "Always did some animal in action, usually with a man riding it."

"This be the painter Komart," said Merlene. "Komart used to be subcommander to Rexart in the warrior corps, but lost his warclaw in a battle with Belator." Rob noticed that Komart had many gold rings on his antennae but no stars of command at the tips.

Komart told them how he had lost his warclaw. "We be penetrating well into the enemy lines and though we be outnumbered, we be slaughtering the cowardly Belators. Mordet be beside me, protecting my flank as Komart be protecting his. More Belator warriors be arriving. Mordet be retreating. Komart be not, and two-fives Belator warriors be giving up their souls before this be happening." Komart held up the stump of his right front claw. There was a prosthesis fixed to the end of it, with a tube at the tip. In the tube was stuck the handle of a paintbrush with bristles made of fine metal wires that looked like aluminum.

"Now Mordet be subcommander to Rexart, and Komart be battling the Belators with a paintbrush." Komart turned and added a stroke to the banner hanging from the side of one of the heullers in the painting. The unfinished work was in various shades of silvery gray that seemed to bear little relationship to what was being represented. For example, what was obviously Brightstar in the background sky was nearly black, the sky was almost white, and the warrior and heuller were represented by patches of gray and silver that were hard to distinguish.

"This painting looks much different from your others," said Rob. "Those are brightly colored, while this looks like it takes place at night—but it can't be at night, because Brightstar is in the sky."

Komart explained. "This be just the microwave underpicture. There come more pictures on top: millimeter wave, deep infrared, infrared, near infrared, visible, near ultraviolet, ultraviolet, and deep ultraviolet."

"He's right!" Selke exclaimed, looking around the room. "Switch from your visible imager to your microwave imager, and then sequence through from long wavelength to short wavelength."

Rob did so. In his microwave imager, the shades in the false-color image of the painting now made more sense. Brightstar was highly emissive in the microwave band, the sky was black, and the various shades on the heullers and warriors were easily distinguishable, although the human choices for the false-color presentation gave the clothing and trappings a clownish overtone.

Rob then cycled through the various wavelength imagers inside the eyeglobe of his telebot as he looked at the completed painting of the two heuller-mounted warriors on the far wall. As he did so, the painting seemed to move like a short animated sequence. In the microwave band, the warriors were well separated and riding at each other at full tilt. In the deep infrared their lances crossed each other; in the infrared each lance was striking the opponent's shield squarely; in the short infrared the lances were cracking under the shock and the riders were being thrown backward by the blow; and the visible band showed the two rearing warheullers, the warriors on their backs, and shattered lances flying through the air. The telebot didn't have ultraviolet imagers, so the last three scenes in the painting were invisible to Rob. He looked around at the other finished paintings and went through the imager cycle again for each one. Some picture sets were in time action sequence, some showed the same image under different lighting conditions, and others added or subtracted background or subsidiary figures as he ooked at them in different wavelengths. None of the separate wavelength images in each multiple painting were sharply clear or properly colored, so Rob knew that the human-made imagers in his telebot were only giving him a blurred and partial view of the "real" painting, compared to what the keracks saw with their larger and more wavelength-discriminatory eye.

"Now I begin to see," Rob said. "What I thought was an ordinary painting when I looked at it with only my visible imager is in reality a series of paintings—a multipainting. What an amazing tour de force! You must have spent ages developing the proper pigments that would allow you to put paintings on top of each other, yet keep them spectrally separate."

"What kind of solvent do you use as a carrier for your pigments?" asked Selke. "I wasn't aware there were any liquids at room temperature on Ice."

"Komart be using ethane as a carrier," Merlene said. She pointed to the oven along one wall. "The oven be used to keep the ethane liquid until Komart apply it to the painting."

Gabrielle said over the audiolink, "He be doing lard paintings instead of oil paintings, then."

Komart demonstrated his technique, working rapidly from pot to brush to canvas, warming the aluminum brushes often by sticking them into the open end of the oven when they got too cool.

"Merlene be helping Komart by finding new colors," he said. "Some colors be available from certain roots and berries, but many colors be not available from nature."

"Merlene be making colors by using spark generator to heat metal wires in various liquids," Merlene added. "Merlene be mostly getting white powder, but sometimes be getting bright colors."

"Most pigments are oxides," Selke said. "But some are other compounds that you might be able to make. You should look up 'pigments' in your Lookman. I'm afraid, however, that most of the colors you will find there are going to be limited to the visible, with some in the near infrared and near ultraviolet."

"We should have a sample of one of Komart's multipaintings to send back to Earth," Boris audiolinked. "Although a four-centimeter-square canvas that has to be kept in a refrigerator to keep the frame from melting and the paint from evaporating is hardly a candidate for a typical showing, it could be exhibited under a magnifying glass."

"The museum would need to use a multispectral imager camera to present it properly anyway," Selke audiolinked. "All they would need to do is add a close-up lens to the camera."

"It *would* be a remarkable miniature," Rob agreed over the audiolink. "And I know just how to get one." Twitching toes to switch back to radio, he walked the telebot over to a completed painting hanging on the far wall. In the visible, it showed an injured Camalor warrior standing over a mortally wounded comrade, trying to protect him by spearing a rearing war-heuller attempting to trample him. The microwave and infrared images showed the two dismounted warriors being injured; the near ultraviolet image showed the demise of the war-heuller. Rob wished that his telebot could see further into the ultraviolet so he could find out the ending, but he would have to wait.

"This is the most remarkable painting I have ever seen," he said. "Every art collector and museum on Earth would love to have it."

"Then it be yours." Komart took it down from the wall and handed it to Rob, who took it with a bow of gratitude.

Selke bowed low as well. "The people of Earth will treasure your most generous gift. The artistry of Komart will be known throughout the solar system." Komart twisted his second and third sets of claws in embarrassment and pride.

They left Komart's studio and Merlene took them to see other artists at work. One was a jeweler who made diamond chestcoat buttons and skirt pendants cleaved from heuller teeth and laboriously faceted by grinding on a copper wheel embedded with diamond dust. The jeweler also used a small wheel to carve multicarat-sized statues and abstract art forms out of chunks of diamond. Selke admired a statue and soon left the workshop with it.

They visited goldsmiths and silversmiths who beat goldberries and silverberries into solid plates and then formed them into artfully curved vessels and utensils. These too were admired, and soon the three had more gifts of art than they could carry.

"We should be taking our treasures back to the base for transshipment to Earth," said Rob. "It is also time we flew the telebots back to the base to replace their trapchips with new ones. The present trapchips are almost depleted of their antihydrogen fuel. If you will help us take these to the microhopper, we will fly to the base and be back shortly."

Merlene paused, wondering how best to ask the question. She wanted very much to learn more about the technology of the humans. "Merlene be showing humans much of her city. Humans be perhaps showing Merlene their base?"

Rob looked at Selke. Neither could find anything wrong with the idea. The microhopper was certainly big enough inside to hold all three of them, as well as their samples and the artworks.

"Certainly," said Rob. "It is almost time to change shifts again. Boris and Gabrielle will fly you and the 'bots back, and I'll get suited up and come out to welcome you."

Boris, Gabrielle, and Merlene made their way across Camalor from the street of the artisans, Gabrielle carrying Komart's painting, Boris carrying Dilene's sculpture, and Merlene carrying a basket full of the smaller pieces of art. They stopped at Merlene's house along the way, where she picked up the pouches full of food samples and artifacts the humans had left in storage there and added them to her basket. They went to the center of the city, into the park, and past the final school to the rocket.

In the field outside the school were gathered all the young males, separated into two teams, the reds and the blues. Boris noticed that each group was led by a larger male sporting a silver ball in addition to the copper rings worn by many of the participants. They were dressed in heavily padded clothing and helmets woven of multiberry plant stems, and each carried a spikeless mace in his large right warclaw, a shield in his left claw, and blunt daggers in his second claws. The larger males in the front ranks carried smooth, lightweight shields that looked strangely familiar; those in the rear made do with heavy, woven-wicker shields. Observing from the sidelines were warriors in casual finery, obligatory daggers in back but no heavy weaponry or armor. Under the command of their leaders, the two teams formed into ranks and charged each other, maces flailing.

Merlene and the humans stopped to watch.

"Jordat be leader of the red battlegroup in his class," said Merlene proudly. "He be getting to wear the silver antenna ball of command."

Once Boris understood that the balls on the antennae denoted military rank, he was able to make better sense of the group of older warriors watching the progress of the mock battle and discussing various participants. These warriors were obviously judges—and perhaps were also sizing up possible future apprentice warriors. Except for an apprentice warrior keeping watch over the heullers tethered nearby, each visiting warrior wore two multispiked "stars" of command. Correlating physical size and quality of clothing with stars of rank, Boris soon figured out that gold outranked silver, which outranked copper. Except for the student warriors, whose balls of command lacked points, the lowest-ranked warrior there had two copper stars, one at the end of each antenna, while the largest and most flamboyantly dressed had one gold star and one silver star. Boris suspected the senior warrior was Mordet, whom he had seen in the parade through the streets on their first day in Camalor many Fifthdays ago. To be sure, he asked Merlene.

"That warrior be indeed Mordet," Merlene confirmed. "He be subcommander to Rexart."

"I notice some of the students have large black shields that are quite thin but very tough. It looks like what we would call high-impact plastic. I have never seen that material before in Camalor. What is it? And how is it formed into that seamless curved shape?"

Merlene was a little taken aback by the question, and almost hicced in stifled laughter before replying. "You not be seeing it before because it be usually covered with armor. Those be carapaces of warriors who have died in battle. They make serviceable shields until a student graduates to become a real warrior and is issued a metal shield made by the armorers."

"Oh," said Boris quietly.

Watching the combatants, it seemed that the purpose of the mace was to knock the weapons or shield out of the claws of the opponent or, failing that, to knock him off his feet. Once an opening had been gained, a warrior closed on his opponent and used his daggers for infighting. The triangular points of the daggers were used to search for weak spots in the armor, and the blade portion near the hilt was used to chop at leg joints. The student weapons were blunt, so the worst they could do was bruise the thick skin under body plates or sting nerves in the leg-joint regions. Boris noticed that some rules applied; no dagger point was ever raised to eye level where it could go through the wicker helmet, but the helmeted eye region was fair game for a spikeless mace. If a combatant lost a helmet, or was struck by a dagger in a vital region, he was counted out and sent from the battlefield.

A loud, shouted command of "Halt!" rode out over the aether, blocking out the noise from the melee, and the warrior with two copper stars strode forward with a baton upraised. The combatants ceased pounding, stabbing, and slicing at each other, and regrouped.

"He is probably the warrior-arts instructor for the school," Selke guessed.

"Selke be correct," Merlene said.

The instructor walked among the bruised and limping battlers and tapped a few of them on the carapace. As they were tapped, the students came forward and presented themselves in front of Mordet, who awarded each of them a copper ring which he placed on one of their antennae.

As she watched the procedure Merlene bragged, "Jordat be also awarded many copper rings for bravery and skill."

When the ceremony was over and the students had marched off, Merlene turned and led the humans to the far corner of the field where the microhopper awaited them. Boris cycled the airlock open. After loading the samples and the artwork, taking care to belt the heavy statue firmly in place against a bulkhead, Boris strapped himself into the pilot bench while Gabrielle made sure Merlene was safely buckled in the copilot bench. Form follows function, and although the microhopper benches and the reading benches in kerack homes had been designed by engineers on two different planets, they were identical in form. There was only one good way to support a kerack body, and that was to rest the front of the abdomen and thorax on a padded bench. There were no other benches or safety harnesses in the microhopper, since it had been designed for only two kerack-sized telebot passengers, but Gabrielle fashioned a suitable harness for herself against the back bulkhead wall out of the cargo-holding belts. Boris turned to look at Merlene sitting in the copilot seat next to him.

"I have your board locked. Even so, do not touch anything. Just hold on to your bench." Merlene obediently lowered all five pairs of legs around the bench beneath her and apprehensively held on. The door closed and Boris reached for a red-colored square on the control display.

"You may feel some discomfort at first," he warned her. "As if you were much heavier than normal. That will soon go away." He pressed the control square and a strong acoustic vibration shook Merlene's shell. The noise increased, and soon Merlene could feel the pressure that Boris had warned her about. It wasn't bad at all, and she was elated when she saw the ground recede below them as they lifted into the sky. Boris tilted the microhopper toward the north, and Merlene could now see the spoke-and-ring pattern of the city of Camalor. Suddenly the roaring noise coming from beneath the microhopper quit.

Merlene screamed.

"My God!" Rob audiolinked. "What's the matter with her!" The scream over the aether continued, blocking all radio communication. Boris turned on the rockets again and the screaming stopped.

"Free-fall," said Boris. "I thought she would have delight of it, but now I think not. I was going to surprise her by unstrapping her and letting her float around in the cabin— the first kerack astronaut."

Gabrielle chided him. "You surprised her, certainly. You should have warned her."

"I was falling and falling and falling . . ." Merlene quavered, the iris in her eyeglobe still contracted tightly shut.

"You'll get used to it," said Gabrielle, trying to calm her down.

"Benever."

"I'll keep us on a flat hover trajectory," Boris said. "Wasteful of fuel, but there is more than sufficient."

After some minutes, the microhopper landed without further incident. Merlene refused to open her eye until they had safely landed, so she missed seeing the layout of the human base from the air. While Boris shut down the microhopper and safetied it in preparation for refueling, Gabrielle unbuckled Merlene and cycled her through the airlock.

Merlene emerged from the exit lock of the microhopper into the glowing heat radiating from two nearby gigantic columns of metal. Contracting the iris of her eye to moderate the bright infrared glare, she raised her head, following the columns up into the sky. A hundred claws up, the columns joined into a single column with an even larger diameter— that went up another hundred claws. On top of the upper column was a sphere of transparent crystal, through which radiated the soft, rounded, glowing countenance of a strange god . . . a god of fire.

Below the head, hanging from the sides of the upper column, were two more columns. These were jointed and ended in a strange claw with five jointed appendages. The god bent over, the glowing appendage of one claw reaching out toward Merlene. She skittered back on six legs, holding her four front legs up in front of her, the three pincers on each claw spread wide, trying to protect her eye from the intense heat of the approaching appendage, which was almost as big around as she was.

The giant spoke, its loud voice bellowing out over the aether, there to be picked up by Merlene's antennae.

"Sorry," Rob said. "Didn't mean to scare you. Just wanted to shake hands."

"Probably not a good idea," Gabrielle said as her telebot clambered out the microhopper exit lock after Merlene. "You're probably too hot to touch."

With her human friend in her familiar kerack-shaped robotic body at her side, Merlene was finally able to overcome her initial awe and take a close look at the glowing countenance inside the crystal sphere.

It was Rob. He looked much different in real life than he did in the projection screen on the telebot. As she relaxed she was able to relate the different parts of the glowing giant towering above her with descriptions she had read of a human in a space suit.

Merlene looked around at the gigantic structures surrounding her. Near the microhopper were some hoses. The giant Rob went to one of them, pulled it over to the microhopper, and attached it to one of the tanks. The hoses led across the snow to some large containers. Merlene knew from previous discussions that these contained liquid air and liquid fireberry juice to operate the rocket. Off in the distance was an even bigger rocket, standing upright on the snow on its three legs. It had brought the humans to Ice. Next to it were other structures that looked like three-legged rockets that had been cut off at the waist. They had been used to bring the equipment and shelter needed by the humans to survive on Ice. Nearby was the shelter itself. It was made of silvery metal fabric with large blocks of ice stacked around and on top of it, except where there was a door or window or view port. The shelter was glowing brightly with warmth, especially through the window area, where not only infrared but optical radiation was pouring outward, illuminating the ice outside. In the window were the faces of three humans looking out in her direction. Although they had a strong infrared glow about them that made them look different from their images in the eyeglobes of the telebots, Merlene identified them as Selke, Elizabeth, and Hiroshi. For a moment she caught a glimpse of something black and furry, but it quickly disappeared.

Soon Boris and Gabrielle had unloaded the cargo of samples and stacked them in a thick-walled box with a thick lid. The outside and inside of the box were of thin metal, and Merlene could see a soft white material between the two sheets—probably insulation to keep the artifacts cold when they were inside the hot human habitat. Using their mechanical claws, Boris and Gabrielle carefully placed the various pieces of art on top of the bags of samples and put on the lid.

"The antihydrogen trapchips are stored out near the nuclear reactor," said Boris. "Do you want to come along with us while we refuel the 'bots?"

"Merlene would prefer to visit the shelter," she said. "It be too hot inside for a visit in person, but Merlene be able to see much from that block of ice in front of the window."

"You *would* be able to see nearly everything in the shelter from there," Boris agreed. "But the top of that block is a good meter off the ground. Perhaps Rob can figure out a way of lifting you up there without touching you with something hot."

"Merlene be not needing lifting." She skittered quickly over the ground to the shelter. As everyone watched in astonishment, she crouched on all ten legs in her black wizard costume, and with a coordinated, smooth, rippling leap that made her look like a ten-footed black panther in a black star-embroidered cape, she easily jumped to the top of the block of ice.

"Square-cube law and fifteen percent gravity," Selke audiolinked. She started setting up a radio link through an outside antenna so the people inside the shelter could talk directly to Merlene without having the conversation repeated through the telebot radios.

"We will be back shortly," Gabrielle radioed from her telebot, as she and Boris took the telebots out to the antihydrogen storage area.

As they came to the first trapchip container Boris said, "Turn around." Gabrielle did. The force feedback on her fingers through her leg controls and on the sides of her feet from her tail control indicated that Boris was pulling up her chestcoat in the back, opening a door, and pulling out the old trapchip.

The trapchips were not rectangular as were the electronic chips used for storing large amounts of data. Since the trapchips needed a magnetic field running through them to allow the micrometer-sized particle traps inside to function properly, the cylindrical superconducting magnetic solenoid wrapped around the trapchip proper determined the basic shape. The silicon chip inside the coil was thus constructed as a long cylinder with the electromagnetic traps arranged in concentric cylindrical layers inside. Each trap held a microcrystal of antihydrogen containing a trillion antiatoms, and there were a million traps, each a few tens of micrometers in size, for a total load of about a microgram of antihydrogen. It had always amused Gabrielle that the antihydrogen trapchips ended up the same size and shape as a triple-A battery, although they contained much more energy—as much as a tankload of gasoline. Each pair of trapchips was in a lightweight insulated storage box. The storage boxes were separated from each other by a distance of ten meters so that they wouldn't all blow up if the containment system on one of them failed. Actually, since the energy release would be in the form of high-energy pions and gammas that would leave the scene of the explosion at the speed of light, the explosion had been calculated to be more of a "poof" than a bang. The theory had never been checked, for so far none of the trapchips had ever failed, and at a billion dollars per load of antihydrogen in each trapchip, they were too expensive to use up in just testing a theory. Still, it would not have been advisable for anyone or any other trapchip to be close to the burst of radiation.

After Boris put in the new trapchip, he said, "Program a power burst to make sure it is functioning properly." Gabrielle turned down the volume on her radio and triggered a deliberate power surge by looking directly at a menu box at the periphery of her vision and giving a deliberate wink. There was a burst of static over the radio as a hundred traps dumped a hundred trillion antihydrogen atoms into the hot tungsten core of the thermoelectric generator that powered Gabrielle's telebot. In the future, the antihydrogen power pulses would be delivered automatically, about every six minutes. The pulse interval was short enough to keep the tungsten heat core at a relatively constant temperature, while not interrupting radio communications with radiation bursts too often.

"Working fine," she said. "Turn around and I'll recharge you. Don't forget to turn off the automatic antihydrogen feed when you get near the shelter so your 'bot won't irradiate everybody inside."

They soon returned to the shelter area. Rob had finished refueling the rocket and taking their box of samples and gifts around to the cold-box airlock behind the shelter, and was waiting there for them. Boris went into the microhopper to insure that the machine was properly refueled and ready to go, while Rob lifted Gabrielle's telebot up on the ice block to join Merlene. A radio link from inside the shelter directly to Merlene's antennae had been established, and Merlene and the humans inside were already communicating with each other through a copy of the telebot translation program.

"Over here is our kitchen where we prepare our meals," said Elizabeth. "We still sometimes use fire on Earth to do our cooking, but most people now, and especially we here in space, cook using electrical heat."

"Merlene be heating wires with electricity," Merlene said. "Betruth Merlene could be cooking with hot wires. But legs of humans must be getting tired making that much electricity."

Elizabeth smiled broadly at Merlene's remark, trying not to break into a laugh that would show her tongue and teeth. She and the others had considered donning handkerchiefs as temporary mouthveils, but had decided Merlene was already used to their naked mouths in the telebot displays.

"We have developed machines that make electricity automatically," she said. "When you get back to your Lookman, look up the entries on nuclear reactor power sources and thermoelectric generators."

Merlene automatically attempted to force a memory of these unfamiliar technical terms, but found that she was so far away from the Spirit o'Camalor that she couldn't. Feeling like her mind was somehow dulled, she pulled her notebook out of her carrying pouch and inscribed a reminder on her list of things to do. She kept it out, for she was sure there would be many other technical terms she would hear this day that she would need to look up and study on the Look-man.

"Over here are the chairs where we monitor the view seen by the two telebots being operated out on the surface of Ice," Elizabeth continued. "In this monitor we see what Gabrielle is looking at through her 'bot. As you can see, it is nearly the same view that you are experiencing yourself. Over here is the inside of the microhopper. That is where Boris's telebot is presently." The view of Boris's monitor changed as he took his telebot through the airlock on the microhopper out onto the surface. The view shifted until Boris's gaze was fixed on Merlene and Gabrielle in the distance, looking in the shelter window. Then it froze as Boris stopped moving.

"I hear Boris's cocoon cracking," Elizabeth said. She moved down the narrow aisle and pointed at the opening telebot controller. "These are the machines that allow us to operate the telebots at a distance using radio signals." Merlene had to move closer to the window to see that far down the inside of the shelter.

Boris's head arose and he lifted off his verihelm. "Hello, Merlene. I am Boris. Welcome to our base." Merlene looked back at the microhopper. The eyeglobe of the telebot standing there was blank.

"I think I will take a break, too," Gabrielle said, and her image blinked off. Soon all six humans were crowded around the window area looking out at the alien from Ice. The table in front of the window had been folded down to get it out of the way. Resenting the fact that he was being ignored, Lucifer jumped to the narrow window ledge formed by the edge of the folded-down table. Merlene, startled by the sudden appearance of the jet-black monster, leapt backward and almost fell off the ice block.

"What be *that!*" she asked.

"This is our pet, Lucifer," Gabrielle said, trying to reassure Merlene by stroking the cat to show that it could do her no harm. "It is called a cat."

"*Your* pet," Selke grumbled, still irritable from lack of sleep. Lucifer, not cooperating, reacted to the pat by turning and biting Gabrielle's finger, showing Merlene plenty of sharp white teeth and pink tongue in the process.

"Merlene be thinking that a creature with teeth that sharp would be dangerous to be keeping around. Heullers be dangerous, but they be useful since they be doing work for us and are good to eat, so we be spending time to train them so they be less dangerous. What be the purpose for which you use these cat creatures? Be they good to eat?"

Gabrielle looked shocked. "We *never* eat cats!"

"Then what be their purpose?"

There was a long pause as the humans tried to come up with a suitable answer. Finally Gabrielle had to admit the truth.

"Cats are not useful for anything. We just feed them, take care of them, and pat them, and they give us company in return."

"Merlene be hearing, but be not understanding. Humans be feeding cat, keeping cat warm, and rubbing cat on back—"

"And emptying its shit out of the cat box," Selke interrupted grouchily.

"—yet humans be receiving nothing in return," concluded Merlene. "Why humans be doing such an illogical thing?"

"You have pets," Gabrielle reminded her. "I remember seeing the princesses and other ladies with their clawpets. What good do they do?"

It was now Merlene's turn to pause and go through a self-examination. What the human Gabrielle said was true. Although she had never had a live clawpet herself, she knew enough about them to know that they served no useful purpose; they demanded and received food and many other services, such as daily grooming of their long hair. The wizard in her was now extremely puzzled. Certainly there must be *some* reason why the clawpets and beautybumps existed. Someday she would have to find out what it was.

"Merlene be having no answer," she finally conceded.

"It's time we were getting the telebots back to Camalor," Rob urged. "We can't let the heat core cool down too much, and I certainly don't want them power-bursting near me."

"It's almost time for our shift to start," said Elizabeth. "Just give Hiroshi and me a little time to get some breakfast and brush our teeth, and we'll take the 'bots back."

"I'll suit up again and go out and lower your 'bot to the surface. You could probably jump down safely, but I don't want Grippen to have a heart attack when he sees the video."

"Gabrielle and I will load up an Earth-return sample capsule before we head for our sleep shift," Boris volunteered. "If you will stay out for a while, you can take the capsule out to the return-rocket launch area."

Gabrielle climbed up on one of the monitor chairs and set the display menu so that it controlled the instruments in the cold box, while Boris made his way to the indented wall between the heads of the two cocoons. He inserted his hands in the manipulator controls, reached the mechanical claws to one side of the cold box, and opened the airlock. Carefully he pulled in the insulated metal box and opened the thick lid. He then opened the storage locker on the other side and pulled out some other boxes that contained samples obtained in earlier forays.

"We are limited to three kilograms of payload in the return capsule," he said over his shoulder to Gabrielle. "Do you have the priority list we worked on last week?"

"I've got it right here on the screen," said Gabrielle. "Even though we sent those two corpses, the heuller segments, and the iceworms back to Earth already, we still have many food and clothing samples, slices of root, and a selection of berries. There was more than three kilograms' worth, so we just drew a line when we reached the weight limit."

"Let me take out and weigh the new items in this latest shipment," Boris said. "We can then discuss their relative priority and insert them in the list at the proper place, then recompute the cutoff line."

"That is going to be difficult," said Gabrielle. "Is a painting of a whole heuller more valuable than a quarter section of heuller?"

"We can only do our best. Besides, there will be other shipments later."

Elizabeth climbed into the cocoon behind Boris. "I would think that sending back some real kerack art would be very important in getting the Earth to appreciate the kerack civilization. Sure, we could laser-beam video pictures of the paintings, sculptures, and other art treasures, but being able to see the alien art in person is so much more emotionally gripping."

"I agree," said Gabrielle. "I go to see the original *Mona Lisa* in the Louvre at least once a year, even though I have a copy in my bedroom at home."

"The first sample is on the balance," Boris said. "A bag containing one deep-fried heuller toe. Looks like about five grams."

Gabrielle read off the screen. "Four point eight grams after the bag weight is subtracted. We already sent some uncooked heuller toes on that quarter segment. I would say very low priority for this item."

"Agreed," said Boris, using the manipulator to change samples on the scale. "This is a gold wire from a spinner worm."

"Twenty-five milligrams. An analysis of the surface structure might give clues to how the spinner worms are able to extrude pure metals. I would put this above a goldberry because the wire probably has the identical material content of the berry, but lower weight."

"Good point," said Boris. "I agree." The two continued on through the box of new samples until they had all been weighed and prioritized. Then they loaded the compartments in the capsule and put the whole thing on the analytical balance. It was several grams overweight, so they had to take some things back out.

"What is the mass now?" asked Boris as he reluctantly removed a precious but heavy inlaid silver bowl from the miniature cargo hold of the express capsule. The cold was beginning to creep back through the mechanical joints in the evacuated cold box that kept the cold kerack artifacts from the hot, reactive, oxygenated air he was breathing.

Gabrielle looked carefully at the balance indicator on the monitor screen. "Still thirty grams over."

Boris, sighing, reached in the capsule hold and pulled out a statue. This was the one by Dilene showing a kerack ballerina poised on one toe. Although kerack bodies normally did not look graceful to human eyes, the artist had accomplished that feat in this work of art, and Boris admired the delicate lines of the ballerina as he set the statue aside on its large and heavy base. The base had to be made of one of the heavier elements, but its color was not silvery like platinum, or gray like lead and tungsten. Had to be some other dense metal.

"Three grams under, now," Gabrielle reported. "Have something small?"

"Nothing that small, I'm afraid. We'll just have to launch the capsule three grams light." Suddenly he had an idea. The important thing about the statue of the ballerina was the figure of the dancer, not the overly large, dense, and featureless hemispherical base. If he separated the statue from the base, the museum curators on Earth could mount the figure on something else once it got there. Certainly nothing of artistic value would be lost.

Boris reached for a wire cutter in the tool rack at the back of the cold box. Carefully he cut the ballerina loose from her base and tenderly placed her in a storage cubicle in the cargo hold of the capsule.

"Nine thousand, nine hundred and ninety eight point two grams," Gabrielle reported.

"Horosho." Boris closed the cargo hatch on the capsule and activated the built-in foaming mechanism that flooded the interior of the storage compartment with a fast-hardening protective foam. Easily lifting the ten-kilogram cylindrical capsule in the light gravity of Ice, he slid the capsule into the airlock tube leading outside. Closing the inner airlock door, he latched it tight.

Boris removed his cold hands from the manipulators, rubbed them together for a few seconds to warm them while he walked back to the monitor chair, then switched on the outside radio link.

"Capsule is loaded, Rob."

"Be there in a second," Rob replied. He crunched over the icy crust, opened the airlock to the cold box, and took out the silvery capsule. Then, switching to a "lunar lope," Rob paced his way to the launch area. The largest structure there was their return rocket, already set up and ready to take them off the planetoid whenever necessary. To one side was a field of eighteen tubes buried upright in holes bored in the ice. Only the top few feet stuck out of the ground. Most of the tubes still had a white protective cap on them, but some were open; these tubes and the ground around them were gray with sootlike material. Right after they had arrived and set up the base, they had taken rock samples from nearby cliffs and deep ice-core samples of the layered snow in the middle of a wide valley and had sent them off to Earth for the planetologists to examine. The two kerack corpses and some early food samples followed. Now the capsules would be taking back more subtle and artistic examples of kerack civilization.

Rob went to one of the pristine tubes and took off the

protective cap. Inside the tube was a long, slender rocket. He placed the sample capsule in the holder designed to take it, closed the clamp around the capsule, and loped back toward the base. A safe distance away, he turned around to look and switched on his radio.

"You may fire when you are ready, Gridley," he said.

"Who is this Gridley you keep talking about?" Gabrielle asked. There was a pause of a few seconds. "Inertial system initialized . . ." She watched the automatic launch sequence take place. "Launch in ten seconds . . . four . . . three . . . two . . one . . ."

The rocket leapt at high acceleration out of the tube and was gone before Rob's eyes could focus on it.

A few hours later the rocket delivered the sample capsule to the main station of the cable catapult in orbit around Ice. The capsule was automatically transferred to the launcher mechanism on the catapult, while the delivery rocket backed away and went off to lose itself in empty space. After Gabrielle had carefully checked over the cable catapult system and found all was ready, the launcher started accelerating down the six cables that stretched 4,200 kilometers outward in space toward the inner solar system. The capsule accelerated at 3,000 gees, its precious cargo protected from the acceleration forces by the foam. Seventeen seconds later it reached the end of the catapult and was traveling at 500 kilometers per second. At that speed it would reach Earth in only four months. There it would be caught by a similar cable catapult near Earth and slowed to a stop, its precious cargo ready to be picked up and examined by Earth researchers.

7

TOURNAMENT AT THE OVAL

"IT BE FI'FIFTHDAY soon," Merlene announced to the humans when they arrived back at her home, having spent the day watching a baker produce breads and berry pies using certain ground-up multiberry plant roots for flour. Some of the pies had looked delicious to Rob, just like ones his mother used to make, with thin strips of crust over bubbling berry fillings. It had been many years since he had tasted a real pie and now he wished his telebot had taste buds.

"Is there something special about every fifth Fifthday?" Rob asked. He had been practicing converting numbers from the kerack five-base number system to the human decimal system. Since the keracks had ten legs, one would have thought that they would have developed a decimal counting system too, but unfortunately, it hadn't happened that way.

"Betruth!" Merlene exclaimed. "The warriors be putting on a tournament. Jordat be now off taking part for the first time as apprentice to the great warrior Laslot."

"Sounds interesting," said Rob. Since the young male was not there, Rob hauled the heavy feastbasket up the stairs to the surface in his warclaw while Fasart managed the sharestand. Selke was up on the surface showing Solene how to skip rope. Solene was fascinated with the new game, and soon was outdoing the clumsy two-leg-pair-gaited human in speed skipping.

At the park, with Solene off showing the other children how to skip and Merlene and Fasart busy setting out the upper layer of the feastbasket contents on the sharestand, Rob and Selke wandered around, looking for something new to add to their sample collections. They had obtained samples of pretty much everything there was to offer in the way of food items, so they collected very little this Fifthday. The tenders of the many sharestands were very disappointed when the humans passed by without taking anything. Then Selke saw a male kerack setting out something different on his sharestand. She recognized him easily because his warclaw was missing.

"That is the painter Komart. I wonder what *he* is giving away this Fifthday?"

"Let's go get a couple," Rob said, clumsily taking a sample bag out of his carrying pouch and lurching toward Komart's sharestand in the awkward two-leg-pair by two-leg-pair gait of the telebots.

By the time the humans got to the sharestand, it was surrounded by young keracks eagerly removing the items from the sharestand as fast as Komart took them out of his carrying basket. When Komart saw the humans coming, he quickly dived back down into the basket and came up with two bowl-like objects. They were the size of the eyeglobe on a small kerack child.

"These be for you," he said with a hic of laughter, handing the bowls to the humans over the outstretched claws and protests of the eager children.

"They are paintings of *us!*" Selke said in surprise.

"They sure are!" Rob looked down at a painted version of himself on the shallow bowl he held in his claw. The bowl looked like it had been cast out of crystal-clear ice. On the outside of each bowl he was giving away, Komart had painted a realistic but exaggerated cartoon likeness of one of the six humans. In place of the irises of the eyes, Komart had left the glass clear.

Rob and Selke looked around at the kerack children. The bowls just fit over their eyeglobes, and with them on, the children looked like miniature telebots with a human face projected onto the inner surface of their eyeglobes.

"They are masks!" said Selke.

"With eye holes so they can see out," Rob added.

Komart's masks were instant hits with the children. At first, they just put them on and looked at each other. This was sufficient to cause hysterical hics of laughter. Then one young male wearing the face of Rob started imitating the awkward gait of the humans, lurching around the park like a drunken Frankenstein monster.

Somewhere in a closet at his parent's home, Rob still had a Frankenstein monster rubber mask that he occasionally wore to parties, where he would take advantage of his height to create a fairly decent reincarnation of the monster, complete with a staggering, stiff-legged walk. Now, here he was being caricatured as a kerack version of a Frankenstein monster. Rob was not sure he liked the comparison.

When the other children saw the awkward gait of their comrade in the human mask, they fell to the ground in fits of hiccing laughter. From the subtle shaking of their bodies it was obvious that the adult keracks standing around and watching the antics were amused as well.

Each time the laughter died away, another child would get up off the ground and repeat the performance, more exaggerated this time, and the children would roll on the ground again. A child with a Boris mask twisted its antennae at awkward and disparate angles as it stumbled around. More hics of laughter. Another, using the multivoice capability of the keracks, imitated the human voice as it was normally heard over the aether, with static and telemetry data missing in the background. Wearing the mask of Selke, she went lurching around to her comrades, carrying an imaginary sample bag, saying in a fairly good imitation of Selke's voice, "Oh! Selkene be wanting a sample of *that!*" She took imaginary objects from her friends and carefully put them in her sample bag with inept, exaggerated motions of her front claw and leg. More hics of laughter.

The children then noticed that Rob and Selke were watching their antics. Embarrassed, they ran off. Soon, however, they were repeating their human-monster performances all over the park, to the general amusement of all. As Rob and Selke walked back to where Merlene and Fasart had set up their sharestand, Rob realized that both he and Selke were now trying to walk more fluidly than they had bothered to in the past.

After the feasting it was time for the Service o'Giving. The humans waited through the hours-long service, and when it was finally over and Merlene, Fasart, and Solene had returned to their sharestand, the human shift change had taken place. Boris and Gabrielle were now in the telebot eyeglobes.

"We be now going to the tournament," said Merlene, leading the way to the Oval o'All. They filed into the amphitheater, Fasart taking Boris around to one side to view from near the royal box, Merlene and Solene steering Gabrielle around to the other side so her telebot cameras could record from that angle.

The royal party filed in and Rexart took his customary place of honor in the center of the royal box. Most of the male escorts that usually accompanied the princesses and ladies were absent. Instead of his lightweight, ceremonial chain mail, Rexart was wearing a more rugged, although still gold-covered, set of full plate armor. His chest and back were guarded with large plates of thick, solid metal, elaborately engraved and inlaid with jewels. There were smaller plates along the sides connecting the chest and back plates that llowed his legs to emerge while still protecting him from a trike from the side. His legs and claw pincers were encased n fitted tubes of armor that imitated his shell, and clever ointed structures covered weak spots that existed in the rmor that nature had given him.

His abdomen was covered with a tight-fitting chain-mail undercoat that fit his lower body like a dancer's tights, leaving nothing exposed. This was covered in turn with piece fter piece of curved plate that gave full protection to the bdomen, without hampering the flexibility a warrior needed in his tail section to climb on and ride heullers or move about on foot.

The most ornate and elaborate portion of his armor was he region around the mouth. The cloth mouthbelt he normally wore was imitated in the seamless armor plate by embossed areas heavily encrusted with jewels. The obscenely large tonguepouches worn by the warrior class in heir daily dress were replicated in their armor almost to the oint of absurdity. Rexart's heavy tongueflap was encrusted vith yellow gemstones and clanked loudly as he made his vay to his place. As he waited for the crowd to settle down, e helped himself to spiritberries from a bowl held by a oung male attendant. Picking up the spiritberries by the lawful with his smaller first-claw, Rexart lifted the hinged ongueflap on the front of his armor with his second claws nd shoveled the berries into his mouth through the small ood hole underneath, one of the few weak points in a varrior's armor.

Finally, everything was ready. Clanking his way to the podium at the front of the royal box, Rexart raised the ceremonial mace of authority and called out, "The tournament be started. The Queen be living ever!"

"The Queen be living ever!" echoed the crowd fervently, ollowed by chirps of applause as the warrior corps, in full battle dress, dashed through the entrances into the stadium on their war-heullers and took up their places around the perimeter.

"One battlegroup be assigned to border-wall duty this Fifthday," said Merlene. "The other four battlegroups be tournamenting today."

"I count five ranks of twenty-five mounted warriors in each battlegroup," Rob audiolinked. "That's 125 in a battlegroup, or five hundred fully armored and mounted warriors. And with the fifth battlegroup out on guard duty, that's six hundred and twenty-five—a twoff in kerack numbers. Then, since each warrior has an apprentice, that means a standing army of something like thirteen hundred males, not counting the armorers, victualers, stablers, and other members of the various service corps."

"The whole population of Camalor is only about ten thousand. That's over thirteen percent of the population doing nothing but playing soldier," Selke calculated over the audiolink. "Even the Swiss don't have that high a percentage on active duty anymore."

With the warriors gathered, the individual challenges started. One of the leaders of a battlegroup rode out to one end of the Oval. On the ends of his antennae were two multispiked balls, like miniature maces, one silver and one gold.

"That be Fi'fifion Gawart," said Merlene.

Rob calculated, "If I counted the number of fi's in that word correctly, that means he commands five times five times five warriors, or a full battlegroup of hundred and twenty-five. The title is roughly equivalent to the Roman *centurion*."

Gawart's challenge was met by another fi'fifion.

"That be Fi'fifion Galart," said Merlene.

The two warriors adjusted their helmets, raised their shields, and lowered their long lances, held firmly in their powerful warclaws. Instead of points, the lances had splayed ends. Kicking their heullers into motion, the warriors charged at each other until they met in the center of the Oval. Both were experienced, so their aim was true and their balance set well forward. Their lances shattered, indicating that they had struck each other squarely and strongly, but neither was unseated from atop his heuller. Having demonstrated before all in the Oval their ability and their equality with an opponent of equivalent rank, they returned with satisfaction to their places at the head of their battlegroups.

The challenges went on until all the fi'fifions had met each other. There was only one slip, when one of the combatants, Fi'fifion Mordet, didn't shatter his lance, indicating that he had missed his aiming point slightly and his lance had slipped off his opponent's shield rather than hitting it squarely. This would not do in a real battle, where the lances were stronger and shatterproof and where a square hit was essential to dismount the opponent and effectively take him out of the battle. Hisses of disapproval arose in the crowd. To recoup his honor, Mordet returned to the challenge position. This time he challenged the commander of all the forces, Commander Rexart.

Rexart accepted the challenge with a roar, clanked his way down from the royal box, and mounted the gigantic war-heuller waiting for him in the Oval. Tying down his helmet and taking up his golden shield and golden lance, he rode to the other end of the Oval to the thunderous chirps of approval and chants of the crowd.

"Rexart! Rexart! Rexart!"

"Now that they are both in similar costumes, it is easy to see that Rexart is bigger than Mordet and the other fi'fifions," Gabrielle said. "And they are bigger than most of their warriors."

"Besure," said Merlene, her eyeglobe fixed on the action. "They be older," she added, as though that was the obvious reason.

Comparing the sizes from his vantage point on the other

side of the Oval, Boris murmured, "Mordet does not have much of a chance."

"Betruth," Fasart agreed, popping a cold fried heuller toe under his mouthbelt and following it up with a spiritberry.

The two warriors set their heullers in motion, and the crowd hushed in anticipation. The resulting crash could be felt through the thin air on Ice, coming shortly after the grunts the two males let loose over the aether as they collided. When it was over, Mordet was on the ground, but both lances had been shattered. Rexart saluted his opponent with the remains of his lance and rode back to his royal box, while Mordet jumped nimbly to his feet and leapt back atop his mount, which his apprentice had brought up to him. The crowd gave Mordet a long cheer of rolling chirps and broke into a chant of approval.

"Mordet! Mordet! Mordet!"

"Why are they cheering him?" asked Gabrielle. "He lost."

"Besure Mordet be losing," Merlene replied. "Rexart be always striking his opponent off his heuller in a joust. Mordet be knowing that fact when Mordet be making the challenge. But Mordet be showing bravery by holding lance steady and causing it to strike solidly on shield of Rexart so it be shattering. Crowd be cheering bravery of Mordet in face of certain defeat."

With the formal and friendly jousts between the battle-group commanders over, more serious battles began. Squads of twenty-five from one battlegroup collided with squads of twenty-five from another. Each squad leader counted up shattered lances and dismounted opponent warriors after each collision and either commended or berated his troops, depending on the count. The winning squad was presented before Rexart, who awarded silver rings, placed on the warriors' antennae by Princess Onlone herself.

Then came claw-to-claw individual combat between un-mounted warriors, carefully monitored by referees to keep the aroused fighters from accidentally killing each other with their blunted daggers in their eagerness to expose a chink in the other's armor. More rings were awarded.

The day drew on, and the human shifts changed. When it was time for the grand finale, Elizabeth and Hiroshi were up from their sleep shifts and in the telebots.

"What is going to happen now?" Elizabeth asked Merlene. There were now two battlegroups and their support apprentices on either end of the oval battleground. The apprentices were dismounted, but each held two spare lances.

"It be much like a miniature war," replied Merlene. "One half be attacking the other half. This time the battle not be stopping when a warrior be unmounted. The warrior must be continuing to fight on foot until vanquished. Unlike a real battle, there be no remounts available. There not be room in the Oval for all the heullers."

"We used to have the same thing in medieval tournaments," Elizabeth said. "It was called a melee."

Four of the princesses came down to the front of the royal box. In their clawpets two were carrying red ribands and two were carrying blue.

"The escorts of those princesses be the fi'fifions that be commanding those battlegroups," Merlene confided to Elizabeth.

The two fi'fifions from each battlegroup rode over to the royal box, where the princesses leaned over and presented them with the ribands. The fi'fifions then rode back triumphantly to their groups and distributed the ribands to their warriors, who carefully tied them to the ends of their antennae.

Elizabeth sighed. "Just like the princesses and ladies in medieval times handing out favors for their knights to wear into battle."

With the two sides now identified, the crowd at one end of the Oval started up a chant:

"A red! A red! A red!"

The crowd at the other end countered with:

"A blue! A blue! A blue!"

With the cheers of the crowd urging them on, the warriors on each side assembled into a simple formation. All 250 warriors lined up heuller to heuller in a single line. Although the opponents faced each other, their antennae were pointed toward the commander of them all, Rexart.

Rexart raised his ceremonial mace, stretched out his antennae for maximum coupling to the aether, and roared the single word: "ATTACK!"

Instinctive primordial drives urging them onward, the warriors on both sides kicked their war-heullers into action and charged at each other with their lances lowered, the grumbles of the hard-worked heullers drowned out by the shouts of the warriors and the cheers of the crowd. The two opposing armies met in the middle of the Oval with a crash and a shattering of lances. Those who were still mounted whirled around and raced back to their apprentices, waiting along the walls, to obtain replacement lances so they could attempt to dismount opponents who were still on their heullers. Those who had been dismounted reformed into small groups and hunted out opponents who were also on foot, or tried to dismount mounted opponents with blows from their spikeless maces.

Although there were occasional arguments over the lethality of a weak blow, most warriors gallantly admitted defeat when fairly struck with a sword or dagger point, and declared themselves dead by taking off their ribands and retiring to the sidelines.

"What a confusion," Hiroshi complained. "I can't make sense of it."

"It be obvious the blues be winning," Fasart replied. "Look, they be still having three mounted warriors and the reds be having only one."

As they watched, the lone mounted warrior with the red ribands on his antennae spurred his war-heuller on, trying to dismount the nearest mounted blue warrior before all three blue opponents could form a compact group that could easily dismount him. But by the time he had gotten close to his targeted opponent, the lance of another appeared. His first opponent's lance knocked the shield from his claw, and the lance of the second shattered on his tongueflap, temporarily flipping it up. The sharp point of the broken lance hilt found the food hole hidden underneath the tongueflap and penetrated his mouth.

There was a shriek of agony over the aether, and the entire Oval was temporarily silent as everyone froze. Waiting chirurgeons rushed from the sidelines to the stricken warrior. The battle continued around them as the chirurgeons dragged the stricken warrior off, yellow-brown blood shooting in a spray from his midsection.

"What happened?" Hiroshi asked.

"He be punctured," Fasart replied. "He be probably struck in the mouth. That be a very serious injury, but at least he be not exploding."

"Exploding!"

Selke's voice came over the audiolink with an explanation. "You forget that the only way the keracks can have a liquid-based body chemistry on this near-zero-temperature planet with a near vacuum for an atmosphere is to have high temperatures and pressures inside their shells. I would estimate that they keep their internal pressure at about five atmospheres."

Finally Rexart called a halt to the battle. The warriors regrouped into their original formations and presented themselves, slightly battered, before the royal box. After consultations with some of the senior warriors who had been acting as judges, Rexart awarded antenna rings to a number of the participants from both sides.

A kerack in a chirurgeon's Cape o'Trade with the symbol of a drop of yellow-brown blood embroidered on it came to the royal box, touched an antenna to that of Rexart, and left.

Rexart retrieved his ceremonial mace from a young warrior attendant and raised it high.

"We be ending the tournament with a Procession o'Soul," he announced. "The Queen be living ever!"

"The Queen be living ever," repeated the crowd, but the enthusiasm they had previously exhibited was gone.

"What was that all about?" asked Hiroshi.

"The injured warrior be dead," Fasart said. "His soul now be taken to the Queen. Tonight his body be in the place of honor at the warrior's feast table, while his shell shall be engraved with his name and dedicated to the final-school warrior corps."

Hiroshi suspected that the place of honor at the feast table was on a serving platter, but he didn't really want to know, so he didn't ask. He was now certain that he would never eat prawns again.

From the entrance to the Oval that led from the nearby Courtyard o'Warriors came a single warrior. It was Fi'fifion Mordet. Between the three large pincers in his warclaw he held a small gray pellet of metal. Rexart and the rest of the royal party came down from the box and led the fi'fifion across the Oval, up the broad stairway that led to the park outside, and through the park to the dance plaza and the Queen's tower.

Solemnly the crowed flowed out of the amphitheater behind them. By the time Hiroshi and Elizabeth arrived at the plaza, the brief ceremony was over and the royal party was returning. Everyone now turned to feasting on the food and the ample supply of spiritberries, while waiting for the Queen to call them for the closing dance to the Fifthday. By the time the dance started, many spiritberries had passed beneath mouthveils and mouthbelts, and the unfortunate death of the warrior had been forgotten.

"The tournaments and melees of medieval times were not without their serious injuries and deaths too," Elizabeth said somberly as they discussed the day's happenings on their way home after the dance. "More than one human king was killed by a shattered lance in a friendly joust."

"In many ways, life here is similar to the romantic ideals of medieval times," Hiroshi said. "The ladies are glamorous and well dressed, the warriors are brave and well equipped and ride large noble steeds, the artisans practice their trades with pride and pass on their knowledge to their dedicated apprentices. There are lots of holidays with spectacular events and shows, there is plenty of food and drink and pageantry and dancing, and everyone is happy and contented. The city of Camalor seems to be just like the fabled city of Camelot. Even the names sound the same."

"That word be not translated," said Merlene. "What be this city of Kam-a-lot?"

"It is a fictional city," Elizabeth replied. "But the stories about it are interesting. We will look it up in the Lookman when we get back to your workshop. I'm sure the *Encyclopaedia Terra Digital* has an entry on King Arthur and his court in the marvelous city of Camelot."

Later that night, Elizabeth and Hiroshi were playing with Merlene's spark generator while Merlene read through the entry on Camelot and King Arthur. The humans had warned her that it was a fictional story, but that there was some underlying truth to it that had been lost in antiquity.

"The story be very interesting," said Merlene. "The ending be especially interesting, where the sword of the king be thrown into the lake and a hand be coming up to catch it. But Merlene be also interested in the 'digs.' "

"Digs?" asked Elizabeth.

"The entry be concluding by saying that human wizards called archeologists be conducting 'digs' in the place called Cadbury in Great Britain. They be hoping to find physical evidence that King Arthur or Camelot be really existing and be not just a fable."

"Yes," said Hiroshi. "Most cities have remnants of older cities buried beneath them."

"It could even be that Camalor has an older city beneath it," Elizabeth added.

"Considering the weather here, it is quite possible," Hiroshi mused. "What happens every time a geyser goes off, Merlene?"

"The air be getting thicker and storm clouds form. Soon everything be covered in a thick layer of snow. Some of the snow be evaporating away with time, and we be cleaning out the Oval o'All and sweeping off the Plaza o'Dance and the Basin o'Sliding, but outside the center o'Camalor we be just adding a step or two to the stairway to the surface and be replanting the bushes."

Elizabeth said thoughtfully, "If Camalor got hit with the kerack equivalent of a thousand-year geyser storm, it could be so completely buried they would have to start all over again." She turned to Merlene. "Do you have any fables of cities buried in storms?"

"Many," Merlene admitted. "But they be always long ago and far away on the other side of the mountains."

"Perhaps they are long ago in time, but not far away in distance at all," Hiroshi suggested. "Maybe they are just a few dozen centimeters down."

Merlene was entranced with the new idea. "Merlene be conducting a dig! Merlene be talking first with the excavators and constructors. They be knowing much about old buildings in Old Camalor." She gathered up her notebook, where she had been entering notes on Camelot, put it back into her carrying pouch, put on her Cape o'Trade, and headed up the stairway.

"Don't forget to make lots of maps as you go," Elizabeth told her before she left. "Before you start, you should make a three-dimensional map of what is known about the location. Then, during the dig, the location of every artifact you find must be pinpointed in all three dimensions and orientations on the map if you want all the pieces to fit together properly." Elizabeth had learned that lesson in one of her first digs, when she and some other students were helping an archeologist from the British Museum exhume an old Cromwell gun battery a Caithness farmer had discovered near John o'Groats.

"She is going to be busy on that project for some time," said Hiroshi. "It will be interesting to see what she finds. Shall we go along with her, or go off and bother somebody else for a while?"

"Most archeology involves a lot of digging for a little bit of information," Elizabeth replied. "Let's go digging at a crèche school instead and learn how kerack children are taught their reading and writing and maths."

Merlene knew exactly where to go to start her search for knowledge about ancient Camalor. She made her way into Old Camalor and entered the home of the metalspinner Patene and her husband, the excavator Covart. As it was still near the close of Fifthday, she knew she would find them and their children home. By the time she reached the first landing, they had sensed her arrival and were waiting for her in the living room.

"Mother. Father. Merlene be feeling good to be at home again. Where be brother and sister o'Merlene?"

"They be studying in their rooms," said Patene. "School be starting again tomorrow."

"Covart be sensing excitement in Merlene. Besure Merlene be here on wizard business."

"Betruth," Merlene admitted. "The wizard Merlene be collecting knowledge about the early days of Camalor, so be visiting those people Merlene be knowing that be living in those early days. Parents o'Merlene be oldest persons Merlene know other than the princesses and ladies who serve the Queen."

"And the Queen herself," Patene said. "The Queen be living ever," she added automatically, and was echoed by both Merlene and her father.

"Who be building Camalor?" asked Merlene.

"Both Patene and Covart be building the Center o'Camalor," answered Patene. "There be many others over time, but we be among the first. Covart be excavating under the Palace o'Princesses and Patene be spinning the Cylinder o'-Support and the many layers of the Dome o'Holies."

Covart began reminiscing. "Progress be very slow at first, for there be few workers. Life in those days be so hard the soul of one be always cold. The clothiers be making only simple, thick, warm garments. There be nothing to eat but black fungus, and an occasional berry or root, for the ice-worms be reserved for the queens and their courts of princesses."

"Queens!" exclaimed Merlene. "There be more than one queen in those days?"

"Queen Une be the mother of two younger queens before she be turning to the task of building Camalor," said Patene. "When the young queens be grown, however, the Queen be evicting them from Camalor along with their retinue of princesses and ladies, in the same manner as Queen Une be previously expelled by the Queen o'Harvamor. One young queen be now the Queen of nearby Belator, while the other be Queen of Zamabor on the other side of Camalor. In those days there be nothing but empty ice where those cities be now flourishing."

Patene paused as she dredged up old memories. "Once the young queens and their courts be sent on their way, life in Camalor be easier. There be more workers and especially more farmers. With more farmers, there be more food. There soon be spare food for the Feast o'Sharing, and spare time for dancing each Fifthday on the Plaza o'Dance. The souls of all be growing warm each Fifthday with the pleasure of the dance."

"But the new workers be needing to be taught," complained Covart. "And once they be finishing their apprentice-ships, they be needing homes and workshops excavated, in addition to the task of excavating under the Palace o'Princesses so the Dome o'Holies could be constructed. Covart and his apprentices be working continuously at constructing new buildings and excavating under the palace, stopping only for the Fifthday dance."

"Patene be working equally long on the many layers of the Dome o'Holies. The High Priest Princess Kitone be telling Patene what the next layer of the dome must be. Then Patene must be learning how to make her spinworm produce that layer in a perfect, seamless way before she be starting the layer. She then be teaching her apprentice spinners to do the same and they be using their spinworms to spin that layer."

"How long ago this be?" Merlene asked.

Patene paused to think. "Merlene be the fi'fifth female child of Patene." After saying this, Patene got distracted and rambled off on a tangent. "Patene be hoping that her five times five female child would be special—and she be! How proud Patene be when Merlene be made the Wizard o'Camalor!"

Merlene was busy calculating in her head. "Since all parents be having a new female child each fi'five twoffdays, that be a threffday before Merlene be a child, and Merlene be five fi'fives twoffdays old herself. That be very long ago." She turned to her father. "When Covart be excavating to make Center o'Camalor, did Covart be finding any buildings or objects or anything else?"

"Covart be finding only ice and rocks."

Merlene was a little disappointed with the answer, but she remembered Elizabeth's admonition. Getting out her notebook and scribe, she said, "Covart and Patene be telling Merlene all about the construction of the Center o'Camalor. Merlene be wanting to draw a map that be having all the details, before Merlene start her dig."

"We not be knowing the details of the Palace o'Princesses, or the Tower o'Queen, or the Heaven o'All," said

Covart. "That be existing before Covart and Patene be children."

"Who be constructing those buildings?" Merlene asked.

"Patene be not knowing. The princesses, perhaps?"

"Merlene be making the map of the Center o'Camalor as complete as possible," Merlene decided. "Those parts that be unknown be left blank and perhaps be filled in later." Raising her stylus, she started her questioning. "Of what be the many layers of the Dome o'Holies composed?"

8

WAR OF THE ICEWORM

A MONTH LATER, the humans were visiting Fasart's farm once again. He had been raising a young heuller and was planning to break it to ride on. Since he was starting fresh with this animal, he hoped to be able to teach it to accept the human telebots on its back, so the humans could take themselves where they wanted to go instead of having to have some kerack drive the heuller for them while they rode behind in a wagon. Since both Elizabeth and Hiroshi had learned to ride horses, Elizabeth on her father's large estate in Caithness and Hiroshi at an American dude ranch, they were picked for the task.

"The secret to training heullers be patience," Fasart explained.

Hiroshi nodded. "It is the same with horses."

"Heullers be gentle animals if they be not frightened. They be most calm when they be with familiar things. So, heuller must be becoming familiar with Elizabeth and Hiroshi." He took them to the ice-brick enclosure in which the young heuller was penned. Hiroshi was relieved to see that the animal was significantly smaller than the old, large heuller Fasart usually rode around the farm. As they approached the enclosure, the heuller backed off to the other side. Like all heullers, it wore an open muzzle that allowed it to eat but kept it from burrowing its way free by eating a hole in the ice.

"It be hungry," said Fasart, opening the gate. "We be not feeding it for two days." He handed them a freshly uprooted multiberry bush with a few berries and thick roots still on it. "You be taking this inside, holding it out, and waiting. The heuller be smelling it, and after some time be coming closer. Humans be not moving. Then heuller be eating the food. While the heuller be eating, humans be talking to the heuller."

"What shall we say?" asked Hiroshi.

"Humans be telling heuller how calm and nice it be. Heuller be not knowing words, but if humans be sincere, heuller be hearing tone. After food be gone, humans leave pen. Come back at the next rise of Brightstar and we be continuing training."

Within two weeks, Fasart and the two humans had trained the heuller to accept the strange robotic bodies of the humans on its topside. Elizabeth had given the heuller the name "Capercaillie" after her horse at home. The three were soon taking training trips along the roads around the farm, Hiroshi and Elizabeth on top of Capercaillie, Fasart on his own heuller. Although the humans were primarily in control of the young heuller through its antenna reins, Fasart kept a loose lead attached to Capercaillie's muzzle, the other end of which was firmly gripped in an upper foot of his larger mount.

One day, their practice jaunts took them along the circular road just inside the low wall that marked the outer boundary of Camalor. From their vantage point on top of the large animals, they could easily see the no-man's-land between the Camalor wall and the neighboring Harvamor wall. Elizabeth pulled Capercaillie to a halt and pointed to something moving around on the barren ice.

"What is that?" she asked.

Fasart stopped and took a look. "It be a stray iceworm," e said. "Sometimes iceworms continue tunneling away om where they be placed in the tunnel instead of coming ack along the path they made. They not be getting the roper nourishment from just fresh ice, so they be coming to urface to look for fungus. Humans be staying here. Fasart be oing back to border gate and going out to capture the stray eworm." He jumped nimbly down to the ground and fas- ned Capercaillie's muzzle lead to the ice with a spiral metal oop.

"You had better hurry," Hiroshi said. "Someone just mped over the Harvamor wall and is running out to get the eworm."

"Harvamors be better thieves than farmers," Fasart mut- red. He jumped back onto his heuller with a single leap and ok off at a rippling gallop, his voice ringing out over the ether.

"To Wall! To Wall! The Harvamors be coming!"

While Hiroshi kept an eye on the Harvamor, Elizabeth oked back at the farm.

"Samart and Dirmat heard him," she said. "They've got eir hauberks on and are riding out on the other heuller, ikes at the ready. Looks like they're going to beat Fasart to e gate."

"The Harvamor has the iceworm," Hiroshi said. "But it is big one and is giving him some trouble. It wiggled away. ow he's got it again."

"You should see the apprentices soon. They just went hrough the border gate."

"He sees them too. Ugh! He just pitched the iceworm ith his dagger."

"He isn't going to make it carrying that worm." Elizabeth urned to follow the riders with her eye. Both humans could ow see all the action. "The boys are going to catch him. ops! He's dropped the worm and is running for the border as fast as his ten legs will carry him. I've never seen a kerack gallop on all ten feet before."

"It's still going to be close," Hiroshi predicted as the apprentices spurred on their mount, their pikes extending well in front of the speeding animal.

"I don't think I want to look." The image in Elizabeth's eyeglobe closed her eyes.

"Uh-oh!" Hiroshi said, and Elizabeth's eyes popped open again. "Here comes a Harvamor border-guard warrior on a war-heuller."

"Those young farmboys will be no match for a trained warrior."

"Samart! Dirmat! Back!" roared Fasart, coming up behind them on his heuller. The young men reined their heuller around and wisely retreated. When Fasart got close enough, Dirmat jumped onto his heuller with his pike so that both animals were partially protected from the warrior's lance. The warrior, although outnumbered three to one, advanced cautiously, driving them back.

"To Wall! To Wall!" Fasart shouted again, and answers came from distant Camalor border guards as they galloped their war-heullers to the rescue. The Harvamor thief who had started the whole thing was now on top of the Harvamor border wall, also giving the alarm.

With border guards on the way to back them up, Samart and Dirmat became braver. When they had backed up to where the dead iceworm lay, they convinced Fasart to hold ground. They stood guard over the iceworm, their heuller grumbling loudly at all the work they had just been asked to do, while the Harvamor warrior drew closer. His lance was slightly longer than their pikes, but he knew that if he attempted to ride at one of them, the other would strike him in the side. He also knew that his armor was strong, and that their pikes were crude and handled by amateurs, but the points on the pikes were sharp, and if they got in a lucky blow he would be the main course at the next warrior din-

ner. Still, there was no way his pride would allow him to
retreat from mere farmers. Coming to a halt at a distance that
would give his heuller time to come up to speed, he growled
a threat.

"You be touching that iceworm and you be pithed like it
be!"

Dirmat had been considering jumping down, quickly
grabbing the iceworm, and jumping back up, but he thought
better of it. Some young Harvamor farmers in light chain mail
and carrying pikes arrived to back up the warrior. Fasart and
Samart backed their heullers away while waiting for the Camalor border guard warriors to ride up and reinforce them.

The Harvamor warrior made use of the temporary advantage of his side. Pretending that he was going to rush at them
with his lance, he instead rode his heuller back and forth
over the body of the dead iceworm. The ninety-six feet of the
multikilogram animal splattered the iceworm's still-warm insides out onto the surface, and the modest morsel of food
became a useless, empty bag of skin surrounded by a splotch
of trampled meat, guts, and blood that soon became a frozen
yellow-brown stain in the dirty ice.

"You thieving Harvamors be stealing your last iceworm,"
threatened one of the Camalor guards as he rode up. "The
alarm be spread throughout all Camalor. Rexart and his warriors be soon turning you cowards into heuller food."

A few more border guards showed up from each side,
and more threats were exchanged. Then from a distance in
both cities could be heard the combined voices of hundreds
of warriors chanting, "To Wall! To Wall!"

"You farmers be going behind the border wall while we
be covering you," said a Camalor border guard with one
copper star on his antenna. "We be then joining you and
awaiting the further orders of Rexart."

Soon both opposing groups had retired behind their border walls. Shortly after that, the perimeter roads behind the
walls were each packed with 625 warriors on war-heullers,

an entire twoff of fully armed, experienced fighters protected by heavy, overlapping metal-plate armor. Following behind were warrior apprentices, also a twoff in number, dressed in lighter chain-mail armor, riding spare war-heullers loaded with spare lances. Following them were the armorers with wagons full of swords, daggers, lances, spare armor parts, and repair tools, chirurgeons and butchers with the tools of their trade, victualers with their wagons loaded with food and spiritberries for the warriors, and stablers with wagons of brush for the heullers.

Behind them was a marching column of young male students from the final school, led by the martial-arts instructor. They were dressed in armor made of pads, helmets made of wicker, and shields made of shell. However, the dull points on their practice pikes had been replaced with sharp metal tips, and there were real daggers in their back scabbards. As they marched past the farmlands between the city and the boundary wall, their ranks were joined by rows of young farm apprentices riding in on farm heullers from the nearby fields, dressed in chain-mail hauberks and carrying pikes, metal shields, and daggers. Behind them thronged on foot most of the rest of the adult population of Camalor, males and females alike, carrying ornamental maces, swords, and daggers, kitchen knives, brush forks, hammers, or any other sharp or heavy implement they had found handy when they had heard the cry "To Wall!" The only people left in the city were the Queen and her court, the children and their crèche teachers, and border-guard warriors on duty at the walls facing the other neighboring cities of Belator and Zamabor.

Fasart and his two apprentices were called before Rexart to explain what had happened. The apprentices were awed by the huge and regal warrior commander, encased in elaborately engraved, bejeweled, gold-covered titanium-plate armor, his antennae solid with gold rings and tipped with multispiked gold stars of command, and holding his helmet with its diamond coronet around a thick diamond eyeglobe guard. Beside Rexart stood Mordet and other subordinate commanders, sporting a mixture of gold, silver, and copper stars of command on their antennae.

"You three be acting well and bravely in the defense of the honor of Camalor," Rexart said when they had finished their account of the events. He made a sign to a young warrior in attendance, who opened a carrying pouch and pulled out a bag. Rexart took three silver antenna rings out of the bag and awarded one to each of them for bravery. They were then dismissed, and the two apprentices joined the ranks of the pike battlegroups while Fasart rode off to collect the humans, who were watching everything from the nearby field where he had left them.

"What is going to happen now?" Elizabeth asked after Fasart joined them.

"There be a war," Fasart said calmly. Then his anger rose and his voice roared out over the aether. "Camalor be teaching those cowardly, lazy Harvamors not to steal!"

"It was just an iceworm," Hiroshi protested. "Considering that it came up about halfway between the two border walls, it could have been an iceworm from either side, as far as you know."

Hiroshi's protest was drowned out by a parade-ground bellow from Rexart. Standing tall on his golden-colored, plate-armored war-heuller, he gave the order, "Warriors of Camalor! Form battle ranks! The Queen be living ever!"

"The Queen be living ever!" the warriors shouted, and the response was echoed by the gathering populace. The subordinate commanders soon had their mounted warriors and pike battlegroups streaming through the gateways, while the foot battlegroups easily clambered over the low border walls and re-formed on the other side. Soon the 625 mounted and armored warriors were arrayed in a line. They were divided into five battlegroups of 125 warriors, each led by a fi'fifion. The central battlegroup of battle-hardened vet-

erans, under Fi'fifion Mordet, were the shock troops, their
flanks guarded by the two experienced battlegroups on either side led by Fi'fifions Galart and Laslot, while the outer
battlegroups of more lightly armored younger warriors led
by Fi'fifions Gawart and Perset were used as mobile cavalry.
Arrayed behind the mounted warriors were pike troops protecting the warrior apprentices on the spare war-heuller
mounts carrying extra lances and weapons. Behind them the
populace crowded along the top of the border wall and
spread out on the flanks where they could observe the battle.
In the meantime, the equally large forces of Harvamor had
arranged themselves in a similar fashion outside their boundary wall. Insults flew, and warriors and civilians on both
sides stoked up their courage with claws full of spiritberries
from their carrying pouches. The acoustic clatter of hundreds
of armored tongueflaps clapping back after a spiritberry had
been popped into the food hole underneath added a surreal
dimension to the tension in the air.

Fasart helped the humans find a place on the wall where
they could observe, and moored their heuller below the wall
in case it was necessary for them to leave. Merlene found
them there and leapt agilely up on the wall next to them, her
wizard's cape twirling about her as she landed. She was
carrying a meat cleaver in one claw and a brush fork in the
other.

"Merlene be bringing the old brush fork Fasart be storing
at home," she said, handing him the sharp, two-pronged
instrument.

"Merlene be remembering my final-school daggers?" he
asked.

"Betruth." She reached into her large carrying pouch and
pulled out two scabbards and belts. Fasart unsheathed the
daggers and removed from each the curved piece of blunted
metal that covered the sharp point and blade edge when the
dagger was used in practice. Soon he too was ready for

battle, with his farm dagger and brush fork in his first pair of claws and his school daggers in his second pair.

"Merlene be staying with the humans," he said. "This war be none of their concern."

He jumped down from the wall and joined the other males arrayed on the flanks of the battle, all armed with at least one implement.

"This looks like total war!" Rob audiolinked. "All being fought over the kerack equivalent of a stolen pig!"

The Camalor troops were ready first, and Rexart didn't hesitate to take advantage of that. Standing tall on his war-heuller behind the front line of mounted warriors, where he could keep a close eye on the whole battle, he straightened out his antennae for maximum coupling to the aether and broadcast, "ATTACK! The Queen be living ever!"

With the paean to the Queen echoing back from their antennae, the line of warriors attacked along a broad front, galloping straight at the enemy lines with their shields raised and their lances lowered. The Harvamor warriors quickly formed themselves and kicked their war-heullers into the attack.

Hiroshi watched the advancing lines carefully. "I notice that Mordet, who started out ahead of his troops, has allowed them to pass him by."

"But there are absolutely no tactics being used in this battle!" Elizabeth exclaimed. "Even Harold had better tactics than Rexart, and he *lost* the Battle of Hastings. No preliminary skirmishes, no cavalry attacks to disorganize their lines, no flanking marches, nothing! Not even a preliminary arrow barrage."

"That last statement of yours brings up an interesting point," Hiroshi said. "The keracks don't seem to have bows and arrows—or any missile weapon, for that matter."

Merlene heard Elizabeth and Hiroshi use the strange military terms and was going to ask them what they meant, but the aether was now full of battle cries and yells of pain as the warriors clashed. Although it took some effort, she forced a phonetic memory of the unfamiliar sound patterns, so she could look up the words in the Lookman later.

The initial collision of the two lines of mounted warriors resulted in the shattering of many lances on both sides. Most of them had shattered on shields, knocking warriors off their heullers. Some warriors had been struck in the armor, and a few unfortunate ones were struck at a juncture between two plates of armor. Many of these collapsed with cries of pain as their blood squirted out, causing their insides to lose pressure and start to freeze. Five exploded, covering those nearby with yellow-brown gore. One of those covered with gore was Mordet. Following behind his front line of troops, he thrust the tip of his lance between the weak side plates of a Harvamor warrior who had already shattered his lance in his encounter with one of Mordet's warriors in the front line.

"Now it looks just like the melee in the Oval," said Elizabeth.

"Except a lot more serious," Hiroshi noted soberly as they heard the death cry of another exploding warrior.

Those warriors who were still mounted and had intact lances whirled and turned to attack enemy warriors who had shattered theirs. Meanwhile, those who had lost their lances pulled out their maces and were fighting their way back to their lines to get new lances. When an apprentice saw his master coming, he would ride out through gaps in the pike battlegroups and deliver it to him. Until they could get back behind the safety of the pike battlegroups, these apprentices, in their light chain-mail armor, were easy prey for the lances and maces of the still-mounted, experienced warriors who had managed to penetrate to the rear of the enemy line.

Warriors who had been knocked off their heullers were soon locked in combat with enemy warriors who had suffered the same fate. Battles with maces ensued, the objective being to first disarm the opponent by battering his mace or shield away, then to damage the plate armor sufficiently so hat a jab with a dagger would penetrate the exposed shell underneath. Occasionally a lucky hack with the sharp, thick, axlike blade of the dagger would sever a first-leg joint. Without his warclaw, the opponent was easy prey.

"Re-form!" came the command from Rexart, followed soon after by a similar command from the Harvamor commander, Tapart. Fighting their way back to their own lines under the protection of their mounted comrades, the surviving dismounted warriors were met by their apprentices, who had gathered their heullers. The apprentices helped the heavily armored warriors remount, supplied them with replacement weapons, and refreshed them with berries—mostly spiritberries. Those with injuries or broken armor retired behind the boundary wall, where their needs were taken care of by either chirurgeons or armorers.

"What is going on now!" Elizabeth cried when she saw keracks on both sides rushing onto the abandoned battlefield. The pike troops were first. They had moved out to provide protection to the regrouping warriors, but now, under the command of minor-ranked commanders, they advanced over ice littered with dead and disabled warriors. Behind them came many civilians.

"Merlene must be going now," said Merlene. "It be her duty to the Queen." She jumped off the wall and ran to join the crowd, meat cleaver held high.

"They are killing the enemy wounded!" Hiroshi exclaimed, watching as a fallen Harvamor warrior with his warclaw cut off and his walking legs paralyzed by a puncture in the lower thorax attempted to defend himself. He had a sword in his one good front claw and both his daggers in his second claws, and was keeping a crowd of about twenty Camalor commoners at bay. The crowd poked at him with sharp implements, but his helmet was still on and his armor was still good, so they were making little progress. When the crowd surrounding him saw Merlene passing by with her meat cleaver, they called her over. One of the males attempted to talk her into giving him the weapon, but she refused. The sword hand of the Harvamor warrior was temporarily pinned to the crust by a farmer's brush fork, and, as Hiroshi and Elizabeth watched in horror, Merlene darted in and chopped through the first-claw joint with her cleaver. One of the males picked up the sword, used it to knock the daggers out of the warrior's second set of claws, and soon the sword point found a chink in the armor. The warrior exploded. Dripping with gore, the crowd hauled the heavily armored body back toward the Camalor boundary, their progress covered by a squad of pike troops. All over the battlefield, similar scenes were taking place as the bodies of dead warriors were retrieved. Some Harvamor warriors had re-formed and were now reentering the battlefield with new lances. They cantered forward, followed by pike troops on the run. They approached Merlene's group, still hauling the heavy warrior toward a distant gate in the boundary wall. Skirting around the defending pike troops, the warriors rode the civilians down, then scattered the pike troops. The Camalor civilians abandoned the corpse of the Harvamor warrior as well as that of a Camalor female who had been run through by a lance. Once the Camalor civilians had left the body, the warriors stopped their attack, and Harvamor pike troops moved up and assumed guard while Harvamor civilians attempted to drag the two corpses back to their side.

Mordet had seen the skirmish, however, and soon he was there at the head of a larger force of Camalor warriors, and the bodies were recovered by the Camalor side without further loss of life.

"You be licking your wounds," Mordet bellowed at the retreating figures. "We be attacking again soon."

"You be licking yourself, you Camalor coward," came the reply.

Merlene soon joined the humans back on top of the wall. The yellow-brown gore on her black velvet wizard's skirt was now frozen, and most of it came off when she picked at it with a claw.

"Merlene be needing a sample bag," she told Hiroshi. He reached into his carrying pouch and pulled out a plastic bag with a self-sealing closure. Merlene carefully put her gory meat cleaver in the bag, sealed it carefully, and put it in her carrying pouch.

"Merlene be displaying her treasure in the living room so that all may admire her part in the rout of the odious Harvanors," she said.

Elizabeth could hardly believe what she had heard. Trying to bring some rationality into the discussion by pointing out that the incident had not been without loss to Camalor, she asked, "Who was the female from Camalor who was killed?"

"That be Arpene," said Merlene, showing little concern. "It be fortunate that her soul be going to our Queen."

"Arpene, the concertleader?" Hiroshi gasped. "The Arpene whose compositions are the delight and wonder of two worlds?"

"Betruth." Merlene picked at a bit of gore on her wizard's cape.

"What was a genius like *that* doing on a battlefield where she could get killed?" Elizabeth exclaimed, her voice raised in annoyance and astonishment. "For that matter, what were *you* doing on the battlefield? You are the Wizard of Camalor, not a warrior."

"Merlene be doing her duty to the Queen." The position of her antennae indicated puzzlement at the question. "All in Camalor be warriors for the Queen."

"I guess we'd better drop that line of questioning," Rob audiolinked.

"They are lining up again," said Hiroshi, looking out at the battlefield.

Elizabeth looked away. "I don't think I want to watch."

"It's about time for a shift change, anyway," Rob said. "Selke and I will 'port in and take over."

After Rob and Selke were installed in the telebots, the whole procedure was repeated: a clash of heavily armored warriors, pitched battles between individuals and small groups, numerous casualties, a call by both sides for a regrouping, and then the civilian task of finishing off the enemy wounded and dragging the bodies in, at considerable risk to themselves. By this time, however, Brightstar was setting in the west. Rexart and his bodyguard rode out and met with Tapart, the commander of the Harvamor forces, and a truce was arranged until the following morning. Both sides pulled back behind their boundary walls. The warriors made camp in the frontier fields, and their food was brought out to them by their victualers.

The chirurgeons loaded up their wagons with injured warriors who had survived their wounds and managed to escape the post-battle slaughter, and hauled them back to the Courtyard o'Warriors to recuperate. Those who had suffered punctures small enough to seal off quickly, before the innards started to boil, suffered mostly from internal frostbite. They would be out of action until the next molt. The chirurgeons would give them lots of bloodberries to build up their body fluids, gasberries to build up their internal pressure, and spiritberries to restore their spirits. The victualers would be instructed to feed them plenty in the coming days to fatten them up and hurry their next molt along. After the molt they would have a new body. Those who lost a warclaw were not as fortunate. The smaller limbs would regenerate, but not the specialized warclaw. But the injured were few. Most casualties of the battle were dead, usually from explosive decompression.

The butchers set up shop and started work on the dead. The souls of all those who died, whether from Camalor or Harvamor, were carefully extracted, cleaned in dry sand, and sent back to the Courtyard o'Warriors in a special wagon.

The shells were removed; and the carapaces of Camalor warriors were set aside for engraving and delivery to the final school to serve as inspiration for future generations of warriors. The rest of the shells were hacked up and fed to the heullers, who made short work of them with their diamond molars.

Soon the whole warrior corps was gathered around large tables, feasting on the fallen bodies of their comrades and foes. Bowls of spiritberries were on every table, and they were kept constantly filled by the victualer's apprentices. Those who weren't warriors, or attending to the needs of the warriors, returned home to make dinner, tend to their neglected businesses, and take over the care of their younger children.

Merlene, knowing that Jordat would be busy taking care of the needs of Fi'fifion Laslot and Fasart would be busy catching up with farm business, got Solene out of crèche school and fed her dinner while telling her all about the battle and showing off her souvenir. Proud of her mother, Solene helped to hang up the meat cleaver with its yellow-brown-blood-stained blade on the living room wall. Then Merlene sent Solene to her room to practice her singing while she went downstairs to her workshop. She went directly to the Lookman and soon found the entry on bows and arrows.

"These be amazing weapons!" she said in astonishment. "They be killing enemy warriors at great distances!" Prompted by key words at the end of the entry, she looked up the entry entitled 'Longbow.'

"The English humans be killing the French humans even though the French humans be wearing heavy armor." The parallels of the Battle of Agincourt with the ongoing battle with Harvamor were obvious. If Merlene could arm the warriors of Camalor with bows and arrows, then the Harvamors would be routed.

"The arrow be like a small pike," she mused as she read

the description. "The bow be like those used by the diamond drillers, except the string be taut instead of wrapped around the drill." It didn't take long for Merlene to make a small bow and notch a stick. Then she realized why bows, although they had existed on Ice as drilling tools for so long their origin was unknown, had never been turned into weapons of war. On a kerack, the legs emerged from the front of the thorax, but on humans the arms emerged from the sides of the trunk. A human could extend one arm out to the side, turn sideways, and still have enough muscle strength to draw the string on a bow back a great distance, bending the bow significantly and storing up lots of energy. A kerack could only pull the bowstring towards its chest, hardly stressing the bow. That was also why keracks didn't throw rocks or sharp pikes at each other—their bodies weren't built for throwing. When Merlene attempted to fire her arrow, it barely made it across the workshop room and bounced harmlessly off the wall and fell to the floor.

"Two!" she swore. She was sorely disappointed that she wouldn't be able to use her wizardry skills to aid Camalor and her Queen. She went back to the Lookman and read some more. She soon found mention of a device called a crossbow, in which a crank mechanism was used to draw the bow. There was no doubt that such a device could be made by Camalor artisans, but the construction of the complex machine would take far too long for it to be of any value in the present battle. She was about to turn off the Lookman and return to taking care of Solene when she ran across a cross-reference to a device called a "footbow" . . .

". . . and he be not noticing Mordet until the lance burst his shell!" Fi'fifion Mordet hicced with laughter. Full of spiritberries and flesh, surrounded by admirers, Mordet was enjoying himself. Then he noticed Fi'fifion Laslot approach his dining table. His demeanor rapidly changed and he was all business.

"Be there problems?" he asked.

"There be no problems, Subcommander Mordet," replied Laslot. "But perhaps there be opportunities. Jordat, warrior apprentice to Laslot, be son of Merlene, the Wizard o'Camalor. Jordat be informing Laslot that Merlene be inventing a new weapon. Rexart be busy at this time, so Laslot be informing Subcommander Mordet."

Mordet knew well that "busy" meant that Rexart had eaten too many spiritberries again. Mordet would not regret the day that Rexart lost his warclaw——or worse. The Queen deserved a better consort.

"What sort this new weapon be?"

"It be killing Harvamors at a distance."

"A long lance?" Mordet queried. "That be too awkward to carry."

"The killing distance be fi'five lance lengths."

"Mordet be seeing this!" He left the dining table. Mordet liked killing Harvamors, but he didn't like having to get close to them to do so.

He followed Laslot to a nearby field, where he invoked the Spirit o'Camalor and immediately knew the identities of the three people who were waiting there. The one in the apprentice warrior Cape o'Trade was Jordat, the one in the wizard Cape o'Trade was Merlene, and the one in the dancer Cape o'Trade was Danceleader Cormene. Cormene was dressed in her dance tights, which showed off the shape of her body. Mordet, having never been this close to a nearly naked dancer before, felt a little uncomfortable.

Some distance from where they waited, propped up against a brush stack, were the remains of a dead Harvamor warrior still in his armor but with his soul ripped out. The butchers had been busy preparing dead Camalor warriors for that night's warrior dinner, and had not yet gotten around to turning the Harvamor dead into food.

Merlene showed Mordet the bow and arrow. She had used her pantograph to trace the outline of a compound bow and had taken it to Icecaster Nirene. Nirene had carved out a mold, arranged some metal fibers in it to increase the strength under tension, and cast a crude bow. Meanwhile, Merlene had visited an armorer, who fixed some lance heads on shafts of various thicknesses for her. Merlene knew, from what she had read in the Lookman, that an arrow was normally kept directed in flight by feathers, but if the head was heavy enough, no feathers were needed. A few experiments with the bow soon determined the right shaft length and thickness, and a short while later, Merlene was back at the border with the bow, arrows, and her choice for archer.

"This weapon be very simple in construction," said Mordet, looking at the curved bow with its taut string and the lance head on its small shaft, notched at one end. "How be it used by a warrior?"

There was a long pause; then Merlene finally answered. "Merlene be trying to teach Jordat to use the bow and arrow. Males be unable to operate it properly. Their warclaw be longer than their other claw. Only females, with both front claws the same length, be able to strike the target accurately. Cormene be now demonstrating."

Cormene grabbed the bow string in the middle with both front claws. Letting the bow hang down, she stepped on it with both back feet, grabbing it firmly with her prehensile back pincers. Then, tucking her tail under and rolling backward, she lay on the ground with her three middle sets of legs stretched out to the side to maintain her precarious balance, and assumed the posture that dancers called the supine position. Merlene reached over and notched an arrow onto the bowstring between Cormene's two front claws, putting the point across the bow between Cormene's two hind feet. Cormene fired, then quickly drew the bowstring and fired again, and again, as fast as Merlene could notch the arrows. Cormene was still learning how to aim, so many of the arrows flew too high or too low, but the last three were buried deep in the Harvamor corpse.

Mordet went down and used his gigantic warclaw to pull the corpse away from the brush stack it had been pinned to.

"These lancelets be going right through both layers of armor and shell like they be lard," he said in amazement. He turned to Merlene. "How quickly can more of these be made?"

"Nirene be already making more molds for both bows and arrow shafts," Merlene replied. "Any metalsmith be having annealing and tempering ovens that be adequate for melting ice."

"And there be plenty of lance heads in the armory," added Laslot.

The danceleader spoke up. "Cormene be pledging two fives fi'fives dancers from her dance troupe to wield the bows. The females can stretch the bows and the males can notch the arrows."

"Two fives fi'fives! That be two battlegroups!" roared Mordet, both surprised and pleased. "Rexart be having to make up a new rank for a two times fi'fifion!" He hicced a loud laugh as he imagined the thoughts of the heavily armored, mounted Harvamor warriors riding forth and finding themselves faced with row upon row of nearly naked dancers lying on their backs. Suddenly he turned serious. "There be not much time before Brightstar rises and the truce be over. Can the bows and arrows be made in time for the dancers to be learning to wield them?"

Both Merlene and Cormene hesitated. Laslot broke the silence.

"Laslot be delaying the start of battle by going out to issue a challenge to a fi'fifion from the Harvamor side for individual combat to the death. The preparations for the combat and the combat itself will gain us sufficient time."

Mordet was taken aback. He himself would not have made such an offer. He was not a coward, but the Harvamor fi'fifions were equal in strength and skill to their Camalor equivalents. There was an even chance of dying. Mordet had not risen to his present rank by taking on those sorts of odds along the way. Indeed, he had always arranged beforehand that the odds would be on his side. Having two extra battle-groups of warriors that would strike at the enemy *before* he had to enter the battle—that was the kind of situation Mordet liked best.

"We be proceeding accordingly!" he decided. "Laslot, if you be assuring that Merlene be getting all necessary assistance from the armorers, Mordet be approaching Rexart and be convincing him of the wisdom of our plans."

Laslot, knowing that Rexart nearly always did what Mordet suggested, told Jordat to make sure Laslot's weapons were sharp and his armor and heüller were ready, then led Merlene to the encampment of the armorers.

Cormene sent out through the Spirit o'Camalor a call for her dancers to don their dancing tights and assemble at once in a field near the boundary wall. She had already choreographed in her mind a series of training exercises that would prepare her dancers so that they would be able to accurately handle the bows and arrows as soon as the weapons were delivered to them by the smiths and casters of the city.

As Mordet was turning to leave, Cormene called after him. "Cormene and her dancers be proud that they now be able to engage directly in battle against the foes of Camalor instead of be only watching from the sidelines."

As Mordet heard those proud words that showed the spirit of the dancers, he had to keep his glance averted so as not to display the unwarriorlike, rapid nictitations of his eyeglobe that her comment had aroused.

The Queen be surely well served by her people, he thought as he strode away towards Rexart's encampment.

The next morning Boris and Gabrielle were in the telebots and up on the wall with the rest of the populace. Merlene, her night's work just completed with the delivery of five fi'five bows and two twoff's of arrows to Cormene's dance troupe, was on the wall next to them. Just as Brightstar started to rise, a single Camalor warrior exited the gate in the boundary wall and rode forth onto the battle plain, his apprentice following behind on a heuller holding spare lances and other weapons in its upward-facing set of feet.

"Isn't that Jordat?" asked Boris. "I recognize him because of the five copper rings and the silver ball on his right antenna."

"Betruth." Merlene pushed out her black wizard's chestcoat with pride.

"What are they doing going out alone?" Boris asked.

"Laslot be issuing a challenge for individual combat to the Harvamor fi'fifions."

"Just as pretentious and macho as the knights in armor of the Normans and Franks in the olden days," Gabrielle muttered.

After many challenges and insults had been passed back and forth, a Harvamor challenger was found for Laslot. It was Fi'fifion Badart. He too rode out on the battlefield supported only by his apprentice.

As everyone watched and cheered, the two knights raised their shields, lowered their lances, and charged. They struck each other's shields with a crashing blow. Lances shattered, but both stayed on their heullers. Wheeling around, they returned to their apprentices, who handed them new lances. Again they kicked on their mounts and charged at each other. Lances shattered again, but this time Laslot was knocked off his heuller to the ice. Badart raced back to his apprentice to get a new lance and whirled with the intent of impaling Laslot from behind while he was running back to mount his spare heuller. Jordat, seeing that Laslot was going to lose the unfair race, kicked his heuller right in between Laslot and the onrushing Badart. Badart's lance ripped Jordat's cape off the neck of his chestcoat; then the two heullers collided, sending both animals and riders tumbling. With Badart unmounted, the battle between the two warriors resumed on equal terms. Maces crashed against armor, the sharp spikes seeking a chink that would allow a disabling puncture. Daggers thrust at bodies and struck at joints. The battle went on and on. Badart lost a midclaw; then Laslot lost two, both the second and third on his warclaw side. But third claws were almost as good as second claws when wielding daggers, and when Laslot was forced to switch both daggers to the same side, Badart was faced with different infighting tactics than he was used to. He made a mistake—and one of Laslot's daggers buried itself to the hilt in Badart's mouth. Badart exploded.

Cheers arose from the crowd as Laslot and Jordat stood guard over the corpse until the butchers came running out to drag it back inside the Camalor wall. Rexart and Mordet rode out to congratulate the warrior on his victory. Laslot was awarded a gold ring for defeating an enemy in individual combat, and Jordat was awarded a silver ring for bravery.

"Be the preparations finished?" Laslot asked, forced to use his elbow joint instead of the claw on his second leg for the heuller reins. "Or shall Laslot be making another challenge?"

"The archers be ready," Mordet assured him. "But as we be riding back, touch antennas, for Mordet be having a plan."

"Rexart still say it be a cowardly plan," Rexart grumbled with a blurred voice. "Full attack be the warrior way to battle."

Laslot realized from Rexart's voice that Mordet had been keeping him well supplied with spiritberries throughout the night.

"We be making a full attack," Mordet assured Rexart. "It just be that having a troop of archers requires different 'tactics.' "

"Laslot not understand. What be this word *tactics* meaning?"

"Tactics be meaning 'battle plan,' " Mordet explained. "Mordet be learning about it from Wizard Merlene."

"Battle *plan?*" Laslot was now more confused than ever. "Battles be not planned. Battles be started, but once they be started, they be having no plan."

Mordet touched an antenna to Laslot's. "Laslot be listening. Mordet be explaining."

Brightstar was high in the sky as the time for the battle approached.

"Here come the warriors out in force," Gabrielle said.

"And the slaughter begins again." Boris's voice was grim. "I was hoping the keracks would be more civilized in their behavior."

"It is no different from what humans did in the Middle Ages," Gabrielle pointed out. "Fortunately they don't have machine guns, guided bombs, or intercontinental ballistic missiles."

Over the audiolink Hiroshi said, "Elizabeth and I were noticing yesterday that they had no missile weapons of any kind. No javelins, slings, bows and arrows, nothing that is thrown at the enemy. I wonder why? Someday we'll have to ask Merlene."

"Not now," said Boris. "The mounted warriors are all lined up in a row in front like they were yesterday. The attack is about to be launched any moment."

Gabrielle suddenly cried, "Look who's coming out from behind the pike troops! They are the dance troupe, in their dance tights!"

The dancers, in two battlegroups, formed in ranks to the right and left of the five battlegroups of mounted warriors, a little ahead and facing each other instead of the enemy.

"They are carrying something," Boris said. He set the visible imager lens inside his telebot's eyeglobe on zoom mode and zoomed down on the strange warriors as they literally danced out onto the field. "The females are carrying bows and the males are carrying arrows."

"Where did they get those!" Hiroshi yelled over the audio-link. "They didn't have them yesterday."

Merlene, proud of her contribution, said, "Those be the archery battlegroups. Hiroshi be talking about bows and arrows yesterday, so Merlene be going home and reading about them on the Lookman. They be simple to make. Camalor be grateful for help of humans."

Elizabeth was going to yell at Hiroshi, but when she looked over from her monitor chair to see his appalled face, pale with shock, she realized he was berating himself enough internally.

Boris sighed. "If only we had known about these wars beforehand. We wouldn't have been tempted to give her the Lookman."

"You can make a weapon out of anything," Gabrielle said cynically. "It will be Camalor's turn to be surprised when the Harvamors show up with improved bows and arrows at the next battle."

"I feel terrible," Boris said. "We have started an arms race."

"We cannot put the genie back in the bottle," said Gabrielle fatalistically. "Better switch your video back to wide view—the Harvamors are attacking."

For once Mordet was out in front of his troops, riding back and forth to keep them in place.

"Mordet!" roared Rexart from his command position in the rear. "The Harvamors be starting their attack. Should Rexart be giving the command?"

"Not yet!" Mordet called. "Not until they reach the archers! Remember, Rexart be first commanding 'Release!' Then Rexart be counting to fi'five. Then Rexart be commanding 'Attack!' " He turned and growled to his men, "Back! Fi'fifion Mordet be saying 'Back!' "

The grizzled warriors of his elite first battlegroup, some with midclaws missing from the previous day's battle, backed reluctantly away from the oncoming enemy, grumbling as loudly as their mounts. When the enemy warriors saw them shrinking from the fight instead of rushing to attack, they spurred their mounts on harder, and the center of the enemy line pushed forward. Meanwhile, to the right and left, Laslot and Galart were also backing up their warriors, but at the same time they were turning them so that they faced the battlefield. The outside battlegroup of lighter-armored warriors held their ground but rotated until they were lined up parallel with the ranks of archers that faced inward.

"Why aren't they launching a frontal attack like they did yesterday?" Boris asked.

"Merlene be telling Mordet about Lookman of humans," said Merlene. "Mordet be very interested and be coming to view Lookman. Merlene be showing Mordet entry on 'Tactics' that Elizabeth be mentioning the previous day."

It was now Elizabeth's turn to feel guilty pangs of conscience.

"Mordet be very interested in tactics at Battle of Ag-incort and Battle of Kre-cee."

"Where the French knights were murdered by English archers," Gabrielle growled. "And we are about to witness a repeat!"

As the Harvamor warriors approached the gap between the two battlegroups of archers, Rexart gave the command "Release!" The female dancers assumed the supine position and pulled on their bowstrings, the males each notched an arrow, and 250 deadly missiles arced into the oncoming horde. The heullers, which had previously endured few casualties, now suffered as much as the warriors, rolling over onto their riders as they attempted to pluck the offending thorns from their topsides. The flights of death from the sky continued, and the outer ranks of the Harvamor horde collapsed toward the center as they tried to evade the deadly barrage.

"ATTACK!" roared Rexart, relieved that the real battle could finally begin. Mordet let his frustrated warriors go, and they thundered past him toward the oncoming front, now so compressed that the Harvamor warriors were getting in each other's way. Laslot and the other fi'fifions also let their warriors attack; only now, instead of a frontal assault, they were attacking from the flanks, where their lances had a devastating effect as they struck enemy warriors from the side instead of the front. The Harvamors were soon completely surrounded by lances. The archers, meanwhile, kept the Harvamor apprentices and pike troops from coming forward to back up their mounted warriors.

Commander Tapart rallied his troops and fought his way back to the Harvamor lines, leaving hundreds of dead and wounded, nearly all of them in Harvamor colors. Camalor pike troops, backed up by the archers, kept the Harvamors at bay, while the cheering populace of Camalor ran onto the battlefield and finished the battle by killing off the wounded and hauling their corpses back behind the boundary wall. Clearing the battlefield took a long time because the number of wounded heullers that had to be killed, butchered into manageable chunks, and dragged off. As the last of the pike troops came through the gate and the Camalor warriors passed around bags of spiritberries, Rexart rode out onto the battlefield with his bodyguard. He was met by the Harvamor commander, Tapart.

"Brightstar be soon setting," Rexart said. "The next day be Fifthday. Rexart and his warriors be leaving the Wall and be enjoying the Fifthday festival."

"Tapart and his warriors also," replied the opposing commander.

"We be not using bows and arrows in future battles. Too many heullers be killed."

"Tapart and his warriors also."

The two groups turned, made their way back through the wall, and the gates closed. As Brightstar set, Rexart led a procession back to the center of the city, the vanguard of warriors led by a leaping, gamboling troupe of elated dancers improvising dance routines using the new tools of their trade, the curved bow and the straight arrow.

"That's it?" Elizabeth said as she watched the crowd leave the scene on the monitor back at the base. "I thought for sure that once they had routed the enemy troops, they would invade Harvamor and at least loot it, if not take it over or kill the populace."

Hiroshi added, "It certainly doesn't make sense. There seem to be no territorial ambitions. It is as if they just wanted some excuse to go out and kill each other. They are acting just like humans!"

"Merlene be going to home to prepare for Fifthday," said Merlene. "Humans be joining?"

"I think we should close down the telebots for a while to discuss what we just observed," Gabrielle told her. "If you leave Capercaillie here, we will ride it in later to join you."

"Merlene be going, then." She hopped off the wall and followed the crowd.

Gabrielle blinked off, but Boris, seeing something that had been left out on the battlefield, paused to zoom his telebot video lens in on the object . . .

It was the trampled skin of the dead iceworm.

9
PARENTS OF THE CHILD

JUST BEFORE THE rise of Brightstar on Fifthday, Rob and Selke rode into town on Capercaillie and hitched the beast next to Fasart's heuller in the yard. Merlene, hearing the tramp and grumble of their heuller, came to the surface to greet them, her kitchen apron protecting her wizard's garments. A short while later the whole family and the two humans were walking into town for the start of the Fifthday festivities.

"The choral concert that be planned for the Oval o'All this Fifthday be canceled," Merlene announced. "In its place be a new dance choreographed by Danceleader Cormene. It be a celebration of the victory of the dance troupe over the enemies of Camalor."

"What happened to the choral concert?" asked Rob, instantly regretting his question when he heard Merlene's answer.

"Concertleader Arpene be killed in battle with Harvamor," she said without emotion. "Without a concertleader to be singing lead in all the parts, the chorus be not functioning properly. The apprentice of Arpene be now communing with the Spirit o'Camalor to extract all the memories Arpene be storing there, but it be many Fifthdays before she be ready to be concertleader."

"Arpene will be missed," said Selke, who already preferred listening to Arpene's music on her Lookman rather than her old Earth-composer favorites.

After waiting in the park through the lengthy Service o'Giving, the humans joined the keracks to watch the new dance in the Oval o'All. In place of music, Danceleader Cormene had formed a portion of her troupe into a percussion band. They had an assortment of battered Harvamor armor and shields on which they beat the time with maces, sending out weak sound waves in the rarefied air of Ice while emitting from their antennae distant-sounding echoes of the shouts and screams of battle. The combined radio and acoustic sounds of conflict formed the background for the artistic recreation of the recent battle from the viewpoint of the dancers who had formed the archery battlegroups.

Two groups of dancers formed in ranks along the sides of the stage, prancing and posturing with their bows and arrows, while between them "rode" blustering male dancers playing the part of mounted Harvamor warriors. They were "astride" female dancers on all two-fives, playing the part of Harvamor war-heullers. At a signal from Cormene, the female archers assumed the supine position while the male archers bent low over them, arrows held in their warclaws. The females pretended to shoot their bows, following which the males carried the arrows across the stage in acrobatic bounds, where they directed them unerringly into the chests of the warrior dancers, who died artistically inspired deaths. The male archers danced their arrows back, where they were fired again and again until there was only one Harvamor warrior left, the lead male dancer, wearing a costume similar to the armor, Cape o'Trade, and gold antenna maces of the Harvamor commander. He died in a spectacular climax when the dancing arrows in the last volley arrived at his chest at the same time, then flew off in all directions as if he had exploded.

After the lengthy applause of chirps from the audience had died down, Cormene led her troupe to the royal box, where each one received a gold antenna band for contributing to the great victory against the enemies of Camalor. When the last of the 250 rings had been awarded, Rexart raised his ceremonial golden mace.

"The war be over. The Queen be living ever!"

"The Queen be living ever!" echoed the crowd.

Rob, turning to leave, said, "I guess we can go back to the park now."

But Merlene put a restraining claw on him and touched an antenna to his. "Not yet," she whispered.

Rob turned back and saw that the eyeglobes of the crowd in the Oval were now looking down at an entrance tunnel at one end of the grounds. Through the tunnel marched a slow, silent procession of Camalor warriors in their best finery. Each one held in his warclaw a small sphere of silver-gray metal.

"It be the Procession o'Souls," said Merlene. Rexart left the royal box and, followed by Princess Onlone, her escort Mordet, and the rest of the noble ladies and their escorts, went down into the Oval and formed the head of the procession. With Rexart in the lead, they left by the long, wide staircase at the far end and proceeded into the park, heading straight for the dance plaza and the Tower o'Queen.

On, and on, and on, came the long line of warriors, as the crowd stood silent and watched. Finally the last warrior passed, and the crowd streamed out the exits and through the park, picking up morsels of food and especially spiritberries from the sharestands set up along the way.

"I counted two hundred and thirty-two souls," Hiroshi audiolinked. "Considering the light losses on both sides the first day, and the heavy losses inflicted on the Harvamors by the archers on the second day, I would estimate that only thirty or forty were from Camalor troops, while nearly two hundred were from Harvamor warriors. Harvamor had only six hundred-some mounted warriors to start with, so they lost nearly a third of their attacking force."

"That's enough to rout any army," Elizabeth audiolinked.

"You forget that one of those souls came from Arpene," Selke said. "She was worth many armies."

Silently, Rob and Selke followed Merlene through the park. She stopped at the edge of the dance plaza with the rest of the crowd to watch the conclusion of the Procession o'Souls. By the time they got there, Rexart had climbed to the top of the Tower o'Queen and had opened the four doors to reveal the Queen on her throne, wearing her elaborate diamond crown around her eyeglobe and covered by her jeweled golden cape. Princess Onlone and the other princesses had gathered at the base of the tower. One by one, the long line of warriors handed the souls they had been carrying to the High Priest Princess Kitone, who turned each soul over and over, scrutinizing it carefully, then passed it on to Princess Onlone. Princess Onlone put the soul inside a door that had been slid open in the base of the tower.

"What is she doing with them?" Selke whispered to Rob, her antenna touching his. "I can't see."

"Neither can I," Rob replied. "Her back is in the way."

After the long, solemn ceremony was over, there was a short pause while everyone went back to the sharestands to stoke up on food and spiritberries. Then the Queen called them back for the closing dance on the plaza. The humans had learned the rudiments of the complex steps by now, and participated out on the fringes with the younger set, who, having overcome their instinctive distrust of strangers, now hicced hilariously at the humans' clumsy two-pair foot action. Rob and Selke took it good-naturedly.

On the way home, Selke brought up the subject of the Queen and her court.

"I notice that only the Queen and the ladies of the nobility have titles. You must have what we humans call a matriarchy, where the crown passes from the Queen to her nearest female relative when the Queen dies."

"Die?" Merlene repeated loudly, turning abruptly so that her eyeglobe and antennae were focused on Selke. "The Queen be living ever!"

"Well," Rob interjected, "I noticed that she and the princesses stayed far away from the battlefield, so there is little likelihood of their getting killed in battle, but sooner or later she is going to have to die of old age. I assume Princess Regent Onlone will be taking over as Queen when that happens."

Merlene halted, as did Fasart and the children. They all looked at the humans with their antennae cocked in puzzlement. "Merlene be hearing the words from the translator, but not be knowing the meaning of the phrase. What be meaning of 'die of old age'?"

Now it was Rob and Selke's turn to look puzzled. Selke tried to explain.

"All life on earth, with the exception of the most primitive organisms, has a finite life. As time passes, the organism grows to its full size, reaches maturity, and stops growing. After a time it becomes less functional, then finally stops living. The process of becoming less functional and ceasing to live is called dying of old age."

"Life on Ice be not like that," said Merlene. "It be growing, and going though a series of molts. Some forms of life be going though changes in form when molting, like eggs changing into iceworms which change into heullers. But as time goes on, the life form just be getting bigger and bigger with each molt, until it be killed, either by accident or deliberately, during harvest or a war. There be no 'dying of old age' in Camalor."

"Then the phrase 'The Queen be living ever' is literally true!" said Rob. "Camalor has never had any Queen but Queen Une?"

"Betruth. It be the same for the princesses. They be the

same since Merlene be a child, except they be molting occasionally and be growing slightly larger each time."

"They *are* substantially bigger than any other females in the city," Selke remarked.

"Since you were a child," Rob slowly repeated. "How long has it been since you were a child?"

Merlene paused to reckon the number of days. "It be about five fi'five twof'fdays ago."

Rob tried to remember the kerack counting system and method of reckoning time. "Let's see. A twof'fday is a kerack year of six hundred and twenty-five kerack days—roughly two Earth years, since a kerack day is thirty hours instead of twenty-four. And you say you are five fi'five kerack years old?" He paused in astonishment as he worked out the numbers. "You're over two hundred and fifty years old!"

"The princesses be many times older than that," Merlene said. "Certainly five, and perhaps many times more. Merlene be not knowing for certain."

"That makes them thousands of years old!" Selke exclaimed.

"The Queen be the oldest o'All," Merlene concluded.

"That doesn't make sense!" Rob blurted. "Living organism *have* to die of old age."

"Why Rob be saying that?" asked Merlene.

By this time they had arrived home, and while Fasart and the children retired to their rooms to change out of their Fifthday finery, Merlene led the humans down to her workshop, where they could continue their discussion. Having a Ph.D. in biology as well as an M.D. in aerospace medicine, Selke took over the conversation.

"One of the major recent breakthroughs in the understanding of the evolution of life on Earth was the discovery of the evolutionary purpose behind death by old age. Originally it was just a hypothesis, whimsically called the 'Solem Pronouncement on Senescence.' It is no longer considered a hypothesis, but a major law of biological evolution. According to the Solem Senescence Principle, the reason death by old age was invented by nature was to produce a better chance of survival for the species as a whole, at the expense of the survival of the individuals in that species. If the older versions of a species don't die and get out of the way, the newer versions that have mutations with better survival characteristics won't have as much room to develop, as they would if the older versions took themselves out of the competition and let the better versions take over. As estimated by detailed analytical models and confirmed by observations of many different species, the optimum old-age death rate for a species should be roughly equal to the death rate by accident and conflict."

"That's why I said that it doesn't make sense," Rob said. "How often do wars like the recent one happen?"

"They be about two twoffdays apart," Merlene replied. "They be going on as long as Merlene be remembering."

Rob calculated again. "About once every four years. This last war cost Camalor thirty or forty killed, while Harvamor lost two hundred—say an average of over one hundred a side. That is one percent of the average population of ten thousand. According to the Solem Senescence Principle a hundred keracks should have died of old age in the same period of time. Yet you say that the only deaths are those due to war and accident?"

"Betruth. There be two deaths by accident in the last twoffday. There be none other until the recent war with Harvamor."

"Then the Solem Senescence Principle is dead!" Rob said.

"I can't believe that," said Selke. "I did a term paper on it in Evolution Theory. The data agreed with the theory too well to just discard it out of hand. We must not be applying it right."

"Or it only applies to Earth," said Rob.

Selke continued, "Birth rate is usually tied to death rate. Although only in a steady-state population, and I presume

Camalor is still growing." She turned to Merlene. "How long does it take for a child like Jordat or Solene to grow before they are ready to start a family of their own?"

"Fi'five twof'fdays."

"Fifty human years," Rob said. "More than twice as long as humans."

"Solene be five-plus-three child of Merlene and Fasart."

"Eight children!" said Rob. "You two have certainly been busy."

Through the audiolink came Elizabeth's warning. "Watch it, Rob. You are treading on taboo territory."

"About one every twenty-five years," Selke calculated.

Merlene paused while she made the conversion. "Selke be correct."

"Jordat has now grown and has left home, hasn't he?" asked Selke, trying to creep up on the subject of procreation.

"He be now living with the other warriors at the Courtyard o'Warriors," Merlene replied. "Soon, a new male child will be entrusted to Merlene and Fasart by Lady Balane, for us to raise."

"What!" Rob said incredulously. "You mean Solene and Jordat are not your children?"

"Rob!" Elizabeth screamed over the audiolink. "Shut up!"

There was shocked silence in the workshop. Finally Merlene said, "Merlene be aware of human method of having children from reading entry on co-pu-la-shun in Lookman. It be true we be the parents of Solene and Jordat. But they be not the result of Fasart and Merlene"——her voice lowered to a staticy whisper as she struggled to find the least embarrassing euphemism——"coupling."

"You get them from Lady Balane," Selke prompted, trying to get off the subject of sex while keeping on the subject of procreation. "Where does she get them from?"

"Lady Balane be getting them from Princess Tormone, who be in charge of the hatchery." She paused, then forced herself on, not wanting the humans to come to the wrong conclusion. "The eggs be coming from the Queen alone. The Queen be not . . . " Here she was forced to pause again. ". . . coupling," she finished in an almost inaudible whisper.

"So Rexart . . . " Rob started.

Merlene pretended she didn't hear him.

"I think we had better be going now," said Selke.

The two humans went up the stairway to the surface, settled their telebots in a safe place, and blanked out.

As Selke took off her verihelm, she was shaking her head.

"Before we left, they kept reminding us and reminding us that we must avoid anthropomorphizing the kerack culture in terms of our human culture. But because we saw a male and a female raising children, we immediately assumed it was a cozy nuclear family just like we had on Earth. Was I fooled! And *I* am supposed to be the expert."

"You were not the only one," Elizabeth said ruefully. "Yet it is a nuclear family in one sense. There are two adults raising two younger ones, but instead of being their genetic children who will pass along their physical gene patterns, they are their 'intellectual' children who will pass along their social 'meme' patterns."

After Rob and Selke had freshened up and returned to the commons room, Hiroshi had something waiting for them on the monitor screen.

"I had the pole-top video camera focused on the base of the Queen's tower during the conclusion of the procession of souls. Look what I saw when I zoomed in on Princess Onlone."

They watched the taped sequence. From the camera's point of view, they could see the side of Princess Onlone. Her clawpets were holding a soul, and she reached in and handed the grayish metal ball to a fat claw just inside the door. Above and below the fat claw were other fat claws. All had large clawpets in them.

"I recognize those claws!" said Elizabeth. "I remember

seeing them in that vertical arrangement when Boris and Gabrielle were down in the tunnels underneath Fasart's farm. Those are *heuller* feet!"

Hiroshi nodded. "They are a direct match. Except they are much larger than any heuller feet we have a video of."

"And if what Merlene told us is correct, then that makes it a very old heuller," Selke added.

"What the hell is a heuller doing in the Que——" Rob paused in his query as the answer came to him. Then he continued, "I remember when I was a kid, seeing a nature program on television of the interior of a termite colony. The termite queen had this enormous writhing belly, hundreds of times bigger than the worker termites that were taking care of her. She was nothing but a gigantic egg-laying machine."

"I saw that program too," said Selke. "No wonder the Queen is always in her tower in the middle of the Palace o'Princesses with all the princesses and other ladies of her court in attendance. She is too big to move."

Rob grinned. "A lot of strange things about the keracks now begin to make sense. That thing they call the Spirit o'Camalor, for one. It is the collective intelligence of the whole colony. The kerack city is a large, intelligent organism where the 'cells' that make it up are the individual keracks—just like the ants in an ant colony."

"I think," Elizabeth said, "that we have found out why the Solem Senescence Principle does not apply to keracks. The evolutionary unit that the principle applies to is not individual keracks, but the whole colony of keracks."

"But keracks are different from ants," Rob protested. "They each have a significant intelligence on their own."

"That individual intelligence might not play an important part in the evolution of the keracks," Selke said. "Most ant and termite colonies run solely on instinct. Every time we have found what we thought was intelligent behavior, upon further investigation it turned out to be just a complex instinctive response to a complex stimulus. I wonder how important intelligence really is to the kerack culture? The intelligence of kerack individuals could be as unrelated to kerack survival as the elaborate playtime mud-bank-sliding of otters. The play activities that otters spend so much time on have practically nothing to do with the real task of otter survival, which is catching fish underwater. Perhaps the same is true with kerack intelligence. Intelligence in individual keracks could be merely a superfluous overlay on the instinctive ant-colony social structure."

10

TEMPERATURE OF THE SOUL

BORIS AND GABRIELLE were in the telebots—video-recording a kerack wheelwright as she shrank a metal rim over a wheel made of cast ice strengthened with metal threads—when the data started coming back from Earth concerning the first batch of samples that the exploration crew had catapulted toward the inner solar system over four months before.

Elizabeth and Hiroshi were still having breakfast, so Rob and Selke read through the reports as they trickled through the interplanetary fax machine, occasionally making comments about the interesting parts.

Selke said, in surprise, "I never have seen technical reports with exclamation points in them before!"

"What's so exciting?" Elizabeth asked, pushing Lucifer away from her plate of scrambled egg powder and rehydrated Spam. "Ouch!" she yelled, and slapped the cat off the table. She looked at the back of her hand. The scratches were already beginning to welt up. Lucifer hissed and leapt back up on the table, growling but keeping an arm's length away. The cat didn't bother Hiroshi—a bowl of steamed rice, bean curd, and pickled radish, daikon, and tsukudani had no attraction for the pest.

Selke glowered at the cat, then answered Elizabeth. "The isotopic analysis of the samples we returned. Although all the ice samples have the normal hydrogen-to-deuterium ratio of seven thousand to one, the organic samples of the plants, animals, and keracks are all heavily deuterated as well as fluorinated."

"I wonder why the selectivity for deuterium?" Elizabeth mused. "The keracks use difluorine oxide instead of water for blood, so I can understand the fluorination of the hydrocarbons, but not the preference for deuterium."

"Must have some importance," Selke said. "Otherwise it would not happen."

Hiroshi sighed. "One more kerack mystery we have yet to solve."

"That is not the only isotopic anomaly," Selke said as she continued to read. "Nearly all the boron in the boron carbide kerack shells is boron 10 and nearly all the lithium in the multiberry tuber-root is lithium 6."

"Are not those the rarer versions of those isotopes?" Hiroshi asked.

Selke looked at the figures in the report. "Boron 10 is only twenty percent abundant. While lithium-6 is seven percent."

"Curiouser and curiouser . . ." Elizabeth mused as she downed the last piece of Spam, ignoring Lucifer's outraged glare.

Selke went on. "The plants seem to do a good job not only of separating elements with different chemical properties, but even partially distinguishing between isotopes, especially if the mass difference is large. But the animal forms are even more proficient than that. Spinworms produce only one isotope out of each orifice. If you feed a goldberry to a spinworm, you get only one gold thread, since there is only one stable isotope of gold. But if you feed it a silverberry, you get two threads, one each for the two stable isotopes of silver, silver 107 and silver 109."

"Heavy silver and light silver," Rob mused. "Now I'm beginning to understand some of the things Merlene said that puzzled me way back then."

Selke continued reading. "What Gabrielle suspected about the radioactive crystals from the iceworms turned out to be true. Iceworm waste crystals are all single isotopes—the radioactive versions of those elements."

Rob held up a page from the report. "This is a commentary by Grippen. The authorities on Earth are very excited by this isotope separation capability of the plant and animal life forms on Ice. By shipping iceworms to Earth or nuclear waste out to Ice, the keracks could solve Earth's nuclear waste problem. The worms and plants could separate radioactive isotopes from safe isotopes, and since each isotope is delivered separately by the spinnerets in the worm, we can set aside those radioactive isotopes that have commercial or medical uses, and only have to store the remainder, which would now be in a concentrated form. This ability to handle the radioactive waste problem would make nuclear power acceptable. Because of this, there is now tremendous worldwide political interest in the keracks. Budgets are being raised and follow-on expeditions to Ice are being planned."

"Grippen must be pleased with that," Elizabeth said dryly. "More people to boss around."

"Well, *I'm* pleased with it," Rob said. "It looks like all the danger and discomforts we six have had to endure over the past four years are finally going to pay off in a big way."

"It is highly likely to revitalize space exploration," said Hiroshi. "I have been concerned that the world, involved with its internal problems, would retreat from deep-space ventures, while to me, the solution to many of those problems is a new frontier."

"Here is something interesting," Selke said. "They were able to find the kerack equivalent to our DNA in the tissue samples we sent them. They are still working on trying to unravel the whole kerack genome, but the preliminary results seem to indicate that each kerack cell contains many different copies of the kerack gene string, each slightly different. Which gene string is expressed would depend upon the environment encountered. Also, all the plant genes, such as the black fungus nodes and the multiberry plants, can be found as 'viruses' hidden in the genetic string, where they would be carried along with the kerack eggs wherever they go. Here is something else. Not only are all the plant genes found in the kerack genome, so are all the animal genes. More correctly, there is only *one* animal gene. The genetic structures of the eggs, the iceworms, the spinworms, the glowworms, the heullers, *and* the keracks are identical. They are just differently shaped expressions of the same basic animal."

"Just like ant larvae," Elizabeth said. "Feed them one kind of diet and they turn into males, while another diet produces miniature nurses, another produces warriors with big claws, another produces sterile foragers. Feed them a special diet and you make another queen. And most ant colonies use their eggs and larvae for food if they're hungry."

"The same applies to the clawpets." Selke read further. "The clawpet genes obtained from that fur skin sample can also be found in the kerack genetic string. The enzyme sequences in the clawpet genetic string are quite foreign to the rest of the kerack genetic string, however, indicating it is probably a true parasite, hiding in the DNA. The gene probably takes over a small fraction of the kerack eggs, and instead of a kerack, a clawpet hatches out. But in order to survive, the clawpets and beautybumps must have some beneficial symbiotic relationship with the keracks. I wonder what it could be?"

"Here is something very interesting," said Elizabeth. "The two kerack corpses that we sent back seem to have been fully functional sexual adults. Wow!" She paused while reading further.

"Wow what!" Rob said impatiently.

"Although they look like different sexes, the male- and female-looking keracks are in reality *equally sexual*. They are *hermaphrodites!* And their sex organs are their *tongues!"*

Rob thought that over for a moment. "Mouthveils and tonguepouches suddenly make sense. But if the keracks are sexually functional adults, why is the Queen the only one allowed to lay eggs?"

The cocoons on the other side of the room stirred, and Boris and Gabrielle rose to take off their verihelms.

Elizabeth put her tray down for Lucifer to lick. "Shift change, Hiroshi. Time to 'port off to Camalor."

Elizabeth and Hiroshi were waiting in the workshop when Merlene came down from her home above to resume her research.

"We have received our first reports from Earth concerning the samples we sent back to be analyzed over four months——" Elizabeth paused, working out the conversion in her head. "——some four-fives fivedays ago."

"What be in the report?" asked Merlene, the wizard in her extremely interested in the results. The translator program, sensing the higher harmonics in the radio signal from Merlene, put an excited tone in her voice.

"Many things," Elizabeth replied. "But one of the most puzzling is that the soul in each kerack is made of pure uranium 235."

"That be not puzzling," Merlene said. "For a long time Merlene be of the knowledge that the soul be made of uranium. Did not Merlene speak of that knowledge to humans before?"

"We suspected it was uranium," Hiroshi said. "But the most common isotope of uranium is uranium 238. Uranium straight out of the ground consists of over ninety-nine percent uranium 238, while the uranium 235 isotope is less than one percent. The sample of the soul we sent to earth was as close to one-hundred percent uranium 235 as the measuring instruments could measure. The purity was amazing."

"Merlene be now understanding the puzzlement of Elizabeth and Hiroshi. Perhaps the uranium here on Ice be different from the uranium on Earth?"

"No," Hiroshi answered. "The chips of different types of rocks we sent back in some of the first capsules had small amounts of various uranium compounds in them. The uranium in those rock samples had the expected distribution of ninety-nine percent uranium 238 and less than one percent uranium 235. The uranium in the metalberries that you called soulberries is merely enriched in uranium 235 to about ten percent, while the uranium soul in the kerack body is pure uranium 235. The rest must be excreted somehow, although no uranium was found in the slop bucket samples."

"What is really puzzling, however," said Elizabeth, "is that the only known use for uranium 235 is to make a self-sustaining nuclear chain reaction, such as a nuclear power reactor or a nuclear bomb."

"Nuclear power reactor!" Hiroshi exclaimed. "That's it! We have found the last link in the missing energy source problem of the kerack food chain. Let me show you . . ." Excitedly, he went to Merlene's smoothboard, erased a large patch of diagrams and equations, and started to scribble on it with a piece of carbon while Merlene and Elizabeth watched. Merlene went to one side of the board, pulled up the rod from a light pot, and ignited it. The diagrams on the board now glowed brightly in the infrared. Hiroshi first drew a box labeled "Long-lived Free Radicals" with a wiggly arrow coming down at it labeled "Cosmic Rays."

"The initial energy source for the kerack civilization comes from the background cosmic radiation, which creates long-lived excited molecules and free radicals in the ice over long periods of time." He drew an arrow leading to another box that he drew in the rotund shape of an iceworm. "Out on the farms, the iceworms and young heullers tunnel through the untouched ice around the periphery of Camalor. They extract free radicals frozen into the pristine ice and use them as a source of energy to grow and continue tunneling. Those long-lived free radicals are the first-level energy source of the kerack food chain, since the iceworms and heullers are harvested as meat. While the worms are doing that, they also extract from the dirty ice all the unstable radioisotopes that the dirt and ice contain." He drew an arrow from the worm shape to a box he labeled "Radioisotopes" and another arrow labeled "Meat" pointing to a crude figure of a kerack.

"Those radioisotopes, concentrated by the iceworms, are then mixed in with organic kerack manure and ground-up base rock from heuller manure and put out onto the surface ice fields. The concentrated radioisotopes produce large quantities of new free radicals in the ice, rock, and manure in the fields, some of them relatively short-lived. The multiberry plants the farmer sows in the fields use that radioisotope-generated free-radical energy source to combine the organic material and minerals into the multitudes of root vegetables and berry fruits that the farmer grows." He drew a plant, then an arrow labeled "Berries & Roots" that went to the kerack figure. "Thus, the second energy source of the kerack food chain consists of the radioisotopes operating through the plants." He continued to add to the diagram.

"The real problem has been the kerack thermal energy balance," Elizabeth reminded him. "The keracks are glowing hot compared to their surroundings, and are losing energy at a rapid rate."

"Merlene be remembering the caloric balance experiment Elizabeth had Merlene do," Merlene added. "Merlene be keeping a careful record of Merlene's temperature, and of all foods Merlene be eating for a whole fiveday. Elizabeth be calculating the energy in those foods be not enough to keep Merlene warm and alive . . ."

"Which is the reason we knew there was still a missing

energy source in the kerack food cycle," Hiroshi said. "But I think I've found it. The uranium 235 is the clue. The missing energy source is the slow nuclear fission of the uranium 235 in each kerack soul. The whole kerack city is a living nuclear reactor!" He drew another box and labeled it "^{235}U", then an arrow labeled "Heat" that pointed to the kerack figure, then another arrow from the kerack figure back to the ^{235}U labeled "Neutrons."

"What a discovery!" Elizabeth said excitedly. "A race of beings that lives off nuclear power. That's in addition to the other amazing abilities of the kerack civilization."

"What other abilities Elizabeth be talking about?" asked Merlene.

"The analyses done back on Earth show that the kerack ability to separate isotopes is not limited to the separation of uranium 235 from uranium 238. Practically every element and compound that comes from a living organism on Ice, be it iceworm, heuller, plant, or kerack, is separated into isotopes. The boron in the shell of a kerack is pure boron 10, although natural boron is only twenty percent boron 10, while the other eighty percent is boron 11."

"Boron 10 is the isotope of boron that has a high neutron capture cross-section," Hiroshi explained. "When it captures a neutron it fissions into an alpha particle and a lithium 7 nucleus, releasing energy in the process. So the boron 10 is a way of converting nuclear energy in the form of free neutrons into heat to keep the kerack body warm. The boron in the shells must also play a part in controlling the fission reaction rate of the uranium 235 pellets in a collection of keracks, by blocking the neutrons from reaching the uranium."

"Merlene be of the opinion that Hiroshi be correct in his proposition. When Merlene feel her soul be too cold, she raises her shell from around her soul and soon it be warm again."

There was a long pause; then Merlene went up the stairway that led to the levels above, slid the first-landing cover door shut, and came back down. Hesitantly she took off her wizard's cape and hung it up, and then, turning her back to them, she self-consciously unfastened and removed her ornately patterned chestcoat but left her skirt on. Making sure first that her mouth was properly veiled, she turned around, naked from the waist up.

"This be where the soul o'Merlene be," she said, pointing to the roughly spherically shaped lump at the base of her now bare thorax. The spherical region was a little less than a centimeter in diameter, and was covered with many overlapping curved pieces of shiny black boron-carbide shell.

"When the soul o'Merlene becomes cold, the shell o'Merlene automatically be doing this." Merlene concentrated, and the overlapping black shell plates pulled apart and opened up like flaps, exposing the pale yellow-brown surface beneath.

"They work like the slats on a venetian blind," said Hiroshi, looking at them with interest.

"There is a small amount of blockage by the slats." Elizabeth lowered her eyeglobe and brought it close so the video camera inside the eyeglobe could capture a good record of the view. "But most of the exposed surface is now skin instead of shell. Neutrons coming from the souls of others nearby can now penetrate Merlene's soul and increase its reaction rate."

"The soul o'Merlene be getting uncomfortably warm," Merlene complained. Hidden discreetly by her mouthveil, her tongue was now sticking out of her mouth and widened to help dissipate her excess heat.

"I have enough video record," Elizabeth said. "Thanks."

Merlene dropped her shell plates back into place and quickly turned away to get herself properly dressed again.

"The suggestion by Hiroshi be an explanation of an ancient puzzlement o'Merlene," she said as she slipped leg after leg after leg into her chestcoat. "When Merlene expose skin under tail shell to cold ground, body o'Merlene cools off. When Merlene expose skin o' . . . " She hesitated over the naughty word. " . . . tongue . . . to cold surroundings, body o'Merlene cools off. But when Merlene expose skin covering soul to cold surroundings, body o'Merlene heats up. Merlene be now knowledgeable of the cause of this anomalous behavior." Halting the process of dressing, the half-naked wizard went over to her notebook, picked up a scribe, and made a long and detailed entry concerning her latest finding.

Hiroshi grinned. "It certainly is fortunate that your shells have boron 10 in them. Otherwise, a large crowd of keracks would be likely to go critical and explode."

"Explode?" Merlene queried, sounding a little concerned.

"I was only making a joke," Hiroshi said quickly. "I am positive that no matter how large a crowd of keracks ever got gathered together, the worst thing that could happen is that their souls would get so warm they would have to take their clothing off and go naked."

There was a moment of shocked silence. Then Merlene spoke, her front claws protectively pulling her chestcoat closer around her to cover her partial nakedness, her twitching second legs indicating her irritation. "Merlene be not amused by the reference to naked bodies. When Merlene be removing her chestcoat in front of Hiroshi and Elizabeth, she be searching for scientific truth, not displaying her body."

"You've done it now, Hiroshi," came Rob's voice over the monitor channel into Hiroshi's ear. "You'd better apologize."

Hiroshi bowed low until he was almost prostrate on the ground, imitating what he had seen commoners do when they had annoyed one of the nobility. "I apologize most deeply and sincerely, my good and valued friend."

"Friend Hiroshi perhaps be not aware of kerack sensitivity to nudity," Merlene replied. "Apology be accepted." She returned to inscribing the new information they had learned in her wizard's notebook.

After Merlene finished her note-taking and had returned to the task of getting dressed, Elizabeth continued with the report of the analyses conducted on Earth.

"In addition to finding the pure boron 10 isotope in the kerack shell, they found that many of the different berries that we sent for analysis are enriched in certain isotopes of each element. The one that is most amazing and difficult to understand is the queenberries. They are enriched in gadolinium 157 and gadolinium 155, just two of the many isotopes of that rare earth. Gadolinium 157 happens to be the isotope with the highest neutron capture cross-section—five hundred times that of uranium 235. Gadolinium 155 is only one-fourth as effective—yet is one hundred and twenty-five times as absorbing as uranium 235. The only Earthly use for these particular isotopes of gadolinium is as a control rod in a nuclear reactor, since they soak up neutrons so effectively."

"The Queen be given all the queenberries for her own use," Merlene mused as she finished lacing up her chestcoat around her thorax.

"Then she must use them somehow to control the reaction rate of the city," Elizabeth concluded.

"That be perhaps the truth."

"Why don't you ask her what she does with the queenberries? Then we'd know."

"Merlene may be Wizard o'Camalor, but Merlene be still a commoner. Commoners be not permitted even to talk to the Queen."

"I don't suppose you could ask a princess—or a lady?"

"Commoners only be speaking to the nobility when spoken to."

Elizabeth changed the topic. "Queenberries are only one example of isotope separation. All the berries they analyzed contained elements or simple compounds enriched in a specific isotope. And it isn't just the plants. The frozen spinner worm that we sent in the last capsule was carefully dissected, and it looks like spinner worms, using a combination of chemical differences and mass differences, are able to separate out practically all of the various possible isotopes up to gold. Each isotope is extruded from a different spinneret in the tail of the spinner worm. That is an amazing ability for such a simple living organism, and the biologists on Earth are completely baffled as to how such an ability could arise through evolutionary processes. They could understand the evolutionary development of an ability to separate out energy-producing isotopes, such as radioactive and fissionable substances, or neutron moderators like gadolinium 157 and boron 10, but *all* the isotopes—from lithium to gold? There seems to be no evolutionary purpose for such an ability. We all wonder why it developed."

Something clicked in the mind of the Wizard of Camalor. "The Dome o'Holies be made of many layers," she said thoughtfully. "The layers be spun using spinworms. Possible answer to question of Elizabeth could be that each layer in the dome be made of a different element, all the elements that be solid at the temperature of Ice, in order, from lithium to gold." She picked up her notebook. Leafing back through the pages, she came to her drawing of the Center o'Camalor that had resulted from her visit with her parents. Showing Elizabeth and Hiroshi the diagram, and knowing that they could not resolve the hieroglyphs of the microscopic text, much less understand what they meant, she began to read the words out loud so the translator program could convert them to human speech.

"The curved wall of the Dome o'Holies be constructed out of many layers, each of a different material. After communing with the most eldest of the metalspinners, Merlene be determining the materials which make up the many layers of the dome. The first of the layers be constructed out of the element beryllium, a strong gray metal. The inside of the Dome be then coated with a thin layer of lithium, to give the inside a soft silvery luster. The outside of the beryllium shell be then covered with a layer of crystalline boron, fol lowed by a layer of transparent crystalline carbon, then by layers of frozen nitrogen, oxygen, and fluorine, separated from each other by thin shield layers of beryllium. These be followed by more layers, each being constructed of one element, such as sodium, magnesium, aluminum, titanium, vanadium, chromium, manganese, iron, cobalt, nickel, copper, zinc, and on-on, for that be what the Spirit o'All had ordained for the metalspinners to spin. In all, there be one fi'five, four-fives plus three layers. The Dome o'Holies be now finished, for it be coated with a final outer layer of luxurious gold.

"The many layers which be found in the Dome o'Holies be compared by Merlene with the 'Periodic Table of the Elements' which be found in the human *Encyclopaedia Terra*. The layers in the dome, from inside out, exactly follow the progression of the elements in the periodic table. Only the few elements that be gases at the normal temperature of Ice, such as hydrogen, helium, and neon, be not represented by separate layers used in the construction of the dome. Why the layers in the Dome o'Holies be ordered in this manner be not understood by anyone. Perhaps someday the Spirit o'All be enlightening us."

Merlene closed the notebook and put it down.

"Well, it certainly makes *some* sense," Elizabeth said, thinking about what Merlene had read, "in that the order of the layers follows the periodic table. But what could be the purpose, other than some esoteric religious mystique?"

"I wonder if the individual layers are single isotopes?" Hiroshi mused.

"Merlene be not sure. But the metalspinners used spinner worms similar to the one sent back to Earth."

"And that spinner worm only produced pure isotopes, so it is highly probable the layers in the dome are single isotopes," said Elizabeth. "If we could obtain a core sample through the wall of the Dome o'Holies we could send it back on the next capsule for analysis and find out."

"That be not allowed!" Merlene exclaimed at the implied blasphemy.

"I didn't think so," said Elizabeth. "Just suggesting it. Still, one wonders why the dome is made the way it is."

"As Merlene wrote in her notebook," Hiroshi said fatalistically, "perhaps someday the Spirit o'All will enlighten us."

"Anyway," Elizabeth said with enthusiasm, "The ability of the plants and spinner worms to separate out individual isotopes from the mixed materials they are fed is very exciting to the scientists and administrators on Earth. If we could successfully start colonies of iceworms and plants on Earth, they could be used to solve the Earth's radioactive waste problem. In fact, it might make sense to send some of those isotopes back here to Ice for you to use as fertilizer in your fields."

"Our supervisor, Frank Grippen, is very excited about the possibilities," Hiroshi observed. "The governments on Earth now realize the potential value of the keracks and Ice to the future of Earth and have asked Grippen to come up with plans for a much larger and better funded follow-on mission so we humans can maintain contact with the keracks."

A haunting call, almost primal in its simplicity, came over the aether, growing in volume as voice after voice was added to it.

"A-i-e-e-i-i-i . . ." Merlene intoned, adding her voice to the others. The humans shivered internally on hearing the ancient and eerie chant.

"Brightstar be rising." Merlene closed her notebook and put it into her carrying pouch. "Fifthday be here and it be time to rest the body and warm the soul." She felt under her chestcoat with her second leg. "Although this day the soul o'Merlene be sufficiently warm already."

"What is scheduled for the entertainment today?" asked Hiroshi, who nearly always enjoyed the cultural activities of Fifthday. Parts of it reminded him of the Oban festivals on

Earth, with feasting, dancing, and honoring of departed souls.

Merlene went into a short trance as her antennae reached out to pick up the subtle, mumbling undercurrents of the constant radio activity existing in Camalor. "After the Feast o'Sharing, there be a concert by the choir and an exhibition of acrobatics by the dancers. They be singing and dancing to a new musical composition by Concertleader Bethene."

"I will want to hear that, even if I have to skip some of my sleep shift," Elizabeth exclaimed. "Bethene is even better than the previous concertleader, Arpene."

"That be because Bethene be able to build on the memories stored in the Spirit o'All by Arpene."

"Now I understand why you were not as heartbroken as I was by Arpene's death," Elizabeth said soberly. "Although her body died and her soul has been given to the Queen, her intellect still survives in the Spirit."

"Betruth."

"I am looking forward to the concert also," Hiroshi said. "Each new composition by Bethene usually means another gold audiochip for her."

Merlene was confused. *"Gold* audiochips? Merlene be of the knowledge that audiochips be made of silicon, like the videochips Merlene uses in the Lookman."

"They are," Hiroshi said, almost breaking into giggles in spite of himself. "But after the audiochip makers have sold a million of them, they present the artist with one that has been gold-plated."

"But gold be a conductor of electricity," Merlene objected, remembering some of the things she had learned from the Lookman about electricity and electronics. "If the audiochip be covered with gold, it will not operate properly."

Elizabeth explained, "It is a token of esteem for good performance. Like a gold antenna ring for a warrior who performs well in a tournament."

"Merlene be now understanding."

"But," Elizabeth continued, "the important thing is that by Earth standards, Bethene is rich, and each new audiochip that she produces will make her richer. She, and the keracks in general, can now pay for things to be sent from Earth by capsule—as long as they are small and can withstand the high acceleration of the cable catapult."

"Merlene be finding that the Lookman be valuable in her work as wizard. It be probable that Bethene be finding a similar device to be valuable in her work as concertleader."

"I wonder how small one could make a synthesizer?" Hiroshi mused. "On my next shift break I'll send off a message to a friend of mine in the electronic musical instrument business."

"Merlene be now leaving to prepare for the Feast o'Sharing."

"And we'll take these 'bots up to the park to wait for the festivities to start," said Elizabeth. "By the time we get them there, our shift will be over and Rob and Selke will be in them."

"They will meet you in the Park o'Pleasure near the video camera pole overlooking the Plaza o'Dance," Hiroshi added. He and Elizabeth clumped up the stairway in the stilted, paired-leg gait the humans used. Reaching the surface, they followed the broadening streets that led toward the center of the city.

Merlene nimbly followed them up the stairs and slid the first-landing door shut after her, closing her work away in anticipation of the enjoyable day to come. The children were not in their rooms, but she was not concerned. Jordat, having finished his molt, was now at the Courtyard o'Warriors. He would soon be transferring the rest of his clothing and possessions there, and Merlene and Fasart would prepare the room for Jordat's new baby brother. Solene was probably outside playing. Just to check, she climbed out the family door and looked around. Off in the distance she could see her playing Blindeye Find in a nearby yard with some other children. The heat from Merlene's soul made itself noticed under her chestcoat, but instead of the discomfort producing a complaint, the wizard that was Merlene converted the discomfort into a question.

"Merlene be now wondering how much *did* the temperature rise? And will it rise further when Merlene be in the crowd in the Park o'Pleasure as the humans predict? Or in the Dome o'Holies during the Service o'Giving? Or in the crowd on the Plaza o'Dance?" She knew that her soul did warm during those times, but how much? And did the amount of warming have any correlation with the number of people around her?

She resolved to find out. It would be some time before Fasart got home from the fields, so she postponed packing the Feastbasket, climbed back down to her study, and got out her thermometer. She put it under her mouthveil and into her mouth, then rolled it around with her tongue until it warmed up. Pulling it out, she read the expected temperature of the blood in her tongue. She then tucked the now-warmed tip between the buttons on the front of her chestcoat, spread the shell plates underneath slightly, and inserted the thermometer so the tip touched the thin layer of skin covering her soul. By adjusting the thermometer position slightly, she was able to hide the outer end of it in her front ruffles where she could still read the scale. It now indicated almost two fi'fives. Her soul was indeed warm. Leaving the thermometer in place, she left her workshop and climbed the stairs again to prepare the feastbasket for the family. Fasart soon arrived home on a heuller pulling the slop wagon. He had picked up Jordat as he passed by the warrior training grounds and Solene from the nearby yard. Jordat was now guiding the heuller, while Fasart, sitting behind Jordat, with Solene between them, gave Solene a welcoming grooming. Merlene was pleased to see her family all together again.

Once the heuller was tethered in their yard and muzzled to keep it from eating through the ceiling of their dwelling below, they all went down to get dressed in their best clothing for the Fifthday festivities. Fasart had to pause for a while to sew a button on Solene's best chestcoat. His large right claw worked with amazing dexterity for its size—but of course it had had a lot of practice, for out in the fields, far from the bag maker, any hole in a berry bag had to be mended or the berry crop was likely to be spilled along the road back to the center of the city.

Merlene was adjusting the jewels on her chestcoat in front of the aluminum mirror when Fasart came back from Solene's room. He stopped to admire her looks.

"You look like a princess," he said, his antennae stroking hers as his arms closed around her from behind, the large warclaw sneaking up under her mouthveil. She flicked a tongue-tip kiss across the back of one of the massive pincers on the claw, but then gently pushed the claw out from under the veil where it didn't belong. The claw accidentally brushed against the end of the thermometer just sticking out from the front of her chestcoat.

"What be this?!?" he asked as he felt clumsily around Merlene's waist, trying to figure out what the rodlike thing was.

"It be a thermometer," said Merlene. "Merlene be conducting an experiment by monitoring the temperature of her soul."

"Oh . . ." Fasart was long used to the strange activities that the wizard Merlene sometimes engaged in. Her last experiment had involved monitoring her mouth temperature while also keeping a record of everything she ate and the amount of clothing she wore. He never did hear what resulted from that experiment.

Once they were all dressed, they walked as a family into town, Fasart easily carrying in his warclaw a large, plump iceworm he had butchered out at the farm just before he headed for home, Merlene carrying the sharestand, and Jordat carrying the feastbasket and occasionally opening the lid to sneak a berry of one kind or other. They were soon joined by many other families, all going in the same direction and all carrying wonderful-smelling feastbaskets.

As they approached closer to the Center o'Camalor and the crowds around them grew, Merlene glanced occasionally at the thermometer dial. There was an increase, but it wasn't large. They met Rob and Selke under the tall pole that the humans had installed in the park with the remotely controlled video camera on top. The camera was scanning slowly over the gathering crowd, its motions controlled by Hiroshi back at the base. The humans were alone, for most of the keracks avoided the alien, mechanical simulations of kerack bodies. Fasart didn't think much of them either, finding them crude in construction and awkward in motion, but he put up with their presence at their Fifthday feasts since Merlene seemed to be learning so much from them. Anything that made Merlene happy made Fasart happy.

The first of the calls for the Service o'Giving came as they arrived, so they left their feastbasket and sharestand next to the humans and moved off with the rest of the crowd toward the entrance ramp, Fasart and Jordat going down the left side and Merlene and Solene down the right. As they started down the ramp, Merlene took another glance at the thermometer. It had definitely risen, and was now two fi'fives plus three, and she had been careful to keep the shells around her soul down.

"The humans be possibly correct in their hypothesis," she mused, as she monitored Solene's performance in the privy.

The two came to the end of the entrance tunnel, where they met Fasart and Jordat, and together the family started down the Spiral o'Holies. Now that they were in the large cylindrical room that contained the ellipsoidal Dome o'Holies, Merlene could see that they were among the first arrivals and the spiral was only partially filled. Only the top third of the downward spiral had keracks on it, and the upward spiral was empty. Remembering the map she had done of the Center o'Camalor, Merlene realized that the number of kerack bodies around her was now substantially smaller than it had been a little while ago when they were all gathered in the Park o'Pleasure. Most of the keracks in the city were still out on the park, far away. She took a quick look at the thermometer scale.

"Two fi'fives plus five temperature marks." She forced a memory of the number and her position on the spiral. "Two marks higher, though there be fewer bodies close to Merlene. The hypothesis of the humans be perhaps not correct. Bethatasitmay, one data point be not a strong disproof." As she made her way slowly down the long spiral ramp that led to the base of the Dome o'Holies, she made observation after observation and forced the memory of the temperature, her position at the time, and an estimate of the number of kerack bodies near her. The temperature of her soul rose after the first few spirals, then dropped again significantly as she reached the bottom of the spiral along the inner wall of the Cylinder o'Support. Yet, at the same time, the number of keracks on the spiral had increased.

"This data be complex," she muttered as she forced another memory, and started up the conical spiral leading to the Altar o'Holies. As she and Solene circled slowly up with the rest of the crowd, Merlene noticed that the temperature of her soul was rising with each spiral. The family deposited their crystals in the Altar o'Holies, after which High Priest Kitone used the close-fitting metal plug to carefully press their contribution into the mass of soft crystals below. They took an awed look at the Heaven o'All high overhead, with its jet-black image coming in at them from every point on the shining inside wall of the Dome o'Holies, and started back down the conical spiral ramp leading away from the Altar o'Holies. As they moved away, Merlene noticed that the temperature of her soul started to drop almost as rapidly as it had risen on the way up, but the numbers were consistently higher. She forced the memory of a number of data points for future analysis while at the same time trying to figure out the strange pattern in her head.

"There be now more bodies near me, since both the upward-going and downward-going spirals be occupied. Yet the temperature o'soul o'Merlene be falling. But the temperature be rising when Merlene entered the crowds in the park, so the humans be partly right—as large numbers of souls approach each other, this 'nuclear reaction' process be increasing and the souls heat up. But there be something else that causes the heating. As Merlene be approaching the Altar o'Holies, her soul be heating up rapidly. Perhaps the altar be made out of the uranium 235 isotope?"

By this time the family had reached the base of the cone that supported the Altar o'Holies, and started the climb up the outgoing spiral. With all the many keracks in front of and behind the family, the spiral walkway was now completely full of bodies moving either downward or upward. Merlene took a data point where the spiral leading down the cone met the spiral heading up the inside of the cylinder. The temperature of her soul had dropped. It was now only slightly higher than it had been at the same spot on the opposite side of the altar. But that was to be expected. Her soul had not had time to cool down and reach equilibrium, and besides, there were definitely more bodies around her now that the spiral ramps were full.

The family started up the ramp to the exit. While Fasart was planning how he was going to arrange the slices of meat from the iceworm, and Jordat and Solene could feel their tongues getting moist from the thought of all the good food waiting for them on all their neighbors' tables, Merlene was busy monitoring the thermometer dial and trying to make sense out of the set of readings.

"The temperature be steadily rising as we climb," she said to herself as she forced a reading about two-fifths of the way up. "Merlene be now level with the altar. If the altar be the source of the excess heating, then the temperature should start dropping as Merlene move further away." They went up a few more spirals until they were well above the level of the Altar o'Holies.

"The temperature be at two fi'fives, two fives and still rising!" Merlene exclaimed to herself as she forced another memory. "Yet the number of people near Merlene has not changed. The source be not the altar."

The family continued to climb, and while Fasart and the children thought that the warming of their souls was a reaction to the Service o'Giving and the awe-inspiring views of the inside and outside of the Dome o'Holies, Merlene knew that there was another reason—and she was determined to figure it out.

As they reached a little over four-fifths of the way up the spiral ramp, the temperature of Merlene's soul reached a peak, then started to drop. Her mind jumped on the peaking of the data points. She wasn't quite sure, for it was hard to estimate from outside, but she thought that she was now about the level where the Heaven o'All was suspended from the top of the Dome o'Holies. Could it be that the Heaven o'All was the cause of the warming of her soul? If so, what caused it? The Heaven o'All was made of jet-black carbon, not uranium 235.

By this time the family had finished their climb up the Spiral o'Holies and had left by the exit ramp up into the park. Merlene took a few more readings and found that the temperature of her soul was rapidly decreasing the farther she got away from Heaven.

"When soul o'Merlene be at its hottest, Merlene be at point that be closest to the Heaven o'All!"

The wizard brain of Merlene thought hard as it tried to make sense of the data. If Heaven caused a heating of Merlene's soul, and if the humans were correct that proximity to the isotope uranium 235 caused Merlene's soul to heat up, then Heaven must have uranium 235 inside it. Suddenly, something clicked in the wizard's mind.

Long ago, when Merlene was in final school, the High Priest Princess Kitone had come to the school to give the students their lessons in religion. She had told them that the souls of those who died in battle, or otherwise doing their duty to the Queen, would go to Heaven. Since then Merlene had always thought that this was merely a fanciful image, since there was no obvious way to get to Heaven except by constructing a large scaffold structure inside the Dome o'Holies.

The general consensus of those who bothered to think about it was that the jet-black Heaven o'All in the Dome o'Holies was just a representation of the jet-black sky that lay beyond the rotating sphere of stars that surrounded Ice, and the "real" Heaven was out there beyond the stars. But now that Merlene had done a careful survey and map of the Center o'Camalor, she knew that the rod coming down from the top of the Dome o'Holies to suspend the Heaven o'All was quite thick. There could easily be enough space inside to provide access to the interior of Heaven.

"And that access be from the base of the Tower o'-Queen," she muttered to herself, her voice leaking out over the aether in her excitement over her discovery.

"Shush, Mother," said Solene in a disapproving tone.

Merlene continued to think, but kept her thoughts out of her antennae. "The Queen be given all the souls of those that die. No one ever knew what became of them——or even wondered——because the Queen always be allowed to do whatever she wants to do, and no one *ever* queries the Queen. Merlene be now of the knowledge where the souls go——they go to Heaven! Just as High Priestess Kitone said! But it be not some imaginary Heaven beyond the stars, but the *real* Heaven in the Dome o'Holies."

The family returned to the pole where the human waited for them. The Service o'Giving was a long one, with the long distance to travel down and up the long spiral ramps, so by the time the family had returned, the faces of Boris and Gabrielle now appeared in the eyeglobes of the telebots. Fasart and the children set up the sharestand and piled up their tasty and fragrant sharings, while Merlene went to talk to the humans.

"Merlene be conducting an experiment during the Service o'Giving. She pulled out the thermometer from underneath her chestcoat and showed it to them. "Merlene be making a record of the temperature of the soul o'Merlene as crowd around Merlene changes."

"Did the temperature go up as the crowd got larger and closer, as Hiroshi predicted?" Boris asked.

"Yes. But there be another source that be producing a larger effect than the crowds. Merlene be going to her workshop to analyze the data to be sure."

"You'll miss the feast and the concert, Mother," Solene warned disapprovingly.

Fasart, accustomed to the strange behavior of his wife, said resignedly, "Leave her be. Once Merlene be in this state, there be no stopping her until her question be answered."

Merlene scrabbled back to their home and her workshop, absentmindedly picking up small morsels to eat from the neighboring sharestands as she passed them.

"I will go with Merlene," Boris radioed back to Gabrielle as he scuttled off. "You remain here and be sure we obtain a good video and audio recording of the concert."

11

Discovery of the Secret

Merlene and Boris soon arrived at Merlene's workshop, Boris carefully two-stepping his way down the stairs from the surface behind Merlene's acrobatic skitter-dive. She pulled up the rod from a light pot on the corner of her worktable, ignited it with a fireberry, and, getting out her notebook, turned back through the pages until she found a diagram.

"This be the map of the Center o'Camalor that Merlene be showing Boris before." She displayed it to him.

"I have a copy of that diagram stored in high-res memory," Hiroshi said through the telebot audiolink. "I'll pull it up so Elizabeth and I can follow things from here."

Merlene set up her pantograph and made a rough copy of the diagram on another sheet of foil. Concentrating, she pulled back, one at a time, the memories that she had forced earlier.

"These be the places where Merlene be measuring the temperature of the soul o'Merlene." She put one number after another on the diagram. "And these be the thermometer readings at those points."

"Get a good look at all those tiny temperature numbers,"

Elizabeth instructed over the audiolink. "I'm going to use them to generate a rough neutron flux model for the Center o'Camalor. Provided I can remember how to set the problem up, that is. The last time I generated a reactor flux map was during a summer job at the Dounreay Fast Breeder Reactor."

Boris bent close to the page until the image from the video camera inside his eyeglobe could resolve the tiny figures Merlene was writing. After she had put down all the data points, with Elizabeth adding them to her model at the same time, she pointed to the peaks in the readings. "Here be a peak in the temperature at the Altar o'Holies, and here be two other peaks. They be at the same level on the Spiral o'Holies, and that level be the same as the level of the Heaven o'All." She paused. "Merlene be of the opinion that Heaven o'All contains many souls made of uranium 235."

"It seems to be a central core to the nuclear reactor energy source for Camalor!" Boris exclaimed.

"She's right," Elizabeth reported to Boris a few moments later. "The neutron flux predicted by my model peaks right at the sphere they call Heaven that hangs from the top of the dome. Now it makes sense why Heaven is made out of graphite—it's an ideal moderator for neutrons and is used in nearly all reactors."

"It is also beginning to make sense why the spinner worms have the ability to separate out isotopes all the way up to gold," Boris said. "By separating out those isotopes that absorb neutrons, the layers of the nearby dome don't react with the neutron flux of the reactor and heat up. If the dome got hot, the frozen ice layers would melt or turn to gas and the dome would fall apart."

"That still doesn't explain the reason the dome is there in the first place," Elizabeth reminded him.

"If it has to do with religion, it does not need a reason. The dome is obviously just an aesthetically pleasing structure to carry out religious services in, like the great cathedrals and temples humans have built all over the Earth."

A message linked in from Gabrielle back in the park. "The concert is starting, and they are setting up the high wires for the acrobatic dancing. Both eyeglobe video cameras will be required if we are going to capture all of the dance action."

"I will be there shortly," said Boris, turning to leave.

"Merlene be staying here to learn more about nuclear reactors," Merlene said. Boris stalked clumsily up the stairway and left.

Merlene went to the Lookman that stood against one wall and turned it on. She first looked up the entry under "Nuclear Reactors" and started to read the human words. There were a few unfamiliar technical terms in the description, but she understood most of the text. It was soon obvious that the nuclear reactors humans had designed had the fuel pellets widely spaced and separated by moderating elements like graphite that slowed the fast-fission neutrons down, so they would be more likely to cause additional fissions. The graphite in Heaven was the moderator for the reactor that was the city of Camalor. Merlene wondered, however, why the Camalor reactor had a clump of fuel pellets at the center. Clumps of pellets could sometimes get out of control, Hiroshi had said.

A little concerned that the mass of souls in Heaven could create a problem in the future, Merlene ran the Lookman back until she came to the section on nuclear bombs. There were some diagrams showing bombs based on the fission of uranium 235. One type used high explosive to compress a subcritical sphere of metal until it had increased its density enough to become critical and explode. The other type used high explosive to shoot a slug of uranium 235 metal into a close-fitting hole in a sphere of uranium 235 metal, rapidly assembling a critical mass, which then exploded.

The text made it very clear, however, that the pieces of uranium 235 had to be in solid metal form and brought together rapidly in order for an efficient explosion to occur.

Relieved, Merlene was about to turn off the Lookman and return to her family in the park when her eye caught the mention of nuclear bombs based on fusion instead of fission. Intrigued, she read on, learning about the various types of fusion bombs and how they could be triggered by fission bomb explosions. Toward the end was an entry on "fission fizzle" fusion bombs that included a diagram. The trigger for the fusion bomb was a uranium 235 fission bomb, as usual, but instead of being highly efficient and producing a high-temperature fireball that emitted hard X rays, the bomb was designed to be a "fizzle" that produced a low-temperature fireball that emitted soft X rays.

The fizzle bomb was placed at one focus of an ellipsoidal cavity with walls made of many layers of metal, while the fuse for the fusion part of the bomb was at the other focus. The soft X rays from the fizzle bomb reflected from the walls of the ellipsoidal cavity and were focused on the fuse, causing it to be compressed and heated until it ignited, starting the fusion explosion in the rest of the bomb. The diagram looked strangely familiar. Merlene forced a search through her memory, and back came an image.

"This diagram be similar to drawing of the Center o'Camalor!" she exclaimed. She opened her notebook to the page containing the map she had drawn of the Center o'Camalor. She held the map up to the screen and compared the two. They were nearly identical. The fission fizzle trigger in one diagram was in the same place as the Heaven o'All in the other, while the fusion fuse was in the place of the Altar o'Holies. The soft X ray reflector was a hollow ellipsoid just like the Dome o'Holies. The layers of metal that made up the X ray reflector started with beryllium and moved progressively up the periodic table of elements just like the layers in the Dome o'Holies—except the Dome o'Holies included more layers, since some elements were either gases, liquids or soft metals at the extremely high temperatures found on

Earth and couldn't be used to make layers in the human-made ellipsoid.

"The Dome o'Holies be a *better* reflector of X rays than the human ellipsoid," Merlene mused as she read in the text how the reflector worked. There was some obscure technical reference to something called a "K-alpha resonance line," but it was quite clear that the curved surfaces of the metal layers acted as a reflector and focuser for the soft X rays from the fireball at one focus. Merlene remembered how the blackness of Heaven came at her from all sides when she was standing at the Altar o'Holies. If Heaven had been a bright light like Brightstar, instead, then the light from that source would pour in on the altar and heat it up. Suddenly Merlene realized that there was one more aspect to a fusion bomb—the fusion fuel itself. In the diagram of the human bomb, the fusion material used in the igniter was a mixture of lithium deuteride and lithium tritide. She looked up the two compounds on the Lookman and discovered that tritium was radioactive and gave off a charged particle called a beta particle. She knew about beta particles, for the humans had taught her how to make a cloud track chamber to detect them. She got out her cloud chamber, primed it with some crystals from a flareberry, and started heating it up to turn the crystals into vapor.

"The fuel that be in the fusion fuse of the human bomb contain radioactive tritium combined with the metal lithium," she murmured as she self-consciously raised her skirt and looked down at her bottom. "The question be . . . what do the Crystals o'Giving in the Altar o'Holies be made of?" Concentrating on the control of her sphincters, she emitted a small amount of white material from number four.

"Not much be available this soon after Service o'Giving," she said to herself, ". . . but it be enough." She set up her spark spectrometer, then, pumping the spark machine hard, dropped a tiny portion of the white material into the spark, which responded with a bright, carmine-colored flash.

"The crystals be containing lithium," she said, seeing the colored lines on the spectrometer that indicated the presence of that metal in the white compound. She looked carefully for other lines. "The only other compound that be present be hydrogen. Be it singly-heavy hydrogen, doubly-heavy hydrogen, or the radioactive triply-heavy hydrogen?"

She then put the remainder of the small speck in the track chamber, and after what seemed an interminable wait, while the cloud crystals melted and the vapor in the chamber stabilized, she finally saw many fine white tracks shooting rapidly out from the speck, then fading away. Number four contained a radioactive component! The white compound was lithium tritide! Just what the encyclopaedia said was needed for the trigger of a thermonuclear bomb!

The thrill the wizard felt upon her realization that she had discovered something that no one had known before was soon swamped by the growing horror of the realization that her city was unknowingly sitting on a doomsday fusion bomb of horrendous power. A bomb of its own making!

"Since it be only a 'fizzle' explosion that be needed, then the souls kept in Heaven be sufficient as the trigger that be needed!" She paused as she worked out the consequences. "And it be possible that the bomb be set off by too many dancers getting too close to the souls in Heaven . . . Merlene must be warning the Princess Regent!" She started toward the steps to the surface, then halted. How was she going to explain such a technical concept to someone in the nobility? Most of the great ladies had little idea of how even ordinary things were made in the workshops of the various artisans. Besides, she might be wrong. She certainly didn't understand all the human words in the text. She would first check with the humans before she approached Princess Onlone.

"Merlene be needing to bring them evidence." She carried the Lookman over to her worktable and placed it on its back, screen upward. Using her pantograph, she quickly traced a copy of the diagram of the fission fizzle fusion bomb n a piece of foil. By adjusting the legs on the pantograph, he was able to make the diagram of the bomb the same size s the diagram of the Center o'Camalor. On another sheet of oil, she traced out the letters in the paragraphs of the human ext that went with the picture. It took her some time to omplete the task, but finally she was done. Adding the foil ages to her notebook, she raced up the stairs to the surface nd back to the park.

When Merlene arrived, the feasting was over and the oncert and acrobatic dance were well under way. The acrobatics show had been choreographed by Danceleader Cormene and was spectacular. The dancers were hauled up o the high wire by pulleys. The high wire was stretched etween two long, flexible poles that acted as springs. By umping upward at just the right moment, the dancers could propel themselves higher and higher with each bound, sus- ended for a longer and longer time in free flight, where they carried out intricate dance maneuvers before returning to the wire below. The dance expanded to leaps between adjacent high wires, then down to lower wires, then back up again, all accompanied by the most exciting music.

It took Merlene some time to find one of the humans. Elizabeth's face was now in the eyeglobe. Another of the human shift changes had taken place. Merlene now realized how long it had taken her to work out her discovery back in the laboratory and verify it with the spark spectroscopy and crack chamber experiments. Elizabeth didn't see Merlene ap- proach, since she was carefully watching the acrobats, cap- turing their action with the video camera that looked out her eyeglobe.

Merlene tapped Elizabeth's antennae to draw her atten- tion. The human didn't respond, and Merlene remembered that the telebot didn't have sensory connections to that part of the robot body because the humans didn't have antennae. She switched her tapping to Elizabeth's back. "Merlene be wanting to tell Elizabeth something!"

"Greetings, Merlene." Elizabeth still did not turn to look at her. "I'm sorry, but I'm very busy right now videotaping this acrobatic act. It is surely amazing what one can do with a small strong body in only fifteen percent gravity."

Merlene, not sure enough yet that her discovery was really the truth, allowed herself to be brushed off and, frustrated, backed away to join her family at their feast and to wait until the end of the show.

When Elizabeth and Hiroshi came back to the pole, Elizabeth said, "Now, what was it you were trying to tell me?"

"Merlene be finding this diagram in the encyclopaedia entry that be entitled 'Thermonuclear Bomb,'" she replied, opening her notebook and pulling out the loose pages on which she had copied the diagram and text from the screen of the Lookman.

"I see . . ." said Elizabeth, looking carefully at the diagram and the accompanying text. "It's not the conventional design for a thermonuclear bomb, but a speculative design that was never actually made and tested."

"Merlene be comparing that diagram with this diagram that Merlene make of the Center o'Camalor." She placed the two drawings side by side.

"They *are* very similar . . ." Elizabeth looked back and forth between the two. "And the bomb diagram has a fission fizzle trigger where the map has the sphere called the Heaven o'All."

"And the Heaven o'All contains souls made of uranium 235."

"And not just a few souls, either," Elizabeth said. "I didn't have a chance to tell you this before, but according to the neutron flux map I was able to generate from your temperature data, there is already at least ten kilograms of uranium 235 in Heaven. That is almost enough for a critical mass if it were concentrated into a solid ball. Luckily it's dispersed into small pellets. It *is* something to be concerned about, however. You wouldn't want the core of the Camalor nuclear reactor to go into meltdown."

"Merlene *be* concerned. But there be more. Merlene be determining that the Crystals o'Giving in the Altar o'Holies be of lithium combined with tritium. The compound lithium tritide be mentioned in the fusion bomb diagram. The other compound mentioned, lithium deuteride, be similar and it be probably also in the Crystals o'Giving, although Merlene be not sure."

"There must be some mistake," Elizabeth said slowly. "The half-life of tritium is only thirteen years. It would have to have been made recently."

"It *was*," Boris audiolinked. "The way tritium is made back on Earth is to put lithium 6 in an operating nuclear reactor. The lithium absorbs a neutron and splits into helium and tritium. Now we know why kerack bodies have so much lithium 6 in them."

"Oh, my God . . ." Elizabeth was appalled. "And the only thing this type of fusion bomb needs to set it off is a crude fizzle bomb made of lots of pellets." Her voice sounded anxious. "In addition to the nearly ten kilograms of uranium 235 pellets in Heaven, I also calculated that the individual soul in each kerack is about four grams in mass—so there is a total of over forty more kilograms in the city. If Camalor has more wars like the last one, one of these days the souls collected in Heaven are going to go critical! At the time I did the calculation, I assumed that evolution had managed to keep things under control—that somehow the Queen would know things were getting too hot and use the gadolinium 157 in the queenberries to control the reactor. In the worst case, if evolution had not progressed that far, the pellets in Heaven would get hot, melt through the graphite, and disperse—stopping the reaction, but making a mess of the Dome o'Holies."

"It now is obvious that evolution didn't stop at the making of a nuclear reactor out of Camalor," Boris interjected. "It has gone further and made Camalor a fusion bomb!"

Elizabeth pointed at the map with a claw tip. "Look! There are some differences in the two diagrams. The Camalor bomb is underground and has a thick cylindrical casing that extends up to the surface—and that is surrounded by concentric rows of privies. There is nothing like that around the human bomb." She turned to look at Merlene. "Merlene? What is the casing made of? And if it isn't too embarrassing to tell us, since you collect your organic waste in the slop buckets at home to put on the fields, what is it that goes into the privies?"

"The cylinder be made of lead," said Merlene. "And the privies be for disposing of lead, uranium, and other heavy metals. There be a surplus of those metals and they would poison the farms if they be mixed with the other body wastes."

"Then in that case, Camalor is not only a nuclear bomb, it's a nuclear mortar!" Elizabeth exclaimed. "The lead in the cylinder and the heavy metals in the privies don't have enough strength to resist a fusion bomb explosion, but their slow inertial response is going to divert the force of the nuclear explosion upwards, tossing the palace, the whole dance plaza, and everybody on it up into the sky."

"And off into space . . ." Boris whispered.

"But why!" Elizabeth said in disbelief. "What possible evolutionary reason would drive the development in that direction? It's easy to see how the Camalor reactor developed. The reactor supplied useful energy to those kerack societies that developed that capability. But a bomb that would *destroy* the kerack societies that developed it? How could that possibly evolve—and for what reason?"

"This be worse than Merlene ever thought!" Merlene was highly agitated now that her worst fears had been confirmed by the humans. "Merlene be now going to obtain an audience with Princess Onlone."

Merlene looked around the park for the knot of glitter that indicated Princess Onlone and the other ladies of the nobility as they made their way slowly through the park after the concert, collecting the queenberries brought to the Fifth-day festivities by the farmers and graciously bestowing their patronage on sharestand after sharestand of the commoners. Pushing her way across the park until she finally reached them, Merlene politely dodged her way through the phalanxes of the nobility until she reached a spot in front of Princess Onlone. She bowed low, notebook clutched to her chestcoat, and waited for the princess to approach. At the same time she chanted the appeal for attention.

"The Wizard Merlene be begging that Her Royal Highness Princess Onlone be asking Merlene to speak. The Wizard Merlene be begging . . ."

Princess Onlone, enjoying a tasty morsel of heuller foot that had been pickled in fluosulphonic acid dissolved in warm blood, was in a good mood, so, instead of passing Merlene by, she stopped. Her clawpet holding the heuller foot took advantage of the distraction and started nibbling away at the princess's food.

"And what great discovery be exciting the Wizard o'Camalor this time? Have more glowing giants in metal kerack bodies arrived?" asked Princess Onlone with a hic of laughter. She calmed down and gave Merlene the needed signal. "The Wizard Merlene may speak."

"There be no more humans coming," replied Merlene. "But the humans that be here have been helping Merlene make a most disturbing discovery." She held forth her notebook so that the map of Camalor and the diagram of the bomb were side by side. "This be a map of the Center o'Camalor showing the Palace o'Princesses and the Dome o'Holies." She tapped the map with her left antenna. "And this be a drawing of the interior of a war weapon made by the humans," she added, tapping the drawing with her right antenna. "The human war weapon be equivalent to a gigantic blood-bomb, one large enough to blow up the entire City o'Camalor!"

There was a moment of shocked silence at that incredible statement; then the entire court burst into a hiccuping chittering of incredulous laughter at the ridiculousness of the idea. Princess Onlone was hiccuping the loudest.

"The brain o'Merlene be so hot with such heavy thinking that Merlene be soon exploding herself," she said, amused at the discomfiture of the wizard.

"But it be *true!*" Merlene shouted back.

"Be silent!" the Princess commanded loudly, highly annoyed that Merlene was aruging with her. In a cold and furious voice she added, "Princess Onlone be of the opinion that the soul o'Merlene be becoming too hot and the heating be affecting the brain o'Merlene." She paused, then commanded, "Merlene be not speaking of this matter again. Do the antenna o'Merlene be receiving the command o'Princess Onlone?"

"Merlene be obeying," she said in a resigned tone, her body bowing low in defeat.

"The time be approaching for the dance," said Princess Onlone to the rest of the ladies of the nobility as she swept by the prostrate Merlene. "We be now taking the queenberries to the Queen and be dressing her in her dancing cloak."

Merlene dejectedly returned to her family and the waiting humans. "Princess Onlone be not listening to Merlene," she said in frustration.

"You can try again later," Elizabeth said. "It's not like the bomb is going off today. There have been three Fifthday dances since the batch of souls from the war with Harvamor were delivered to the Queen. Nothing happened during those dances, so nothing will happen during this dance. When the next war happens, we will go with you and help you convince Princess Onlone not to give the souls to the Queen."

"Merlene be hungry?" asked Fasart, tempting Merlene

with a sweetmeat made of a thick paste embedded with a collection of berries of different tastes. Merlene took the offering, tucked it under her mouthveil, and licked the berries off one by one.

Princess Onlone climbed up the inner steps into the second-story chamber in the Tower o'Queen. In one clawpet she was carrying the basket of queenberries she and the ladies had recently gathered from the crowd. In the other was the Queen's dancing cloak. The Queen had lowered herself into the second-floor chamber from the viewing pavilion above, but had left the heavy closure door slid back in its holding frame. Two ladies, one on each side of her, were shoveling basketful after basketful of food into the Queen's gigantic heuller mouth, trying to keep the enormous body fed.

"Here be the latest collection of queenberries from your faithful subjects." Princess Onlone held the basket out, expecting the Queen to eat them.

"Queen Une be having no need of them any longer," said the Queen. "The previous basket be sufficient for Queen Une to complete the Collector o'Souls."

"Then the building of Camalor be now finished?" Princess Onlone asked with rising anticipation. She came forward holding the Queen's dancing cloak.

"It be time for the Final Dance," the Queen intoned.

With Brightstar approaching the horizon, the people of Camalor gathered at the plaza for the usual closing dance. In the center of the plaza, the Queen rose back up to her throne on the top floor of the Tower o'Queen, where she was attended to by Princess Onlone and a number of the ladies. Rexart was standing respectfully behind the throne, dressed in shining gold chain mail woven through with patterns of red, blue, and green thread. The Queen stretched out her antennae and gave the call to the dance. The people gathered and the dance started.

"Closer!" she called after a while, and obediently her people moved onto the Plaza o'Dance, all adding their voices to the simple, rhythmic, ancient dance chant while their hind legs clicked in time to the beat on the smooth black surface of the plaza. They were soon arranged in concentric circles around the Tower o'Queen at the center of the Plaza o'-Dance.

Merlene, having finished the sweetmeat, now realized she was famished, and opened the feastbasket to find some leftovers.

"Merlene be hungry," she said to the others. "You be joining dance and Merlene be coming along shortly."

"Shall we join the dance, Elizabeth?" asked Hiroshi, waving his warclaw in invitation. The two humans joined the outer ring of dancers, which was made up of younger keracks who were still learning the complexities and careful timing of the dance. The humans, with their two-by-two gait, would never be good enough to participate in the intricate formations of the inner circles. Out here with the novices, their clumsiness was not so obvious. Also, the youngsters didn't seem to mind the presence of the metallic aliens as much as the older keracks did.

"Closer!" the Queen commanded, and the dancing crowd responded, moving faster as the circles contracted inward. Merlene soon had enough to eat and moved to join the dancing crowd. Not wanting to leave the humans entirely alone, she joined Elizabeth's circle as it cycled back and forth to the complicated movements of the dance.

"Closer!" the Queen commanded again, and the circle near the center contracted once more as the pace of the dance quickened. Elizabeth and Hiroshi, near the outskirts of the whirling crowd, could see little but those about them. Boris kept watch on the dance through the video camera up on the pole in the park, moving it back and forth and occasionally zooming in on a particular pair, while Gabrielle monitored the eyeglobe views from the two telebots. The tempo of the dancing crowd had now increased significantly, almost to a frenzy. Boris watched as the dance came to its peak. It was about time for the Queen to give her last command of "Flee!" At this command, the crowd would disperse, tired and hot, to gather up their families, feastbaskets, and sharestands and head for their homes.

Instead, the Queen broadcast a command that she had never used before.

"Enjoy!"

Boris was astonished to see the Queen drop her cape, revealing that she had nothing on underneath except her mouthveil, and soon that was stripped away, revealing a gigantic heuller mouth with a huge long tongue hanging out, swollen with hot, yellow-brown blood.

"The Queen is acting strange!" Boris muttered through the audiolink to Hiroshi and Elizabeth, at the same time putting the long-range view from the video camera on their peripheral screens.

"Cast off your clothing and enjoy!" continued the Queen. "Belly to belly! Mouth to mouth! Tongue to tongue!"

"They are all taking off their clothing!" Boris said in astonishment.

"It is orgy!" Gabrielle cried over the audiolink. "I am putting the recorders on high-data-rate mode."

"Maybe Grippen can sell copies through the kinky-porno shops," Elizabeth remarked sarcastically as she watched her young male partner of the moment toss off his cape, mouthbelt, skirt, and chestcoat.

"Rexart has left the Queen. He has stripped off his clothing and joined the crowd," Boris reported. "The Queen is staying on top of the tower, while the noble ladies have gathered around the base of the tower, wearing nothing but their pets."

"The crowd seems to be moving from one partner to another every few seconds!" said Gabrielle.

The Queen broadcast another command from the tower.

"Closer!"

Despite their frenetic coupling activities, the crowd obeyed. There was an ecstatic cry over the aether from someone in the crowd, and a column of black powder shot into the air. This was followed by another and another.

Merlene found herself unable to resist joining the dance. Her brain, operating at its highest level of intelligence, attempted to make her body ignore the music. It couldn't, and Merlene moved inward with the rest. The tie-strings that held on her wizard's cape had become knotted, so she was working on unbuttoning her chestcoat with one claw while holding her cape over her nakedness with the other.

"Keracks on the inner circles are bending over. Their thoraxes are splitting open!" Boris reported. "The souls are falling out of their bodies, and they're glowing hot!"

"My God!" yelled Elizabeth. "The reactor is running away and overheating!" Elizabeth's meetings with each kerack partner had become more physical. A large male, eyeglobe in a blank daze, whirled around from an embrace with a partner in an inner circle and grabbed her. Ripping off her mouthveil with one claw, he tried to rape her with his tongue. Elizabeth, forgetting that she was in a robotic body, screamed in fright, and the attacker withdrew in frustration when he found she had no throat or tongue behind the artificial teeth. She quickly sought out Hiroshi, and the two clung together in a desperate embrace to keep from being attacked while they watched the behavior of the frenzied crowd around them.

"They're switching partners every few seconds," Elizabeth gasped.

"As if they wanted as many different gene combinations as possible."

The Queen's voice pealed out once again. "Closer!" All about them, the keracks moved obediently closer to their Queen.

Elizabeth and Hiroshi sidled outward against the flow of

the in-gathering crowd. On the outskirts they came upon Merlene, who was struggling with a nearly berserk male who was trying to strip her wizard's cloak from her. She begged them to drag her away, for she was feeling herself giving in to her instinctive desires. The two humans pulled the male away and lifted Merlene bodily. Carrying her in their strong mechanical claws, they struggled out of the crowd and into the park, where they could look back.

In the center of the dance plaza both male and female keracks were exploding, their upper torsos flying high into the air, trailing a cloud of black powder behind them. Around the exploding keracks were others who were merely blowing streams of black powder into the air.

"That black dust must be eggs," said Hiroshi.

"More like spores," Elizabeth observed. "Probably just the right size to be pushed through space by light and solar wind."

"And the bomb will toss them there!" cried Merlene.

Soon more and more keracks turned into empty shells surrounded by black mounds of fine dust, their uranium souls glowing brightly in the infrared beside them.

"Those insane princesses are collecting the uranium pellets and giving them to the Queen!" Hiroshi yelled. "Soon there will be enough to cause an explosion! *Abanai!* Let's get out of here!" Running at the fastest gait he could manage, he headed for their microhopper in the cleared area at the outer regions of the park. Elizabeth put Merlene down and scuttled her telebot after Hiroshi's as fast as her fingers could twitch.

"Take Merlene with you!" Merlene screamed.

"Hurry along, then!" Elizabeth replied. Merlene folded her antennae over on each other, so as to short out the sirenlike radio signals from her demented Queen, and started running as fast as she could. Elizabeth soon found herself trailing behind, as Merlene galloped past her on all ten feet and shot through the open door of the small rocket ahead of her. Elizabeth slammed the door shut, and Hiroshi rocketed off on a flat trajectory that took them quickly behind the nearby mountain range and toward the human base thirty kilometers away.

Elizabeth switched the view screen on her tiny engineering console so it displayed the signal broadcast by the miniature television camera monitoring the activities on the dance plaza. It was a scene of hellish chaos. The last few keracks on the outskirts of the dance plaza gave the last ecstatic screams as, in each one, the glowing ball of uranium burned its way out through their waists, separating their thoraxes from their abdomens and setting free the black spores inside.

The scene shifted as Boris, back at the base, scanned the video camera around the outskirts of the plaza. There were a number of bewildered, sexually immature children there, still dressed in their Fifthday finery. Boris recognized one of them, and zoomed the camera in on her. It was Solene, trying to straighten out the folded and blasted body of a young male lying next to a red-hot soul. The young male was unclothed, but by the pattern of tournament rings on his antennae, Boris recognized the body as that of Jordat. From the manner in which Solene's antennae folded and unfolded, Boris knew she was sending out urgent calls for help, but the plaintive calls of the child were lost among the screams of pain and ecstasy coming from all over the plaza.

A princess came by. Ignoring Solene's pitiful cries, she picked up Jordat's soul and carried it off toward the Tower o'Queen. There, along with the souls of all the others who had once been the inhabitants of Camalor, it was given to the Queen, whose clawpet-covered heuller feet accepted all of them, one after the other, and stuffed them down below.

12

SUICIDE OF THE QUEEN

QUEEN UNE COULD feel a sublime pleasure rising within her as she called to her people once again.

"Closer!" she commanded, all her energy going into the penetrating cry that radiated from her stiffened, outstretched antennae. Her people responded, coming closer to her.

"Closer!" she commanded again, and the crowd near her tower contracted inward and whirled faster, their voices speeding up the tempo of the ancient chant, their souls searing within them. Queen Une's soul warmed yet again in response, so hot it was painful, but the pain produced ecstasy, not agony.

Queen Une looked out with pleasure at the whirling crowds of her people around her, hind legs skittering nimbly across the ebony Plaza o'Dance, meeting pair by pair, grasping front claws, the gigantic right male claws dwarfing the dainty female claws, pulling together, almost mouthveil to mouthbelt, pausing in anticipation, then pulling back again, then a whirl around and off to the next partner. The dancers grew more and more frenzied, and soon mouthveils and tonguepouches were wet from the flickering tips of the swelling tongues trapped behind them. Queen Une, sensing the mood of the crowd and feeling at the same time the intense heat at the base of her thorax, knew in her soul that the time had really come for the Final Dance. She raised her voice again in an electrifying tone to give a command she had never given before and would never give again.

"Enjoy!" She dropped her cape, then pulled off her mouthveil and cast it aside. "Cast off your clothing and enjoy! Belly to belly! Mouth to mouth! Tongue to tongue!" Following her example, capes and clothing of rank and trade were soon abandoned, and veils and belts were stripped from ten thousand mouths. Her now-naked people danced from partner to partner, bare tongues flickering in and out between flashing teeth. Rexart, who had been standing quietly beside the Queen in his usual position beside her throne, became restless when he saw the naked couples cavorting below him. He looked at his Queen, also now naked, and hesitated, driven by conflicting emotions.

Queen Une flicked her gigantic heuller tongue at him and hicced with laughter. She would enjoy sport with Rexart, but she had more important things to do. "Go join them!" she commanded. In a flash Rexart scrambled down the side of the Tower o'Queen and disappeared into the crowd, leaving warrior cape, chain mail, and mouthbelt behind.

Below, at the base of the tower, the other high warriors who were consorts to the ladies of the nobility found that with the Queen's last command, the rules of the dance had changed. Mordet, his soul hot within him, twirled Princess Tormone on to her next partner and whirled himself around to face Princess Regent Onlone. At the same time, he instinctively obeyed his Queen and dropped his cape and mouthbelt, letting loose a large tongue that had swollen to fill his tonguepouch and was now hanging lasciviously from his mouth. Mordet stumbled to a halt in front of Onlone and his tongue pulled back into his mouth in surprise at the sight of her. She had stopped dancing and had taken off her mouthveil, cape, and skirt. Her clawpets were now making short work of the task of removing her elaborately jeweled chestcoat, revealing the four fur-covered beautybumps on her thorax. She was looking coldly at him with her large staring eye, her nakedness inviting, yet the position of her legs and belly indicating that his approach was not welcome.

Mordet, frustrated and greatly confused, looked around at the couples in the outer circles. Most were in close embrace, almost mouth to mouth, tongue flickering lightly over tongue, while others were skipping from one partner to the next, all naked and enjoying themselves. He turned back to look at Princess Onlone, and then realized that she and the other highborn females were different from their commoner sisters. Their tongues were short and unswollen, as if their bodies could not feel and respond to the sexual tension that choked the aether. What bothered Mordet the most was that Onlone's thorax lacked a bulge at the base.

"You have no soul!" he exclaimed as he stared at her narrow waist.

Princess Onlone ignored the comment. "Go join the crowd," she said, dismissing him. "Onlone be tending to the Queen." She turned and headed for the base of the Tower o'Queen, where she was joined by the other ladies of the nobility, all free of clothing but still burdened with beautybumps and clawpets. There they waited patiently, their rear feet tapping to the rhythmic singing coming over the aether, watching the commoner crowd whirl by on the dance plaza.

Up above, at the top of the Tower o'Queen, Queen Une's tongue flickered from side to side between her giant heuller teeth, getting longer and more rigid as it did. In the whirling crowd of dancers, furtive licks between passing tongues grew to longer and more passionate embraces. Tongues grew yellow-brown as they engorged with blood and became longer and more rigid. Involuntary spurts of white liquid came from tiny holes in the tip of each tongue as the dancers whirled around to approach other partners. Soon partners no longer passed each other with a quick whirl, but stayed locked in each other's forearms for whirl after whirl while they danced mouth to mouth, each shoving an engorged and pointed tongue deep inside the mouth of the other, the tip searching wildly in an effort to deposit the gift of Eros to a willing and waiting cavity in the back. Once the joint gift had been exchanged, the partners quickly broke and whirled about to find yet another partner, there to repeat the process. Partner after partner after partner they went.

Queen Une's tongue was now fully extended and an almost continuous stream of milky white fluid gushed from the tip. She almost wished that she was down there dancing, with her tongue pushed deep into someone's mouth, but now was not the time for sensual pleasure. She had a more sublime task ahead of her.

"Closer!" she commanded again, her antennae almost vibrating in her passion.

Obediently, her people, most of them now coupled together, whirled nearer to her. Their heated souls grew even warmer as they crowded closer together. Their blood coursed faster through their bodies as it attempted to cool the heated soul, and the blood became hotter in the process. The dancers nearest the Queen screamed in a combination of ecstasy and agony as their now searing souls caused them to stop dancing and bend over at a nearly impossible angle until their eyes were between their hind feet. The continually increasing heat emitted by their souls turned the liquid nitrogen in their blood into vapor. The pressure inside their thoraxes rose higher and higher until their carapaces burst, sending up a powdery stream of tiny black spores pushed by a jet of high-pressure nitrogen, soon followed by a short, globular gout of bubbling blood and guts. Without the blood to cool it, each soul now turned glowing yellow, burned its way out through the thin skin between the plates at the base of the thorax, and fell to the surface of the Plaza o'Dance.

The princesses, who had been waiting patiently at the base of the Tower o'Queen for this moment, moved quickly out and picked up the glowing souls, their heavily furred clawpets and beautybumps providing protection from the extreme heat for their claws and thoraxes, although the pets suffered. By the time the first of the ladies had returned with the souls they had saved, the princesses had rolled back the four heavy sliding doors that led to the Queen's abdomen. Inside each door was a column of large, heullerlike, clawpet-protected feet that took each soul and passed it down, at the same time keeping the surface of the soul cooled by intermittent jets of nitrogen gas.

Queen Une's thorax was now hot and rigid with blood approaching the boiling point. Her eye was almost blinded by the infrared self-radiation emitted by her hot blood, but she could still sense the surrounding presence of her people with her antennae. Her tongue was flattened and sticking straight out in an attempt to keep her thorax cool. Fortunately she had a large quantity of blood and nitrogen stored in her large heuller abdomen to keep the lower part of her cool. She shivered in pleasure as, on all four sides, she felt the souls traveling down the length of her abdomen, where her bottom four feet found just the spot to put them. These were all perfect souls, smooth and round. None went to the reject areas to one side; all were placed tenderly into one of the outer ring of holes in the Collector o'Souls at the base of the Tower o'Queen. Her lower feet could feel them rattling down the holes to be added to the souls in the Heaven o'All. There was more for her to do, however.

"Closer!" she commanded yet again, and those still dancing on the outskirts of the crowd whirled obediently closer. Queen Une felt a rapid surge in heat output at the base of her thorax as the souls of all around her reached out and energized each other. She had expected it, had prepared herself for it, and now reveled in the painful sexual pleasure it gave her. The searing heat of their souls was too much for many in the crowd. The nearer ones, the blood in their abdomens heated to the cavitation point, exploded, sending their thoraxes flying high in the air, spraying out a trail of spores as they did. The souls, being dense, fell to the plaza nearby, where they were quickly picked up by ladies and taken to the princesses, who took them with the insulating pelts of their now-dead clawpets protecting their claws. These souls were carefully examined for flattened surfaces before being handed inside the doors to the feet of the Queen.

Those farther from the Tower o'Queen didn't explode, but emulated the first group by bending over and putting their heads between their feet, until their heated souls pressurized their thoraxes to the bursting point, jetting more spores into the air. Soul after soul was brought to the Queen by the scurrying ladies of her court.

Queen Une looked out over the scene with her nearly blind eye, as ecstatic cries pierced the aether into her antennae with each explosion and jet.

"This be good," she said to herself in satisfaction. "This be the way it should be." Below, she felt her lower feet on her abdomen as they placed soul after soul in the outer holes until the Heaven o'All was full. She now started to fill the inner holes in the Collector o'Souls. More souls would be needed, but there were still many more out on the Plaza o'Dance. She would call in the souls of her people so that they might all be joined into one supreme soul, the Soul o'All.

"Closer!" she commanded again, and again the whirling dancers moved inward toward the Tower o'Queen to join those who had gone before, and more souls were collected. Soon all the holes in the Collector o'Souls were full.

"It be time to retire to my chamber," Queen Une said to herself. She lowered herself through the close-fitting hole in the top floor of the Tower o'Queen into her chamber on the floor below, her elongated waist contracting as she did so. Reaching up, she slid the heavy disc-shaped plate into place overhead. Nearly blind from the infrared radiation coming from her overheated body, the sensitivity of her antennae numbed by the repetitious chant from the remainder of the crowd outside, she turned her mind to the feelings in her lower body.

The holes in the Collector o'Souls at the base of the tower beneath her lower feet were full, and that was good. Her many feet around her body still held about five-fives of souls, all searingly hot and painful despite the protection of the clawpet pelts, but the pain meant only joy to her. She lowered the souls, and all the souls in her feet, as well as her personal soul in her waist, became hotter. She raised the souls and they cooled off. She lowered them and they heated up again. She rippled them up and down, feeling out her control over the Soul o'All below her. She could tell that the Soul o'All was now ready for the final climax.

The blood in her abdomen was heating up rapidly as her body began to run short of the nitrogen gas that jetted out of her body orifices to keep her cool. She was exhausted and began to feel faint.

"It is time."

She dropped all the souls that she held in her feet. As they fell toward the multitude of souls stored below her, the temperature of the soul at the base of her thorax rose until it was white hot. Queen Une screamed in fused agony and ecstasy—and exploded.

When the pellet of uranium 235 in Queen Une's thorax exceeded 150 degrees Kelvin, it became hot enough to boil the pressurized difluorine monoxide blood attempting to keep the pellet cool. The first few vapor cavitations in the blood caused only a sharp acoustic snap as they burst into being, but finally one became violent enough that it started a chemical chain reaction in the highly unstable yellow-brown liquid. Queen Une's blood exploded, releasing large volumes of hot free fluorine and oxygen gas inside the Queen's chamber. Small spurts of unexploded yellow-brown difluorine monoxide vapor, greenish-yellow fluorine vapor, and colorless oxygen vapor initially leaked through the fine cracks between the sliding doors and the ceiling closure to the chamber. But these soon sealed tight, as the pressures inside the chamber raised to a level normally found only in the firing chamber of a large artillery piece. With the pressure contained in those directions, the expanding gas thrust downward at the glowing uranium 235 pellets waiting in the arrays of holes made in the solid plug of gadolinium 157 at the base of the tower.

With the high pressure of the fluorine and oxygen gas pushing on them, the stacks of uranium 235 pellets burst through the weak retaining barriers across the bottom end of the round cylindrical channels, as if the gadolinium 157 plug was a Gatling gun firing all its barrels at the same time.

As the uranium 235 pellets left the protection of the gadolinium 157, they encountered a rapid rise in neutron flux. They grew rapidly hotter, as fission after fission occurred in the uranium 235 nuclei, releasing even more neutrons to increase the neutron flux in the region. The thousands of streaming pellets of hot uranium 235 shot down across the short distance from the gadolinium 157 plug toward the cylindrical cavity in the center of the collection of uranium 235 pellets in the graphite sphere called the Heaven o'All.

As the high-speed slug of uranium 235 pellets approached the pellets waiting in the graphite sphere, the rate of uranium 235 fission in each pellet rose dramatically as the neutrons from one batch of pellets induced fission reactions in the other batch, which released more neutrons that traveled back to induce even more fission reactions in the first batch. The pellets were just beginning the slow physical process of melting when the cylindrical slug of moving pellets entered the cylindrical hole in the sphere of stationary pellets, creating a complete sphere of uranium 235 pellets. The neutron fission chain reaction went critical, and the sphere of melting uranium 235 pellets exploded into a glowing fireball of heat, light, X rays, gamma rays, neutrinos, alphas, betas, protons, neutrons, and fission fragments.

The resulting nuclear fission explosion was a very inefficient one, with the sphere of pellets blowing itself apart before less than one ten thousandth of a percent of the uranium 235 fuel had burnt up. This "fission fizzle" released the energy of only a few hundred kilograms of TNT, and attained a surface temperature of only four million degrees Kelvin.

The explosive force of a few hundred kilograms of TNT would have been sufficient by itself to toss the Plaza o'Dance with its cargo of spores off a small comet or icy asteroid a few tens of kilometers in diameter, where the surface gravity would be less than one percent of earth gravity and the escape velocity would be less than 500 meters per second. The explosion would not have been sufficient, however, to drive the plaza off Ice, which had an escape velocity of 2,700 meters per second. For that, a more powerful explosion was needed.

Being at a temperature of four million degrees Kelvin, the fireball emitted photons over the entire electromagnetic spectrum from gamma rays to X rays to light, with the peak in the radiation spectrum occurring around the soft X ray wavelength of 10 angstroms, one thousand times shorter than typical light wavelengths. The photons, traveling at the speed of light, moved much faster than the neutrons, protons, electrons, and fission fragments in the explosion.

The soft X rays shot radially outward from the spherical fireball at one focal point of the ellipsoidal dome and struck the inner surface of the dome. Those few photons with a short ultraviolet wavelength between 200 and 350 angstroms were closely matched in wavelength to the K-alpha resonance line of the inner electrons of the lithium metal atoms that lined the inner wall of the Dome o'Holies. Because of this resonance, a large number of these photons were reflected from the lithium inner wall, to be focused onto the spherical altar at the other focal point of the ellipsoidal dome. The larger number of short ultraviolet photons with wavelengths between 80 and 200 angstroms passed through the inner wall of lithium as if it were transparent, but reflected from the next layer made of beryllium, and were focused on the altar. Those soft X ray photons between 50 and 80 angstroms reflected from the next layer made of boron. Those between 40 and 50 angstroms reflected from the carbon layer. Those between 20 and 30 reflected from the frozen layer of nitrogen. This continued until the last layer of gold reflected those photons with a wavelength around 0.5 angstroms. Thus, each successive layer in the dome reflected a shorter and shorter wavelength of the total spectrum coming from the fireball and focused all that radiation down on the spherical altar at the other focal point of the dome.

So, before the fireball had time to expand and destroy its smooth ellipsoidal perfection, the dome had carried out its purpose and had transferred the radiative energy from the fireball to the altar and its gifts within. The outer shell of the altar absorbed the intense dose of photons coming in from all directions, and was instantly vaporized and turned into a cloud of expanding plasma. As the plasma expanded away from the surface of the altar, it produced a reaction force in the opposite direction that imploded inward on the mixture of lithium deuteride and lithium tritide contained within the altar. The intense heat and pressure this implosion produced was sufficient to cause the deuterium nuclei to fuse with the tritium nuclei, producing helium nuclei and neutrons, plus a large amount of energy which caused the heat and pressure to rise still further, causing more deuterium-tritium fusions to take place. The fusion chain reaction soon turned into a detonation wave, which propagated into the rest of the mixture of lithium deuteride and lithium tritide stored under the altar, resulting in a large thermonuclear fusion explosion.

Surrounding the explosion was a thick cylinder of lead, surrounded in turn by the heavy metal contents of the privies. The inertia of this thick cylindrical wall of heavy metals constrained the explosion and directed the explosive force upward, where it struck the under-surface of the Palace o'-Princesses under the Plaza o'Dance. The Palace o'Princesses had been fabricated of seamless black boron carbide, which was almost as strong as crystalline diamond and could withstand higher temperatures. The rooms in the Palace o'Princesses had been made hexagonal in shape, producing a structure that had the greatest strength for the least weight. As a result, the Palace o'Princesses maintained its physical integrity as the shock front of the thermonuclear explosion hit it. The palace accelerated rapidly upward, driven by the directed thermonuclear explosion, until it and the cargo of spores on its upper surface attained escape velocity and were thrown into interstellar space.

"Faster, Hiroshi! Faster!" Elizabeth was watching the view from the monitor camera on the pole overlooking the plaza. "The princesses have stopped bringing uranium pellets to the Queen and are sliding the doors back into place. Now I know why the doors had to be so massive."

Spurts of yellowish smoke shot from cracks around the doors, and a heartbeat later, the plaza floor rose as a single piece, carrying with it the piles of spores on its upper surface. There was a blinding flash of light, and the camera monitoring the plaza stopped working . . .

They had witnessed the destruction of an intelligent civilization so that a gene might propagate itself.

"Gone . . ." said Merlene sorrowfully. "All the knowledge, all the art, all the music . . . all gone."

"It's not all gone," Elizabeth said, trying to console her.

"Although Camalor, the city, has been destroyed, the best part of the Camalor civilization still exists within you. As long as you are alive, the city is alive."

"Which may not be for long!" Hiroshi said in a tense voice as he watched a monitor screen that showed the view from the rear of the rocket. "Look at that blast wave move! *Kita! Kita!!*"

Racing toward them through the almost nonexistent atmosphere was a sharp, almost vertical, cylindrical cloud, getting larger and taller, but fortunately less dense, as it neared. As it rushed past them, the tiny rocket ship shook violently and Elizabeth's telebot was slammed against the bulkhead. She was suddenly in blackness. Her scream of panic echoed loudly in her pitch-black virtual helmet.

Elizabeth felt a deep, menacing rumble as the first underground pressure waves of the shock arrived at the base ahead the air blast. She ripped off her verihelm and looked around the familiar control room in fright. Boris's and Gabrielle's faces, initially showing just surprise at seeing her back so soon, tensed with fear when they felt the rumbling too. The human base was over thirty kilometers from Camalor. Was the bomb big enough to reach it? The rumbling became stronger, the shelter shook violently as the shock wave passed, and the lights went out . . .

Then, through the porthole in the darkened control room, Elizabeth saw sunrise for the second time that day as the nuclear fireball rose over the distant mountain chain. There was no mushroom cloud, for there was no atmosphere to hold back the nuclear ball of fire. It grew larger, and larger, and larger, and finally faded away like a gigantic firework balloon. In the fading light of the ball of hellish fire that had once been Camalor, she could now see a small rocket ship coming down to a wobbly but safe landing on the ice-covered rock not far from the shelter. Beside her, the control cocoon for the other telebot removed its arms from the virtual sleeves and took off its helmet.

"That was a close one!" Hiroshi said into the hell-lit blackness of the control room.

Emergency lights finally flickered on, revealing a shocked Boris and Gabrielle sitting alert at their monitoring consoles and a disheveled Rob and Selke rolling out of the bunks in their sleepwear, not yet quite awake.

"What the hell happened!" Rob asked.

Hiroshi shook his head. "Camalor was destroyed by a self-made hydrogen bomb."

"Destroyed for now, but soon to be recreated," Elizabeth corrected. "Recreated in two ways. The spores will recreate the body of Camalor on some other icy planetoid, while the wizard Merlene will go out to recreate the spirit of Camalor in all the other kerack cities on Ice. With the knowledge she will transfer to them, perhaps the kerack race can gain intelligent control over the direction of their future evolution."

"Let us hope they will be wiser with their self-knowledge than the human race has shown itself to be so far," Hiroshi commented.

There was a pensive look on Elizabeth's face as she looked out the porthole at the tiny figure of Merlene crawling out of the open door of the rocket ship, her large single eye looking over at the distant glow of destruction.

Merlene was awed by the magnitude of the catastrophe that had befallen her city. Because her vision extended well into the infrared, the gigantic nuclear fireball that was now invisible to the humans was still bright and growing to her as it expanded upward toward the stars. Her large eyeglobe enabled her to make out the speck of glowing light far above that was the white-hot base of what used to be the Palace o'Princesses, carrying its cargo of spores, rocketed into space by the bomb that had destroyed her city.

13

UNDERSTANDING OF THE MEANING

". . . so WE raced to the microhopper, and streaked here as fast as we could," Hiroshi continued.

"The blast wave caught up with us, knocked my 'bot into the wall, and it stopped working—so I 'ported back," Elizabeth added. "Just in time to get hit by the blast wave again—in person this time." She suddenly had a thought and looked around at the video monitor hanging over the controller cocoon for her telebot. The monitor showed a view of the inside of the microhopper, indicating that at least the video system of the telebot was working again. She went over to the controller, put on the verihelm, and ducked down into the sensuit. The image on the monitor moved as she shook herself into the scene and checked out her claws and legs. "The 'bot seems to be working fine now," she reported over the audiolink. A few seconds later, she was back with them again.

"It's nearly time for shift change," said Rob. "Why don't you and Hiroshi take a well-deserved s-'n'-s, that is, if you haven't had all the 's' scared out of you, and let me and Selke take over."

"Good idea," Elizabeth said, getting out of the sensuit

and heading for the bathroom. "But we shouldn't leave Merlene alone at a time like this."

"I will 'port back and inform her of the impending shift change," said Hiroshi, raising his verihelm. "I will stay with her until Selke arrives in the other telebot."

They watched on the telebot eyeglobe monitor as Hiroshi shook himself into the scene, then used his walking legs to turn from the pilot position on the control deck and made his way out through the lock onto the surface of Ice. Merlene was waiting there, absentmindedly rubbing her second pair of legs together while the claws on her front legs moved nervously over her body, adjusting her mouthveil, touching the closure on her carrying pouch, and fussing with a tear in her wizard's cloak.

From the view out of Hiroshi's telebot eyeglobe, the humans could see themselves standing in the brightly lit window of the shelter beyond Merlene. They listened to Hiroshi greeting her over the telebot link.

"How be Merlene?" he asked solicitously, hoping that the translator program could pass on the tonal nuance.

"Alone . . ." Merlene replied in an unusually flat voice. "They are gone . . . gone forever . . ."

"She is in a poor state," Gabrielle remarked, listening to the haunting tone coming over the link. "There is a possibility she is losing her mind."

Selke sighed. "Considering that a portion of her original mind was distributed out among the rest of the keracks in the city, she *has* lost at least some of it. I would suspect that a large portion of her instinctive drives and her social strictures—what Freud would call the id and superego—are gone. Fortunately, she still has the ego—the part that contains her individuality. We'll soon find out if it is strong enough to survive on its own without going insane."

Selke climbed into the sensuit Elizabeth had vacated, put on the verihelm, shook herself into the scene, and went out the airlock on the microhopper to join Hiroshi and Merlene on the surface of Ice.

"Making sure Merlene is OK is important, but we also have other responsibilities," Rob reminded them as he got ready to replace Hiroshi. "Since Elizabeth was an eyewitness, she ought to work up a summary report of what happened to send to Grippen. Boris, it might be a good idea if you activate the engineering console and take the whole base through a systems checkout. There are no emergency alarms, but you might find that something has been damaged——like the outside waste line getting blocked. Gabrielle, Grippen isn't going to be satisfied with what little Elizabeth can report to him in the first message. Why don't you activate the imaging cameras on the orbiters? Program them to take hi-res shots of the terrain around where Camalor used to be, so we can assess the extent of the damage."

One of the sensuits opened and Hiroshi rose to take off his verihelm and climb out.

"She is still in a state of shock," he told Rob. "I recommend just letting her talk until she has herself back under control."

"I understand." Rob prepared to climb into the sensuit. "Do you think she needs food or anything? We have some small samples of kerack berries we were going to include on the next capsule shipment back to Earth."

"We *will* have to worry about food for her in a day or so," said Hiroshi. "But under the same circumstances I doubt that *I* would be concerned about eating."

"I'll just hold her claw, then." Rob put on the verihelm and settled into the sensuit. Hiroshi watched the monitor for a few seconds as Rob teleported to the nearby robot and took over.

Selke noticed the large, blank round eye on the telebot next to them light up with Rob's face and shake its head.

"Ah! Rob has arrived," she said with false cheerfulness.

"Greetings, Merlene and Selke," he said, trying desperately to think of something else safe to say.

"Merlene be appreciating the presence of her good friends Rob and Selke," Merlene said. "It be good to feel voices coming in through my antennae. That be what Merlene yearns for most. Perhaps Merlene be soon returning to Camalor to listen and perhaps hear if there be any others that survived."

"I hate to say this," said Rob, "but we humans have experienced what Camalor has gone through. We know the extent of damage that thermonuclear bombs can cause. Two human cities, each many times larger in physical size than Camalor, were subjected to similar explosions and both were thoroughly destroyed. I am almost certain that Camalor is completely demolished and all that were in it were killed."

"Merlene be still desiring to see for herself."

"Even that would not be safe," said Rob. "There was probably a lot of excess uranium in the fission trigger for that Camalor fusion bomb. The radioactive fallout will be heavy for kilometers around. You keracks are pretty tough, but I don't think you could survive long in a megarad environment."

"Merlene be not understanding."

"Remember your cloud-track chamber for observing radioactivity?" asked Selke. "The samples of radioactive materials shot tiny particles out, and the particles made cloud tracks in the vapor. Imagine materials that shot out larger particles, so heavy and fast that they could shoot through the walls of the chamber and all the way through your whole body like an arrow. Each particle would make a small hole in you. Now imagine millions and millions of holes in you."

"Merlene be now aware of the danger, but Merlene be still wishing to return to Camalor to look and listen."

"Gabrielle has activated the video cameras on the spacecraft we have orbiting Ice," Selke said. "We soon should have pictures showing the extent of the damage. From that, we can estimate how close we can approach the center of the explosion."

Rob added, "Hiroshi is also planning to refuel the microhopper so we can fly it over the site to see what happened to it. You can go along with us when we do. Until then, we must wait."

"Then wait it must be." Merlene reached into her pouch, pulled out a spiritberry, and chewed it thoughtfully, letting the crystals dissolve in her mouth, then swallowing the stimulating liquid. It made her feel warm inside. Seeing Merlene eat something, Rob remembered their small stock of berries.

"We have a small amount of kerack food stored here," he said. "They are extra samples that we gathered of the various berries that grow on the farms. You may have them if you are hungry."

"Merlene be not hungry, but Merlene be knowing that she must eat to stay strong. Merlene be most grateful for any berries Rob may have."

"They are stored in the cold box," he said. "I'll get Boris to put them outside the lock." The background hiss of his voice over the airwaves disappeared as he switched to audiolink mode to talk to Boris inside the shelter. Then he was back talking to them.

"We have to go around to the airlock at the back of the shelter." He led the way around.

Rob thought that the food would cheer Merlene up, but it had the opposite effect. Each different-tasting berry triggered another memory in her mind, memories of happier days in the glory that had been Camalor.

"Bloodberries!" she said, taking one of the yellow-brown berries in her mouth. As the taste of the melting crystals flowed over her tongue, memories of Solene's first molt came pouring into her mind . . .

Merlene and Fasart helping the tiny child—ugly in its wrinkled new shell—struggle from the crack in its old carapace. Then the parents putting bloodberry after bloodberry in the tiny mouth until the baby had visibly swelled to its new size, young Jordat looking on with awe at the process. Finally, relief as Solene's shell slowly hardened to protect the child until the next molt.

"Gone . . ." Merlene mourned. "Solene gone . . . Fasart gone . . . Jordat gone . . . Camalor gone . . ." She reached into her carrying pouch and pulled out her notebook. "This be all that I have left to remind me of Camalor."

"That is *all!* That's *wonderful!*" Rob exclaimed. He took the notebook from Merlene's claws and flipped carefully through the thin foil pages, filled from edge to edge with microscopic script. Although the large kerack eye could easily read the tiny hieroglyphics, they were barely visible through the telebot eyeglobe video camera.

"Merlene be taking the notebook to Princess Onlone to show her those pictures when the end came."

"This is very valuable information," Selke said to Merlene. "May we make videoprints of it for transmission back to Earth?"

Merlene, glad to have something constructive to do to keep her mind off her sorrow, readily agreed. To get a video camera with a powerful enough lens to image the tiny characters, Boris had to take apart the microscope in the analytical laboratory and jury-rig a power and video link so the microcamera portion could be operated outside. The field of view of the microcamera was not large, so many overlapping pictures had to be taken of each notebook page.

Once the microcamera was operational, they kept at the long and tedious task of copying the notebook until it came time for shift change. Rob teleported back while Selke waited alongside Merlene, stroking her back and antennae the way she had seen keracks do to unhappy children back in Camalor. Selke was sure that she wasn't making the right kind of motions, but Merlene didn't move away, so she continued the stroking.

* * *

"How is Merlene?" Boris asked as Rob took off the verihelm and started the laborious task of climbing out of the sensuit.

"Better, but still not happy," Rob answered. "Selke has decided to stay with her until you and I switch places. That way she won't be left alone. That seems to be Merlene's major problem, the complete loneliness that she feels now, plus the sure knowledge that she will be alone for the rest of her life." Rob pulled his personal urine acceptor from the tubing inside the suit, and Boris reached in to insert his own in place.

"It must be like losing your soul," Elizabeth said, handing Rob his orange coveralls as he headed toward the bathroom. "For all her life, Merlene was continuously in radio contact with all the thousands of people in her city, thinking their thoughts, dreaming their dreams, responding to their feelings, calling to them when in need and getting an instant response . . . Now she is alone."

"Any response from the Griper?" Rob asked.

"Not due for another six hours."

"Ten-to-one he's going to find some way to blame us for what happened."

Elizabeth snorted. "He isn't going to like the loss of the isotope separation capability of the iceworms and the plants. He was counting on using that springboard to jump a couple of levels on the promotion ladder."

"He can still have that. All we have to do is make a deal with some kerack colony on the other side of the globe that survived the explosion and fallout. Merlene can help us establish contact."

"You're beginning to sound like Grippen yourself, Rob," Gabrielle said. "Shame! Whole cities destroyed and you go on with business."

"What *was* the extent of the damage?" he asked, sobered somewhat by Gabrielle's reminder.

"Difficult to tell," Elizabeth said. "The video cameras on

those shoddy orbiters Grippen foisted off on us don't have very good resolution. There is a big cavity where Camalor used to be, while the spiderweb street pattern of the nearby surrounding cities are mostly obliterated by debris from the explosion. There are also indications that small explosions took place at the center of Harvamor and Belator, for the dance plazas there have been displaced from the center of the pattern. In the case of Harvamor, the plaza has been tossed a few hundred meters and overturned. We can't tell if anyone survived in those cities, or what the extent of the damage is in the other cities. Once we have the microhopper refueled, we can go out and get a closer look."

Boris reminded them soberly, as he snuggled down in the sensuit, "I am afraid we humans will not be able to help the keracks much."

"We'll do what we can." Rob sauntered to the bathroom. "But first I'm going to get my s-'n'-s before Selke pupates and beats me to it."

Boris put on his verihelm, and the image on the console video monitor swerved from side to side as he cued in his visual system to the virtual reality.

"Boris has arrived!" Selke said, seeing the telebot beside her shake its head. "It is time for me to go." She stopped stroking Merlene's back.

"Must you?" Merlene replied, her second arm-pair twisting and twitching in anxiety.

"Unlike keracks, we humans need our rest," Selke said firmly. "Gabrielle will 'port in shortly, and she and Boris can finish videoprinting the contents of your notebook. It was very fortunate that you had it with you, for it is the only physical record of Camalor that is left—other than yourself."

"Merlene's notebook is not the only record we have of Camalor," Boris reminded them. "We also have recording of the video and sound that passed through the telemetry links from the telebots while we were there, and video records from the monitoring cameras we had set up around the Plaza."

"That will help us humans reconstruct things when we get back to Earth," Selke agreed, "but it will be of little value to Merlene as she attempts to explain to the rest of the kerack cities what happened to Camalor and what that means to the future of the kerack race. I will go now. Gabrielle will be here shortly to take my place." Selke's telebot froze, the face in the eyeglobe faded out, and she was gone.

"Merlene be not able to explain to them," Merlene said, her confidence gone. "They be not believing Merlene, a stranger from another city—a city that no longer exists." She emitted a low, heartrending wail over the aether. The last time Boris had heard that cry, it had been in the city when a young kerack child had been accidentally separated from its parents in a crowded street. At that time, all keracks in the vicinity, immediately upon receiving the wail through their antennae, had dropped whatever they were doing and had rushed to the aid of the child. Although he was not a kerack, Merlene's wail elicited the same immediate response. He moved quickly toward her and awkwardly took her in his arms, his claws clumsily grooming her antennae and carapace as he tried to calm her. It didn't help, for the wail grew louder until it reached a painful shriek that went on and on . . .

"Well!" Gabrielle said in surprise as she shook herself into the scene and saw Merlene in Boris's arms. Then she too heard the wail and was impelled to rush to Merlene in an attempt to comfort the distraught alien. The wail finally faded into silence.

"You feel better now?" Gabrielle asked, releasing her hold on Merlene.

"Merlene must be not behaving as a child," Merlene said sternly to herself. "Merlene must be thinking!" She paused. "But the thoughts o'Merlene be not as sharp as they used to be. Merlene be needing time. Merlene be going off to think. You be staying here and waiting until Merlene returns."

Boris and Gabrielle backed off, and Merlene turned and clambered up a rocky slope to the top of a nearby hill. Boris turned off his radio link to her and spoke to Gabrielle through the 'bot-to-'bot audiolink. "It appears she has much to think about and will not be back down for some time. Let us two teleport back and discuss our next steps."

As Merlene went upwards, her antennae instinctively searched the aether for the incessant babble of radio communication that had always linked her with everyone else in Camalor. There was nothing. She was truly alone. And she was right that her thoughts were not as sharp as they used to be. She knew that her memories used to be much more extensive than they were now. Only her personal quarters were clearly visible in her mind. The rest of the city, which she used to know intimately, now seemed a blur. And now it took forever to think through a problem. Before, she would know instinctively what the right answer to a problem was, and she never had to check, unless perhaps some complicated mathematical calculations were involved, and in most cases her instinctive guess had been right on the eye. She now had a very difficult problem to solve, and the answer did not come to her, so she must reason it out using intellect rather than instinct.

Once Merlene had reached the top of the hill, she put herself into the analytical mode that had served her so well in the past as the Wizard of Camalor.

"Merlene be knowing a truth," she began. "And it be a truth, for Merlene be witness to it." She paused and thought further. "The humans be witness to it, also. Their machine eyes have made a record of that truth, and that record can be seen again and again on their Lookman viewers."

That last thought comforted her somewhat, for with the availability of the video record of the last days and moments of Camalor, she knew that the truth was independent of herself and her now untrustworthy memory. She then realized that the existence of the video record and the Lookman viewers meant something else.

"When Merlene be telling others on Ice the truth, they be believing Merlene if they be shown the truth on the Lookman. Merlene be asking the humans for a Lookman to take along when Merlene be explaining the truth to other cities."

Inside, Merlene shrank from the idea of visiting a strange city. Much preferring her own people, she disliked strangers intensely. Now, however, her own people were gone, and as much as she disliked it, she would have to visit strange cities and talk to strange people. But what could she tell them other than the bare truth? That if they continued in their present fashion, they would blow themselves and their civilization to pieces, with nothing left except a cloud of spores traveling through space to the next comet to repeat the whole fruitless process over again. Yet, wasn't that the way it was supposed to be? Weren't the keracks made to do just that and no more?

"No!" she blurted out. The intellectual in her rejected that thought. The gallantry of the heroic multipaintings by Komart and the beauty of the spin-sculptures by Dilene passed by her eye, while the majestic music of Arpene and Bethene coursed through her soul. The artistry of the destroyed kerack civilization of Camalor had been valuable. Even the very advanced and very alien humans thought the art and music was valuable, and had sent examples of it back to Earth where it had been admired by everyone there. Everywhere on Ice there were other cities with other artisans whose works were doomed to destruction unless Merlene saved them with her knowledge.

Then there was the knowledge of the wizards of those cities. That knowledge had value too. As Wizard of Camalor, Merlene had not had sufficient time to produce knowledge of value to the much more advanced human wizards, but she had definitely helped her own people with her knowledge, and if Camalor had not exploded, and she had continued on to live for the twof'fs or thref'fs of fi'fifthdays that she knew she could have worked, she certainly would have produced knowledge of value even to the human wizards. Then there were the chirurgeons. What did they produce that was valuable? And the warriors, and the priests . . .

Suddenly the genius that made her the wizard she was, clicked inside her like two pincertips of a claw successfully picking up a pin. It couldn't be done by just wizards or chirurgeons or artists or warriors or priests alone; it would have to be a combined effort.

The wizards would have to learn how to control the dance so that sufficient energy was generated by the uranium in the souls of the people to keep them warm and active without allowing an explosion to occur. The chirurgeons would have to learn how to control the sex act so that only a manageable number of children were produced. The warriors would have to lay down their weapons and the cities would have to learn to live in peace, so there would be no large buildup of souls in Heaven. The priests would have to use their new knowledge to restructure the religion so that the emotional taboos against sex were eliminated and the present destructive course of action would be avoided.

Merlene paused. The major problem in each city she visited would be the Queen and her court, especially the high priest. Would they listen to Merlene and her message? Would they believe? Would they change? She did not know, but she must try. And if that failed, she must convince the commoners not to obey their Queen and her court.

Perhaps all this could be done, but would the keracks still be the same people? She paused to think. No . . . they wouldn't. She paused again. Who *was* this commoner Merlene, who dared to play Queen to her race?

All this thinking and planning took Merlene to her limits.

Why was she doing this? Why was she striving so hard? Perhaps she should give up . . .

Exhausted from the strain of reasoning with only her own brain to aid her, she made herself stop thinking so furiously. She forced herself to relax and rest.

After a long and delicious period of calm and contentment and peace, her mind lost in the blankness brought on by the lack of radio communication, she heard a faint sound coming over the aether. She had not heard it before, for she had been accustomed to the continual loud radio roar of living in Camalor, or the hissing noisiness of the humans and their digital telemetry, but now the roar of Camalor was gone, and for once the humans and their machines were quiet.

Just above the radio hiss of the stars she could hear a call, a living call. There were occasional audible words, usually some imperious command but sometimes a distant call for help. The aether faded and undulated as solar plasma streaked past the planetoid, sometimes focusing, sometimes scattering the distant voices.

"That be the voices of all the others on Ice," Merlene whispered to herself. "That be the Spirit o'All. Merlene be not alone. There be fourffs, nay, fiveffs of others, living and working out there, all trying to create a better future for their children and the people in their city. Yet, Merlene be knowing that they work only to create a senseless death for their entire community. They be deserving better, and Merlene be saving them! Merlene be bringing them the truth, and the truth be making them free!"

Resolved and invigorated by her decision, Merlene turned and purposefully strode back down the slope toward the dark and silent telebots waiting below.

After leaving Merlene at the top of the hill and teleporting back into the shelter, Boris and Gabrielle took off their verihelms and looked around the cramped quarters. Elizabeth was operating the airlock controls, cycling Hiroshi back into the hut from his task of refueling the microhopper. By the time Hiroshi had gotten out of his suit, Rob and Selke had both completed their cleanup, and Rob had warmed up some beef stew for their shift-break lunch. While Rob and Selke ate, and Gabrielle at the monitor console kept a watch on the distant figure of Merlene as seen from the eye of her telebot, the six went over what had happened in the last few hours and tried to understand what it all meant.

"What amazes me," said Elizabeth, "is that until Merlene looked at her culture from our outside point of view, none of the keracks could see that their civilization was on a self-destructive course. Yet there were all kinds of clues, like not being allowed to have sex, and a religion that involved the building of strange structures like the Dome o'Holies that had no functional purpose. There was also the ritual collection and storage of nonessential materials like uranium pellets and lithium deuteride and lithium tritide crystals."

"A culture can be very blind for a very long time," Boris reminded them. "Look at Soviet Union. For seventy-five years it blindly followed the idealistic principles of Marxist Communism, even though it should have been obvious after the first few years that Communism wasn't working."

"I wonder if the human race is itself blind to some self-destructive future?" Selke said thoughtfully. "Perhaps if we think about ourselves as if we were an alien scientist, we can see some things that we should be doing differently, and change our ways."

"It's not hard to find them," Elizabeth replied. "Until the Soviet Union broke up, the US and the USSR were on a suicidal nuclear-arms buildup that could have destroyed the entire human civilization on Earth as thoroughly as the keracks of Camalor destroyed their civilization."

"Fortunately, that threat is gone now," said Rob.

"Diminished, yes," Elizabeth agreed, "but not gone. Both the US and Russia still have enough warheads left to cause plenty of damage to each other and to the rest of the world. And we still have many smaller wars, most of them based on esoteric religious differences. Look at the Irish problem in the UK. Both sides even believe in the same God and the same messenger from God. The only thing that divides them, and makes them murder each other, is their disagreement over the exact form of the bureaucracy by which the word of God's messenger is passed down to the people. There are many worse examples, where the religious beliefs of two warring factions are essentially incompatible, like the Jews of Israel and the Muslims of the Arab states, and whole nations are on one side or the other. One of those conflicts could easily get out of hand and lead to a nuclear exchange. In view of that, what kind of craziness makes us humans keep *any* of those weapons of mass destruction around?"

"There is an even worse problem," Selke interjected. "There are too many people in the world. Everybody knows it is a problem. But no one will talk about it."

"Or *do* anything about it," Rob added. "Again, religious beliefs are making us blind to the obvious."

Elizabeth said thoughtfully, "I think perhaps that as soon as Merlene has finished her job here on Ice warning the other kerack nations, she ought to come to Earth and give *us* a good talking to."

"I wonder if there is something else we do that is crazy?" asked Boris, trying to think.

"There most likely *is* something. But if we are blind to it, how can we see it?" Hiroshi asked epigrammatically.

"I wonder what it could be?" said Gabrielle, absentmindedly stroking Lucifer, who irritably responded to the caress by attacking her with all four sets of claws and her teeth. She withdrew her badly scarred hand and tried again at a less sensitive place on the beast.

"We'll probably never know," said Selke. "Until it is too late."

Gabrielle, who had been keeping an eye on the telebot

eyeglobe monitor, called out, "Merlene is starting back down the hill. Time to 'port back, Boris."

The visages of Boris and Gabrielle were back in the eyeglobes of the telebots by the time Merlene made her way down the slope. As she approached, she spoke to them.

"Merlene be now engaged in important work that must be done. Merlene be a wizard—a wizard with knowledge—knowledge that be important to every city on Ice. Merlene will be taking that knowledge to all! You will be taking Merlene in your flamewagon to the nearest city. We be taking with us a Lookman with all your records of Camalor."

"Very well," said Boris. He was surprised, yet pleased, by the firm, commanding tone that she used. "We'll be glad to help you, but we need to make some preparations first. We'll need something to carry the Lookman in, and you'll need some food and other supplies."

"And we have yet to complete the video copying of the pages of your notebook," Selke reminded her. "That should be done before you leave the camp . . . unless you are willing to leave the notebook with us—"

"No! That be all that Merlene have!"

"I didn't think so," Selke said. "I will continue the copying while Boris prepares for the expedition. Fortunately, Hiroshi has already refueled the microhopper."

Their first trip in the microhopper was a short hop to the damaged city of Belator to get food supplies for Merlene. After checking the radiation level to calculate how long Merlene could stay in the city without getting a radiation dose equivalent to more than a few months' worth of the normal cosmic-ray radiation level on Ice, they entered the less damaged portion of the city on the side opposite to Camalor. Merlene listened to the aether very carefully, but there were no voices emanating from the city.

They found supplies of frozen meat and eggs, bags of roots and berries, and a small wagon to haul the food and the

Lookman. Merlene was able to find the home of the Wizard of Belator. The wizard, like most of the populace, was lying in two pieces—burnt in two by the pellet of uranium at the juncture of her thorax and abdomen, heated white hot by the neutron flux from Camalor. From the wizard's workshop, Merlene was able to gather some precious pieces of blank writing foil to add to her notebook, a few writing styluses, a heating plate suitable for cooking on, a few pots and pans, and the wizard's calculating rods.

That evening, as Brightstar set over the mountains surrounding the valley where the humans had set up their base, the seven of them sat down to dinner together, Merlene on the ice block just outside the one window of the shelter, and the six humans inside, three crowded around the small table, the other three either sitting in the monitor chairs or standing. Merlene was enjoying a filet of iceworm smothered in bloodberry gravy, while the humans each partook of one of their reconstituted "special" dinner packs. Lucifer, satiated by a corned-beef entree sacrificed from Elizabeth's stocks, was contentedly washing his face in one of the bunks, locked away to keep him from interrupting the meal.

Merlene, being the only one of the seven able to talk while eating, dominated the conversation with a detailed discussion of her plans to take her message of salvation to all the cities on Ice.

"That is going to take a long time," said Gabrielle. "There must be thousands of cities that need to be visited. It is going to take years."

"Merlene be having nothing but time, now."

"Speaking of time," Hiroshi interjected, "I have been thinking. This mission was originally designed to be a one-time visit of six months' duration—although we brought down enough food for twelve months in case it was desired to extend the visit time on the surface. Things have now changed, and UNSCO is planning to send additional crews that will set up a permanent base and establish and maintain continuous contact with the keracks. Unfortunately, until UNSCO builds a much larger cable catapult system capable of reaching higher launch velocities, and gets one of the terminals out here and set up, they will have to use the present catapult system. It will take the first of the follow-on crews over forty months to get here. Since we have been here almost six months already, the longest we can stay before we run out of food is another six months. That leaves a gap of thirty-four months with no humans on Ice."

"Normally, that wouldn't be a problem," said Rob. "If Camalor was still functioning, the follow-on crew could just reestablish contact with Merlene and continue on where we had left off. This means that although we can give support to Merlene for six months, we will then have to abandon her."

"Merlene be not liking the idea of human friends leaving. But if it must be, it must be," she said fatalistically, tucking a chunk of iceworm under her mouthveil as she spoke.

"I would like to propose a solution to that problem," Hiroshi continued. "If you five leave Ice now, and go back to Earth, then there will be thirty-six person-months of food left in the food storage locker. By skipping an occasional meal, that should be enough to keep me alive until the next crew arrives. This would allow me to monitor Merlene's attempts to take her message to the other kerack cities. Also, I could help her out of any difficult situations she may encounter, by producing an occasional high-tech miracle, or rescuing her with the microhopper."

"That is a most noble offer on your part, Hiroshi," said Rob. "But as mission commander I can't allow you to stay here all by yourself. This is a hostile planet, and there are just too many ways you could get into trouble. You could even get yourself killed! Sorry, but you'll have to catapult back with the rest of us."

Instead of replying to Rob, Hiroshi turned and looked at Elizabeth, then Selke. "You two are the physicians," he said. "You saw the response of my heart to thirty gees after three years at fifteen percent of Earth gravity. I died. Fortunately you were able to revive me. I've now gone another six months at fifteen percent gravity. What are the chances of my dying again when we catapult toward Earth? Then add in another three years at fifteen percent. What are my chances of surviving thirty gees then?"

Neither Selke nor Elizabeth would answer. Hiroshi turned back to Rob.

"Catapulting back with the rest of you will *certainly* kill me. I'll take my chances here on Ice." He paused as he thought more about the serious problem that faced all the kerack cities on Ice. His upbringing had taught him to reach out with compassion to help all living creatures in this universe. Now, here was a whole species that was in serious trouble. "Besides," he continued, "that way I can help Merlene save her people."

"Merlene be most grateful for companionship of friend Hiroshi," she said.

There was a long pause as Rob considered the pros and cons. "OK," he said finally.

"Good!" said Gabrielle. "Lucifer can stay here to keep you company!"

Hiroshi turned to glare at her and opened his mouth to protest, but Gabrielle interrupted.

"Small kittens can stand thirty gees protected by bedding. Lucifer is now much larger. Like you, he too can no longer go home."

That thought sobered Hiroshi and he began to feel a sense of compassion for the loathsome cat, even a sense of comradeship. Gabrielle was right. Both he and Lucifer could no longer go home. Even when the larger catapult system became available, it would still operate at many gees, and by that time he would have lived so long at fifteen percent gravity that even those lower gee levels would kill him. Even if they didn't, and he was able to get back to the inner solar system, he would probably have to spend the rest of his life on either the Moon or Mars. He might as well stay on Ice where he would be able to do the most good.

After a long and thoughtful pause, Hiroshi turned to Rob.

"I would like to send a message to the Secretary-General of the United Nations with a suggestion and a request," he said to Rob, finally.

A few days later, Merlene and Hiroshi were out on the ice next to the waiting microhopper. They were both looking up into the sky, Merlene with her large single eye, Hiroshi with the zoom lens behind the eyeglobe of the telebot he was inhabiting. On the other side of the camp, the ice was streaked where the ascent stage of the lander rocket had blasted it during the launch of the other five humans on the first leg of their long journey home to Earth. Far above them floated the terminal of the cable catapult.

"The capsule be starting to move," said Merlene.

It took a little while before Hiroshi's less sensitive telebot eye could discern any movement of the tiny dot at the end of the long cable. Then it finally did.

"Sayonara," he said softly. Then he too began to feel the terrible sense of abandonment and loneliness that he knew Merlene was still suffering. The two of them—small cold kerack and giant hot human—now had only each other for companionship.

In less than three minutes the capsule reached the end of the catapult. Soon it was gone from sight, lost in the glare from the bright star in the sky toward which it was heading.

"It be time for us to be proceeding with our task," said Merlene, turning to head for the open door of the microhopper. Hiroshi followed her in. The other telebot was there, fastened into the pilot's seat, its empty eyeglobe staring blankly out the window. He fastened Merlene into the copilot's seat and strapped his telebot into a safety harness against the wall. Then, with the touch of a toe in the controller cocoon back inside the shelter, Hiroshi switched telebots.

His face disappeared from the telebot in the wall harness and reappeared in the pilot telebot. Soon the microhopper was headed for the nearest kerack city on the less damaged part of Ice on the opposite side of the human base from Camalor.

The microhopper landed on an outcropping of rock, well outside the city. Merlene and Hiroshi climbed down the rock and headed for the city, Hiroshi's telebot pulling the wagon carrying the Lookman. Merlene adjusted her wizard's cloak around her so the mended tear was hidden by a fold. As they approached the outskirts of the city, their way was blocked by a young border guard warrior riding a heuller. He wore a cape of white edged with intricate patterns of gold and silver and red. His lance was long and polished, and the points on his mace had the sharpness of never having been tested. There was an arrogant tone to his voice as his gold-ringed antennae broadcast his challenge.

"You be eyeing the great warrior, Nokset o'Misufor. Why be you approaching Misufor, wizard? Go back to your own city where you belong, and take that 'thing' in kerack shape with you."

Merlene stepped bravely forward. "This wizard be named Merlene. Merlene be having no city." She pointed an antenna at Hiroshi's telebot. "This being be named Hiroshi. Hiroshi be now appointed ambassador to all keracks on Ice from the glowing giant gods on the great city-planet Earth. Merlene be coming to Misufor with a message. A message from the Spirit o'All." Her voice shifted to a commanding tone, a tone so imperious that the warrior had only heard his Queen use it before.

"Nokset be getting down off heuller and be giving it to Merlene!"

The warrior, greatly bewildered, hesitated. All his life he had instantly obeyed the imperious orders of those above him in station——ladies, princesses, and his Queen. This person looked like a low-class female wizard, a female not from his city, yet her tone was that of a Queen. Merlene didn't give him time to think. She repeated her command, her strong, demanding voice radiating through the aether.

"Give Merlene your heuller! Merlene be having need of it!"

Off in the distance, Hiroshi could see some farmers out in their fields looking their way, antennae spread wide to catch Merlene's signals. At the same time there were incredulous queries passing back and forth over the fields.

"Who be this strange wizard that be speaking like a Queen?"

"Who be this Queen that be walking among the people like a commoner?"

The warrior, confounded by Merlene's queenly tone, finally obeyed his instinctive response to authority and got down off his heuller. Turning the beast around so it was facing the city, he handed over the reins to her. Hiroshi pulled the cart carrying the Lookman forward and put the ends of the shafts in the upper hind claws of the heuller, where the well-trained beast grabbed them.

"Do you be the Queen?" the still bewildered warrior asked in awe, trying to reconcile the voice with the appearance.

Merlene hesitated, not having really thought things out this far. She was surprised at her ability to use her voice to command people to her will.

Hiroshi noticed the hesitation and realized that Merlene needed help. Her message was the truth, but it was such a big truth that it was going to be hard for the average kerack to swallow it. What was needed was a big lie to make the big truth easier to swallow, and, as the detested Nazi Goebbels had once found out, the bigger the lie, the easier it was to sell. Although it bothered him greatly to do so, Hiroshi decided to lie for Merlene.

"Merlene be not the Queen of the city Misufor," he said, using kerack sentence structure. "Merlene be the Queen of all on the entire world of Ice! She be having a message for you! Listen to it!" He hoped that Merlene would be able to take it from there. The warrior believed the big lie and bowed so low as to almost prostrate himself.

"What be your message, great Queen of Ice? And what should Nokset be doing to serve you best?"

"The message Merlene be bringing be not just for you," she said. "The message be for all to hear." She handed the reins of the heuller back to the warrior. "You be taking Merlene and Hiroshi to the plaza in the Center o'Misufor. But first you be laying down your weapons, for the Queen of Ice be traveling only in peace." The warrior rapidly dropped his spear and mace, then used his second set of claws to extract two daggers from their crossed back-scabbards and added them to the pile. Hiroshi, realizing their value, picked them up from the road and put them in the wagon, but the warrior went to the wagon, pulled them out again, and used the mace to beat the spear and the daggers into useless shafts of metal, in the process dulling the spikes of the mace until it too was worthless.

"The Queen of Ice be traveling only in peace!" the warrior said fiercely to Hiroshi. "She be having no need of weapons!"

Merlene approached them and tapped the warrior's antennae with hers. "Merlene be pleased with Nokset. From this time forward, you shall be traveling with Merlene, helping to take the message around the globe of Ice."

"Nokset be following Merlene from pole to pole and back again," said the warrior. He took off his cape and added it to the pile of blunted weapons. "Nokset be casting off the Queen o'Misufor as he be casting off the cloak o'Misufor, and be following a new Queen, the Queen of Ice!"

Nokset helped Merlene up on the middle of the heuller, then climbed up in front of her. Hiroshi clambered into the wagon with the Lookman and clamped his claws firmly on the low rail. Starting the heuller moving with a few kicks, Nokset and Merlene headed off toward the distant city, the heuller pulling the cart behind. With the journey started, Hiroshi locked the telebot claws to the cart rail, set the sensors behind its eyeglobe for automatic scan and hi-res recording, and teleported over to the pilot telebot in order to return the microhopper back to base. Just before he left the telebot in the cart, Hiroshi could hear Nokset broadcasting over the aether. His voice, strong with the certainty that he was representing a Queen, had also switched to a commanding tone that instinctively brought obedience.

"Make way for the Queen! Make way for the Queen of Ice!"

Attracted by Nokset's call, the keracks of Misufor gathered alongside the road to watch the two riding into town. As they passed each group of keracks, Merlene, using her queenly tone, commanded them to follow. Controlled by their instinctive response to an imperious command, they instantly obeyed.

"You be following Merlene!" she called. "You be listening to the message o'Merlene—a message for all. You be believing that message—and you will be *saved!*"

Notebook o'Merlene

Notes by Merlene on the human decimal system of counting.

Human Number		Kerack Number	
1	one	1	one
4	four	4	four
5	five	10	five
6	six	11	five plus one
9	nine	14	five plus four
10	ten	20	two-fives
20	twenty	40	four-fives
25	twenty-five	1'00	fi'five
49	forty-nine	1'44	fi'five, four-fives plus four
50	fifty	2'00	two fi'fives
100	one hundred	4'00	four fi'fives
125	one hundred and twenty-five	10'00	five fi'fives
250	two hundred and fifty	20'00	two-fives fi'fives
625	six hundred and twenty-five	1'00'00	twof'f
15,625	fifteen thousand, six hundred and twenty-five	1'00'00'00	thref'f

Notes by Merlene on conversion of the scale on the thermometer o'Merlene to the human absolute temperature scale.

[Convert Marks from fives notation to decimal notation]

Kelvin = 1.4 Marks [decimal notation] + 14

Marks [decimal notation] = 0.71 (Kelvin − 14)

Physical Meaning	Absolute (Degrees K)	Thermometer Scale (Marks [fives notation])	
[Absolute Zero]	0	− 20	minus two-fives
[Hydrogen Melts]	14	0	zero
[Surface of Ice]	28	20	two-fives
	42	40	four-fives
[Oxygen Melts]	56	1'10	one fi'five, five
[Kerack Body Temp]	70	1'30	one fi'five, three-fives
	84	2'00	two fi'fives
	98	2'10	two fi'fives, five
	112	2'40	two fi'fives, four-fives
[F$_2$O Blood Boils]	126	3'10	three fi'fives, five
	154	4'00	four fi'fives
	169	4'20	four fi'fives, two-fives
[HF Melts]	190	10'00	five fi'fives
	•		
	•		
[H$_2$O Melts]	273	12'14	five plus two fi'fives, five plus four

Notes by Merlene on the structure of the Center o'Camalor:

The Center o'Camalor be arranged as be shown in the illustration. The Queen herself be resident in the Tower o'Queen, which starts at the base of the Palace o'Princesses and rises up above the Plaza o'Dance. The central chambers of the tower, down for many layers, be the private quarters of the Queen. Only the princesses have access to the Palace o'Princesses and the Tower o'Queen, so details of the arrangement of the rooms inside be unknown to Merlene.

Below the Palace o'Princesses be the Dome o'Holies. The Dome o'Holies be most beautiful in construction. Merlene be calculating it be a perfect ellipsoid, with the Heaven o'All hanging down from the top of the Dome o'Holies to one focal point of the ellipsoid, while the Altar o'Holies rises up out of the floor of the Dome o'Holies on its conical pedestal to occupy the other focal point. The conical pedestal of the Altar o'Holies be continuing downward and outward from under the Dome o'Holies until it be meeting the thick walls of a metal cylinder which surrounds the Dome o'Holies and supports the Palace o'Princesses. At the base of the metal cylinder be a thick metal disk. The disk be under slow but constant lowering by the periodic use of iceworms to remove a thin layer of ice from beneath the disk. The cone, disk, and cylinder form a container for the Crystals o'Giving which be placed into the Altar o'Holies.

The curved wall of the Dome o'Holies be constructed out of many layers, each of a different material. After communing with the most eldest of the metal spinners, Merlene be determining the materials which make up the many layers of the dome. The first of the layers be constructed out of the element beryllium, a strong gray metal. The inside of the Dome be then coated with a thin layer of lithium, to give the inside a soft silvery luster. The outside of the beryllium shell be then covered with a layer of crystalline boron, followed by a layer of transparent crystalline carbon, then by layers of frozen nitrogen, oxygen, and fluorine, separated from each other by thin shield layers of beryllium. These be followed by more layers, each being constructed of one element, such as sodium, magnesium, aluminum, titanium, vanadium, chromium, manganese, iron, cobalt, nickel, copper, zinc, and on-on, for that be what the Spirit o'All had ordained for the metal spinners to spin. In all, there be one fi'five, four-fives plus three layers. The Dome o'Holies be now finished, for it be coated with a final outer layer of luxurious gold.

The many layers which be found in the Dome o'Holies be compared by Merlene with the "Periodic Table of the Elements" which be found in the human Encyclopaedia Terra. The layers in the dome, from inside out, exactly follow the progression of the elements in the periodic table. Only the few elements that be gases at the normal temperature of Ice, such as hydrogen, helium, and neon, be not represented by separate layers used in the construction of the dome. Why the layers in the Dome o'Holies be ordered in this manner be not understood by anyone. Perhaps someday the Spirit o'All be enlightening us.

The Dome o'Holies be reached by two ramps which be coming down from the park above, below one side of the Palace o'Princesses. The left ramp be for males and the right ramp be for females. The males be following a corridor which circles around under the Palace o'Princesses to the left, while the females be following a corridor which circles around to the right. All along both corridors be the privies for the cleansing of the bodies of the offerers before they be entering the Dome o'Holies. As each privy hole be filling up, the privy be capped and a new privy hole be made further out. The two corridors be meeting at the opposite side of the Palace o'Princesses. At this meeting point be the entrance tunnel which leads under the Palace o'Princesses to the Spiral o'Holies and the Dome o'Holies.

The beauty of the Dome o'Holies can be viewed from the Spiral o'Holies, a spiral ramp which be starting from the entrance tunnel, and be spiraling down the inside of the cylindrical cavity which be containing the Dome o'Holies within, and then up to the top of the Altar o'Holies where the Crystals o'Giving be deposited each Fifthday. An interleaved spiral exit ramp then be winding down the altar and back up the inside of the cylinder to an exit tunnel on the opposite side of the cylinder from the entrance tunnel. This exit tunnel be leading directly to the exit ramp which rises up to the surface between the two entrance ramps.

Covering the Palace o'Princesses be the Plaza o'Dance. Both the plaza and the walls of the palace be made of boron carbide, the strongest material known except for crystalline carbon. Surrounding the plaza be the park, covered with moss and berry bushes, and containing many places for various entertainments. Radiating out from the park be the broad main streets of Camalor.

This be the ending of the description of the Center o'Camalor.

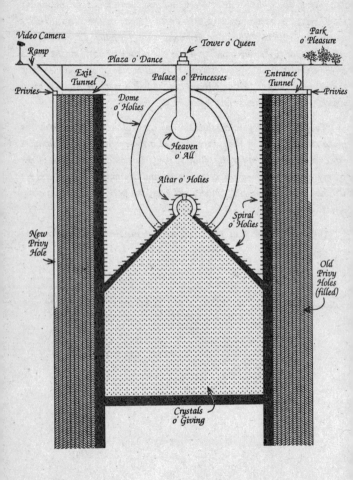

Illustration of Center o'Camalor

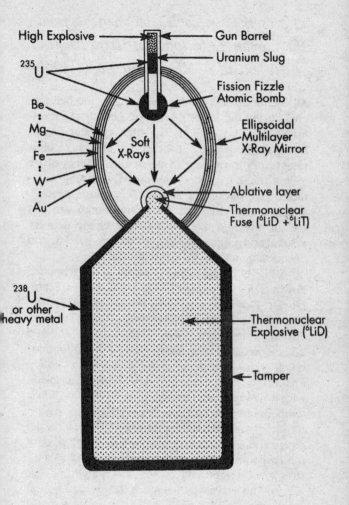

Fission Fizzle Triggered Thermonuclear Bomb

Notes that be copied by Merlene from the human Encyclopaedia Terra Digital, entry entitled "Thermonuclear Bomb."

All thermonuclear bombs designed by the belligerents during the long "Cold War" period which followed World War II used a high efficient fission bomb as the trigger. In the design of a thermonuclear bomb, it was important that the efficiency of the fission-bomb trigger be maximized, since this minimized the amount of fissionable material needed, which in turn decreased the overall bomb size and weight, lowered the size and cost of the delivery system, and reduced the amount of long-lived fission products generated by the explosion.

A highly efficient fission bomb is not essential, however, for triggering a fusion explosion. For example, Dr. F. Winterberg, in his book *Physical Principles of Thermonuclear Explosive Devices* (Fusion Energy Foundation, New York, 1981), showed it is theoretically possible to ignite a thermonuclear bomb with a low-efficiency fission explosion, called a *fission fizzle*. Whereas an efficient fission explosion with a typical fission fuel burn-up of 10% reaches a temperature of 66 million degrees Kelvin, a fission fizzle only reaches a temperature of 3.6 million degrees. The wavelength corresponding to the peak of the radiation emitted at this temperature is 13 angstroms, corresponding to the wavelength of soft X-rays. This wavelength is much longer than typical wavelengths at the much higher temperature of a fully developed fission explosion. As a consequence of its longer wavelengths, such radiation can be reflected from a metal surface if the wavelength is matched to that of the K-alpha line of the discrete

X-ray spectrum of the metal. For a wavelength of 13 angstroms, the K-alpha resonance reflection occurs for a substance with an atomic number Z of 11, which is the metal sodium.

A temperature of 3.6 million degrees, however, produces radiation over a wide spectrum of wavelengths around the peak wavelength of 13 angstroms. To make a K-alpha resonance mirror covering the many wavelengths to be found in such a broad spectrum, the mirror should be constructed of many thin layers of substances varying from light elements inside to heavy elements outside. For example, lithium reflects X-rays with wavelengths around 228 angstroms, beryllium reflects 114 angstroms, carbon 45 angstroms, magnesium 10 angstroms, iron 2 angstroms, selenium 1 angstrom, and gold 0.5 angstroms. The softer X-rays with the longer wavelengths would be reflected from the inner layers of the mirror made of the lighter elements, while the harder X-rays with the shorter wavelengths would penetrate the inner layers of lighter elements and reflect from the layer made of the element whose resonance line matched the wavelength of that particular X-ray.

As is shown in the figure, a soft X-ray mirror for use in a fission-fizzle-triggered thermonuclear bomb would be made of many layers of metals shaped into an ellipsoid with the fission fizzle explosion at one focus of the ellipsoid and the thermonuclear fuse at the other. The soft X-rays from the fission fizzle at one focus would reflect from the curved multilayer mirror and converge onto the thermonuclear fuse at the other focus. The X-rays strike the ablative layer covering the thermonuclear fuse and are absorbed in the ablative layer. The ablative layer, heated by the X-rays into an incandescent plasma, explodes. The recoil from the ablated material exploding from the outer surface of the fuse causes an implosion of the thermonuclear fuel inside the fuse, igniting a fusion explosion. The explosion of the fuse then propagates through the remainder of the thermonuclear fuel in the bomb.

Not all elements can be used to make soft X-ray mirrors, since many elements are gases, liquids, or soft metals at room temperature. For example, the four elements between carbon and sodium on the periodic table are gasses (nitrogen, oxygen, fluorine, and neon), while the poor mechanical characteristics of the very soft metal sodium makes it of dubious utility in the construction of a weapon subjected to rugged environments. The inability to use these materials in the design of a soft X-ray reflection mirror leaves large gaps in the reflection spectrum of the mirror. This is no doubt partially the reason why fission fizzle bombs were never taken seriously by weapons designers.

The thermonuclear fuel in a fusion bomb is made of isotopes of the element hydrogen. A hydrogen atom normally has a nucleus consisting of just a proton. There are two heavier types, or isotopes, of hydrogen atoms. The first is deuterium, with a nucleus consisting of a proton plus a neutron. The second is tritium, with a nucleus consisting of a proton plus two neutrons. The optimum thermonuclear fuel is made of equal parts of LiD (lithium deuteride) and LiT (lithium tritide). The lithium holds the deuterium and tritium atoms in a compound which is a stable solid at room temperature and pressure, and thus is easily handled and stored. This eliminates the necessity for storing the normally gaseous hydrogen isotopes at either low temperature or high pressure.

When the fusion fuel is heated to a sufficiently high temperature, the deuterium nucleus (one proton plus one neutron) fuses with a tritium nucleus (one proton plus two neutrons) to produce a helium nucleus (two protons plus two neutrons) and a free neutron. The neutron carries off the excess energy, making the reaction proceed more easily. If the lithium used to hold the hydrogen isotopes in a solid form is the lithium 6 isotope instead of the more common lithium 7 isotope, the free neutron released by the fusion of deuterium and tritium can react with the three protons and three neutrons in the lithium 6 to generate a helium atom (two protons plus two neutrons) and a new tritium atom (one proton plus two neutrons). The new tritium atom can then fuse with an additional deuterium atom to add additional fusion energy to the reaction. The ability to collect these isotopes of hydrogen and lithium and convert them into an easily handled solid form has made it possible to create fusion reactions in devices compact and reliable enough to be transported and used as bombs.